Cathy Williams can remember reading Mills & Boon books as a teenager, and now that she is writing them she remains an avid fan. For her, there is nothing like creating romantic stories and engaging plots, and each and every book is a new adventure. Cathy lives in London. Her three daughters—Charlotte, Olivia and Emma—have always been, and continue to be, the greatest inspirations in her life.

Canadian **Dani Collins** knew in high school that she wanted to write romance for a living. Twenty-five years later, after marrying her high school sweetheart, having two kids with him, working at several generic office jobs and submitting countless manuscripts, she got The Call. Her first Mills & Boon novel won the Reviewers' Choice Award for Best First in Series from *RT Book Reviews*. She now works in her own office, writing romance.

Also by Cathy Williams

Emergency Engagement
Snowbound then Pregnant
Her Boss's Proposition

Secrets of Billionaires' Secretaries miniseries

A Wedding Negotiation with Her Boss
Royally Promoted

Also by Dani Collins

Marrying the Enemy
Husband for the Holidays
His Highness's Hidden Heir
Maid to Marry
Hidden Heir, Italian Wife

Discover more at millsandboon.co.uk.

RECLAIM ME

CATHY WILLIAMS

DANI COLLINS

MILLS & BOON

All rights reserved including the right of reproduction in whole or in part in any form. This edition is published by arrangement with Harlequin Enterprises ULC.

This is a work of fiction. Names, characters, places, locations and incidents are purely fictional and bear no relationship to any real life individuals, living or dead, or to any actual places, business establishments, locations, events or incidents. Any resemblance is entirely coincidental.

Without limiting the author's and publisher's exclusive rights, any unauthorized use of this publication to train generative artificial intelligence (AI) technologies is expressly prohibited. HarperCollins also exercise their rights under Article 4(3) of the Digital Single Market Directive 2019/790 and expressly reserve this publication from the text and data mining exception.

® and TM are trademarks owned and used by the trademark owner and/or its licensee. Trademarks marked with ® are registered with the United Kingdom Patent Office and/or the Office for Harmonisation in the Internal Market and in other countries.

First published in Great Britain 2025
by Mills & Boon, an imprint of HarperCollins*Publishers* Ltd,
1 London Bridge Street, London, SE1 9GF

www.harpercollins.co.uk

HarperCollins*Publishers*, Macken House, 39/40 Mayor Street Upper, Dublin 1, D01 C9W8, Ireland

Reclaim Me © 2025 Harlequin Enterprises ULC

Billionaire's Reunion Bargain © 2025 Cathy Williams

The Greek's Wife Returns © 2025 Dani Collins

ISBN: 978-0-263-34473-8

07/25

This book contains FSC™ certified paper
and other controlled sources to ensure responsible forest management.

For more information visit www.harpercollins.co.uk/green.

Printed and Bound in the UK using 100% Renewable Electricity
at CPI Group (UK) Ltd, Croydon, CR0 4YY

BILLIONAIRE'S REUNION BARGAIN

CATHY WILLIAMS

MILLS & BOON

To Emma, for all the help and inspiration.

CHAPTER ONE

Leo relaxed back, half-closed his eyes and for a few brief minutes enjoyed the quiet purr of his chauffeur-driven car as it silently cruised away from Manhattan towards his mansion in the Hamptons.

The drive would take well over an hour and a half. In his world, where time was money, this was a luxury when he could have taken the helicopter. It would have covered the distance in less than half the time.

But, for once, he'd needed to relax.

He opened his eyes and glanced out at a cold, grey world outside. It was early December and winter had descended with sudden urgency in the past week. Freezing blue skies and a stillness in the air had given way to the slow, inexorable promise of snow storms and blizzards. The weather reports were full of warnings to everyone in Manhattan to prepare to batten down the hatches.

Leo was accustomed to this. He usually spent the winter months in his penthouse overlooking Central Park because it was close to his offices and work never stopped, not even for Christmas.

This time, though, a spate of high-level deals meant that his feet had hardly touched the ground for three months. He'd spent more time out of the country than in it and, when he *had* been in it, he'd had to endure the low-level, passive-aggressive complaints from his current girlfriend who had had to deal with last-minute cancellations and late arrivals with monotonous regularity. He hadn't had a leg to stand on when it came to any counter-arguments, but it had just been another headache to deal with.

Two days ago, he had broken up with her.

'It's not you, it's me,' he had said, internally wincing at the platitude. 'I can't help my schedule and it's never going to change. You deserve better.'

Leo was shocked at how fast his blonde-haired, blue-eyed catwalk-model girlfriend, who had the face of an angel and a butter-wouldn't-melt-in-her-mouth expression, had turned into such a foul-mouthed, oath-spitting, shrieking harridan. She'd sworn revenge and told him that he might be rich but he was a loser who would never be happy, not if she had anything to do with it. Then she had changed tack and pleaded and begged. Finally, in the face of his unyielding silence, she had stormed out with the parting shot that he could forget it if he thought she was going to return any of the things he had given her.

He hadn't, as it happened. So here he was—sitting in the back of his BMW and pleased to be leaving behind the annoyance of an ex who would no-doubt make it her duty to irritate the living daylights out of him, at least until she got bored and moved on to someone else. Which, with any luck, wouldn't take long.

Maybe he should give up on women for a while. The older he got, the more predictable the outcome of his relationships seemed to be. It was as though a thirty-one-year-old bachelor was a lot riper for the picking than a twenty-two-year-old one, especially when the older version had money to burn. His last five girlfriends had become varying shades of nightmare. They had stampeded through all the warnings he had delivered about not wanting to commit to anything permanent and, after the honeymoon period of a handful of months, had begun with gusto a serious pursuit of 'something a little deeper'.

It was tiresome.

How hard would it be for him to ignore his libido for a while and focus on work?—They were a lot more straightforward than the demands of women.

He slid back the partition separating him from his driver and asked him to put on some music.

'Classical,' he said.

'Music—classical?'

'Why are you looking so shocked, Eddie?'

'I didn't think you knew what music was, sir.'

Leo grinned. Eddie, the fifty-seven-year-old veteran who had been with him for six years, was probably the only person on the planet who felt free to speak his mind to him. Leo had rescued him from life on the streets, taken with the placard he'd been holding which had said, 'you see where you'd be if you'd walked a mile in my shoes'. He had given him money, clothes and eventually counselling and a job with him and he hadn't lived to regret any of it.

'Every day is a school day, Eddie. Keep the volume low. I might try and get some sleep.'

'Good idea, Mr Cruz. You work too hard.'

'Thanks for the advice, Dad. I'll make sure to keep it in mind.' He smiled, slid back the partition and settled back to sleep.

Just a few emails to check and he would kill his stress by actually relaxing and switching off his phone.

He flipped open his phone to check his emails. He had three PAs working for several arms of his businesses with a remit to siphon off any work correspondence that belonged in his junk bin. Any legitimate acquaintances who wanted to contact him personally would already have his private email address.

So how had this email got through? How had it not been automatically binned when the address was just a name and the subject matter had been left blank? But there it was, sandwiched between an email from suppliers in China and one from the CEO of a microchip company wanting to arrange a conference call about a takeover.

Then Leo saw the name and every muscle in his body tensed as shock slammed into him. He sat up. All notion of catching some sleep was gone.

C. Farraday.... Cassie—Cassie Farraday.

He had spent eight years making sure that name was erased from his mind; eight years forgetting her. But now, fingers a little shaky as he opened the email, Leo realised that the past might not have been buried quite as deeply as he had hoped.

Cassie sat back in her chair, closed her eyes and thought that the last thing she felt like doing on a Saturday afternoon was working her way through a bunch of accounts that were never going to add up to anything but grief, misery and heartache.

The deeper she dug, the more the debris rose to the surface, and she'd been digging away for the past five months. In between holding down her day job as a caterer, she'd done nothing but dig, dig, dig. How many more gaps in her family's finances was she going to find? How much more money had disappeared into the ether?

And how on earth had she not spotted that her dad had been sinking as he'd done his best to cope with years of her mother's ill health? He'd taken his eye off the ball and his company, once his pride and joy, had paid the price through mismanagement and poor investments which had never been properly scrutinised.

Everything she and her mother had been left after her dad had died was slowly draining away to pay bills that had been piling up for weeks, months and in most cases years. The holiday cottage by the lake had gone; the cars had already been returned to the dealership; most of the artwork accumulated over the years had been sold…and the very worst of it was that the family home was hanging on by a thread. Thank God the baying wolves at the door couldn't lay claim to her little runaround and the company van or that would be her livelihood swept away in the torrent as well.

Cassie sighed, stood up and stretched. She was a leggy, athletic girl used to the great outdoors but stuck in the little space she rented to do her company accounts as she tried to sort out the chaos of a life rapidly unravelling.

She was twenty-seven years old but right now she felt like a hundred. She couldn't remember a time when she'd been truly happy, without a care in the world, whistle-while-you-work happy with her heart intact and a future radiant with hope and optimism. Or at least she could… but those days were long gone.

She idly fiddled with the elastic band and released a curtain of poker-straight dark hair which hadn't been cut in so long that it was now almost down to her waist, and then she absently switched off the computer. Nothing; not a word from Leo yet, but she couldn't blame him. It had been a long time since they'd been a clandestine couple, too young to realise that they would never have the happy-ever-after ending they'd wanted. When everything had fallen apart, he had walked away and never looked back.

For the hundredth time, Cassie swallowed down the bile of bitter regret that she had sent him that email a week ago. She shouldn't have, but she had just come from seeing her mother and desperation had overtaken her. She had returned to her tiny rented place twenty minutes away from where her mother still lived in a handful of rooms in the fast-crumbling family mansion, and had sat in front of her computer and sent the wretched begging email.

She gritted her teeth, blanked out the memory and headed out. It wasn't yet two in the afternoon and she had to go and help Frankie finish off their order for the Samsons, which was a big job for thirty people with a million different dietary requirements. And then straight home, a quick shower and she would check in on her mother.

This Saturday was going to resemble all the other Saturdays she had spent over the past few months.

Leo debated how to get to the place he had once called home.

Should he drive? Too far, especially in deteriorating weather, even though he quite fancied the freedom of a road trip. There'd be a lot of time to think and over the past eight days, ever since he'd read that email, he'd found that his thoughts had been very satisfying indeed.

However, there was only so much time out he could spare and, tempting though the thought of taking to the road was, he was regrettably going to have to give it a miss. The length of time he'd spend there would definitely not warrant a couple of days on the road with some high-end stop-overs along the way.

Leo planned to deliver what he had to say to Cassie in record time. He could have said what he wanted to say via email but curiosity had been too persistent.

What did she look like now? What was she doing? Was she seeing anyone? Presumably not, because if she was she surely wouldn't have come to him with her begging bowl. What self-respecting man would allow his woman to ask favours from an old flame? He would take his private plane to Vancouver and get a driver from there.

She had emailed him with every possible contact detail he could ask for, from her telephone numbers to her address. Leo had thought long and hard about calling her but he wanted the element of surprise. Why? It had been eight years, a lifetime ago, and during those years he had become a different man—tough, hard and, more to the point, successful beyond his wildest dreams.

He was complete and, if mistakes had been made in his youth, then surely he was over them by now? Surely the pain and searing disillusionment had scarred over? But, if that was the case, then why had that email from her, the first contact since he'd turned his back and walked away, had such an effect on him? Why hadn't he laughed and deleted it? Or replied with some casual, dismissive response?

Instead he'd sat on it for a week and allowed memories to infiltrate his mind and take him back to a time when he'd been a very different person from the one he was now.

They'd been so damned young when they'd first met. She, only eighteen, the beauty queen born with a silver spoon in her mouth....and he, twenty-two, from the wrong side of the tracks with an immigrant father who could just about manage to make himself understood in English. An immigrant father who'd worked all the hours under the sun so to make sure his one and only kid could have the new trainers, the new school uniform and the new backpack. An immigrant who'd done his best to make up for the absence of a mother because his wife had upped and left him when Leo had barely been out of nappies.

Leo had grown up looking at the rich kids who went to the exclusive school by the lake, little knowing that, as the clocked ticked past, he would meet and fall for the richest girl there. The girl whose father had practically owned the small town where everybody knew everybody else.

Except no one had known about *them*. No one had known how they had met at one of her father's construction sites where she'd been doing a something-and-nothing job during the long summer holidays. He'd already been there, working with all the other builders, earning money because he'd had no choice but to study at night until he couldn't keep his eyes open.

No one had known about that whirlwind eight-month courtship. Six-three, with killer looks and the hard body of someone used to heavy manual labour, Leo had already been experienced when it came to the opposite sex, but then he'd met Cassie and...

God, he'd fallen hook, line and sinker. He'd already had one foot in MIT. He'd been accepted on a generous scholarship, had finally saved enough to cover his accommodation for at least a year and he had just...*stopped*. For the first time in his life, he had heard the beating of his heart and he had listened to it. He'd put drive and ambition on hold because he'd let her into his soul and had wanted to wait until she left high school.

They'd already made plans. Where she would go: somewhere close to MIT where she could go to culinary school. What they would do together while they both studied... He had let himself peer into a future that had never been on his radar. He had forgotten the hurt he'd carried inside and the painful legacy of abandonment by his mother, never discussed but always felt. He'd actually allowed himself to be vulnerable.

She'd enchanted him. She was tall with that dark, dark hair, blue, blue eyes, dimples whenever she laughed and that expression of delight, innocence and absolute joy and trust whenever she looked at him. For the first time in for ever, he had felt at peace with himself.

That brought bitter memories because even then, with all that adoration shining in her eyes and the soft words of love and devotion, she had known where she belonged— and it hadn't been with a guy like him. All those thoughts had slammed into Leo as he had sat on that email and processed it.

From the luxury of his mansion in East Hampton, a glorious place sitting in twenty acres of prime land overlooking the Atlantic ocean, Leo had finally come to the conclusion that, while he was no fan of the unexpected, there was no denying that sometimes the unexpected could hold all sorts of appeal.

Such as now. For the first time in eight years, Leo was going to temporarily park the predictability of his highly organised, ordered, controlled life and take a little walk on the wild side, back into the past. If it hadn't been buried properly, then this was surely going to be the opportunity to put the final shovels of earth on the grave and seal it up for good…

It was after five in the afternoon by the time Cassie and Frankie finished delivery to the Samsons and setting up the meal which Claudia Samson's own staff would take over as soon as they left. Cassie knew the couple well and so did Frankie. They'd been to school with one of their kids who was now living in Europe and working in finance.

She'd phoned her mother, all prepped to head there straight from their job. She would spend a couple of hours, prepare one of the meals she had batch-cooked the week before and then head back home but, as it turned out, Mary Farraday was tired.

'Darling, you should go out and have some fun,' she had said. 'It's Saturday. You should be having a good time and not trekking over here to see me.'

'Oh, I'm way too tired to go out with my can of red paint,' Cassie had said airily. 'The town will have to wait another week for me to decorate it.'

But, as she walked to her car, mobile phone pressed against her cheek while she fiddled in her bag for her car keys, Cassie couldn't help but feel a certain amount of relief.

She was tired—one-achingly, brain-achingly *tired*. Tired of the steady drag of financial worries as the house of cards continued to topple down around them at pace. Tired of pretending to her mother that things were really not half as bad as they seemed and that every cloud had a silver lining. Tired of trying to find ways and means of getting them out of the hole they were in. How on earth would her mother cope if they lost the house?

As it was, Mary Farraday was becoming more and more anxious and panicked as she saw things being sold off to clear debts neither of them had known anything about. It was heart-breaking. Just thinking about her mother was heart-breaking, come to think of it. It was heart-breaking that her once proud parent—who only twelve years ago had set up the thriving animal shelter that had twice been featured on national television, had lectured at the nearby university and given dinner parties that had been the talk of the town—had been reduced to a shadow of herself.

Her multiple sclerosis, diagnosed all that time ago, was now so much worse. More often than not, she was so fatigued that she could barely walk for more than minutes at a time and the muscle spasms and stiffness which had come and gone were now mostly present, making a mockery of normal life.

The stress didn't help.

'Sure,' Dr Lewis had said several weeks before, 'A little low-level stress does no harm, but long-term or excessive stress... Well, you'd be surprised how much that can impact on your mother's overall wellbeing. Pain, fatigue and anxiety are all going to make everything seem and feel a lot worse. I understand if I were you I would consider taking her on a little holiday—somewhere warm, perhaps. You can take a couple of weeks away from catering, can't you?'

He'd patted her arm and smiled. 'Let some of us slightly overweight residents do without your excellent food so that we can make way for the full Christmas onslaught.' He'd looked at her thoughtfully. 'And you look as though you could do with the break as well, Cassie.'

A little holiday somewhere warm could not be further out of her reach financially. However, Rob Lewis had no idea what was going on within the Farraday household, like everyone else in the town with the exception of Phil, the bank manager, who could be counted on to keep a secret.

She got into her car with her thoughts still messy and depressing. It was busy. Christmas beckoned and it was the sort of town where every single person celebrated the festive season in flamboyant style. In a week's time, the big houses in the suburbs would be groaning under the weight of decorations, and no tree in any public place would be safe from a display of Christmas lights that would probably be visible from space. The shops were now open for longer hours to cope with the start of the crazy spending season and, although it was freezing cold and dark, everywhere was buzzing.

It was a small town, a former logging and mining place, one of many such communities that were scattered across the vast lake which was the beating heart of the region. In summer, the lake was a deep, dark blue of calm and the towns circling it were like a child's drawings of pastel-coloured houses with green gardens sloping down to wide streets and trees everywhere.

The mountains could be seen rising up to form an impressive backdrop, and the air was so clear that on a bright day she could almost make out the million different shades of green in those mountains as they towered up into a misty blue haze that seemed to touch the clouds.

Now, at this hour on a cold winter's evening, they were just a rising dark mass all around the town, mysterious and beautiful. Pinpricks of lights advertised the ski runs and chalets that formed part of the winter business for all the towns in the vicinity.

Cassie had never flown far from the nest. It was just the way her life had panned out in the end. She had gone to catering college in one of the bigger towns an hour's drive away. For half the course, she had shared a place in the town with Frankie but, for the remainder of her course, she had lived at home. It was a life that couldn't have been more different from the one she had once breathlessly yearned for.

With all the problems now pressing on her, for the first time the huge open spaces and big skies made her feel claustrophobic. She wished she could run away. She never, ever would, of course, but wouldn't it be nice to run the way Leo had, all those years ago…

He'd run far away to make his fortune. His dad had hung around, but only for another few months, and then he too had left. For such a long time, Cassie had nursed her grief and turned away from the memories of what had happened between them.

She headed back to her apartment with unhappy thoughts of Leo joining the swirling mix of problems she was trying to sort out. By the time she swung into the courtyard in which her apartment block sat, a beautiful squat building surrounded by trees, Cassie was exhausted…and it wasn't yet six-thirty.

There were lights on in most of the flats. It was a wonderful, communal hub comprised of twenty reasonably large apartments in a fantastic location between the shores of the lake and the town. From her bedroom window at night, Cassie could make out the black, still water, in winter dappled silver by moonlight.

She drew to a stop and remained sitting in her car for a minute while the cold air gathered around her, pressing against her thick waterproof. She'd missed three calls. She was very strict about taking no calls when driving. In a place where winter darkness made driving tricky and the roads away from the main drag could be twisty, it would be a dangerous indulgence.

Eyes still half-closed, Cassie pulled the phone out of her backpack and silently hoped that her mother hadn't phoned, asking her to pop by after all, because she was exhausted.

There'd been two calls from prospective clients with whom she had already had a couple of meetings.

And the last call…unknown. It had gone to voicemail.

She expected another potential customer. She wondered who it could be and whether she would know them. She was well-known in the area but had recently feverishly begun to try and drum up business further out to maximise her client base. Maybe it was paying off.

It only took a couple of seconds for Cassie to register the voice—the low, dark drawl; the same voice that had sent shivers down her spine when she'd been a teenager, wildly and madly in love with the boy she'd known was off-limits.

Leo… Leo's voice. Eight years' worth of painful memories slammed into her with the force of a freight train and she could feel her heart pick up speed as she sat up in the car, mouth slackly open as the recorded message told her that he'd got her email.

'So I thought I'd revisit my old stamping ground and pay you a little visit.'

Cassie's breathing was jerky and uneven. Yes, she'd emailed him, but that had been a week ago and she'd expected just an email back, if anything—not a phone call, or a visit out of the blue. Her brain could barely compute it.

She disconnected the message and remained where she was, immobile under the sheer weight of unresolved memories. If she was being honest, she'd wondered whether he'd got her email at all. He was a bigshot now, with tons of money and apartments on every street corner in every city. After they'd broken up, she'd tried her best not to follow what he was up to on any social media platform, and that had been easy because he hadn't been on any.

He'd simply disappeared. Random strands of news had reached her about what he'd been up to over the years but he really hadn't kept in touch with anyone.

He'd moved to the town with his dad when he'd been fourteen and he had seemingly chosen never to put down roots, even though he had gone to school there for years, even though his father had worked in her father's company and even though, for a while, he likewise had worked there as a labourer.

He'd been the sexiest construction worker on the planet. One virginal look at him and Cassie had been lost, and she'd remained lost long after their eight-month-long clandestine relationship had crashed and burned. Long after he'd gone. The memories of him had continued to burn bright inside her along with those of that one perfect night they had spent together when she had just turned nineteen, when neither of them had been able to resist the other any longer.

It was only in the past few months that she'd started checking to find that his name was everywhere on the Internet. He'd gone from Mr Nowhere to be Found to Mr Everywhere because he'd made a fortune, and in record time.

He'd been beyond bright; she knew that, just as she knew that he had been accepted by MIT. What she couldn't have known was just how far he would soar, that he would use everything he had picked up working on that construction site to formulate programmes that would speed up big building projects by weeks, in some cases months. He had revolutionised areas of structural engineering, sold his knowledge for millions before he'd even graduated and, from there, the millions had expanded over the years until now, at the ripe old age of thirty-one, Leo Cruz was rich beyond anyone's wildest dreams.

It was all there on the Internet: his rise to power, money and fame catalogued with loving respect.

And so, a week ago, she'd had that stupid idea... It had been a silly impulse, really, but she had just left her mother, having been to the bank first where Phil had patiently explained to her that the wolves were baying at the door and that there was only so much time left before the house would be repossessed.

'You should start laying the groundwork to prepare your mother, Cassie,' he had told her kindly. 'You're not going to be able to put off the inevitable. I know Clive never expected to go without warning, but he did, and what he left behind was, quite frankly, an unholy mess.'

Except her mother had been having one of her bad days and Cassie just hadn't been able to broach the subject. She'd remembered what the doctor had said about stress, everything in her head had exploded and she'd got back to her apartment and...written that email.

And now...

Her mobile buzzed and Cassie breathed in deeply and accepted the call. She knew who it was. She just didn't know what he was going to say.

'Cassie.'

Leo had booked himself into one of the five hotels in town, the most expensive one. He could remember actually having worked on an extension at the back a thousand years ago when there was no way he would ever have been able to afford to stay in any of the rooms. Now he could buy the entire hotel and it would be small change for him. Now, there was a thought...

He sat back in the old-fashioned sofa by the window and gazed out at a picture-postcard scene of the network of busy streets, brightly lit and filled with Christmas paraphernalia. There were garlands of lights strung from lamp post to lamp post and the bustle of people was getting into the spirit of Christmas spending. He'd forgotten what a production they made of the festive season here.

He dragged his eyes away and sipped some of the excellent red wine he had ordered without bothering to check the price. The room had been cleared of people. He had wanted complete privacy for this call and he hadn't wanted to be cooped up in a bedroom to make it. They had obliged because, as he had discovered over the years, money talked.

No amount of money, though, could quell the sharp jag of memory as he dialled her mobile. Right now, sitting here with her on the other end of the line, it would be stupid not to recognise that he was nervous.

'Leo.'

Leo sucked in a sharp breath and straightened because the sound of her voice, breathy and husky, was like a body blow.

'I'm staying at the Imperial.'

'I... Leo...you're...you're here already?'

'I'm here. Not surprised, are you, Cass? Do you remember the email you sent me a week ago?'

'I shouldn't have contacted you.'

'But you did. Meet me here.'

'Why have you come?'

'Wasn't that what you wanted?'

'I thought... You could have just emailed me back... if anything.'

'And miss the pleasure of catching up with you face to face?'

'You don't really want to see me, Leo. We both know

that. After things ended between us… You still hate me, so why would you come? It was a mistake getting in touch with you. I just… It was…'

'You're stumbling over your words, Cass. Am I making you nervous? No need to be, and you couldn't be further from the truth, as it happens. I don't hate you, not at all. Why should I?'

'I'm sorry. I know I hurt you.'

Leo stiffened, lips thinning as every defence barrier he had ever erected slammed firmly into place.

'Cassie, Cassie, Cassie…' he drawled in a cool, low voice, 'I think you're over-estimating the impact you had on me. We were young, we were infatuated and the truth is that I would never have made it the way I made it if I'd had you harnessed by my side.'

'That's an awful thing to say.'

'Is it? I prefer to see it as being truthful. A young, spoilt bride tagging along would never have been able to weather the years of blood, sweat and tears I've spilled into making my fortune. University…then climbing the ladder, rung by arduous rung… You wouldn't have had the stamina to go without for so long.'

'If you came all the way here to insult me, Leo…'

Had he come to insult her? No. He had come because that email had stirred thoughts of unfinished business, had opened wounds and summoned up memories that should have been dealt with a long time ago.

She clearly wanted money—what else? The minute Leo had made his first million, he had realised that he suddenly had a lot of friends and that an awful lot of them wanted money from him. Cassie was no exception. He was no longer the boy from the wrong side of town, her brief, clandestine secret. He was a billionaire and, if he hadn't come to insult her, he had come to assuage the pain she had dealt him when she had turned him away.

He had come to see her to hear her stumble her way through an explanation of what had gone wrong over the years and then politely but firmly to tell her that, if she wanted money from him, then unfortunately she wasn't going to be in luck. What was wrong with settling a score or two?

'So, I'm taking it that you don't want to see me?' he inserted smoothly.

'I...'

'Because I'm more than happy to have a look around the place for old times' sake and then head back to my house in the Hamptons.'

'I...'

'What do you want to say? I'm all ears, Cass. Your email was brief but you want money from me. So, now that I'm here, have you decided that you no longer need a handout?'

'I never asked for a handout from you, Leo.'

'Perhaps a handout is a little harsh,' Leo agreed. 'You talked about a *loan*, which is such a loose term between friends. Sure you meant a *loan* and not a donation, for old times' sake?'

'I would pay you back every penny, Leo.'

'On an amount that hasn't been specified...interesting. You don't even know what interest rates I might apply.'

The tension had left him. He felt relaxed, triumphant even, because he could sense the rock and the hard place between which she was caught. She hadn't said what the money was for. Personal debts? Had she spent beyond Daddy's generous allowance? He couldn't picture it, but maybe she had developed an insatiable addiction to diamonds and pearls. In the space of eight years, she certainly wouldn't have remained the sweetly innocent thing he had loved so hard and lost so fast.

She'd sent one text message dumping him after the best sex he'd ever had. She'd walked away from him, just as his mother had done, and he was certain the reality of seeing her again would kill off whatever scraps of nostalgia he discovered hadn't quite been exorcised yet.

His lips thinned in grim anticipation. He could have done a little digging and found out what the problem was. He could have delegated it to one of his PAs, although that held no appeal, because this intensely guarded slice of his life wasn't for sharing with anyone, even on a casual level.

However, Leo decided that he would wait and hear what she had to say for herself. There was nothing wrong in prolonging this enjoyable interlude in his life.

'Meet me here in an hour, Cassie. For me, time is money. If you're a no-show, I'll take it that you've had second thoughts and decided that you don't need your so-called loan after all.'

CHAPTER TWO

Half an hour?

There was no time to have a shower and change, even though that was what Cassie would dearly like to have done. She could barely think straight but at least a shower and a change of clothes might have put her in a more composed frame of mind.

Leo! Here, back in the sleepy town he had vacated so hastily, leaving her alone with her misery, her guilt and her sadness. She could remember that text she had sent him as though she'd sent it yesterday. A final goodbye—after all the plans they'd made and the dreams they'd shared, she'd walked away because she'd had no choice.

Cassie rested her head on the steering wheel and closed her eyes as the winter cold seeped around her and settled. She didn't want to think about what had happened between them. She had felt so confused and helpless at the time, torn in a thousand different directions. Leo had been the one guy who could have given her the support she'd needed, her rock for eight of the sweetest months of her life—but of course he had been the problem, so confiding in him had been impossible. She had done what she'd had to do.

It would take twenty minutes to make it back to town and to the Imperial, which was the nicest hotel for miles.

On the spur of the moment, she phoned her mother from the car, turning on the engine just to get a little warmth circulating.

'You don't sound yourself, Cassie,' Mary said after she'd talked about how she had spent the day.

'Mum...' Cassie hesitated. She was an only child and had always been very close to her parents; she had always confided in her mother until she'd met Leo and discovered that there were limits to how much she could ever tell someone else, especially an over-protective parent.

Now, though, she would dearly have loved to tell her about Leo and the nightmare on her doorstep, but she had gone from child to protector the minute her dad had died. Telling her mother about Leo would open up the can of worms that would lead to disclosing the disastrous state of the family finances, and that in turn would ratchet up her mother's stress levels, and she didn't need that.

'Darling?'

'It's...it's nothing.'

'You sound exhausted. Was the catering job more complicated than you expected? I know Claudia Samson and she's never been able to make her mind up about anything.' Mary chuckled. 'I'll bet she made so many changes to the menu that you and Frankie were cooking up to the last minute.'

'She asked after you. She really wants to come and see you.'

'And she can, just as soon as I feel...my old self again.'

'You keep saying that. Honestly, your friends know the situation. They're all so sympathetic.'

'I do see Martha and Elizabeth.'

'Yes, you do. And that's great.'

Cassie ended the call soon after. It was hard to tell the

exact moment when she had become her mother's protector, always careful to put her mental wellbeing ahead of her own and gradually giving up on ever returning to that place where again she might find her mother back able to provide support when she needed it.

When she looked at the clock on the dashboard, it was to see that she would at least not arrive early to meet Leo. Early would equal 'desperate'. The call to her mother had, however, clarified the road she knew she had to take, whether she liked it or not.

Her mum was so proud that she had even retreated from the vibrant friendship group she'd had for over forty years. Yes, she kept in touch with a couple of friends from childhood, but Cassie knew that she didn't want to look feeble and reduced to too many others. She had gone from the society belle of the ball to a woman who could no longer control her own movements, who forgot stuff and who had lost her confidence. To lose the roof over her head would kill every last shred of pride she had left and Cassie wasn't going to put her through that, not if there was the slightest chance she could prevent it.

So, whether it stuck in her throat or not, she was going to go and see Leo, and she was going to lower her eyes and beg. There was no more any bank could do for her but Leo, a billionaire, now...he could help without anything leaking into the public domain and, if he chose to make her pay in blood, then pay in blood she would.

'Shall I keep the room clear for you, sir?'

Leo looked at the manager of the hotel and wondered whether the old man recognised him. It had been a long time ago, but was there a vague recollection in that fuzzy brain somewhere of a young lad of twenty-one who had once asked for a glass of water from the kitchens? He'd been told that he couldn't enter through the main lobby, that he was to return to the extension the team were building and wait for refreshments to be sent out in due course. Their clientele wouldn't take kindly to a sweaty labourer in the foyer. He should *know better*...

'Until I say otherwise,' Leo murmured. 'It's Jenkins, isn't it?'

'Yes, sir.' The old guy reddened and smiled, clearly in awe of the mega-rich guy who was sitting in the chair by the bay window, his long legs extended and loosely crossed at the ankles.

'Do you remember me?'

'Should I sir?'

Leo hesitated.

'No.' He smiled. 'It was a long time ago and I was just passing through. I realise this might be an inconvenience for you, but I want privacy and, like I said, you'll be more than adequately compensated for your trouble. By the way, arrange for another bottle of wine to be brought along with the best you have to offer by way of something to snack on. Lobster and crayfish would work for me.'

'Of course, sir.'

Leo remained where he was as the old guy shuffled his way out of the room.

Hearing Cassie's voice again... He couldn't believe that he was still affected by it. He presumed that that was a simple case of the past colliding with the present, creating rose-tinted glass with a prism through which everything seemed distorted.

He knew that the minute he saw her reality would kick in hard because she wouldn't be the young girl he'd fallen for. The young girl who had given her virginity to him and at the same time bestowed on him the most earth-shattering sex he had ever experienced. That was a joke, really, when it had been followed up by her walking away without a backward glance.

He was sipping his wine, half-looking at the door, half-gazing out at the spectacular view, when he heard the faintest sound of approaching footsteps and every muscle in his body tensed in automatic anticipation.

He shifted, watching as the door was gently pushed open and then...there she was.

She was still leggy, that hair longer now than it had been, but just as dark... He saw that intensely pretty face and those eyes with the long, long sooty lashes...eyes that used to slide sideways at him, giving small, shy glances that had stoked his libido to fever-pitch.

For everything he had gone through as a child; for all the sadness he had endured at his mother's abandonment, the questions he'd asked his dad when he'd been five, six and seven... For all the hardness that had settled inside him as he had come to understand just how badly his father had been affected by his mother leaving him... For all that, it was the woman hovering in the doorway now who had made him the man he was today.

She'd taught him the most valuable lesson he'd ever learned, one he should have learned from his own fractured background: that control was everything. She had been the final nail in the coffin when it came to his view of people, the world and life in general.

He'd broken his own rule and had dared to love and open up to someone and in return...?

'So you made it.' He looked at her, not moving a muscle, his arms hanging loosely over the arms of the chair, his body language advertising someone utterly relaxed.

'And on time, as well. Come in, Cassie. Don't stand there hovering in the doorway—close the door behind you. I thought that, as this was the grand meeting after eight years, I'd make sure the room was cleared for us. If memory serves me right about this place, nothing ever gets past the gossip-spreading grapevine for very long.'

She was wearing a pair of faded jeans, trainers, a worn striped jumper and a thick coat which she had removed but was hanging onto for dear life, along with a backpack that could have accommodated the kitchen sink and then some. She'd tugged her long hair over one shoulder and it hung in a tangled dark mass over her breasts, reaching almost to her waist.

She looked older, more careworn, and yet somehow just as fresh-faced and young as he remembered her. Just as impossibly sexy, and he'd dated enough catwalk models to be an efficient judge of female beauty.

There had always been something about her that went beyond bone structure and body type. It was something about the expression on her face, the timbre of her husky voice and the way she smiled that could make a person feel a thousand feet tall.

Not that he needed any of those attributes now. Too much water had flowed under that bridge. If he wanted to feel a thousand feet tall, he had the proverbial little black book stuffed with candidates who would fall over each other to audition for the role of companion for the night. He would never need any such thing, though, because he was emotionally impregnable. He would hear her out and bid his goodbyes, having put his curiosity to rest.

Yet, for all that, Leo could still feel the unwilling drift of his eyes over her lithe body, the full breasts pushing against her jumper and the length of her legs. He could remember the feel of her as though he'd touched her only minutes ago.

'Sit or go, Cassie,' he said, shifting to adjust to the alarming physical response.

Cassie sidled into the room.

Her stomach had been knotted with nerves for the short trip back into town. Twice she had been tempted to spin the car around and turn back, but then she'd thought of her mother, gritted her teeth and accelerated on.

Being shown to the room by the manager of the hotel had made her feel faint with trepidation. Of course, Bob Jenkins recognised her and asked after her mother but politely refrained from asking about Leo. He obviously hadn't recognised him, which suited Cassie just fine.

And now here she was and, by God, Leo hadn't changed.

He was still as shockingly gorgeous as he had been as a young man, but those good looks had been refined over time and given a harder edge and a more arrogant stamp. He was the guy who had carved out a fortune for himself through blood, sweat and tears, as he had said, and it showed in the sense of ruthlessness lying just beneath the surface.

His hair was still raven-black but was now cropped very short and he was as bronzed as he always had been, the burnished colour of someone whose roots lay somewhere hot and sunny.

She knew that, if he stood up, he would still be six three of compact muscle and sinew and she felt faint just thinking about that. No change, and yet so much—from boy to man. From jeans and tee-shirts to hand-made shoes and cashmere. He wore a black jumper, black trousers, and a matt chrome watch which was unmistakably from a luxury brand.

She sat down in the chair facing his with relief, because her legs were wobbly.

'You look a little shaky,' Leo murmured. 'Don't worry, I've ordered some wine, but you're free to have something stronger if you'd like. First, though...' He reached for his glass that he had set on the table next to him and sipped, before tilting his head to one side and gazing at her over the rim of it. 'How are you?'

'I'm...'

'Not fine?'

Cassie shifted uncomfortably. He'd always been able to read her every shift in mood and it felt as if not much had changed on that front, which was worrying.

'We could spend time going over stuff you're not interested in, Leo but, as you know why I've come here, we could just cut to the chase.'

'I'm not sure I want to take that shortcut just yet, Cass.'

'Because you want to see me squirm.'

'What makes you say that?'

'You know what,' Cassie muttered under her breath. She glanced down at her fingers which were linked on her lap, barely aware of someone bringing two trays, one with wine and glasses and another with finger food. She was ravenous but the thought of eating made her feel queasy.

'Look, I'm sorry, Leo. I'm sorry about the way things ended between us.'

'You mean the way you texted me to tell me that we were unfortunately over? You'd had a think and decided that you were too young to make any serious decisions about your future, especially one that involved leaving this godforsaken little town?'

'I *was* only nineteen.'

'Loosely translated, your parents laid down the law and

you caved in because, when it came right down to it, leaving town with your dirty little secret just wasn't going to do.'

'Don't say that! You were never that!'

'Oh, Cassie, it's the truth.' Leo sighed. His face remained calm and indifferent but inside he was seething at the way he had been drawn into this pointless disinterment of the past. It wasn't why he'd come here. But just seeing her had catapulted him back to where he had been eight years ago and resurrected all sorts of feelings he thought he'd left behind.

His dark eyes cooled and he looked at her without bothering to disguise his masculine appreciation. 'So you went through with the catering course,' he said, changing the subject, and this time there was genuine interest in his voice. He dragged his eyes away because he was tempted to keep on staring at her and somehow that felt like a weakness.

'Yes.' She drew in a steadying breath and hesitated for a few seconds. 'I... I always wanted to go to culinary school, as you know.'

'How could I forget?' Leo said politely, 'When you made such a convincing show of checking out courses near MIT?'

'Leo, please...' She paused but then continued in a rush, 'I opened up a catering business with Frankie—you might remember her.'

'Not really, no.' Leo lowered his eyes. His body was still surging with a physical pull he couldn't seem to control and the drift of the conversation wasn't in a direction he had time for. 'Have some wine.' He poured her a glass and nodded to the plates of food that had been brought in for them. 'And you can see whether the offerings here are as good as you can do yourself.'

'I'm not hungry. Thank you.'

'Suit yourself, but Cassie, my advice is this—when you're on a begging mission, it's often a good idea to approach your potential benefactor with a smile on your face. Why did you get in touch with me when you could have gone to your parents anyway? Or at the very least, the bank manager?' He looked at her narrowly when she didn't immediately answer then he smiled slowly, with dawning comprehension. 'I get it.'

'What? What do you get? And, Leo, you know why I'm not smiling. You're not exactly making this easy for me.'

'You may have a point there, although I'm wondering why you think I should,' Leo conceded with a shrug. 'The past can cast a long shadow.'

'You were going to tell me why you think I came to you...'

'If you wanted money for something straightforward, you would have gone down the straightforward route. However, you haven't. The fact that you've bitten the bullet and contacted me after eight years suggests that, whatever you want the money for, it's for something you want to keep under wraps.'

Leo watched the colour crawl into her cheeks and was almost disappointed that he'd struck the jackpot. Had he secretly hoped that he would find the same innocent girl he had fallen for, however unlikely that would have been?

'What have you been up to?' he asked speculatively. 'Spending beyond your means on things your parents might disapprove of? You're not doing drugs, are you?'

'Of course I'm not doing drugs! I don't even smoke! There's no point playing guessing games, Leo. I'm here... I've come to you because...'

* * *

Their eyes tangled and Cassie felt a shiver of awareness that was threaded with the treacherous stir of sexual excitement, the same sexual excitement she had felt all those years ago when she'd lived and breathed only Leo.

She didn't even know this man sitting in front of her with the unfeeling, superior expression and his contemptuous manner. Wealth had changed him and bitterness had instilled a cruel harshness that had never been there before. He'd forgotten nothing.

She felt a surge of protectiveness towards her family, towards her ailing mother. She would have to admit to the financial difficulties sitting on her doorstep, but she wasn't going to confide in him about anything else. She would do what she had to do and forget that they'd once shared a past.

'Because…?'

'It's the family business, Leo. There have been problems and now…' Cassie felt tears gather in her eyes and rapidly blinked them away.

'You've been to the bank? And why are you the one coming to see me? Did your parents think that you might be able to find a way to me where they would never be able to?' He shot her a curling, derisory smile. 'Was your father too proud to come with the begging bowl?'

'This isn't going to work.' Cassie leapt to her feet and began turning away.

'Stop!'

That single command brought her to an abrupt standstill and she swung round to glare at him.

'Why?' She swept some of her hair away from her face and tilted her chin at a defiant angle. 'We both know that the only reason you came here was to watch me beg you for money you have no intention of lending me!'

Leo flushed darkly.

'You're still bitter about what happened between us but, even if that's the case, Leo, I never thought that you could be as cruel as you're being now.'

That hit home and she saw Leo's jaw clench. He'd probably told himself that he wasn't here for revenge but of course he was.

She'd hurt him once upon a long time ago and so he'd returned to repay the favour.

'Tell me why you need the money, Cassie. And have something to eat. The food will otherwise just go to waste.'

Cassie looked at him for a few seconds. For the first time since she'd entered the room, his tone wasn't openly aggressive. She thought of her mother and all the horrible changes and distress she would have to endure if the house was repossessed. With that thought uppermost in her mind, she tentatively sat back down.

'So?' Leo prompted.

'First of all,' Cassie said quietly, 'My dad died several months ago. I know that, after everything that happened between us, you thought the worst of him. I know your father worked for the company, and you never openly said anything, but you didn't like the divisions between the men on the ground floor and the managers who gave the orders. I *know* you pigeonholed Dad as rich and maybe uncaring, but I loved him, and he honestly wasn't like that.'

'I confess I didn't know him aside from the glimpses I had now and again,' Leo said gruffly. 'But it's true that I resented what he represented—the boss who seldom checked in personally on the lowly blue-collar workers. How did he die?'

'Heart attack, out of the blue. He... When he died... I mean afterwards...lots of things came out that my mother and I didn't know about.'

'Ah.' Leo sat back and looked at her. 'He left behind debts you knew nothing about. It happens, I'm afraid. Bad management, poor investments, over-extending... take your pick.'

'It was a huge shock.' Cassie sucked in her breath. 'He'd always been protective of both of us, was always so proud that he could provide for us, so neither of us really delved into any of the company finances. He took his eye off the ball, made bad decisions and even worse investments. He'd dug into all the savings and he'd taken money from the company. He'd borrowed from Peter to pay Paul.' She looked away and swallowed painfully. 'I've spent months unravelling all sorts of debts and selling stuff to pay creditors. I came to you because the house is on the line and it would kill my mother if we lost that.'

'Why?'

'Why what?'

'Why did he take his eye off the ball?'

Cassie lowered her eyes. She didn't know why, exactly, but she could make a pretty educated guess. Tracing back through, it had all begun a few years after her mother's diagnosis. On the surface, he had been dealing with it all, but underneath he had been slowly collapsing and no one had noticed.

They had always been a close couple but Mary had been the force behind the union, the one who had always been there for him—his backbone in many ways. He just hadn't been able to cope with her diagnosis and the fact that there was so little light at the end of the tunnel.

There was a limit to what she wanted to reveal to Leo, however. She hadn't come asking him for pity. She had come asking for a loan. He hated her for what she had done to him and most of her could understand why. She had walked away from him, and she hadn't been able to tell him why, so he had been left without any explanation. God, it had been so hard.

Looking at him now, she recalled the night she had excitedly, finally, told her parents that she was in love with Leo, that she wanted to go to catering college close to where he would be studying and that they had dreams and plans of a future together.

In response, her parents had brokenly told her about her mother's diagnosis which they had been keeping to themselves and, because they'd begged her not to leave, just like that she had found herself in a hole with no way out.

She felt the weakness of tears sting behind her eyes and gritted her teeth against the temptation to cry now. The past was the past. Leo had walked away after she'd texted him and had never looked back over his shoulder once to find out what had happened to her, and he wouldn't be sitting here now if it weren't for the fact that she had reached out to him.

He'd forged a prosperous life for himself and, as he had told her, was relieved to have left her behind because she would only have held him back. They stood on opposite sides of an impenetrable wall and she could never forget that.

'These things happen. He didn't leave a journal giving his reasons.' She shrugged.

'How is your mother?'

Cassie thought of her proud, frail mother and ached for her. She couldn't bear Leo to be privy to the absolute vulnerability of her situation and she wasn't going to discuss something she felt as very private with a guy who, painfully but understandably, no longer felt anything for her but dislike.

Even though his tone of voice was neutral right now, what lay in his heart would always be bitterness.

'If you don't mind, I'd rather we stuck to business, Leo. I haven't come prepared with facts and figures, but I can tell you that the catering company is doing really well and we're on the verge of expansion.'

'How much are you asking for?'

She told him, not pulling any punches. It was a vast amount of money but what would be the point in pretending otherwise? He didn't so much as wince at the figure.

'I know it's a lot—' she cleared her throat '—and it will take a while for me to repay you in its entirety but the catering company is mine and I would do whatever it took to repay any debts from whatever profits I made. I would even be willing to let you have a share in it... surely an arrangement could be made...something that would work for you...'

'You would never be able to repay me entirely, Cassie. We both know that. A catering company is a catering company, however successful it is, and the fact that you're operating here, where the population density is low, restricts just how big it could ever get.'

'So that's it, then. Okay.'

'Why not just sell the house and downsize?' Leo shrugged. 'Why would your mother object to that?'

'She would find it very stressful,' Cassie hedged, glancing away.

'There's no such thing as a life without stress,' Leo said flatly. 'I could put you in touch with my father if you want to learn all about that.'

Cassie tensed. It felt hopeless. He had no intention of lending her any money. Had she contacted him because, like he'd pointed out, she'd subconsciously hoped he'd help her out for old times' sake? If she had, then she must have been crazy because his memory of those *old times* would never have him running along the track of being happy to help out.

'Okay,' she said quietly. 'I'm glad I tried anyway and I'm sorry again about…everything, Leo.'

'Wait a minute, Cassie.'

His voice, so low and velvety, as rich as the darkest of chocolate, settled around her, making her want to swoon.

She stared at him and licked her lips nervously.

CHAPTER THREE

WATCHING HER, Leo noted every shift of expression on her face, so familiar and yet so alien after all this time.

Curiosity had propelled him here. Curiosity and a stupidly childish desire for revenge, whether he liked to admit it or not, because revenge was a petty emotion, beneath him. Take away those two things and only one thing remained which would account for his response to her, a response which defied logic and infuriated him: unfinished business.

'I think I can help you out…provided you're ready to take the deal I offer.'

'Deal?' Cassie asked hesitantly.

'Interested?'

'I thought you said that my catering company could never repay any loan you offered.'

'Who said anything about a loan?'

'Do you really think I would ever believe that you'd just *give* me money after everything that's happened between us? I know how you feel about me. I can see it in your eyes and hear it in your voice. At any rate, I would never take money from you if it *wasn't* a loan, Leo.'

Leo countered that with a slow, curling smile.

'Gifts often come with price tags but, that aside, I expect you might very well take money from me if I threw it your way. One thing I've discovered is that people often say one thing very loudly but can always be persuaded to do the exact opposite when sufficient money is dangled in front of them. In the nick of time, they're usually prone to remembering the saying about pride coming before a fall.'

'You've changed so much, Leo.'

'From what?'

'You used to be so…gentle and kind.'

Leo flushed.

Gentle? Kind? It was a reminder that wasn't welcome because he'd been as tough as nails from way too young. By the time he'd met Cassie, he'd been so tough, he'd been pretty much untouchable. Working in construction wasn't a career that called for anyone of a delicate disposition.

But with Cassie, yes, he'd become a guy he'd barely recognised, though he'd liked that part of him—the part that *had* been gentle and kind. The part that had put her first.

He had let her tame him and he would never forgive himself for that misjudgement. She had opened a door behind which his emotions had been kept under lock and key and, when she had walked away from him, he had returned those emotions to their vault but this time he had thrown away the key. It would never be used again.

It was good that she could see just how far he'd toughened up. For the deal he was about to put on the table, she'd do well to remember that he would never be up for grabs.

Once she'd been the rich girl and he the poor boy. Now the shoe was on the other foot and that was pretty much the beginning, the middle and end of it.

'Want to hear the deal?' Leo drawled and, when he

knew he had her full, undivided attention, he sat forward, arms on his thighs and looked at her until she nodded.

'We made love once and I haven't forgotten just how good it was. You got cold feet and ran for the hills before we had time to really explore one another sexually.'

'It wasn't like that. I know it seems that way but I didn't run for the hills. At least, not like you seem to think.'

Leo let her finish. 'Let's not get bogged down in details that don't matter. Time's moved on from then. What I'm proposing is that we pick up where we prematurely left off…'

'You mean you want me to *sleep* with you?'

'You catch on fast.'

'How could you suggest such a thing?'

'Unfinished business for me, Cassie.' Just talking about it was a reminder of how good that one passionate encounter had been. It had been mind-blowing. Sleep with her again, and he was sure he would discover fast enough that his rosy memories of that magical experience could be a thing of the past. He'd never found that level of passionate fulfilment with anyone else. It was time for that particular ghost to be exorcised, and sleeping with her would definitely do the trick.

'Not for me!'

'Oh, we both moved on with other people, but neither of us is married and I'm currently unattached. What about you?'

'I'm not going to have this conversation.'

'But you haven't heard what you get out of it.'

'I'm not interested!'

'Everything. Every single debt will be paid in full: no nasty creditors at the door; no unsympathetic company turning off the central heating as winter approaches; no stressed-out mother wringing her hands in despair at having to show the world how far the powerful Farraday family has fallen...'

Cassie stared at the man opposite her.

He was so devastatingly, sinfully beautiful and so casually ruthless. She should spring to her feet right now and march out of the door, whatever the consequences!

Then she thought of her mother...thought of how she would collapse when she knew the full extent of their penury. Thought of the disease burrowing inside her, which would be unleashed to run amok by the stress which would surely cripple her.

'Why would you want that, Leo?'

'Like I said, there's unfinished business between us, Cass. I hadn't realised till I got here just how powerful that can be and this is my golden opportunity to slay that particular dragon.'

'You would force me into a situation like that? How would you be satisfied knowing that you'd manoeuvred me into doing something I didn't want to do?'

Leo shook his head reprovingly. 'You know me better than that. I would never force you into anything,' he said softly. He looked at her with his head to one side. 'You're not married, are you?'

'No.'

'The lack of a wedding ring was the first thing I noticed. I'm surprised.'

'Why?'

'Given you listened to your parents when it came to getting rid of me, I would have imagined you'd also have listened to them when it came to hooking a suitable husband.'

'I'm not a doll, Leo, to be positioned this way or that without any say in the matter.'

But Cassie blushed. Her parents had been appalled when she'd told them about Leo. She'd been so excited, so flushed with love, tripping over her words as she'd laid out all her fairy-tale plans. Then had come the revelation about her mother's illness and their dismay that she would consider leaving Canada. They'd insisted they needed her there because these times were frightening and uncertain. The fact that it would have been Leo taking her away and not one of the boys she had grown up with, who would have been a known quantity, had filled them with dismay and confusion.

Oh, how she could remember the painful conversation, the way the enthusiasm to spread her wings with the man she'd fallen in love with had seeped out of her. Her dad had actually cried and it had been the first time she'd ever seen him do that. Never had she felt the burden of responsibility on her shoulders weigh more heavily as she had listened to him brokenly explain the hard road that lay ahead of them all.

Her mother had started to cry as well. The thought of losing her daughter to an unknown future far away with someone she'd never even met had been too much. She'd said she would worry about Cassie, worry that she'd made a terrible mistake, that she'd be too far away to come home if she had to. The worry would kill her before the illness did. Her diagnosis was something Mary had insisted on holding close until she'd grown used to the horror of it. She'd said no one could know, not yet—it was too raw. She needed her family around her, just until she grew strong enough to face the inevitable. She'd said she knew it was a big ask, knew that her baby had to fly the nest some time, but not yet.

So, Cassie had stayed put. She had ended their relationship by text, without telling Leo the truth, because there'd been no way out. What would be the point of meeting up to discuss it, talking about something that was already a done deal, the details of which she couldn't even share with him?

She'd promised her parents that she would say nothing to anyone, least of all Leo. And she'd known, in her heart, that if she *had* met up with Leo, he would have seen the secret she was trying to keep. What would he have done? Would he have sacrificed his bright future at MIT for her? Promised to wait for her? If he'd decided not to and walked away, how bad would he have felt at having had to make that decision? She couldn't have clipped his wings, never. It had been easier to cut the ties between them completely.

But something inside her had died that day. She blinked and surfaced to what he was saying now, some response to her comment about her not being the sort of doll who could be positioned this way or that.

'Although,' he murmured, 'I very much enjoyed your positioning the day we made love.'

'Leo!'

'I never forgot the feel of you,' he said huskily. 'Did you—forget the feel of me?'

'Why does it matter?'

'You still haven't told me if there is someone else on the scene for you. Is there?'

Cassie blinked and looked at him. She tugged her thoughts away from where they'd been, dwelling on the past. No, she'd forgotten nothing. The memory of him had been preserved in her mind in all its wondrous glory.

'That's none of your business...' She breathed.

'It is if we're going to become lovers. I'm not into treading on any man's property.'

'*Property?* I would never be any man's *property.*'

'You'd be mine if we were together.' Leo kept his dark eyes levelled on her annoyed face in unashamed appraisal before standing up and flexing his muscles. 'I'm like that...'

He stood tall, hard as rock, with the body of someone honed to physical perfection. Cassie's heart was beating fast. His offer had penetrated her brain but she still hadn't really registered the enormity of it. She took a step back because his physical presence was so overpowering.

'I'm guessing there's no lucky man on the scene,' Leo murmured, moving to stand so close to her that she could breathe him in, and she did, nostrils flaring, eyes reluctantly and defiantly pinned to his face. She couldn't tear them away. That dear, dear face she had held in her hands so many times, crazy in love and wanting a future with him more than she'd ever wanted anything in her life...

'Good,' he murmured with satisfaction.

And then he reached out, very, very gently pushed some hair away from her face and cupped her cheek with his hand. That was it—nothing more—and his hand barely rested on her for longer than a few seconds but that touch sent her body racing towards meltdown. She could feel the heat pour through her, lighting her up inside until her skin was burning.

'So?' Leo stood back and shoved his hands into his trouser pockets. 'What's it to be, Cassie—a trip down memory lane with all your financial worries sorted along the way, or no deal? Because, if you go for the *no deal* option, then there will be no turning back, ever. Whatever money worries you have to deal with, you'll have to manage them on your own. I will walk away and you'll never see me again.'

Cassie's mouth went dry.

'And if I agree? What exactly would you have in mind?'

Leo smiled slowly. 'Terms and conditions to be agreed but, as I'll be running the show, I'll be honest and say that they'll mostly be *my* terms and conditions.' He paused. 'The one thing you'll have is my signature on the dotted line that all your financial worries will be over.'

Cassie's head was spinning.

Leo…as a lover…? The very thought of it made her want to pass out. His offer was brazen, arrogant and utterly selfish but could she say no to what he had put on the table? Yet, if she did agree, what would those *terms and conditions* amount to? She had a lot of thinking to do but he wasn't about to indulge that need. He'd thrown his offer down and he was waiting for her answer. Say no, and he would walk away and she would never see him again.

She should have been outraged and she was! Yet underneath the righteous anger that he could use his power and money to twist her arm the way he had was a certain simmering excitement that she didn't want to feel but which she couldn't seem to suppress.

Oh, she had relived their love-making on a loop, night after night, week after week, year after year.

To have that again…

He would give her ten minutes to consider his proposal.

He left the room, ordered coffee to be brought to them and by the time he returned he had decided that, from here on in, things would move in a business-like direction. So much for his original decision to make an appearance, listen to her sob story, see how the years had treated her and then walk away. An eye for an eye.... He hadn't looked at it as revenge. He didn't do revenge. He'd justified it as simply doing whatever it took to lock the door for ever on memories that had no place in the present.

But then he'd seen her, and every single bit of him had known that a baseless act of walking away would never kill the hold the past still seemed to exercise over him. She had stood there in the doorway, with that look of defiance, innocence and trepidation on her face and he had seen the blushing shy girl who had stolen his heart and managed, somehow, to keep a piece of it in the palm of her hand.

Her body was long and strong, athletic rather than willowy. Her breasts, those breasts he had held and kissed just that one, beautiful time, were full and round, her legs were shapely and slender and they made him think how badly he wanted the feel of them wrapped around him once again.

Walking away, knowing that he was in a position to deny her the money she wanted, would mean he'd never get rid of those feelings she still stirred in him. The love might be gone but the memories were still too sharp. He'd tuned in to her as though no time had passed.

What was surprising, though, was that it hurt to see her in the position of supplicant when he'd thought he would feel satisfied. But he refused to let nostalgia and whimsy get the better of him. He'd moved on from that place but something inside had twisted when she'd told him about her father's debts.

No, to destroy whatever hold she still had over him,

he would have her again, feel her body move beneath his again and touch her in all the places he remembered with a clarity that shocked him.

If she accepted his proposal, he would soon know whether the physical pull was still there for her as it was for him. He thought it was. He'd felt the tremor in her body when he had touched her.

Of course, he would have to lay down some ground rules…

'Coffee is on its way.' He closed the door behind him. She was sitting now, frowning and chewing her lip. Her eyes were distant and thoughtful when they met his.

'Is this the part where you tell me that I need a clear head…?'

'I hadn't thought of that,' Leo drawled, amused, 'But a clear head might be a good idea.'

'You already know what I'm going to say,' Cassie said quietly, pausing as coffee was brought in and deferentially put on the coffee table. She continued when they were once more alone. 'I told you how awful the situation was. I accept your deal.'

'So let's relax and talk about the terms and conditions. I wouldn't want any crossed wires or misunderstandings when it comes to this little arrangement.'

He noted her casual outfit with satisfaction. The lack of designer gear was a turn-on for him because it reflected something authentic about her he used to find irresistible. He imagined ripping her clothes off, and then he imagined her ripping them off herself, wanting him so much it hurt.

Leo wasn't trying to conceal his thoughts and, watching him, Cassie could feel the hot burn of his desire, the anticipation of touching her.

She freed her own thoughts and admitted that it was the same for her—that pull of lust and desire to touch the thing she'd been denied for eight long years.

How many nights had this man surfaced in her dreams? Since Leo, she'd had only one brief, disappointing affair and, after that, she had abandoned that side of her. She'd pushed forward with her life, and enjoyed her work, just as she enjoyed spending time with her friends, but he'd stuck in her head and she had never managed to rid herself of the memory.

So maybe this was her time to clear her head of him once and for all. She could never feel about him the way she had before, but she could see this as a situation that benefited them both.

Why not? Why should she play the shrinking martyr, dragged into something because she had no choice? She had a choice. *This* was her choice and she was going to own it. Sleeping with Leo wasn't just going to be about doing something for the sake of her mother. It was also going to be about doing something for *herself.*

'I have one or two terms and conditions of my own,' she said coolly.

'Have you? Interesting. Fire away, but bear in mind that I reserve the right to completely disregard them.'

'I want a timeline to this situation.'

'What did you have in mind?'

'A week.'

'But what if you decide that you want things to keep going for longer?' Leo purred.

'That's never going to happen.'

'A week sounds about right. I can't see either of us wanting to extend things beyond that.'

'Agreed. I want to have closure as much as you do. I

also want to finish what we started eight years ago. And a week? Perfect, just long enough to exorcise old ghosts.'

'Never a word truer spoken. Anything else now that you're on a roll? I'm keen to hear if there are any more conditions I'm willing to allow.'

Cassie ignored the sarcasm. 'It'll have to fit around both my work and family commitments.'

'I'm afraid,' Leo said mock-sadly, 'That particular condition falls into the category of "to be jettisoned".'

'Why?' Cassie cried.

'Because I want my time with you to be uninterrupted and it's going to be interrupted non-stop if we're here—catering emergencies, phone calls from friends, your mother popping round... None of that's going to work for me. Not on any level.'

'What do you mean?'

'A change of scenery might be in order and, before you continue protesting, you're not going to change my mind on that.'

'A change of scenery to where?' she demanded.

'To be decided. Let's stick to the programme in the meanwhile. You'll be having a week off from your routine and you'll need to sort that out.'

'But my mother's already stressed with everything that's happening. I need to be here for her.'

'A week is hardly an eternity in the great scheme of things.'

Cassie looked down at her hands knotted on her lap. She pretty much lived with her mother, looking in on her once a day, sometimes more. How was Mary going to cope without her around? She would have to depend on the two friends she actively kept in touch with. Would that be enough? Could they be relied on? People had their own lives to live.

'What are you not telling me?' Leo pressed.

'Mum's not in the best of health,' Cassie confessed unwillingly.

'What's wrong with her?'

'I... I'd rather not discuss that, if you don't mind.'

The silence lengthened between them.

'There's something serious in your expression. I'm sorry,' Leo said quietly. 'I know you have a close bond with your mother. Is that why you've agreed to do this?' His dark eyes were suddenly shrewd and speculative.

The last thing Cassie wanted was for Leo to feel sorry for her. The very last thing she needed was to soften towards him. He'd moved on. She meant nothing to him now and, if he hadn't once looked back in eight years to see how she had fared, maybe she just hadn't meant all that much to him back then. Yes, she'd broken up with him, but hadn't he ever been tempted to glance over his shoulder and see whether she was okay? Or had she been so easily disposable in the end?

'Like I said, yes, I'm doing this because I need the money, but also because we *did* leave things unfinished between us and we *do* both need closure.'

'I'm very happy we're on the same page,' Leo murmured, looking at her pensively. 'I'm sure your mother will be capable of coping for a week...won't she?' He looked down and clenched his jaw.

Was he already regretting their deal?

'I also want it in writing,' she added.

He glanced back up. 'What?'

'The money side of things.'

'You don't honestly think that I would make a deal with you and renege, do you?'

He looked genuinely shocked and Cassie's mouth tightened. 'I don't know who you are any more. You're not the boy I used to know.'

'Very true. That said, I'm a man of honour and I always have been.' His voice had cooled. 'But,' he continued, 'I'll make sure my signature is in all the right places. Is that the sum total of your conditions?'

'Yes.'

'Good. We can move on to mine now.' He poured himself some water, sipped it and looked at her for a few seconds. 'We have one week together and I want that week to be spent...' he smiled slowly and ran his eyes over her until she blushed '...productively.'

'What does that mean, exactly?'

'We had one night together...and now I want all the fantasies I've had on the back of that for the entire week we're together. I don't just want great sex. I want great sex with all the bells and whistles.'

Cassie went bright-red because his very words, husky and sexy, were making her damp between her legs. She could scarcely breathe as dark, forbidden excitement raced through her.

'So, here's the deal. I want you to wear sexy underwear—maybe no underwear at all. You can surprise me, but no granny cotton panties and bras designed to repel wandering hands. I want to touch your bare skin without having to unclasp anything and I want the feel of lace and silk on my fingers when I pull your panties aside so that I can touch your moistness.' He raised his eyebrows when she didn't object and smiled slowly. 'I'm not hearing any howls of horror yet.'

'How do you know I don't already wear sexy underwear?'

'Now, there's a remark to turn a guy on. Do you?'

'I'm afraid you'll have to wait until you sign our agreement,' Cassie told him coolly.

She could feel a pulse throbbing between her legs as distant fantasies began to take shape, reminding her of how he used to make her feel—as though she was on a permanent high, plugged into a socket, with every waking moment spent in heady anticipation of seeing him.

The situation was nothing like that now but the slow build of that familiar lust told her that she had done the right thing, agreeing to his proposal. He was getting what he wanted but he couldn't know just how much the very same thing applied to her.

'Also,' Leo continued, 'No pining to be back here. One week, but you're all mine, with all your attention on me.'

'I agree, as long as I've sorted my affairs before I leave. But I'll still need my phone with me at all times, just in case.'

'I'm not going to be holding you prisoner, Cassie,' he said wryly. 'You'll be able to contact the outside world if you want to but I'm guessing you might want to keep this little arrangement of ours under wraps.'

'Yes,' Cassie admitted. 'So it probably works that we won't be here.' She looked at him curiously and for a moment her mind wasn't on the weird arrangement ahead of her. 'Has anyone recognised you?'

'Not to the best of my knowledge,' Leo said, relaxing and looking at her with amusement. 'It's been a while and, believe me, put a man in different clothes and the world assumes he's a different person.'

'I guess so.'

Leo hesitated. 'How have you coped?'

'With what?'

'The lack of money.'

'Believe it or not, my rich background didn't turn me into a spoiled brat. Course, it's been difficult dealing with the bank and having to sell family stuff to pay off creditors, at least as many as I've been able to, but...' She looked at Leo with open honesty. 'No one knows.'

'No one?'

'I wanted to protect Mum. It's been tough for her after Dad died. She knows we now have money troubles, but not just how deep the problem is, and I couldn't expose her to the shame of having everything fall apart around her. I wanted to protect her a bit longer.'

Leo looked at her thoughtfully.

He'd sensed that about her even back then; she'd always been unaffected by her background. It was what, in part, had made her so irresistible. He'd accused her of dumping him because she couldn't bear to lose the status she'd grown up with, because her parents had weighed in on the subject, but he uneasily wondered whether there'd been more to the story. She'd sent that text and he'd walked away from her and never looked back. The pride and bitterness had been too powerful. All too clearly he'd remembered his mother and the way her vanishing act had affected his dad...had affected *him*.

He'd moved on immediately. There was no turning back the clock now, and he wouldn't want to anyway. No way was he ever going to be vulnerable again but he could only admire her attitude now.

'Whatever you say about wanting this, if tough times

are calling the shots, I want you to tell me. Drop the pride and tell me the truth.'

'What would you do if I said yes?' Cassie looked at him sadly. 'Would it change anything? You have me where you want me.'

'I would call the deal off.'

'I need the money. You know that.'

'You would have the money,' he said roughly.

'Sorry?'

'I meant what I said at the start, Cassie. You say you want what I want, that you want to finish what we started, but you have to mean it. I don't want an unwilling woman in my bed. If this comes down on the side of hard cash, then you can have the hard cash without being my lover.'

'You would *do* that?'

'No big deal.'

'That's not what you were saying when I first showed up here, Leo.'

'You want to take the money and run? Tell me now and I'll transfer the lot to you within the day.'

Their eyes met. Hers were wide and on the side of disbelieving and, for a couple of seconds, Leo was rocked by an urgency for her to turn that particularly generous offer down. He wanted her. He wanted her badly, more than he could ever remember wanting any other woman. One night with her had been off the charts and he wanted more. He needed more. He had to get her out of his system.

But, however much he wanted her, however much he wanted to finish this once and for all, and however much he had uncomfortably admitted to himself that payback had played a part in his decision, the thought of sleeping with her when she might not be one hundred percent invested in sleeping with him brought a sour taste to his mouth.

He wanted her to want him in equal measure and to mean it, or else what would be the point? Wouldn't that just make the whole thing linger more destructively inside him over time?

'Why would you do that?' Cassie demanded.

'Because it's not my style, like I said.'

'You also said that if I didn't take your deal you would walk away without a backward glance.'

Leo flushed darkly. 'I had no idea your mother was ill,' he said brusquely, keen to get off the topic of his sudden change of heart. 'Naturally, that changed the landscape somewhat.'

'In that case...'

Leo tensed.

'I'm not going to walk away, Leo.'

'Good,' Leo returned, heady with satisfaction that he had given her the option of walking away with the money, pleased that he now knew for certain that the desire was as great for her as it was for him.

'Which,' Cassie said, 'Doesn't mean my ground rules don't stand.'

'I wouldn't dream of thinking that.' Leo waved one hand in a magnanimous gesture. 'Of course they stand but, now that we're on solid ground, there's just one more thing I want to add before any signing on dotted lines takes place.'

'What's that?'

'You and me... We might be sitting here talking about sex but that's where the conversation begins and ends.'

'What do you mean?'

'I shouldn't have to spell it out, Cass, but I will anyway because the last thing I want is for something unfortunate to happen.'

'Do you honestly think I would make a mistake, Leo? Do you think I'm *that* stupid? If you must know, I'm on the contraceptive pill, so you don't have to worry on that front.'

Leo laughed shortly. 'I actually wasn't talking about that but, just for the record, I have never taken chances in that area. When you're as rich as I am, you quickly become hyper-vigilant about women who see you as more than just passing through. Scrape the surface of every accommodating woman and you'll soon find one who has dollar signs in her eyes.'

'What were you talking about, in that case?'

'You had me once,' he said neutrally. 'You won't be having me again.'

'Meaning?' she asked again.

'One week, as per your timeline, and then you exit my life. I don't know how active or inactive your love life has been, Cass, but there won't be anything between us other than some extremely satisfying sex.'

'It's very arrogant of you to think that I might start looking for anything more.'

'Once upon a time,' he said quietly, 'There was the promise of more, but it's far too late now. One week and I will be walking away.'

'Like you said earlier, we're on the same page.'

Leo stood up, conversation over, and Cassie hurriedly leapt to her feet as well.

Between them, the tray of finger food remained untouched but that wasn't surprising, Leo thought, considering the conversation they'd just had. Now that they were embarking on this unexpected adventure, Leo could feel the libido he had tried to stifle when he'd first seen her rear into action.

He gazed lazily and leisurely at the fall of her thick, dark hair and the soft curve of her cheeks. He breathed out slowly, reining in the erection that was already growing rock-hard. He swerved to stand in front of her and looked down into her eyes.

'You're even more beautiful now than you were back then, Cass.'

'You don't have to do the compliment thing.'

'I never do anything I don't want to do and I seldom say what I don't mean. That's the one thing vast wealth brings a person—freedom to do just as you please provided no one gets hurt. You're not going to get hurt, are you?'

'I've told you, Leo, that's not on the cards.'

'Good. In that case...'

This time his touch wasn't fleeting and light. This time he pulled her towards him and, as his mouth descended, every single thought in his head flew away as she surrendered to the one thing he'd spent eight years trying to forget.

CHAPTER FOUR

Had she made the right decision?

It was a clear-cut deal and, in the end, he hadn't forced her into anything. He had given her an opt-out clause and, when he'd heard about her mother's ill health, had been gracious enough to offer the money without the stipulations. He might no longer have feelings for her outside a basic physical attraction he wanted to kill off but he hadn't rammed her into a corner and forced her hand.

He'd never been that kind of guy. Underneath the tough exterior, she had always seen the gentleness inside him. Life had toughened him up, and bitterness had scarred his memory of her, but he essentially remained a fair-minded man despite the ruthless streak that had propelled him to the top of the food chain.

Cassie knew that she could have taken him up on his offer to claim the money and walk away, but she'd rejected that, because seeing him had fired up her own memories of what it had felt like for her body to yearn for his. She, too, had buried those sexual feelings and presumed them to be dead.

One look at Leo's handsome face and the past had rushed back at her, bringing everything with it, and the force of that resurrected past had made her agree to what he was offering.

She'd wanted the strings attached. The difficult bit had been telling her mother, who'd been confused and alarmed at her daughter's sudden need to disappear for a week. Cassie could hardly blame her. One minute she was saying that she was far too busy to have a life, that the skies were falling down around them, and the next minute she was doing a disappearing act to shores unknown for a much-deserved break.

'Can we afford it?' her mother had asked worriedly, and Cassie had immediately put her mind to rest on that score by telling her that things were looking up on the financial front.

It had been a good prelude to the news that would materialise within weeks that all their money problems had been solved. Cassie had no idea what she was going to say to explain that. A lottery win? A kind investor who wanted to buy the unprofitable dregs of the family business through the goodness of his heart? A mysterious donor who had read about their situation and decided to hand them a wad of cash, no strings attached?

The last might be the most accurate, bar the attached strings, but there was no way she was going to breathe a word about Leo. She knew her mother would be appalled if she suspected that her daughter was going to sleep with the guy who had broken her heart for an injection of cash. Even if she tried to explain the situation, to reassure her mother that the decision was entirely mutual, she knew that Mary would be bitterly disappointed, and at the back of Cassie's mind was all that stuff about trying to make sure her mother had to deal with as little stress as possible. It didn't bear thinking about, so she'd have to cross all the bridges regarding their sudden good fortune when the time came.

For the moment... Standing by the window of her

apartment, waiting for Leo's driver to arrive, Cassie felt yet another attack of sheer nerves.

It had been a week since she'd seen him.

'That should be long enough for you to sort out whatever you have to sort out.'

'It might not be,' Cassie had immediately objected. 'A week isn't much time to get things in order with work... and then there's Mum.'

'You've laid down your ground rules, Cassie,' he had told her coolly and firmly. 'I'm giving you a week. My driver will collect you and I'll email you everything you need to know about where we're going.'

Cassie had conceded defeat. He'd already been exceedingly generous; she wasn't going to start pushing her luck. She got the feeling that Leo had become a guy who didn't have much of a soft side and she'd already used up some of it. Besides, the sooner she did this, the better.

She looked at her case on the ground next to her and hoped that the clothes she'd packed were going to do the trick. Lots of hopes, fears and keyed up nervous tension built but, as she settled into the back seat of his chauffeur-driven car and peered around to catch a departing glimpse of the town, already turning white under light flurries of snow, the thread of excitement also wended its way through her veins.

She rested back and prepared herself for the journey that lay ahead.

Leo relaxed back and gazed at a blazing sunset. He actually hadn't been in his villa here on Mustique for over a year. He was extremely satisfied with his choice of destination for their one-week interlude: sun, sea and sex; what could go wrong?

He glanced at his watch. All arrangements had been made for Cassie to be delivered to his villa. He would have made the trip with her, but he had already been in Europe on business and had flown straight from his apartment in Paris.

Still... Leo swirled his drink in one hand and smiled with a warm glow of anticipation...it wasn't as if she wouldn't be travelling in style. She'd fly first class to St Lucia where she would be ushered to a special lounge to wait to board the tiny eighteen-seater plane which he had commandeered for her sole use.

Life throws curveballs, he couldn't help but think.

Back in the day, he would have been the one too strapped for cash to take a domestic flight, never mind a long-haul one, while she would have been the one waving bye-bye to Canada as she boarded a jet for somewhere exotic. Obviously, nowhere near as exotic as this, but who was going to split hairs?

It was a pleasant thought and he enjoyed it until he heard the sound of his doorbell. Every muscle in his body tensed in heady anticipation but he didn't rush as he sauntered away from the wraparound porch with its fine view of sky and ocean, both submerged in inky darkness, and headed towards the front door.

There was no need to rush. He had a whole week and he intended to make sure he took his own sweet time... She was going to be enjoyed in ways that would make her blush. He'd had one taste of her and it had been never forgotten. A feast now awaited.

Cassie was a bag of nerves.

She hadn't quite known what to expect aside from the fact that she would be going somewhere hot, that the trip would be quite long and that she should bring casual clothes.

I'm not usually a fan of surprises, he had written in his email, *but, since this whole situation has come as a surprise, why not go with the flow?*

Cassie hadn't argued.

He had already begun the business of sorting out all her financial woes and her relief had been so huge that she would have willingly hopped on a rocket to Mars to meet him. Everything, from his driver collecting her to arriving here now, had been pretty amazing: first class flight to St Lucia, with such attention paid to her that she'd felt like royalty, then ushered into a lounge clearly designed for very rich people before catching a connection to one of the most exclusive islands on earth. Then she'd been met at the airport here by a wonderful guy called Walt who had ushered her to a bright-red buggy that had reminded her of a bigger than average golf buggy.

And how glorious it was to feel the breath of warm air on her skin, to hear the sound of the ocean in the distance and the harmonious noises of insects going about their nightly business in the lush bushes and dense undergrowth that spilled all around them. How glorious to remember what it felt like not to be plagued with worry every waking moment.

The small roads were empty, as apparently no cars were allowed on the island. Instead, transport was via buggies.

She doubted anyone would want to do much driving here. She quickly got the feeling that people came here to escape and that meant doing nothing but soaking up the sun and sea in utter privacy. Massive villas hid behind the coconut trees and the lush vegetation of tropical foliage. She could almost hear the sound of expensive batteries being recharged. She could smell the ocean in the salty air as the breeze blew her hair around her face. All around, the silhouettes of palm trees leaned into the breeze, the fronds whispering in the night.

She'd dressed in light clothes, but even so the jeans and shirt felt hot and stuffy. It would be good finally to relax and unwind but right now, standing in front of the door and hearing the bell reverberate inside the villa, nervous tension banished all thought of relaxing or unwinding.

She heard the echo of Leo's footsteps before the door was pulled open and then there he was, standing in front of her, and the punch to her gut made her feel as though she hadn't just seen him a week ago. He was barefoot and in a pair of low-slung, slim-fitting khaki shorts that were almost knee-length. His tee-shirt was grey, loose and designer.

'On time…come in. That's all for now, Walt, I'll take it from here.'

He reached down to grab her case and then stood aside so that she could precede him into the villa.

And what a villa. It was all on one level, but that one level was vast and circled by a broad veranda with white, wooden railings. Inside, the tiles were cool, white marble and, as she followed him through, she noticed they were replaced with blond wood. Everything was open-plan and overhead fans were scattered here and there.

There was a lot of white, so the place felt vast. She walked past a cluster of white sofas arranged around the pale, pastel shades of a silk rug and beyond that she could see enormous glass doors that had been flung open to a vista of sprawling lawn illuminated by the moon and outside lights.

Various other rooms lay further down, but they were

making their way to three broad steps that led to a balustraded area. She assumed the bedrooms were there.... nerve-wracking thought.

'Hungry?'

He stopped, looked round at her and smiled, a smile that managed to ease some of her tension away.

'Look, Cass,' he said quietly, 'I get that this is an unusual situation but don't be nervous.'

'I'm not.'

'That's not what your expression is telling me.'

'Maybe it's telling you that I'm exhausted after nearly a day on my feet and you're confusing it with nerves. Don't forget, I *chose* to come here.'

Brave words but, as he stepped towards her, she swallowed hard and just about managed to maintain eye contact. He reached out and stroked her bare arm. She shivered and gazed down at his long, brown fingers running up and down her much paler skin.

Of course, this was why she was here. Not to make chit chat or get to know the man he was now. For Leo, she was here for the sex.

And it was the same for her.

'So you did. Okay, it's been a hell of a day for you, but are you hungry? Thirsty? The place is fully stocked and I've had a private chef prepare a week's worth of meals for us so that all we have to do is turn an oven on and stick one in.'

'I'm a caterer. There was no need for that. I'm perfectly able to cook food.'

'You're not here to be a caterer, though, are you?'

'No.'

He looked at her in silence for a few seconds.

'Okay, come and I'll show you to the bedroom. You

can have a shower and refresh and then, if you decide you want something to eat or drink, that's fine, or else you can just sleep it off.'

'Thanks.'

He didn't move. He hoisted her bag over one shoulder and continued to stare at her until she blushed.

'Okay,' Cassie admitted. 'I'm nervous. I wasn't sure what to expect and I guess now that I'm here, it all feels... very real.'

'It's not meant to be an ordeal,' Leo told her wryly. 'And, if it is, tell me and I'll try and brush up on my seduction moves.'

'You have seduction moves?'

'Tried and tested.'

Cassie fell in behind him as he led her towards the bedroom...*their bedroom.*

The very thought set up a riot of butterflies in her tummy but she was going to play it as cool as he was. This was the very reason she wanted to do this, to sleep with him.

'It's a beautiful villa, Leo.'

'It is.'

'Does it get much use? Everything feels very new.'

'I have someone come in twice a week to make sure everything's in order. To answer your question about how often it's used?' He paused. 'Not very. I've come a couple of times to unwind, and I've hosted a few meetings here with overseas clients when absolute privacy has been necessary because of the sensitivity of the deal being completed. My father came once but told me that he didn't care for the atmosphere—too quiet.'

'That's what's so wonderful about it. The roads were empty on the way here.'

'Quiet only suits some people.' Leo grinned. 'Too few bars here for my father. I also don't think he feels comfortable with the guest list.'

'Why?'

'Why do you think, Cass? He spent his entire life taking orders and obeying other people's commands. He never learnt the valuable lesson that because someone has more money or power than you doesn't make them a better person.'

'You've always been so sure of yourself, Leo.' She blushed because that felt like an overly personal remark. 'Why did you buy this villa if you didn't plan on making much use of it?'

'Because I could,' Leo drawled and shrugged as he pushed open one of the doors at the very end of the villa. 'When you grow up with very little, the ability to treat yourself to *a lot* can be tempting.'

'I guess it's a good investment,' Cassie murmured, half-smiling at that very human revelation of his, although a fanciful part of her wondered how much of his life had been put on hold as he'd climbed the ladder to success. Had the ability to kick back been sacrificed to his thirst for success, to make his future better than his past? He had been so much less icily controlled when she had known him. Had her rejection helped to shape the block of granite that now seemed to enclose him?

She knew that this was pointless speculation that didn't belong in their current situation. 'I guess it would be a brilliant holiday place for when you have a family of your own.'

'Oh, that's not ever going to be on the cards. Those sorts of plans don't figure in the present trajectory of my life. And, word to the wise: don't bother going there.'

Well, that told her.

Cassie took the hint and fell silent as she stepped into a bedroom suite that took her breath away.

The door opened into a luxurious sitting area where the pastel shades had been left behind in favour of bursts of colour in the furnishings and local artwork on the walls. Beyond the sitting room was a door which was ajar, leading to the bedroom, and she could just about make out an enormous bed and lots of wood.

Floor-to-ceiling doors opened out onto the deck where sofas and chairs sheltered under a sloping roof overlooking the lawns to the back.

'Wow.'

'Tomorrow you'll see that there's an uninterrupted view of the sea from out there,' he told her as he followed the direction of her stare. 'We can access the beach from here and, trust me, there will never be anyone there to interrupt us. Paths seldom cross here unless by arrangement. It's a place where privacy is highly valued.'

Cassie turned away and eyed the bed, soon to be the main focus of their carnal pleasure. Simmering excitement warred with nerves.

'Maybe I could have a shower, like you suggested?'

'Bathroom's adjoining the bedroom. I'll bring you something to eat...or drink? Tea, coffee, water...?'

'You mean you'd shove something in the oven for me that's already been prepared?' She looked up at him and smiled, easing herself out of her nerves. 'You used to complain about cooking.'

Leo laughed and this time there was genuine humour in his laughter.

'My father could be very fussy for a mild-mannered guy. Not spicy enough...too spicy...did you remember salt?...too much salt... He hated cooking more than me and I had to do it because, if he did, I was never sure just how safe my stomach would be.'

'How is he, Leo?'

'Very contented, as it happens. I bought him a house in Spain close to many of his relatives and he's busy in retirement. He deserves the best.'

They looked at each other for a heartbeat and then he turned away abruptly.

'I'll be half an hour. I'll bring you some tea and toast. I can manage that, and I don't suppose you want anything heavier.'

Cassie nodded, backing towards the bathroom.

Now that she was facing the inevitable part of the deal she had agreed to, all sorts of practical worries reared their heads, the biggest of which was, *what was he going to expect from her in bed?*

They'd had one time, one spectacular moment in time together, but her experience was limited beyond that. Her one short-lived relationship after Leo had been the opposite of a sexual adventure and she had retreated into work after the break-up.

When she'd looked up Leo online and plucked up the courage really to look at his profile, she had seen dozens of images of him with women; lots of leggy models clinging onto him for dear life. Of course, now he possessed the trappings that would make him the most eligible man on the planet. God knew how experienced he was in bed. Would he expect a similar level of experience from her—someone acrobatic, creative and maybe into weird stuff?

She quailed at the thought of that. Her nerves were all over the place when she emerged from having a quick shower and she was relieved when she realised that he wasn't there in the bedroom waiting for her. He'd brought in her case and she dressed quickly, sticking on some soft jogging bottoms and a tee-shirt and then, barefoot, she strolled outside and forgot everything.

The breeze was warm and she could smell the salty ocean in the air, tangy and fragrant. In the distance she could make out the view of the sea and hear the gentle rolling of the waves lapping on the shore.

Even where she lived, surrounded by nature, there were still the daily sights and sounds of life being lived to be heard: the far-away noise of cars interrupting the silence; the romantic, dull glow of street lamps switched on in winter; and in summer the pleasant background thrum of lawnmowers, kids playing and cars taking people here, there and everywhere.

Here, there was nothing but the breeze and the ocean. It was lulling and peaceful and she jumped when she realised that Leo had come to stand next to her. Cassie shivered and slid a sideways look at him. She dared let her imagination take flight.

What if...?

What if there had been no roadblocks? Would things have worked out between them? She'd been so deeply in love but had that been just a first, immature kind of love that wouldn't have lasted anyway? Was he right when he'd said that she would have hindered his progress through life?

But if everything had worked out, wouldn't it have been heaven to be here now, in this most romantic of places, with Leo by her side and the love between them not blighted?

'Leo...' She turned to him impulsively and gazed up

at the dark shadows and angles of his face. 'Do you ever think about…what might have happened if…if…?'

'No.'

That flat answer sliced through her daydream and brought her swiftly back to reality.

'And,' he continued heavily, 'Don't let the romance of this place get to you, Cassie. What we had began and ended the day I left town. What's happening now is a very different beast.'

'I know. I just wondered…'

He moved to stand with his back to the wooden railing, leaning against it and looked at her steadily and coolly.

'Then don't. If you get the misguided temptation to try and rekindle what happened between us eight years ago, then you'll find that you're barking up the wrong tree. I don't make the same mistakes twice, Cass. What we had is done and dusted.'

'I'm not a fool, Leo. Do you think I would ever want to climb back into any kind of relationship with you?'

'I don't know, Cassie,' Leo said smoothly, his voice slamming down shutters on her brief departure into the sort of emotionalism he had warned against. 'When you start going down the dangerous road of "what ifs"?'

'Forget I said anything,' she said abruptly, swinging round and walking back into the bedroom suite. 'We might just as well get this over and done with.'

She was hurt—hurt at the cold, flat hardness in his voice even though she knew that it shouldn't have come as a surprise. She was also angry—angry at herself for falling into the trap of nostalgia and whimsy because he was right, that wasn't what this week was all about. She would have to make sure that the past remained where it was, separate from the present, with no overlap.

* * *

Leo watched her as she walked briskly back into the bedroom, leaving a vague, clean, flowery scent behind her. For a minute there, the softness on her face when she had strolled back into the past, wondered aloud about a future that had never happened, had taken him with her but he had instantly fought back against that.

A happy-ever-after life with love, optimism and hope? He'd had a taste of that with her before it had all turned sour and he wasn't about to repeat the mistake. He seldom thought about marrying and settling down. He had no particular desire to leave his mark behind him in the form of a child. If he ever changed his mind on that count, then love wouldn't be the guiding force behind any union he entered.

Learning curves were there for a reason. He'd ignored his own learning curve growing up. He had wilfully chosen not to remember the pain of his mother's absence from his life, a pain he saw every day on his father's face, and had succumbed to hope with Cassie—never again.

Nor did he want her getting any ideas about longevity with him. This was going to be an uncomplicated week during which demons that had floated to the surface would be put to rest once and for all.

She was waiting for him in the bedroom, her stance defiant and belligerent, her clothes still on. Leo enjoyed the anticipation of how that was going to play out over the course of the week when she would be standing there greeting him completely naked and definitely with no arms defiantly folded.

He tugged off his tee-shirt, stripping it over his head, watching the way her colour rose, and the way she was trying her hardest not to look at his bare chest. Her eyes flicked there, and slid away just as fast, but then were compelled to return to a sight she didn't want to enjoy, but enjoying it she certainly was.

He felt a kick of satisfaction.

'Your turn.'

'I'm tired—jet lag.'

'You don't look tired.' He grinned when she yawned. 'I'm very good when it comes to waking women up.'

'You have a lot of experience of women falling asleep on you?'

Leo burst out laughing and rocked on his heels, looking at her and appreciating every single inch of her beautiful body. He looked at the well-built body with strong, full breasts—nothing like the wafer-thin models he was accustomed to dating.

'I have a lot of experience of waking them up at night so that I can make love to them again... It's your turn, by the way.'

'I beg your pardon?'

'I've taken off my top. Your turn now.'

'Leo...'

Leo could smell the desire in her and that was a massive turn on.

'I've always liked the way you say my name,' he murmured, moving towards her until he was so close to her only a sheet of paper could have been slipped between their bodies. 'You have a great voice, husky...sexy...'

He trailed his finger over her arm but didn't do anything else but look at her.

'Leo, there's something you should know...'

'Now is not the time to tell me that you're having second thoughts, Cassie.' He pulled back and raked his fingers through his hair.

'I'm not!'

'Then there's nothing else I need to know.'

'Leo, you may have moved on with a thousand different partners but...but... I haven't had time to. I've been so busy growing my business that... Of course, I had a relationship after you but, if you're expecting a wild, experienced lover then you might be in for disappointment.'

Leo smiled slowly.

'I get the picture and you don't have to worry on that front. I'm not a guy who expects anything from the women I sleep with.'

'You date models, Leo.'

'You've been reading about me?'

'I've seen pictures of you prancing here, there and everywhere with six-foot blondes!'

'I'm not sure I like the picture of me you're painting.' He was grinning now. 'I try so hard not to *prance*. But I have to admit to the six-foot blondes. Were you a tiny bit jealous when you snooped around and saw those images?'

'No! And I wasn't snooping. I was curious...considering the situation I was about to embark on.'

'Good. I don't like jealousy.'

'As a matter of fact, nor do I.'

'So,' he said, 'Now that we've covered that particular topic...'

Before she knew what was happening, he swept her off her feet and deposited her unceremoniously on the bed, eyebrows raised with amusement as she struggled up onto her elbows, glaring at him.

'One thing I can tell you,' he whispered. 'I've never made love to a hellcat and, now that you're here in my bed, I realise that one time with you wasn't nearly enough. Disappointment isn't going to be anywhere on my radar.'

He put his hand on the zip of his shorts.

'I'm still waiting for you and your top to part company,' he crooned, 'But, if you don't want to oblige, I'm very, very happy to do the honours.'

He pulled off his shorts without taking his eyes off her and then he sauntered towards her, completely naked but for his boxers...and his erection.

Cassie's heart was beating so fast, she could scarcely breathe. Not in her wildest imagination had she ever thought her body could behave the way it was behaving now. She wanted this man. She wanted him with eight years' worth of pent-up, frustrated passion.

There wasn't a shred of objection in her as he moved to stand right next to the bed, touching himself and watching her as she watched him.

'I've waited a thousand years for this moment,' Leo said huskily. 'Although, in fairness, I'm only realising that now. Take your clothes off.'

Cassie slid off the bed. She was standing right in front of him as she reached to pull the tee-shirt over her head. Underneath was the laciest bra she had ever owned. When he had told her that he wanted her to dress in sexy underwear, she had been more than happy to oblige.

She'd wanted that as well. *She* wanted the feel of lace to scrape over her nipples; wanted to expose the fullness of her cleavage to his gaze; wanted to see his eyes darken with desire.

Maybe he wasn't the only one to have had that youthful fantasy.

'So, you followed the brief,' Leo murmured with rampant masculine appreciation, 'I can't wait to see the other half of the set. So much more exciting than boring, practical underwear, and you certainly have the body to pull off those little bits of lace.'

Cassie looked down at her cleavage spilling out of the skimpy bra and then sucked in a shaky breath as his finger dipped between the valley of her breasts to trace a tantalising, feathery line that made her shiver in response.

Heady passion and recklessness swamped all the apprehension she'd been feeling. If he'd been waiting a thousand years for this moment, then so had she.

One week…and then her life would reset and she would be on another track, with no debts hanging over her head like a hangman's noose and no shadowy memories of lost love darkening her dreams and clouding the roads she chose to follow.

CHAPTER FIVE

THE HUGENESS OF what she was about to do made Cassie freeze for a couple of seconds but she liked that he wasn't rushing her, that he was taking his time. He was being patient.

Maybe it was because he wanted the experience to be good for him—maybe it was all about him—but maybe it was because, underneath the bitterness and the toughness that had come with age, that same streak of consideration that had been there eight years ago was still there. If she commented on that, she knew he would burst out laughing and give her another pep talk about not having any illusions about him.

Her hand hovered on the waistband of her jogging bottoms but, before she could begin wriggling out of them, he stepped fractionally closer, inserted his fingers under the elasticated waistband and tugged. And then he lowered himself so that he was kneeling in front of her, sliding the joggers down, down, down until they pooled in a bundle at her feet and she stepped out of them.

She reached for her panties, more lace and rudely skimpy, but he stayed her hand and raised his eyes to hers.

'I really like what I'm seeing,' he said, kneeling at her feet as she gazed down at him breathlessly. 'I'd wondered,' he confessed hoarsely, 'Whether my memories might have been wrong. God, they weren't. You're as beautiful as I remember; as delicately, gloriously, sexily beautiful.'

She reached down to sift her fingers through his dark hair and felt a shudder of absolute, erotic, heady giddiness. She was so damp between her thighs that she wanted to rub them together to alleviate the itch, or at least get rid of the damn thing altogether, but before she could do that he gently pulled aside the crotch of the panties and flicked his tongue against her crease, tasting her just a little bit.

It was just enough to make her want to collapse as her legs turned to jelly. Just enough that she remembered it all too, and those memories flooded through her, memories of that one and only time when he had tasted her untouched femininity and had sparked a conflagration inside her that had blown her apart. Her fingers tightened in his hair and she drew in a sharp breath as the questing tongue made deeper, more insistent inroads inside her, searching for the nub of her clitoris and finding it.

She groaned. Her legs trembled. She was barely aware of him pulling down the panties or of her stepping out of them so that they could join the discarded jogging bottoms to the side. Through glazed, half-opened eyes, she looked down at her own nakedness. She was tall but she wasn't slight. Her breasts were more than a handful, the nipples two big, circular pale-brown discs. Her waist was slim but her hips were generously rounded and her legs were long and strong. She absently took in all this, as she did the broad width of his brown shoulders and the intense darkness of his hair.

She couldn't see what he was doing exactly but she didn't need to. His tongue flicked the sensitive bud, driving sensations to screaming pitch. She could hear herself moaning and see herself writhing as she lost herself in what was happening with her body.

When he parted her thighs with the flat of his hands, she obediently allowed him to so that he could burrow deeper against her core, driving her to a fevered pitch of wanting.

'Not yet,' he murmured unsteadily when she would have climaxed against his mouth. 'I want to savour every morsel of you.'

He laid her down on the mattress and looked at her with hot desire, loosening any inhibitions she might have had. She was still throbbing between her legs from where he had caressed her. Now, she parted her lips on a sigh as he lowered himself to continue caressing her body.

She arched up as he swirled his tongue over her nipple, licking and suckling until she was moaning with wild pleasure. She clasped his head, driving him to take more of her into his mouth, to suckle harder until she was on fire, burning up inside and out. She pushed her hand down, down to where the orgasm he'd denied her was building again with hungry, demanding impatience.

He rubbed there, found the perfect rhythm and touched her until she could no longer withstand the crescendo building inside her. She spasmed against him with a long, loud cry of pleasure, head flung back and eyes tightly shut.

When she opened her eyes to look at him, his dark eyes were hot with satisfaction. 'We've only just begun, my darling,' he whispered. 'I had a taste of honey eight years ago. I won't be rushing this banquet now.'

'Do you think *I* want to?' She reached up to nuzzle the thick column of his neck, hands lightly clasped around him. 'Don't forget I had the same taste of honey as well...'

He'd satisfied her and now it was her turn. She might not have his vast experience in the bedroom but her body knew what it wanted and, guided by instinct and desire, she reversed position so that she was the one in charge now. She licked him as he had licked her, flicking her tongue over his flat, brown nipples, then she trailed her mouth and her fingers lightly along his muscular torso. She grazed his skin with her teeth and felt him shudder under her.

She reached to circle his thick erection with her hand and then slowly began caressing his stiffened member with strokes that were firm, slow and sure.

He covered her hand with his and half-groaned, 'Okay. Any more and I won't be able to help myself.'

'I'd like that…' Cassie breathed. 'To see you helpless.'

'You already have, once upon a time.'

'You don't want to rush this, Leo, and neither do I.' Cassie moved lower, her body sliding against his. She angled herself over him so that she could take him in her mouth, so that he could taste her at the same time and so that they could satisfy one another slowly and seductively.

Leo was the first to break their erotic contact with a hoarse groan.

'Cas-s… I can't stand any more. I need to feel myself in you now—right now.'

He adjusted himself so that he could fumble for a foil packet containing protection, finding it in the nick of time, because he was so on the brink of losing it. He breathed in deeply, gathering some of his self-control, then it was his turn to lie over her, raised on both hands so that he was looking down at her.

'That first time with you, Cassie… It was unmatched.'

'For me as well.'

'This time round?' He laughed huskily. 'Concerns about disappointing me were vastly misplaced...'

He could barely rip open the packet and when he entered her, seconds later, feeling her tightness around him was bliss.

He'd died and gone to heaven.

He didn't want to rush. He thrust long, deep and slowly, moving rhythmically and feeling the excitement rising in her as he continued to move inside her. The past collided with the present. He was touching the girl she had been and the woman she had become. It was...perfection.

He came and it was an explosion, sending him soaring into orbit, forgetting everything but being in the moment, and knowing that he'd never had such a powerful orgasm before in his life. Spent, he lay back and stared up at the ceiling, enjoying the weight of her against him as she lay in a similar position with her head on his shoulder.

One week... He had never felt so good, so complete. He'd thought he might have to revisit the crazy benchmark from all those years ago; surely his memory had played tricks on him, and time would dim the ferocity of her appeal?

But making love to her just then... He felt the stab of disappointment that a timeline of only a week had been set, but just as fast he dispelled that weakness, because how could he ever trust her? He couldn't. She'd walked away once and there was nothing to stop her doing it again. After his mother's betrayal, after Cassie's, trusting a woman again would never be an option for him. A week would be plenty.

'What sort of food do you do?' He opted for harmless conversation because the alternative would be to disappear down a rabbit hole he didn't want to explore.

'When?'

'For your catering business.'

'Every possible kind of food,' Cassie said sleepily. 'Although, Frankie is the pastry queen, so I leave all the desserts to her. I enjoy making savoury food and the more complicated the better.'

'Do you enjoy what you do?'

'You're being very polite.' She stifled a yawn.

'And you're sleepy. You also haven't eaten.' He absently pushed her hair from her face. 'I would suggest we have a shower together, and then you can get some sleep, but I might get turned on under running water and then who knows where that'll lead us?'

Leo paused, waiting for a response that never came. When he shifted and looked at her, she was sound asleep. It had been under a minute.

Just for one second, one fleeting second, he felt *happy*...happy and at peace.

This was *exactly* the right thing to have done. This was what it felt like to scratch an itch he'd never known he had. Stupid concerns about timelines had been put to bed. By the end of the week, he would be a very contented man indeed and, after months of working all hours round the clock and dealing with an increasingly demanding and indignant ex-girlfriend, contentment couldn't come fast enough.

Cassie stretched.

It took her a couple of seconds to register that she wasn't in her own bed; that striped curtains weren't opened onto a wintry Canadian sky outside and that the noises weren't ones with which she was familiar: the whirring of an overhead fan; the chirrup of birds... And, when she opened her eyes, sunshine found a way through the white shutters and filtered into the bedroom.

It all came flooding back to her: Leo, and making love to him right here in this bed where he had made her feel so wonderful that she hadn't wanted the sensations ever to stop.

Things felt right in the world, and she almost didn't recognise the feeling, because she'd lived under a cloud for so long. She felt weightless. Her body still thrummed from the pleasure of the night before—pleasure she wanted to sample again, and soon.

It was after nine in the morning. A routine would have to be established. One week had to be filled, and they couldn't stay in bed every minute of every hour, so what was the routine going to be?

As she padded towards where she felt the kitchen should be, Cassie felt more apprehensive about those waking hours when they wouldn't be in bed than the ones when they would be. What would they talk about? So much was off-limits.

She slowed her pace and looked around her, fully appreciating the immense luxury of her surroundings.

It was open-plan so that the sunlight pouring in through the floor-to-ceiling glass doors was maximised. Pale colours melded with the pale wood and the furnishings were shades of white. The living area, or one of the living areas, had clusters of off-white sofas and chairs overlooking the wraparound veranda. Beyond that, in the daylight, she could see the landscape stretching outside was a glittering, bewitching blend of greens from the fruit and coconut trees, interrupted by vibrant shades of reds, oranges and purples of flowers that seemed to push out of the shrubbery in random profusion.

And it was hot. Even with the breeze wafting through the villa, she could feel herself perspiring in the shorts and loose vest top she had flung on.

Everywhere she looked was magical. She'd travelled with her family when times had been good, but she had never been somewhere like this, and for the first time in her life Cassie appreciated just how that tiny percentage of super-rich lived.

Why bother with a hotel when you could have this? The only window coverings were white shutters and pale voile that billowed in the gentle breeze, so that the outside felt as though it was made an inroad into the interior of the villa.

She could have dawdled for ever, but instead she fumbled her way through, following her nose, until the kitchen was there and, sure enough, Leo was standing there helping himself to coffee. His laptop was on the eight-seater pale-grey concrete kitchen table and she wondered how long he'd been up.

'You're awake,' he said.

'I don't normally sleep this late.' His lazy, dark gaze made her blush but she boldly held his gaze, as she felt her body heat up at the memory of their love-making.

'Jet lag. Hits us all. Would you like some coffee? There's fresh bread in the oven.'

'You've baked for me?' This was to lighten the atmosphere and break the compelling need to keep staring at him. It worked because he smiled, a genuine smile that she remembered from the past when their lives had been entwined and smiles had been easy to come by. 'I'd love some coffee.'

The kitchen was vast. Over-sized marble tiles were cool underfoot and everything was in keeping. Much of the villa was pale, bar the bedrooms, from the walls to the sleek fitted cupboards and granite countertops that complemented the grey streaks in the marble flooring and the grey of the table.

'Sit.'

'I can help.'

'Like I said, you're not here to do anything in the kitchen.' Leo poured her a cup and strolled to join her at the table. 'And we won't be playing at domesticity.'

'It's all about the sex... I know. You honestly don't have to keep drumming it in.'

'All about the *great* sex,' Leo murmured, his dark eyes roving over her flushed face.

'Great' didn't come close to describing it, Leo thought.

He'd had to resist waking her from her beauty sleep at five-thirty, when he'd woken up.

Already, at that hour, tendrils of sunlight had begun filtering through into the bedroom and he had propped himself up on one elbow and stared at her.

She'd flung off the covers and was lying on her side, her hair a wild, dark tangle, her mouth parted, and he could just about make out the curve of her full breast pressed under her arms. She'd looked young, soft and sweetly innocent and he'd had to remind himself that the days of falling for her elusive charm were long gone.

He'd known that, if he roused her, she would come to him and the thought had been such a turn-on that he'd had to suck in a shaky breath and quietly slide off the bed before he'd done something about it.

She deserved a good night's sleep. She'd barely had any sleep for over a day and she'd been a bundle of nerves when she'd showed up the evening before. But she'd wanted him, and he thought of the way she'd opened up to him, tentative at first, but then responding without any inhibitions at all... There'd been no playing games, no practising any tedious arts of seduction; they'd had each other once, for one blissful moment, and for him having her again had felt like coming home.

The week stretching ahead of him couldn't get any better.

'So, plans for today...' he said briskly, heading to the oven and bringing some piping hot bread rolls to the table along with some butter and a jug of fresh orange juice. 'The beach. I suggest we go as soon as you're ready and catch the sun before it becomes too hot. Should be empty as well. At its most packed, this place only ever has a handful of people on any of the beaches. While we're away, my housekeeper will tidy and be gone before we get back. Last thing I want is someone hovering underfoot and popping up in unexpected corners.'

'Very inconvenient, I'm sure,' Cassie said dryly, blowing on the coffee and looking at him over the rim of her cup. 'What time did you get up?'

'Before six. I had work to get through before the day begins.'

'I'll have to check some emails as well,' Cassie said.

'What did you tell your mother and your friends? And your helpful bank manager who's guiding you through your financial woes? Although that process should swiftly be wrapped up. I would love to be a fly on the wall to see his expression when the cash comes flooding in. Let's hope he's discreet or the world and its granny will know all about your personal situation before you can blink.'

'He's very discreet.' Cassie reddened and distracted herself by buttering one of the rolls he had produced from the oven. 'I just said…er… I was going away for a few days…'

'No further details? No where, how and why? Very tactful. Who bought that story—surely not your mother? If she knows about the mess your family business is in, then wouldn't she question your sudden desire to go on holiday with funds you don't have?'

'I said things were looking up on the financial front, if you really must know.'

'Very diplomatic. What will you tell her when all the money worries have been miraculously sorted?'

'I haven't thought about that yet,' Cassie admitted, reddening yet further.

Leo's eyebrows shot up and he grinned. 'If you blush like you're doing now when you make up whatever fairy story you're planning, I can tell you straight away that she's going to smell a lie.'

'As long as she never finds out that I spent the week with you here and that you were the guy responsible for saving us.'

'"Saving" is a big word, Cass. Why would she be upset anyway?'

'Why do you think? She'll figure out that I traded myself to you for money. I don't even like to say that out loud and I can't imagine… Well, it would devastate my mum if she thought that.'

'Well, you'll just have to come clean and tell her that you threw yourself into the situation as enthusiastically as I did.' He pushed his plate to one side and looked at her thoughtfully. 'Or maybe she might still be attached to the idea that I'm too undesirable for her daughter, even though I've made so much money I could buy the town you all live in, never mind the house that's collapsing round her head!'

'It's nothing like that,' Cassie muttered, tensing.

'Forget I said that, Cassie,' Leo said eventually, raking his fingers through his hair. 'It was out of order.' He smiled at her. 'And not exactly conducive to the mood I'm aiming for today.' He reached forward and tilted her chin so that he was looking at her. 'No more bringing the past into the present. My fault.'

Cassie smiled back but tentatively.

'What sort of mood were you aiming for?' she asked.

'Relaxation. This place is made for that.'

'Then why don't you come more often? Who doesn't like down time?' She poured some juice for herself, drank it and watched him. Her shrewd gaze made his neck itch.

'Anyone who has an empire to run. Down time tends to get in the way of that. I hope you've brought a swimsuit with you, as per my instructions?' He turned the subject briskly.

'I'm wearing it under my clothes.'

'In that case, meet me by the front door in half an hour. I have a couple of calls to make.'

Cassie was there promptly. The one-piece black swimsuit, which she wore for serious swimming at the local pool, was prim and proper and she couldn't wait for him to strip it off her.

She'd had some qualms before she'd come but she knew that she was doing just what she was meant to—weaning Leo out of her system. The key was to avoid getting wrapped up in the past too much and, if she did, then it was important she keep her thoughts to herself. All roads led to a past they were never going to discuss. If that hurt, then she'd have to suck it up because, even if they could sit down and talk about how things had broken down between them, it wouldn't get them anywhere.

She was standing, staring down at the floor and frowning, as Leo approached.

He paused to look at her. The navy shorts showed off the length of her legs and the loose, white vest top the toned slenderness of her arms. Like everyone else in the town where she lived, she was a proficient skier, someone who engaged in a lot of outdoor activities. That part of the world was made for that kind of life, a life of being tuned into nature.

Her body was lithe and strong and he liked that more than he could have imagined, given that he had really only dated extremely slim models. He liked the fact that she was straightforward. He'd always liked that, especially as it had been so contrary to her privileged background. He liked that she didn't tiptoe around him. He'd become accustomed to women falling in line with what he wanted. His last girlfriend had, and he took the blame for that entirely, as she'd had to endure a lot before she'd finally had enough.

He enjoyed the way Cassie glared at him, ready to fight, even though she should have been subservient and eager to please, considering he was sorting out all her money problems.

What he didn't like was the way his thoughts strayed so easily from the physical into the murky waters of a past he didn't want to explore. He knew that the two were deeply entwined, that the two of them were only here because of their previous relationship, but something deep inside him cautioned against trying to analyse and confront their past. He'd done enough of that eight years ago.

He snapped out of his introspection and she glanced up as he strolled towards her. 'Ready?'

'What about…er…towels and stuff?'

'Someone will deliver towels and a picnic hamper when we get there.'

'Really?' Cassie rolled her eyes and stepped back as he opened the front door. 'You're very spoilt now that you're a millionaire, aren't you, Leo?'

'Billionaire, and I'm not complaining on that front.'

'You're so arrogant.' But she glanced across at him and laughed.

'I'm both confident and adorable.'

'I stand corrected.'

They walked out into bright sunshine and a cloudless blue sky. The ocean glittered in the distance, a band of blue beyond the coconut trees and abundant foliage. They strolled towards the buggy parked outside in the massive courtyard.

'It's so stunning here,' Cassie said, sitting next to him as he eased the small, eco-friendly vehicle away from the villa. 'Tell me all about it.'

She rested back, breeze blowing in her hair, eyes drifting to his long, brown fingers on the gear stick and listened as he told her about the island. He gave her facts and figures and told her about the royal connections, the coral reefs that protected the many private coves and the yachts that passed through as they sailed down the Grenadines.

It took them no time at all to hit the beach and, as Leo had predicted, it was empty. Within minutes of their arrival, another buggy pulled up and, sure enough, towels and an enormous hamper were delivered before the buggy trundled away, leaving the two of them the only occupants on the beach.

White sand as soft as caster sugar led down to turquoise water as calm as a lake, and behind them coconut trees swayed between dense vegetation in all shades of deep green.

Cassie yanked the vest over her head and stood still for a few seconds, eyes closed, breathing in the salty fragrant air and tuning in to the soft lapping of waves barely breaking against the shore. The sun was absolute bliss on her skin.

'Don't overdo it.' Leo's voice was soft and his breath against her neck had her opening her eyes fast enough. 'You don't want to get sun burnt...and, by the way, why is your swimsuit so severe? Did you come here planning to compete in some swim trials?'

Cassie turned to look at him. He was in an old, soft tee-shirt and shorts and was barefoot. He'd kicked off his shoes and, when she glanced past him, it was to see that he had set up a huge towel just behind them in the shade. He shucked off the tee-shirt and she placed her hands squarely on his chest and splayed her fingers.

Deliberately, she licked a finger and idly teased one flat, brown nipple, feeling it tighten under the pad of her finger.

'So is that how you intend to play this?' Leo murmured with a slow grin. He moved his hands to cup her breasts.

'Leo, we can't! Not here.'

'I don't see anyone around, do you?'

'No, but...'

'Have you ever had sex outside of a bedroom?'

'That's none of your business!'

'For this week, everything about you is my business.'

His hand crept to caress her cheek and his dark eyes were lazy, serious and amused, and such a turn-on that Cassie could feel herself melting. She thought about her one semi-serious affair and how much she had longed for it to be the real thing so that it could help her get over a broken heart. Adventure had not been part of that relationship.

'Well?' Leo prompted, grinning. 'No need to answer that, Cass. I can read the answer in your eyes. Unadventurous lover, was he? Dull as dishwater?'

'I'm hot. Let's go swim.'

Leo burst out laughing. 'Again, no need to answer that one.' He stepped out of his shorts down to swimming trunks and grinned as her eyes traced the outline of his erection pushing against the trunks.

'I know,' he said piously. 'Look at the effect you have on me.' He guided her hand to his erection and smirked at the burning colour that invaded her cheeks and the frantic way she glanced across the perfectly deserted beach.

'Cassie... I like it that boredom was the lynchpin of the relationship that didn't work out. Frankly, hot sex is pretty vital when it comes to any relationship.'

'I never said anything about *boredom*, Leo.'

She began heading to the water, leaving her discarded clothes on the sand and feeling relaxed despite the annoying man trying to needle a response out of her.

'You didn't have to. I get the picture.'

He slung his arm over her shoulder and pulled her against him. When he leant in to kiss her, it was the gentlest kiss—a brush of his cool mouth on hers, the soft probing of his tongue lingering and exploring as he took his time tasting her.

They were at the water's edge and she could feel the

tiny pull of the ebbing sea, her feet sinking slightly into the sand.

Bliss. She could lose herself in this. She could start thinking about 'for ever'…

Just like that, Cassie came crashing down to planet Earth. Just like that she had a vision of how easy it would be to be seduced into a daydream that bore no resemblance to reality. Leo, with his many and varied relationships all filled with hot sex, had moved on from her a long time ago. But had she moved on from him in the same way?

She'd thought she had but, instead, had she replaced him with a catering business after that one unsuccessful attempt at a relationship? Had she let work take over the desire to get out there and experience *life*? Life with all its complexities, possible broken hearts and ups and downs…

She had become engrossed with her mother over time, involved in the drama of her ill health, her father's concerns and a life overshadowed by the presence of tragedy. But where had *she*, Cassie Farraday, only twenty-seven years old, *been* while all this had been happening—hiding somewhere waiting for life to happen without going out to find it?

'Race you?'

She pulled back and looked at Leo who, she reminded herself, was nothing like the young guy she had once adored to distraction.

'I know you're a good swimmer, Cass, but are you forgetting that the last time you challenged me to a race you were still in the shallow end by the time I'd reached the other side of the pool?'

Cassie remembered it all too well, that sneaky night visit to the swimming baths in one of the other towns, far enough away for them to be strangers.

'Bit of an exaggeration, Leo, and besides aren't we supposed to be pretending that we never had a past together?' But she laughed, sprinted away from him and forgot the tangle of her thoughts as she struck out into the warm, turquoise sea. The water was clear and shallow. She was a brilliant swimmer, her strokes long, fluid and rhythmic as she swam away from shore and away from all those disturbing questions that had pushed their way to the surface.

When she looked to the side, she could see Leo keeping pace with her with ease. Amazingly, she could still touch the sandy bottom when she finally paused and stood, and then she laughed when he asked her if that was the best she could do.

The sun glinted off his broad shoulders and when he pushed his fingers through his wet hair water cascaded over him.

'I know you were struggling to keep up with me, Leo,' she teased. 'I probably get a lot more practice than you. I still go once a week to clear my head so, unless you and whatever girl you're going out with swim against one another, I'd bet I'm in better shape in the water than you are now.'

She was laughing, relaxed, revitalised after thrashing out into what these calm seas had to offer and as good a swimmer as she'd always been.

Leo felt invigorated. He knew that not a single one of those women he had dated over the years would have enjoyed swimming in the sea. They would have shown up at the beach in expensive designer gear and dipped a toe in the water but that would have been it—no wet hair, no make-up washed off, no physical exertion. He felt a sharp pang of something remembered from long ago and cleared his head of it immediately.

'Now, now,' he crooned, gathering her up to him, two wet bodies pressed against one another in the heat with the water lapping around them, 'You know we men have very fragile egos. You wouldn't want to hurt me, would you? I might just have to punish you otherwise...'

'How?' Cassie wrapped her arms round his neck.

'I can think of lots of interesting ways but let's start with this...'

And he reached down under the tight crotch of her swimsuit and felt her shift her legs, parting them to accommodate his searching, questing, penetrating finger....

CHAPTER SIX

Cassie left the *en suite* bathroom, towel-drying her hair as she walked towards the chest of drawers to fetch some clothes.

It was day five and already nearly eleven o'clock; they'd enjoyed a very lazy bout of love-making when they'd got up. From his vantage point propped up on the pillows, arms folded behind his head, Leo was being treated to a sight that was second to none.

She was completely naked, her generous breasts swinging as she vigorously dried her long hair. She stopped, straightened, looked at him with raised eyebrows and smiled.

'Come back to bed, Cass.'

'The beach is calling me, Leo.' She laughed and tossed her towel at him and he caught it with one hand and dumped it on the ground. 'I want to make the most of being out here. After all, I won't be seeing much sea or sand, or sun for that matter, when I get back to Canada next week.'

'But on the plus side you also won't be seeing bailiffs knocking at the door to take away the TV and the dining table.'

'I had an email from my bank manager yesterday,' Cassie told him, 'And everything is slowly being put in place. Debts are being cleared and suppliers paid off and my father's company can be revived on a smaller scale. There are a couple of interested parties willing to buy it now that it won't come with any encumbrances.'

'So everything is sunshine and light in the Farraday family?'

Cassie looked away, fetched her swimsuit and began putting it on, her back to Leo and his all-too-perceptive dark gaze.

Her mother wasn't in the loop about the fast-progressing events. That would be a conversation Cassie would have with her face to face. She'd been vague in her text messages to Mary over the past few days and breathlessly in a rush on the phone. She had made reassuring noises about the state of their finances, and vaguely said something about talking to people interested in buying the carcass of the construction company. It was just awful but Cassie hadn't even been able to tell her where, exactly, she was.

'Offshore... I don't want to go into the details, Mum, just in case I jinx this deal that's happening...'

'I think today we're going to do something a little different,' Leo drawled, and Cassie swung round to look at him.

'But I love our routine.'

Cassie couldn't help wondering whether this was the start of things changing between them. Their routine had been one of making love, hitting the beach, eating delicious food, then the pool, dinner and making love again.

But the time limit for their bubble was always there, at the back of Cassie's mind, and she felt a jolt of panic at the prospect of any change in their routine. It was a wake-up call: two more days and then reality would resume and pick up where it had left off. She didn't want to wake up, at least not yet.

A deeper panic stirred. What was going on inside her? It felt as though the clock had been turned back on their relationship. How had that happened? This was *nothing* like what they'd shared eight years ago. Now, there were no promises of anything, not one. They talked, laughed and chatted but vast grey areas remained out of bounds. There was no mention of what life had been like for them when they'd only had eyes for one another, and *definitely* no mention of the wedge that had finally driven them apart.

So why did she feel so comfortable around him? Why did she think of them parting ways with a sinking sense of dread? How had she gone from doing this for herself—purging herself of memories with the bonus of money on the tablet—to feeling that weakness around him, that desperate want and craving that had ruled her years ago?

Pride stiffened her spine.

'I want to take you out and show you off.'

'Really? Here? I don't think I've actually seen anyone else since we've been here.'

'I've wanted to keep you to myself, for obvious reasons.'

Cassie tried on a smile for size, because a reminder of how important the sex was to him hurt even though she tried to bank down that reaction.

'Where is there to go?'

'There *is* an infrastructure here,' Leo said wryly, 'Although it's small, and caters very much to an exclusive clientele. Anyway, it would be nice to see a bit more of the island before we leave.'

'On the subject of which…' Cassie stepped into a pair of denim shorts and pulled over her head the pink tee-shirt she had taken out of the drawer. She kept her voice light and breezy but her heart was thudding because this was the taboo subject she had been careful to avoid.

She watched as Leo levered himself out of bed. He was a work of glorious art. It was what she thought every single time she looked at him. Eight years had not diminished him: broad shoulders tapered to a whip-slim waist; strong, muscled legs had just the right amount of dark hair that accentuated the bronze beauty of his skin tone.

'Whatever it is,' he said, heading for the bathroom, 'Let's discuss it once I've had a shower, or preferably later. I have a bit of work to do. I'll be an hour at most, so help yourself to breakfast...coffee...you know the layout of the land.'

He vanished into the bathroom and Cassie took herself off to the kitchen. Breakfast was delivered daily. It was a real treat to not cook. She missed it, but it was so relaxing to be taken care of. It made her realise that the privileged childhood she had taken for granted had been overtaken by so many financial and emotional concerns that she had forgotten what it felt like not to worry.

She was finishing a hot roll with local guava jam when Leo strolled into the kitchen in a pair of khaki shorts, a white designer tee-shirt and loafers.

The sun was pouring through the windows, which she had flung open. Someone was doing the garden and she could hear the distant sound of a lawnmower. There was some manicured garden but much of it was wild, a tumble of bushes, flowers and trees and, nestling amongst the lush growth, was the swimming pool.

He helped himself to some coffee, remained standing and then strolled towards her and deposited a kiss on the top of her head.

'Ready for some shopping?'

'Shopping's on the agenda? I had no idea there were any shopping centres on the island.'

'There are a couple of shops. No one could really call it a *centre*, as such. I want to buy you something luxurious, ultra-sexy and feminine to wear tonight because I'm taking us both out for dinner. Again...it's no metropolis when it comes to choices of restaurant, but I think you'll approve.'

'Luxurious...ultra-sexy...feminine...' Cassie murmured as they headed out in the blazing sun towards the buggy parked at the front. 'Not quite me.'

'I know.' Leo grinned. 'I remember you in jeans and trainers or shorts and hiking boots.'

'You know that part of the world.' Cassie smiled. 'There's not a lot of opportunity for the feminine stuff.'

She twisted to look at him as he eased the buggy away from the villa, taking his time.

'Did you...?' She paused and fell silent because she was so tempted to stray into forbidden territory.

'Did I what?'

'Nothing. It doesn't matter.'

'Want to hear the plan for today?'

'Yes. Shopping, but not in a shopping centre, and then...?'

'And then, back to the villa. The gardener will have cleared off by then and we can relax by the pool. We can have a reasonably early dinner. There might be music.'

Leo looked at her. He had swiftly steered her away from reminiscing because, in that tentative question of hers, he had detected the scent of questions waiting to be asked, questions to which he would not want to give any answers.

In fairness, she hadn't strayed from the ground rules.

He had told her what he wanted—a brief fling in the here and now, gone in the blink of an eye, with no harking back to the past. Some stuff was unavoidable but he had been determined to keep it real.

He'd seen her and had known that he hadn't forgotten her. It had been the same for her. Neither of them was here to build ties and pick up where they had left off. They were here to put the past to rest.

Except, as they trundled towards the main drag of the island, he felt a spike of curiosity to hear what she had wanted to ask before she'd stopped herself. Doubts about whether this one week would be enough had pushed against the vault into which they'd been shoved days ago, after that first time they'd made love once again, and it felt like a physical effort to keep them there.

They'd been careful never to go near the subject he knew would shatter what they were enjoying and, besides, he had long ago come to the conclusion that post mortems were a waste of time because they never changed anything. They'd broken up, and that was the end of that, and nothing to do with what was happening now, which was simply the physical residue of what they had once shared.

Emotions had been drained away and yet... He contained himself, content to watch her as he introduced her to the bit of the island they had yet to visit. Away from the solitude of the magnificent beaches was the leisurely bustle of a life that catered largely to a handful of uber-wealthy visitors to the island.

He took pleasure from her reactions. Her face lit up when they walked round the small town. He smiled when she told him that it was like being transported into a picture-perfect postcard. The small boutiques were in pastel shades of pinks, greens and baby blues, and the swaying coconut trees cast moving shadows on the lacy, old-world wooden facades.

She tried on frothy, silk creations in one of the boutiques while he sat, watched and enjoyed the view.

By half-past two they were back at the villa but not by the pool.

'It's too hot to be outside,' he said as soon as they were in the cool interior of the villa, with the breeze billowing through the windows. 'Besides, seeing you in some of those outfits was too much of a turn on... I'd rather be in bed with you than swimming in a pool.'

The curiosity was still needling at the back of his mind as he began undressing her, not waiting for the bedroom, too hot for her to take his time. He buried his mouth against her neck, propelling her back, back against the door and relishing her whimpers of pleasure as he kissed her, nipping her soft skin with his teeth while he pushed his hands up under her tee-shirt.

He could barely bear the brief pause as he yanked the tee-shirt over her head and then he kissed her, long and deep, the rhythm of his tongue against hers matching his movements against her pelvis. The rub of his erection through his shorts against her stomach made him want to groan out loud.

He tugged down the straps of the swimsuit and inched them apart to appreciate the lush swell of her breasts, the big, circular discs of her nipples swollen, the tips stiff and growing stiffer as he rubbed them with the abrasive pad of his thumbs.

'I have to calm down,' he said hoarsely, 'Or else I'm going to do something I've never done before.'

'What?'

'You know what, Cassie. No man is ever proud to lose

control of himself in his clothes. You're trying hard not to laugh, aren't you?' There was shaky amusement in his voice. 'You have a cruel streak I've never noticed before.'

'How do you plan on calming down, Leo? And what if I don't want you to?'

Leo gritted his teeth when she reached for the button on his shorts, flicked it open and then shoved her hand underneath, pushing against the zip which smoothly parted, allowing her to circle his throbbing erection with her fingers.

'No, no, no...' He groaned.

They did a sideways shuffle from the door against which she was pressed. It was a matter of just a small swivel away from the door and they turned to the six-foot-high wooden-framed mirror that stood in the massive hallway.

'Much better,' Leo said in a husky, shaky undertone.

She was standing in front of him now, her back to his stomach. In the long mirror, their eyes met and for Cassie, it couldn't have been a bigger turn on.

His head was dipped against her neck. The swimsuit had been tugged down to her waist, exposing her breasts, which were flushed and roused. She'd never seen him so uncontrolled and it fuelled something inside her, a similar wild craving. Like him, she couldn't have made it to the bedroom if she'd tried.

He moved against her and she could feel his hardness on her back, big and demanding, and she uttered a loud, guttural moan. She covered his hands on her breasts with hers and then continued to touch herself when he removed his hands, all the better to get rid of her shorts.

She wriggled out of them. It seemed to take for ever,

but at last she kicked them aside and looked at them both in the long mirror. Her body was so pale compared to his, even though she had developed a nice enough glow over the past few days. Her legs were spread wide and his head was still buried into her neck as he stroked her between her legs.

She watched the plunge of his fingers there with bold fascination. Very quickly, though, those strokes became too much to withstand. She closed her eyes and arched back against him. Her hands dropped to tightly circle his wrists and she came with a long, powerful shudder and a sweet release that made her giddy and euphoric.

She sagged against him, turned round and curved into him so that she could wrap her arms around his neck for a few seconds.

'Time for a bed.' He reached to lift her.

'Don't even think of sweeping me off my feet,' she murmured on a contented smile and he ignored her.

He swept her off her feet.

Leo thought that he didn't have any choice because, instead of banking down his desire, that beautiful little diversion in front of the mirror had stoked it even further. It seemed as though she wasn't the only one for whom new experiences were to be forged.

He made it to the bedroom with her in his arms but, before he deposited her on the bed, he paused and glanced down at her flushed face.

God, she was beautiful. She took his breath away A couple of days and this would go, this sudden fever inside him; it would disappear from his life for ever. The memory of her would be expunged.

Wouldn't it? Wouldn't it...?

Her eyelids were fluttering shut and her cheeks were still flushed from the force of her orgasm. He laid her on the bed, watched her shift for a couple of seconds then found himself some protection. Sex would clear his head.

He took it slow. It was the opposite of what had gone before. He touched her everywhere until her body reawakened and she touched him everywhere in return until, when he eventually entered her, his whole body was on fire.

He came in a shameless hurry. She knew just how to excite him to fever-pitch and he wondered whether that was just natural for them or whether some weird bond that had stretched through the years made him feel more comfortable with her than he ever had with any other woman.

Maybe it was the freedom. There were limits and a timeline on what was going on between them, so there was no danger of crossed signals, coy hints or leading questions to get him to a place he wasn't interested in visiting. They already knew exactly where they stood with one another.

Leo flopped back and stared up at the ceiling.

'Well...' He turned to her, propping himself up on one elbow and staring at her. 'That was a tidy end to the afternoon.'

How...? Why...? Why had it all crashed and burned?

He'd walked away, and he'd kept on walking, and he'd shoved those questions down so deep that they hadn't resurfaced until now, until she'd come back into his life. Or maybe those questions had always been there, just waiting for the right opportunity to present themselves.

Leo shook his head to clear the nagging urge to delve back into the past, which he had emphatically promised himself, and told her, he had no intention of doing.

'Very tidy.'

'We should think about leaving shortly... Now I've made a dinner reservation, I almost wish I hadn't. You could have got into that floaty little number you chose today and I would have been an appreciative audience of one.'

'I'm looking forward to going out!' Cassie laughed. She slid her long legs off the side of the bed and resisted the insistent tug on her arm to climb back in. 'A girl needs to show off now and again, especially when there's a new dress involved, and an audience of at least one who's appreciative.'

Leo grunted. He could have stayed put for the next twenty-four hours. He realised he didn't want to show her off—he wanted her all to himself. It was a disturbing thought, but one that wouldn't go away, even when they were back in the buggy and heading off to the beach bar that served amazing local delicacies.

She was wearing a floaty, silk wraparound dress in apricot and green that worked well with her colouring. Her long, dark hair tumbled over her shoulders and down her back and she wore strappy, tan flat sandals. She looked completely natural. In that regard, he was pretty sure she would stand out, given where they were heading. When Leo thought of the other men who might be there, looking at her, he had to clench the steering wheel hard to focus himself.

'This is amazing.'

Cassie looked around her as they arrived at the bar. It was very informal, with a massive wooden deck perched over the water on which tables and chairs were arranged in little clusters.

She couldn't give it her full attention, though, because Leo was on her mind. He was in a weird mood and she couldn't quite work out what that was all about.

There had been something fierce, urgent and desperate when he had caressed her in the hallway of the villa, and then afterwards in bed... It had been lingering and languorous, which in itself had carried a different kind of urgency.

She wondered whether he was tiring of her. Her body said *no*, but in the absence of any other explanation her mind said *yes*.

She would be careful to keep it light. Light was what made him comfortable...and if light was getting to be a strain for her that was something she would keep to herself.

She blinked her way back to the here and now. In the background there was the soft sound of steel drums being played. The fairy lights strung from the beams were intimate and subdued, and flickered on the dark water, illuminating it with streaks of silver here and there.

'Fantastic music, and I just love how open it is, and rustic!' There was a buzzy vibe, waiters coming and going, couples sitting at the tables laughing, talking in low voices, and gazing out at the dark, dark sea which ebbed and flowed softly against the wooden decking.

'At lunchtime, the birds come to pick up whatever scraps they can find. That I do remember from the last time I was here, which was a while ago, but I doubt anything's changed on that front. All looks the same here.'

'Have you ever brought anyone here, Leo?'

'Not counting my fussy old man?'

Cassie laughed and their eyes met over the flickering candle between them as they sat at the wooden table to which they had been ushered.

She flushed because she could see the perceptiveness in his dark eyes as he understood what question she'd really been asking. Jealousy raced through her, unsettling and unwanted.

It was a relief when a charming and chatty waiter came to take their drinks order. She could still feel Leo's lazy, piercing dark eyes on her, working out what she was saying, processing what she might be feeling.

'I'd go for the rum punch,' Leo suggested. The waiter was chatting with him, laughing and friendly without being intrusive. He heard himself chatting back, discussing the menu, asking about the mahi-mahi, but his mind was on Cassie and that question she had asked.

Had he ever brought anyone to the villa with him… Was she jealous? This was dangerous territory.

He remembered that time when he had been exposed and vulnerable, and recalled his resolve never to go there again. Yet, when he thought about her being jealous, he wasn't annoyed, he was pleased—more dangerous territory.

When he'd embarked on this plan to take the thing he'd once been denied, to tie up loose ends, it had seemed very clear-cut: sex. He would get her out of his system because he'd realised the thing he still hankered for, through all the bitterness, was physical. He could deal with that.

But things felt complicated now. He hadn't taken into account how the feel of her warm body next to him would play tricks with his resolve. He hadn't predicted how her laughter would cut through his iron-clad defences or how the past would keep making inroads into the present in ways that were small but significant.

None of this worked for him. They had a couple more

days left here and it wouldn't hurt to remind them both of exactly why what they had came with a deadline. Why there was no room for nostalgia, jealousy or any emotion bar the straightforward one called *desire*.

Maybe it was time the past was discussed after all. It would leave an acrid taste in both their mouths but it would put things into perspective before she started over-inflating what was going on between them.

Before *he* started over-inflating what was going on here between them, a little voice whispered. Before he weakened. No way was he going to do that.

'Have you decided what you're going to eat? Everything's freshly prepared here, so it's wise to order well in advance, because the main meal can easily take a while to arrive.'

'Any recommendations?'

'I would go for the fish. You won't get anything like it in Canada.' He paused and waited until the waiter took their order.

He made no effort to lighten the very subtle shift in atmosphere between them and he could see that she was as conscious of it as he was. Something inside Leo twisted at the thought that he was hurting her, and he gritted his teeth, irritated that she could still have some kind of weird power over him without even trying. He wasn't that gullible boy any longer!

'When we came here,' he said heavily, 'I told you that the past wasn't a place we would be returning to.'

'And I haven't,' Cassie told him quickly. 'If there was the occasional reminiscence, then that's inevitable. We're not robots, Leo. I don't think we have to beat ourselves up if we sometimes go back down memory lane. It's not as though we spent a lot of time there.'

* * *

She tilted her chin defiantly and gulped down some of the rum punch.

She'd been right—he'd been acting weird and now this. It had been stupid to kid herself that she hadn't imagined an undercurrent swirling just beneath the surface.

She was guiltily aware of the feelings for him resurfacing. She didn't want to acknowledge them but she would be a coward not to. Was it just the old pull of friendship; the feeling of being with her soulmate?

Or was it more dangerous than that…? Was she falling back in love with a man who no longer had similar feelings for her?

Oh, no, please no.

Cassie's heart picked up speed. Had he noticed it as well? Was he about to cut short their week? Cassie was horrified to realise that she didn't want that. She didn't want this glorious interlude to end but if *for ever* wasn't meant to be then the here and now was something she would grab with both hands.

She finished off the rum punch and made a fuss over the starters that had been brought to their table.

Desperately trying to think of something, anything, that might lighten the tension, she looked up when he said seriously, 'I was wrong.'

'Wrong? Wrong about what—coming here? We can leave any time you want, Leo!'

'Wrong about thinking it would be possible for us to sleep together without discussing what happened eight years ago—and I don't mean a little jaunt down memory lane where you remind me of something I once said or I remind you of something you used to do. You're right—

we're not robots. I'm talking about how things ended between us.'

'You said there was no point to digging that up.'

'And yet I find that there probably is. So...where do we start with this one?'

He sat back, signalled to one of the waiters without taking his eyes off her face and ordered a beer for himself, another rum punch for her and a bottle of wine. The silence lengthened until Cassie sighed and sifted her fingers through her tumble of hair.

'It's not going to change anything, Cass,' Leo told her quietly. 'But it's beginning to feel like it's more of an effort avoiding the landmines than just risking an accident in an attempt to defuse them. Your parents persuaded you to dump me because they didn't think I was good enough for you, is that it? Is that why you dumped me without any explanation? Was it easier?'

'I didn't have a choice. I had to do what I did and there would have been no point meeting up to talk because... because it wouldn't have made any difference.'

'Shocking turnaround for a girl who'd not a day earlier been joyously talking about sharing a future with me.'

His voice had cooled and, in that coldness, Cassie could see the bitterness that had crept into him and mushroomed over the years. The sex was mind-blowing but, for Leo, there would never be forgiveness. The sex would never give way to love because he could never forget.

'Yes, my parents convinced me that it wasn't the right time for me to leave, to follow you wherever that might take us. I mean, it would have meant not just leaving town, but leaving Canada. You wanted to spread your wings. You wanted an Ivy League university and a career that could only happen in America. You wanted out of small-town living completely.'

'And you didn't, Cassie? I wasn't the only one with wings that wanted spreading. I'm guessing the fact that my father was a lowly employee at your father's construction company played a part in ending the whole wing-spreading thing?'

'That's not it at all…'

'Oh, really? Enlighten me, Cass. Now that we've started down this road, there's no point shying away from full disclosure.'

'There was other stuff going on,' Cassie muttered.

'What other stuff?'

'Leo, why are we picking away at this now?'

'Is that what we're doing? Or are we just discussing something that's become a rather large elephant in the room?'

'It's a bit late in the day for us to start acknowledging the elephant, isn't it, considering we're winding down to going our own separate ways?'

A treacherous part of her longed to hear him tell her that he didn't want what they had to end. But he didn't.

'Maybe I would rather not have the elephant following me once I return to reality. Maybe,' he said with cool, relentless persistence, 'Both of us need to wrap things up properly, and there's no reason why we shouldn't after eight years. It's not as though we're involved with one another beyond what we have here. So, talk to me.'

'And after we've finished talking?'

'We enjoy our dinner and head back to the villa and have fun for the remainder of the time we're here.'

'I was so young, Leo. My parents… When I told them

about you, yes, they were shocked. They'd had no idea we were together. Well, no one had known.'

'No, the secrecy angle was a big deal for you, wasn't it, Cassie?'

'Can you blame me?'

'No. No, I don't suppose I can.'

'I know you don't mean that but there was more than just… There was…' Cassie shook her head. She felt raw inside. Maybe he was right. Maybe they had to part company with everything out in the open so that they could finally be rid of one another. Yet, when she thought about that, she felt a little sick inside.

She hadn't moved on, not in the way that he had. She just hadn't realised how deeply stuck she had become over the years. Perhaps this would be a release for her in a way she couldn't have predicted.

'Things were going on on the home front that I'd known nothing about. Things had been going on for a while, maybe a few months, and Mum and Dad might have kept it all quiet if I hadn't told them about our plans to leave town and me go to America with you. You wanted to make it big, to go to MIT, and I wanted to come with you. I told them that we planned to marry, that I loved you.'

'And I'm guessing that spooked the life out of your over-protective parents,' Leo said drily.

'My mum had been having tests,' Cassie told him in a low voice.

'Tests? What are you talking about—tests for what?'

'She'd been having a few bad turns. I hadn't really noticed. I'd been so busy living my own life that I'd barely registered what had been happening. Two days before I broke the news to my parents about us, the consultant in Toronto confirmed that she had the onset of multiple sclerosis.'

'What?'

'It was devastating, Leo. I didn't know what to do. It was like the ground suddenly opened up under my feet. Everything was in disarray. They didn't want to tell anyone, no one at all. My mother had always been a proud woman. She said she couldn't stand the thought of people pitying her.'

'I can't believe what I'm hearing!'

'There's no timetable for that illness. She could have lived happily with it for years with just minor flare-ups, or she could have started declining immediately. She told me, though, that she would be hollowed out if I left, that she needed me there with her. And my father begged me to stay. They both cried, Leo. I was devastated. I thought about you…about us…but I knew that I couldn't walk away from that crisis. They swore me to secrecy.'

'So you sent me a goodbye text.' It looked as though his mind was reeling with shock; with anger that she hadn't breathed a word and a deep sadness about a situation he'd known nothing of.

'I knew that it would have been unfair on you to have said anything. Even if I'd decided to go against my parents' wishes and told you about Mum's diagnosis, there was no way I would have wanted you to be conflicted about what to do. You had your future in the US all mapped out. Whichever way I looked at it, I knew that I had to sever the ties between us completely, even if that meant…even if it meant that you would walk away thinking the worst of me.'

'I really can't believe what I'm hearing,' he repeated.

'You had your dreams and you were always meant

to follow them, Leo, and there was no way I could have borne the guilt of thinking that I had somehow got in the way of that because of my own family constraints. I couldn't have lived with myself.'

'So you simply removed that choice from me by making it yourself.'

'You have to see that I did what I thought was best. I did what I did because I loved you.'

'You walked away from me.' He looked at her as though he knew that her intentions had been honourable, but also that her abandonment had rendered him helpless in a way he'd sworn he'd never be again. 'I never told you about my mother, Cassie. She did that to me as well.'

His mouth twisted. 'Maybe with less honourable intentions, but she walked away from my father and me and left me to spend my childhood picking up the pieces of her desertion.'

'Leo...'

'You swore your love to me. You should have trusted me with the truth, trusted that I would have known how to handle my own response. An impossible situation, I agree...but, yes, you could have taken the risk.'

'Leo, I'm so sorry. I had no idea about your mother. We never talked about her... I never knew...'

He drained his glass and looked at her, 'No matter now. It's done. What it does prove, though, is why this thing needs to end in two days' time. We were too young. I was impatient, eager to move on with my life. You had problems you couldn't bring yourself to tell me about. We were two people who deserve to be right where we are—together, but never for ever, because neither of us can ever return and fix what got broken eight years ago...'

CHAPTER SEVEN

They'd been young…impatient… It was a relationship that had never been destined to survive heady, crazy youth. She'd turned her back on him eight years ago and he'd walked away without a backward glance, all his armour plating sliding into place the further and faster he'd walked. And eight years had passed without him giving much thought to the repercussions of what had happened all those years ago.

He'd been shocked by her confession. Even now, a week and a half later, with sun, sea and sand just a fading memory, he was still shocked. Multiple sclerosis! How could she have kept something that big to herself? Yes, she had eventually confessed everything, but of course it was way too late for that now.

There'd been too much water under the bridge by the time he'd heard what she'd had to say. She could have told him at the time instead of sending an anodyne text message breaking things off between them! He had deferred a future to wait for her, making sure that she never felt pressured. He'd been tough and cynical and had known that women could break a man. He had resolved never to have that happen to him the way it had happened to his father, and yet…

He had met her and all those resolutions had flown

through the window. He'd acted out of character and he'd enjoyed it; he had felt young, hopeful and *normal*, without the cynicism weighing him down. And still, she'd broken up with him, and hadn't trusted him enough to tell him the truth as to why!

That really hurt. It made a mockery of the love she'd professed to have for him. With love, there was always trust. She hadn't trusted him. He'd been right to walk away. He'd given himself to a woman who hadn't trusted him against every scrap of better judgement.

He told himself that, because it would be easier to see the tableau in black and white. But there was nuance to the situation and Leo knew that could be his undoing because she'd acted with the purest of motives. Would he have put everything on hold indefinitely for her if she'd explained the situation to him? If he had, it would have been a dreadful mistake because she was right—he'd worked hard for a future that was opening up in front of him, too promising to be denied. But he hadn't, so had guilt eroded the very future he'd embarked on?

He had genuinely meant it when he'd told her not to beat herself up for decisions that had been made a long time ago in good faith. The doors were shut between them but that was just the way things sometimes worked out.

The remainder of their time on Mustique had not been uncomfortable. It should have been but, in fact, they had fallen into one another with the fierce desperation of two people who'd known the end was imminent. Nothing more had been said about the past, and there'd been no more dwelling on what had happened between them. They'd both known that the air had been cleared and that there was nothing left to talk about.

They'd parted company on Mustique, she to make the

journey back to Canada and he to stay on for another day before flying to Europe to close several deals that had been put on hold.

'I really thought long and hard about coming here—to do what we did,' she'd told him, just before she'd boarded the little plane that would hop away from the island and take her away from him for ever. 'But I'm glad that I did.'

'Always good to scratch an itch,' Leo had returned blandly, already giving the impression of someone whose mind was moving on.

She'd insisted on going to the airport on her own so that she could get her thoughts together about practical issues to do with the family home, now that it wasn't going to be repossessed.

He hadn't argued. Everything had been clear cut, in the end, so why did he still have this strange sense of emptiness inside him?

Leo looked around at the stunning minimalism of his Manhattan apartment. It was blindingly white and somehow he found that irritating. The memory of turquoise water, bright-blue skies and colour everywhere clearly hadn't faded as anticipated.

His apartment had clear, uninterrupted views of Central Park and much of Manhattan from its perfect positioning twenty-two storeys up, and from the floor-to-ceiling windows that were spectacularly dramatic because there were no shutters or curtains to contain the sensation of the giddy heights outside pouring in.

On a clear day, the view was unsurpassable. On a cold winter's night with a bottle of whisky on the table next to him, Leo couldn't have cared less about the view.

His phone beeped with a text and he groaned. He had responded to a handful of texts his ex, Aimee, had sent him while he'd been in Mustique. The communications had been annoying but had seemed harmless enough. She was sorry for having blown a fuse when they'd broken up... She'd been round to his place to get some stuff she'd forgotten...was that okay? Jimmy had let her in and mentioned that he was away...where was he...?

But now the trickle had become a flood and, if she wasn't threatening hellfire, damnation and revenge, she was pleading for them to get back together. He would have to deal with the situation soon, but the thought of doing that was exhausting and irritating at the same time. He wasn't mean-spirited enough not to realise that this was happening because he'd taken his eye off the ball.

His phone beeped again. He picked it up, glanced at the beginning of a message on the screen, frowned, sat up and opened it... He read the message quickly, then more slowly.

And, just like that, the tenor of his evening completely changed. He stood up, flexed his muscles, which had stiffened from lying on the sofa for too long, and then he smiled.

It seemed that catching curve balls was getting to be a way of life for him and this one was very interesting indeed...

Cassie was watching telly on the sofa in her apartment, feet up, busy wondering how all her money worries could be sorted only for her now to face different but equally stressful anxieties, when the buzzer on her intercom went.

She almost couldn't be bothered to get it. Snow had started falling outside. It was as yet just wispy flurries, but flurries with a plan, and the plan was getting worse.

Mustique felt like a hundred years ago. Had she really

swum in the crystal-clear sea, laughed with Leo and made passionate love with reckless abandon? It felt like a dream.

After she'd told him why she'd backed away from leaving with him eight years ago and why she'd stayed with her parents, morally and emotionally obliged to do what she'd known she'd had to do as the loving and dutiful daughter, she'd had a moment of wild hope that things would change between them. That he would revisit the past, return to that fateful moment and see it from a different perspective.

Their time together in the bubble of his villa had been so special that she'd felt all those emotions from the past return in a whoosh, stronger and better than ever, because they'd lived life in the intervening years and were now wiser, more mature and, she'd hoped, capable of forgiveness.

If she'd learned to accept the anguish he'd caused when he'd walked off without looking back over his shoulder even once, then he might be able to forgive the way she'd decided not to start the adventure they'd planned together and see that, ultimately, she had done it all for him. She'd certainly recognised that the feelings stirred up being there with him, making love with him and much more than that, had gone way beyond desire that needed satisfying.

She'd been so wrong. After the initial shock, he hadn't raged. He'd told her that he understood. He'd also told her that nothing could ever reopen the door that had slammed shut between them.

And he'd told her about his mother. He hadn't been the only one with a shocking revelation. She'd had no idea how deep his feelings of abandonment had run but, back in the quiet of her flat with her thoughts for company, she had begun to wonder whether things would ever have worked out between them.

Deep down, was he too scarred by his past ever to have put all his trust in her? The fact that he had never tried to get in touch with her—not even once, even though he'd known at the time how big a deal it had been for her to have lost her virginity to him—told a story, didn't it?

The fact that he had been so casual about ending things after their week together reinforced what she had begun to suspect—that he was not a man who could ever give himself to the vulnerability of loving someone else. He hadn't been able to resist killing what old demons remained by sleeping with her, and in fairness it had been the same for her, but killing those demons had opened up a different door for her. For him, no door had been opened at all.

Sex was what he'd offered her, sex was what she'd agreed to—willingly and happily, and there were no regrets there—but that was all there was to it for him.

Cassie was so glad that she hadn't done the unthinkable and poured out her heart and soul to him. She'd put a smile on her face instead, and had thrown herself into making the most of their final days on the island.

She groaned and walked towards the door on the third ring of her buzzer. Whoever it was wasn't going away. Outside the flurries were picking up pace, which made her think that she would need more time to deliver two catering jobs in two days than she and Frankie had factored in, not to mention also needing a minor miracle on the weather front. Driving was difficult in poor conditions, and the snow in this part of the world tended to pile up in great white mounds which meant that there were many times when there was just too much to clear.

Cassie pressed her intercom and then froze when she

heard a familiar dark, sexy voice telling her to open up and let him in. Leo was the last man she'd expected to be standing outside. The last man she'd expected and also the very last man she wanted to see. Her heartbeat quickened and a wave of panic and nausea washed over her. Her thoughts raced, becoming a tangled mess that made her feel faint.

'Leo…'

'Open up, Cassie. It's snowing outside and I'm not dressed for it.'

'What are you doing here?'

'What do you think I'm doing? Here's a clue: I'm not passing through and just deciding to drop in and say hi. Now, open up.'

'Leo…'

'I'm not going until you let me in, Cass. We need to talk and I'm guessing by your prevarication that you know exactly what we need to talk about.'

Cassie sucked in a shaky breath and buzzed him in.

It was nearly seven in the evening. She was dressed in thick tracksuit bottoms and a long-sleeved tee-shirt and, frankly, it couldn't have been a worse time for him to have showed up on her doorstep. She felt under-dressed and under-prepared for what she knew was coming.

But he'd been knocking on her door before she'd had time to do anything about either of those worries. She drew in a long breath, counted to ten and then pulled open the door with a rictus grin that wouldn't have fooled anyone.

'Cassie.'

'Hi, Leo.' It was as if she was seeing him for the first time in all his sinful, devastating beauty, as tall, as dark and as mesmerising as she remembered—more, if anything. 'This is a surprise. I wasn't expecting to see you…er…'

'I know,' Leo murmured soothingly. 'But life is full of unexpected surprises, or at least it certainly seems that way ever since you re-entered my life. Can I come in or shall we have this conversation with me standing on the threshold?'

Leo didn't take his eyes off her flushed face.

He could all but see the word *guilt* writ large on her forehead in bright neon lettering. He'd actually debated whether to show up on her doorstep or phone her to discuss the very interesting piece of information that had landed in his lap but it had been a very quick inner debate.

He'd wanted to see her. In fact, for the entire trip back here, his mind had been exclusively occupied with thoughts of her and he had to admit that he hadn't exactly complained at the prospect of showing up unannounced.

It also helped that his ex had demanded a meeting with him to 'talk things through'. Coming here had been very handy, given the fact that talking to Aimee was the last thing he wanted to do. He'd already had two conversations with her, being polite but firm, and he might as well have talked to a brick wall.

Under any other circumstances, he wouldn't have dreamt of showing up unannounced on a woman's doorstep at night, in the depths of winter, but Cassie... She'd been his lover not so long ago and, as things stood, well, this was definitely a conversation to have face to face, where he could see exactly what she was thinking.

She was wearing some old clothes—grey jogging bottoms in some kind of fleecy material and a long-sleeved tee-shirt that reminded him very forcibly of just how beautiful her breasts were and just how much he could lose himself in them with agonising speed.

Leo shifted.

'I suppose you should come in, but I wish you'd called in advance, Leo.' Her voice was grudging and wary.

'Is that what we are now, Cass—strangers making appointments to see one another? I'm disappointed.'

He briefly noted the heightened colour in her cheeks and brushed past her into a light, airy space that was bigger than he'd expected, and perfectly proportioned. It was a modern apartment, tastefully done on two levels with airy rooms and an open-plan layout. The block was horizontal rather than vertical and fronted with a generous circular courtyard that was currently turning white under the snow.

'Terrible weather outside.' He strolled around the apartment, unashamedly taking in the framed family photos on the modern bookshelf with its pale unevenly spaced shelves, the paintings and the rich colours of the comfortable seating.

As he walked, he divested himself of his charcoal-grey cashmere overcoat, dropping it over the back of one of the chairs, before ambling to the living room window to stare outside at the now thickly falling snow.

When he eventually turned around to look at her, she was standing in the same position with her arms folded.

'You're not exactly giving me a warm welcome here, Cass.'

'I'm just curious as to why you've shown up.'

'Nice try.' He raised his eyebrows and grinned. 'I would have enjoyed a little more small talk before cutting to the chase, especially given our new-found relationship…'

'We don't have a *new-found relationship*.'

'That's very hurtful after our many lazy, hot, passionate encounters in my villa.'

'You know what I mean.'

'Admittedly, at the agreed time our week came to an end, but I would still say that it's a lot more of a relationship than we had eight-odd years before that.' But there was something under her bravado; Leo could sense it in the way she couldn't quite meet his gaze and how her fingers were biting into the soft flesh of her arms—no surprise there.

'And,' he continued, heading towards the living area which occupied a pleasant spot next to a bank of windows that overlooked the area at the back, 'It seems that our *new-found relationship* isn't quite as dead as I'd thought.'

He sat on the sofa and patted the space next to him.

'In fact, it seems that it's very much alive and kicking, although I'm disappointed that my wife-to-be hasn't seen fit to tell me about our engagement herself…'

Of course, the second she'd heard his disembodied voice on the other end of her intercom, she'd known exactly why he'd shown up.

'So you found out. You weren't meant to,' she muttered.

'Really? Pretty major situation to keep under wraps, wouldn't you say?'

'How did you find out, anyway? And really, considering you live a million miles away, I thought… I assumed, naturally, that…'

'That I would be none the wiser?'

'Something like that.'

'It's been a long day for me. Actually, a long and restless night as well, bearing in mind that I couldn't remember for the life of me when I was supposed to have proposed to you. Care to bring me up to speed?'

'I know you must be furious,' Cassie managed with as

much defiance as she could muster. She shuffled to one of the chairs facing him because the last place she fancied sitting was right next to him on the sofa.

'I'm too shell-shocked to be furious.'

'I suppose I should get you something to drink,' Cassie said, resigned now to the inevitable and without the faintest notion of where things were going to end up—not in a happy place, was her prediction.

'Excellent idea. Let's skip the tea or coffee, though. I think something a little stronger would work, at least for me.'

'I have some wine.'

'Why not? Great apartment, by the way. Was this also on the chopping block before I came to your financial rescue?'

'Can you please stop being sarcastic?'

'I'm finding it hard to be casual and amiable in a situation like this. It's not every day I find out that I'm about to become a married man. Okay, Cass, tell me how all of this happened.'

He followed her into the kitchen, which was separated from the main area by a long island under which three bar stools were neatly tucked.

He pulled one out, sat down and looked at her as she went to the fridge, opened it, took her time fetching the wine and then pouring them a glass each.

'I haven't eaten,' she prevaricated.

'Nor have I.'

'I have some leftovers from the last catering job. Nothing fancy—finger food that wasn't quite perfect enough to be presented.'

'Suits me. Cassie, look at me for a minute.'

Cassie looked at him reluctantly. On the one hand,

he hadn't hit the roof. On the other hand, maybe it was a slow burn and he was building up to it. He certainly wasn't going to be overjoyed with what she'd thrown at him, considering he'd been more than happy to see the back of her when their week had come to an end.

She paused and looked at him as instructed, but with cautious, narrowed eyes. 'I'm sorry,' she said, clearing her throat. 'Like I said, you weren't meant to find out.'

'What I'm hearing is not that you're sorry you dragged me unwittingly into a deception of which I was completely unaware but that you're just sorry I happened to find out about it.'

'Maybe.'

'I'm not going to explode, so you don't have to look as though you need to be dodging bullets,' Leo told her wryly. 'It is what it is and now it's a case of what happens next. So, first and foremost, what happened?'

Cassie sighed in painful, grudging resignation. 'Mum found out about us. Your name was on the bank transfer. Lord knows, she must have been eagle eyed to have spotted it. So she put two and two together and came to exactly the right conclusion, which was that my week away "sorting out the finances" was a deal I'd done with you that involved...involved...'

'Lazy nights and even lazier mornings and a lot of hot sex?'

'She was absolutely horrified.'

Cassie could feel tears welling up when she remembered her mother's crushed, shocked and disappointed expression.

'She said she would rather have had bailiffs beat down the doors and take the roof from over her head than to think that her baby girl had slept with a man she didn't have feelings for simply because he could afford to pay her family's debts off.'

'So I'm guessing you didn't mention that it was a two-way street,' Leo murmured drily. 'No hint that you were as hot for me as I was for you?'

'I was thrown into a tailspin. We were sitting right there in Phil's office. Mum might have been able to wait before she said what she was thinking, but she'd had a bad morning, and the shock of it... Well, I ended up telling her that you and I had been communicating for a while... that I wasn't going to mention anything to anyone just yet but that we were a serious item. I implied that it was something of a loan between two people who had...found love all over again.'

'I'm not seeing the ring on your finger.'

'I was coerced into saying that we were engaged,' Cassie confessed. 'The minute I told Mum that I hadn't jumped into bed with you in exchange for a bailout, she perked up. She asked whether we were engaged, whether this was more than just a flash in the pan relationship for you, because she knew that I wasn't that kind of girl, and I said the first thing that came into my head...'

'Ah.'

'It all seemed to happen so fast. How did you find out?'

'I got a congratulations text from Phil, who remembered me, I have no idea how.'

'You were highly memorable back then,' Cassie said glumly. 'You may not have hung out with us because you didn't mix in our social set, but all the boys knew just who you were. I think most of them envied you.'

'That would explain it. Small town and news that travels at the speed of light. You can imagine how stunned I was to be congratulated on an engagement I didn't know the first thing about.'

'Please don't pretend that you're not angry about this, Leo. I can take it.'

'Like I said, it's a bit late for that. Anger isn't going to change anything. How were you going to deal with the situation, had I never found out?'

Cassie swallowed some of the wine that she had forgotten about. She could feel it going straight to her head on an empty stomach but the thought of breaking off the conversation to go and do something with leftovers was crazy. Her nerves were stretched to breaking point.

'I... I was going to take some weekends away,' she confessed, reddening as she looked down at her clasped fingers. 'It would have been easy to use the excuse that you couldn't make it here because of your work schedule. Mum asked a lot of questions about you, and I made sure to stress just what a busy guy you were, running your empire.'

'Go on. I'm all ears.'

'Gradually I would have become disillusioned with the amount of time you spent abroad wrapping up deals and doing what billionaires do.'

'Ah.'

'We could have had an argument about you not wanting to relocate here because you thought it was a backwater.'

'Of course. Makes sense when you remember I walked away and never returned for any school reunions. It would have been typical billionaire behaviour.'

'Maybe you would have had an affair.'

'Now, that I find unacceptable.'

'You would never have known.'

'And wouldn't your mother have found it a little odd

that the guy who put the ring on her daughter's finger couldn't make time to meet the woman he was going to call his mother-in-law?'

'I don't know, Leo!' Cassie cried, leaping to her feet, then jerkily preparing the leftovers with her back to him, all too aware of his dark eyes keenly on her. She was shaking as she flung a quick salad together, topping it off with home-made mushroom tartlets and salmon bites with crème fraiche.

What on earth was her mother going to say when the truth came out? Not only would she become the daughter who had slept with a guy for money, but the daughter who had been happy to lie shamelessly about it. She was still flushed and agitated as she dumped food on the kitchen counter along with plates and cutlery.

'Maybe you were on your way here but you…you lost control of your car and had an accident! Nothing serious but enough for you to have to return to New York to recuperate—a broken leg…'

'Very creative. And now that I've found out and I'm here? What do you suggest happens next?'

'I'm going to see my mum tomorrow,' Cassie told him with a quiet sigh. 'I guess we should both go and try to explain the situation to her. You've returned to your life and I know the last thing you want is for there to be any continuing connection with me.'

'Not, I suppose, that there would have been any bearing in mind that our last contact would have seen me in hospital with a broken leg before the whole thing was called off, because I turned out to be a workaholic who might or might not have been having round-the-clock affairs.'

* * *

Leo watched her avoid his gaze at all costs. She was stabbing the lettuce leaves in the desultory fashion of someone waiting for the Grim Reaper to make an entrance.

She'd asked him if he was angry and Leo knew that he should be. Without any input from him, he'd been actively used to deceive someone and, from everything she'd said, his entire character would have been impugned; whether he'd been present or not to suffer the consequences of that was irrelevant.

However, for reasons that escaped him, he wasn't angry. In fact, when he looked at her downcast head, part of him wanted to burst out laughing.

Part of him was strangely pleased to be back in her company. Why? Surely he'd accomplished what he'd set out to do when he'd whipped her off to Mustique? Surely sleeping with her had killed off those last dying embers of what he'd once felt for her? Feelings he hadn't even realised had been there until she'd contacted him out of the blue.

Yet he realised now how much more he'd missed than just her sexy, willing body. He frowned because that was an unsettling thought. It nudged something deep inside him that was a little frightening because he couldn't control whatever it was that had been stirred up.

Getting a grip, his mind automatically turned to a more logical train of thought. One that made sense of him sitting here, eating leftovers with her and realising that this could be another temporary situation that suited him as much as it suited her. He had an ex who was becoming increasingly strident in wanting to reignite what they'd had. A phoney engagement to Cassie was beginning to look like a walk in the park compared to Aimee's tearful, pleading, stalking behaviour.

So a legitimate and serious relationship might serve him very well. It would even suit him to go public with it, and in due course Aimee would fade into the background and that particular inconvenience would become no more than a learning curve.

'Nice leftovers, Cassie. If this is the standard of your food, then I'm not surprised you're doing well.'

'Thank you.'

'I don't want to be responsible for any, how shall I put it, fracture in your relationship with your mother, Cass. As an only child, and given the situation you've both been in, I know that for all of this to unravel would cause immense stress.'

'It would.' She looked at him in silence for a few seconds. 'My mother is very important to me, Leo. I know after what you went through, how you felt when your mother left, that it must take a lot for you to recognise the value of a mother, and to appreciate and empathise with me in this situation when your own experiences were so different, so painful. A situation which, I'm ashamed to admit, is of my own making—and for that, again, I'm really sorry.'

'I think we can do away with the psycho-babble, Cass, and stick to the basics. So, here's what I propose,' he continued, relaxing back and waving one hand in a magnanimous gesture. It was discomforting to think that she knew parts of him he barely knew himself and he certainly wasn't about to start any touchy-feely conversation with her about that. 'We go along with the charade you dreamt up.'

'What? We do?'

'We play a part which will realistically involve the minimum effort from either of us, and it can die off in just the way you predicted—but naturally without the accident being necessary, and certainly no philandering. I find that sort of thing very distasteful, if you must know. That I'm a workaholic, however, strikes the right note and happens to be the truth. My hours are ridiculous.' He thought of the many times he'd bailed on girlfriends in the past and winced. 'I'm not even averse to people knowing, or to playing the part of your fiancé as and when, until problems inevitably arise and we part company.'

He looked at her steadily. No need to tell her that what suited her likewise suited him. He was perfectly happy to be the good guy in all of this, and what was wrong with that?

Returning that steady gaze, Cassie almost couldn't believe what she'd just heard. She'd expected him to be livid. She'd pretty much accepted that at the very least she would have to do a full, unabridged confession to her mother and just swallow the consequences.

But now…for him to agree to go along with the charade…why?

Then it slowly dawned on her why that would be: the sex. He probably fancied that he could call on her as and when he wanted in the guise of her fiancé until such time as he got bored of her. Perhaps he hadn't had quite enough of her by the end of the week and this would be a pleasant opportunity for him to take what he thought might still be on offer, and legitimately on offer, in the eyes of the outside world.

But gut instinct told her that this wasn't going to do. He played by his own rule book but she had feelings for him—deep, true feelings that ran all the way back to the girl she'd been eight years ago. The love she'd felt had never been killed off by absence, hurt, disillusionment or anything else.

And to fall into bed with him again for whatever reason would be a catastrophe. Her heart would never withstand it. He was doing her a favour, but she had to do herself a few favours as well. She had to have control over the narrative she'd set in motion.

'I can't believe you're agreeing to do this, Leo,' she said quietly. 'It means a lot to me.' She drew in a shaky breath and managed to hold his gaze. 'But I have a condition, I'm afraid.'

'What's that?'

'This won't be about the sex. This will be about friendship.'

'No sex?'

'We've been there, done that and, as I see it, we won't be in one another's company very much to pull this off anyway, but when we are...well... I don't want any unnecessary complications.'

'Such as?'

Cassie stiffened imperceptibly. *Such as me falling gradually, inexorably more and more hopelessly in love with you.*

'Such as,' she quipped lightly, allowing him a smile, 'You getting ideas that there could ever be more to us than one week's worth of sex.'

'Sizzling sex,' Leo corrected. 'And agreed—the fewer complications, the better. This favour is simply for old times' sake.'

CHAPTER EIGHT

'HAVE YOU BOOKED a hotel?'

Cassie looked at him. *Her fiancé!* Pretend fiancé, of course, but just thinking about Leo in those terms made her heart skip a treacherous beat.

He'd pushed up the sleeves of his black cashmere jumper and her eyes were compulsively drawn to the dark hair curling round the matt silver band of his watch. She looked away before he had a chance to see her staring at him.

'I thought about it but, in the end, I decided that it was probably not the best of ideas,' he replied.

'What do you mean?'

'Join the dots, Cass. If I'm here and we're supposed to be engaged, then what if someone in the hotel vaguely recognises me and, when the gossip hits the streets, puts two and two together? It's very busy out there. The entire town seems to be out and about. Why would I be staying there if my fiancée is holed up in her house twenty minutes away? Wouldn't the loved-up couple be spending their hard-won time actually in the same place?'

'So you came here with the expectation of staying in my apartment?'

'I actually came here in the expectation of driving back to the airport and taking the next flight back to New York. Believe it or not, I'm accustomed to flying at any hour of the day or night. If it was too late, or I was too tired to drive to the airport here, it wouldn't have been a problem to get a driver to take me, and there would always be the option of having a private jet ferry me back to civilisation.'

'So you came here to...'

'To find out what the hell was going on. Call that natural curiosity. I was a single man when we parted company, and now I'm suddenly on course to be married, and the odd thing is I can't remember proposing.'

Cassie squirmed. Of course he would have been curious. Of course he would have come to see her. One minute she'd vanished, the next minute she had mysteriously become his fiancée. Leo wasn't the sort of guy to shrug that off as a misunderstanding. Everything he said made sense and she was an idiot for concocting a scheme that had more holes in it than a sieve.

'Okay, I get that.'

'That's very understanding of you.'

'Can you please stop being so sarcastic?'

'Like I told you, that's tricky, considering the situation I find myself in.'

Their eyes tangled and the atmosphere was suddenly static with electricity. *No sex: that was the important stipulation.* But, looking at him like this, all she could think about was sex, touching him and having him touch her. She could feel her heart beating so hard that it felt as though it might burst out of her rib cage.

'Keep looking at me like that,' Leo ground out in a rough undertone, 'And I might start asking whether you're serious about the *no sex* rule, Cassie.'

Cassie breathed in sharply, mouth tightening.

'You're so egotistic, Leonardo Cruz.'

'Is that what you want to call it?' He shrugged, although his dark eyes remained on her with laser-like intensity. 'Okay. I'll let it go.'

'Just tell me what you intend to do now.' Cassie dragged the conversation back to a practical level because she was finding it hard to bring her disobedient body to heel.

'Now it looks as if you and I are going to be spending the night together.' He held up his hands as though she'd interrupted him, even though she hadn't. 'I'll take the sofa. There's no need to fret that there's going to be anything further between us.' He stood up, stretched and began gathering things from the table. Stuff had been eaten but she couldn't remember eating it.

'I wasn't going to *fret* about that, and there's no need to help clear away. I can handle this.'

'Slight fly in the ointment is the fact that I haven't brought a change of clothes with me because a sleepover was the last thing on my mind.'

Because it's well and truly finished between us, was how Cassie translated that, and it hurt.

She covered the sting of his remark with a tight smile, 'Surprisingly, there are no spare men's outfits hanging in any wardrobes here.'

She began clearing away, and despite her objections he helped, creating a fake domestic-bliss scene that made her grit her teeth because it couldn't have been further from the truth.

'Is that department store by the church still up and running?'

'Mel and Acton?' Cassie asked, sliding a glance across to him and he nodded. 'Yes, why?'

'Will it be open now?'

'With Christmas just round the corner, nothing shuts

till ten. As you pointed out, everywhere's packed, stuffed full with people on red alert to recognise you.'

'Now who's being sarcastic?' But he grinned. 'I'll call them; get them to deliver the basics to me here.'

'They don't deliver.'

He looked at her and smiled slowly. 'You'd be surprised what rules can be changed when there's sufficient money on the table.'

He pulled out his mobile, scrolled for a couple of seconds and then turned away to begin talking on the phone. Cassie watched, fascinated, as he strolled off back into the sitting area, for all the world as though he owned the place. In a way, that wasn't so surprising, because he'd become the guy who gave the impression of owning the space around him, wherever he happened to be and whoever he happened to be with. Maybe he'd always been that guy, she thought.

'Done,' he said with satisfaction, returning to the kitchen and propping himself against the wall to look at her as she blinked her way back to reality and carried on tidying.

Eventually, with the dishes neatly stacked on the draining board, Cassie turned round to look at him. 'Very impressive,' she said politely. 'Did you manage to get what you were after?'

'Isn't it? And, yes, I did.'

'Would you like some coffee? Or would you rather I show you where you'll be sleeping? I have two bedrooms, so there won't be any need for you to toss and turn on a sofa overnight.'

'You almost sound as though you're trying to get rid of me.' He looked at her, assessing, with his head tilted to one side. 'Did you get a two-bedroomed place so that your mother could stay over now and again?'

'How did you jump to that conclusion?' Cassie returned his steady gaze and was suffused with a heady, drowning feeling. To do something, she spun round to put the kettle on and reached for a couple of mugs.

In Mustique, she had been on safe ground. They'd both been there for one thing and one thing only: sex. Within those very defined parameters, she'd known how to operate, and being so far from everything she was accustomed to had made it even easier for her to stick within the confines of their deal.

This was very different. She was aware of her feelings now, sensitive to the impact he had on her and the way her heart was open to him, although he didn't know it. She was alert to danger, and with him here in her apartment, big, powerful and darkly, sinfully sexy, danger seemed to be everywhere.

Her skin tingled with it and she ached from the absolute necessity to keep a physical distance between them because it felt as if she might go up in flames if she got too close.

But he knew her.

'We go back a long way, Cassie,' he said, practically reading her mind. 'Underneath the outgoing, popular girl back then, there was a gentleness I always recognised in you and found appealing. I also knew how much your family meant to you.'

'Then you should understand why I did what I did, why I ended it with us. I know I said this to you before, but I really and truly believed that it was for the best that I let you go—let *us* go—to give you the chance to pursue your dreams. I knew how much leaving here meant to you back then. If I'd explained the situation, you would have been conflicted.'

'You took away my agency, my right to have an input into the decision-making,' Leo said coolly. 'Like I think *I've* said before. Which reminds me that there's no point walking down this road again. It's always going to lead to a dead end.'

Took away his agency... Put like that, in those stark, bleak terms, Cassie could see how her choice to break up with him without any explanation put her on par with the mother who had taken away all his choices by disappearing. It was a different situation, for different reasons, but still—a scar that had formed long before she knew him had been torn open.

How could he ever forgive her? She'd been unaccountably crushed that he hadn't made the slightest effort to find out how she was, at least to try and discover why she had done what she'd done, but now she could see that there would have been too much pain inside him at the time and over the years that pain had crystallised into bitterness.

Cassie lowered her eyes but she could feel the anguish surge through her. If only he knew how deeply she still cared for him, how easy it had been for those feelings to reawaken because they had never really gone away. But for Leo... For Leo, he could separate the physical attraction from any emotional connections because those connections had been completely severed eight years ago.

She clenched her jaw but couldn't quite manage to drag herself away from the memories of past suffering and hurt—not just her hurt but the hurt she had unintentionally inflicted on the man she had loved so deeply.

'What we shared, Cass, was the pure, unencumbered purity of sex. If sometimes a memory surfaces of whatever else there was between us, it's just that—a memory—nothing more.'

His eyes darkened and she could see the sensual intent there, banked down but simmering patiently under the surface, waiting for her. He wanted her, still wanted her, and he knew that she still wanted him, even though now they both knew the folly of getting physically involved all over again.

She, more than him, knew just how idiotic that would be. But that lazy, assessing, *patient* look in the depths of his eyes... Cassie went weak. Her mouth trembled and everything, every nerve in her body, trembled because the air sizzled with the tension of emotions that had been locked away for eight years and because of the finality of what he'd just said. Her hands shook and she felt herself drop the tray as if it was happening in slow motion.

Aghast, she watched everything fall: not the coffee, because that was still brewing in the cafetière, but everything else on the tray went flying through the air in an aerial bombardment, landing with a resounding crash at their feet.

'Cassie!'

He pulled her towards him and she buried her face against his chest, trying and failing to staunch the tears that were finally released. Her sobs were broken and wretched.

'I'm sorry,' she whispered, when they finally eased to shaky little hiccups.

'You're crying for the past.' Leo tilted her face so that their eyes met. 'And for the future we never had.'

He kept his voice level and unemotional but his heart constricted. God, had he ever wanted any woman the way he wanted this one? Her tears seemed to soak into his soul and revived all those feelings from the past. She hadn't been the only one to cry for a future denied. He'd thought the pain of his mother's abandonment couldn't be matched but he'd been wrong.

No way could he revisit that dark place from which he had surfaced and propelled himself into the one he occupied now. He slammed an iron door against the weakness of a tenderness that was trying to push its way into him.

'But the past is the past. Tears will never change it.'

'Leo…'

'Go sit. I'll tidy all this mess.'

'I… Leo…'

'We need to leave this alone, Cassie. We need to stop picking away at it. This isn't where we are now.' But his voice was just a little unsteady and he stood back to thread his fingers through his hair.

Cassie nodded and did as he said even though she could still feel the searing pain of hearing him slam shut the door on things inside her that felt raw and unfinished. She could still hear the harshness of his response, the absolute, painful sincerity in his voice.

There would never be any point appealing to a side of him that might not have shut down completely, because he didn't have that side left. The past was a subject she would never slip into again.

She was back in control by the time he'd cleared away the broken bits to replace them with new mugs and this time no accident happened when he set the coffee in front of them. The atmosphere had settled into something approaching normality and for that she was grateful. He might be bitter in retrospect, but he had moved on. He wasn't hung up on a past neither of them could change.

'Will you leave tomorrow?' She cleared her throat and

shot him a quick look from under her lashes. 'Like I said, I'm due to go see Mum, and then there's a small break with the catering before things pick back up in a couple of days, mostly with office parties.'

'Clothes are being delivered by ten this evening,' Leo murmured, 'And then I think I'll play the devoted fiancé and come with you to see your mother.'

'No need.' Her voice was more terse than she'd intended but, after that crying jag and feeling his arms encircling her, she just wanted some time out to recover some of her sapped emotional strength.

'Very peculiar if I didn't, wouldn't you say?'

'She has no idea you're here.'

'You can tell her. Think of the awkwardness if she found out afterwards. What if the kind, helpful person who delivers my clothes recognises me and word gets round? Your mother shouldn't belatedly find out that she's missed me because I couldn't be bothered to visit her.'

Cassie frowned. 'It just feels as though…as if…'

'As if what?' Leo queried. 'Play with fire and you might end up getting burnt, Cassie. You got found out in a lie and decided that it wouldn't do any harm to take the easy way out by making up a story about me, thinking that it would be a safe bet because I wouldn't be around. You could say what you wanted about me, turn me into the villain of the piece and I would never be any the wiser.'

Put like that, it sounded pretty awful, but there wasn't much there she could disagree with. 'Not necessarily a villain…'

She'd roped him into a charade for her mother's benefit and, now that he'd found out, he'd understandably come to find out what was going on. Much to her heartfelt relief, he'd decided to go with the flow when he could have demanded she tell Mary the truth. Underneath the tough exterior, there was a core of empathy that had moved him to see just how much it meant to her that she not hurt her mother if she could help it. It was the same empathy she had felt wrapped around her when she had cried against him—a weakness that wouldn't happen again.

'It just might be easier to get rid of you if you never actually put in a physical appearance,' she said truthfully.

Leo glanced down.

He had to try hard not to burst out laughing. She'd always had a way of making him less serious, less cold, less driven. And, more than that, making him feel ten feet tall, as she had when she'd sobbed in his arms, although he wasn't inclined to find that amusing. It had been disturbing, if anything.

Right now, however, her honest statement made his lips twitch. He also couldn't fail to appreciate the gaping difference between Cassie and the ex-girlfriend currently caught up in a stalking game. One wanted him to conveniently disappear, the other would have pinned him to the floor with super-glue so that he couldn't move.

'You have a way with words, Cass. You make it sound as though what you wanted was a puppet you could create a story around before consigning him to the scrap heap. I almost feel I should apologise for showing up and spoiling your fun.'

'You know what I mean.'

'I'll try to be underwhelming.'

'I don't think that's possible, Leo,' she said without thinking.

'I'll take that as a compliment,' he murmured. With his dark eyes pinned to her face, he felt a familiar stirring, an awakening of desire that was now off-limits. It was easy to recognise just why anything further between them would be a real complication. Her softness reached into him, stirring up all sorts of things. They'd both felt something when he'd held her, but had both shied away from it.

But his libido still had some catching up to do with his common sense. He thought of her as he'd seen her in bed, naked, willing and wanting him.

He thought, too, about seeing her out of bed—laughing with her head flung back, frowning at something he'd said, teasing him every time she thought he might be getting a little pompous. Those thoughts were a lot more unsettling, and he refocused on her, but this time there was genuine curiosity in his expression.

'Did your parents approve of the last one?' he asked and he could tell that she wasn't following him. 'The ex of yours who failed to make the grade in bed.'

'That's…'

'One hundred percent my business, bearing in mind we're engaged.'

'But we're not.'

'What if your mother asks me something I should know? Granted, I might be able to give her your favourite colour or your favourite annoying reality TV show when you were nineteen, but what if she decides to talk about the dearly departed boyfriend who couldn't cut it?'

Leo knew that he was brazenly fishing but he was unapologetic about that.

'You know my favourite colour?'

'It was hard not to when you wanted lilac trainers for your birthday present, and a matching lilac sports top, and white ankle socks with lilac trims. What was wrong with the guy?'

'Nothing was wrong with him, Leo. We just weren't on the same page.'

'Next you'll tell me that he was perfectly *nice*, which is the most damning word in the English vocabulary. We'll have to get our stories straight about this so-called relationship of ours and how it mysteriously developed off her radar. What have you told your mother, exactly?'

'As little as possible,' Cassie admitted.

He remembered those lilac trainers... He knew her favourite colour...

Something inside her warmed and melted just a little. Maybe he wasn't doing this just because he had a kind streak. Maybe he hadn't agreed in the hope that sex might be on offer as an added bonus. Could he be here because something deep inside him had actually missed her, something he could barely consciously acknowledge? Was it buried underneath all the lessons he'd learnt from what had happened between them?

Of course not...but her mind still played with the fantasy. She knew it was crazy to think like this but her thoughts grew wings and flew, and she let it happen. The memory of those strong arms made her head spin and her heart race with crazy wishful thinking.

At least for a short, indulgent few seconds then she reminded herself that he wasn't going to stick around, finding excuses to be in her company because he'd missed her. He'd made that perfectly clear. There wasn't a trunk of clothes stashed in the boot of his car *just in case*. She surfaced at the sound of his dark, velvety, amused voice.

'Yes, I suppose when it came to the back story, the minimum was always going to work best, bearing in mind you would have killed me off in record time. I guess you would have needed to leave some leg room to tire of my philandering ways as I flew back and forth around the globe, but not much more than that.'

'I would never have killed you off! I wouldn't have turned you into an actual villain!'

Leo's eyebrows shot up and he grinned. 'I'll put in an appearance tomorrow and then leave you to it. I have meetings to get back to by the middle of next week and, in actual fact, they do involve me crossing a few time zones, so the workaholic angle can genuinely stand up in court.'

His phone buzzed and he stood up and looked down at her.

'Clothes are here.'

'I'll get your room ready.' Cassie leapt to her feet as he was spinning round on his heels, heading to the door so that he could fetch whatever he had ordered.

'Don't lock me out,' he threw over his shoulder. '"Fiancé spending the night in the snow" would be on par with "fiancé spending the night in a hotel". Both options would be open to question if anyone found out, the only difference being one could see me in hospital with hypothermia.'

'I won't,' she flung back at him. 'And, if I'm not around when you get back in, I'll be in bed!'

She threw a towel on the bed in the guest room and hurried to her own room, locking the door behind her, and then leaning against it for a few seconds because she needed to catch her breath. This situation felt intimate and she wondered whether it was because she was going to be presenting him to her mother, that in double-quick time most people in the town would know about their phoney relationship or because just the notion of being engaged to this man made her heart flutter.

Or because there was still that thing, that dangerous

chemistry, simmering just below the surface, undermining the polite conversation.

Determined to not give it any more head space, Cassie made sure not to emerge when she heard the distant click of her apartment door opening and the sound of his footsteps when they eventually padded past her bedroom.

The snow had picked up pace overnight. Cassie headed to the kitchen at a little past eight the following morning to find Leo up and sitting at the kitchen counter in front of his laptop, with a mug of coffee and a plate with a half-eaten piece of toast on it next to him.

He was in a pair of black jogging bottoms and a black jumper, and he'd obviously had a shower, because his dark hair was still slightly damp. She had her own *en suite*, and had never been more relieved about that, because she couldn't imagine how embarrassing it would have been for them to bump into one another en route to the bathroom—even though they had been lovers recently. It made no sense, but then neither did the tumult of her emotions.

He looked up as soon as she entered.

'Hope you don't mind...'

'Making yourself at home?' Cassie tilted her head to one side and folded her arms. 'Not at all. I don't suppose you've made yourself sufficiently at home to do the ironing, have you?'

Leo burst out laughing, which brought warm colour to her cheeks, and she turned away to make some breakfast for herself. The same as his—toast and coffee.

'I try and avoid household chores like that.'

'Why is that?'

'When time is money, a guy can't afford to let household chores get much of a look-in. Doesn't make financial sense.'

'Of course.' Cassie sat next to him with a decent distance between them and was very conscious of him manoeuvring the bar stool so that he could look at her as she ate. In turn, she grudgingly angled her own stool so that she felt less like a goldfish in a bowl, inspected while she munched her toast. 'I'm guessing you rope girlfriends in to do it for you, while you lock yourself in your home office so that you can start work at six on a Sunday morning?'

'Is this in keeping with the "workaholic" storyline you had prepared as part of the reason for our unfortunate break-up?' His expression was shuttered. 'Just for the record, women and household chores don't make good bedfellows, as far as I'm concerned.'

He thought of Aimee, who had done her utmost to move in with him, and who had *conveniently* forgotten personal possessions at his penthouse in Manhattan, as though marking territory she wanted to permanently occupy. He had broken the news of his 'engagement' to her last night and, when she'd laughed and told him that she didn't believe him, he hadn't hesitated to tell her the story of the girl he had once loved and lost but who was now back in his life. Even to his own ears, it had sounded like a cheesy tale.

'I'm back in the little town in Canada I used to call home,' he had said gently, but with steel in his voice and with the right level of wistfulness which, oddly, was a little like how he'd felt. It had surprised him, because he wasn't the sentimental sort. 'And you know what they say about the way to a man's heart being through his stomach? Cassie Farraday, my fiancée, is the resident town chef, and she's done the impossible and captured my heart. Although, I might add, she's managed that through more than just her cooking.'

The conversation had lasted fifteen minutes. Finally, he'd had enough and had abruptly told her that it was time for her to let go. 'I can't keep telling you to step out of my life, Aimee,' he'd said flatly. 'You need to stop obsessing over me. I'm more than happy to pay for therapy for you but, in the meantime, any more texts, phone calls, emails or showing up at my place is going to be met a lot more robustly.

'Put it this way—I don't want to have to get a court order to keep you at bay. If you imagine damaging my reputation for the sake of payback would make me lose any sleep, then you're way off the mark. But consider what you might lose if word got out that I had to take out a restraining order against you.'

Leo surfaced with a frown from his internal meanderings and reverted to what he'd been talking about. 'If I want home-cooked food, I'm very happy to pay for someone to prepare it in their own home or kitchens and deliver it to me.'

'Mum's going to be very surprised at the guy you've become,' Cassie mused lightly.

Leo purred with silky confidence. 'Oh, she will be, when I lay on the charm.'

'Which you won't be doing.'

'The opposite of being low key isn't being an arrogant bore,' Leo returned smoothly. 'I don't think your mother will buy you falling for some guy who dominates the conversation by shouting everyone else down.'

Cassie felt that familiar, warm tug of shared humour, something that had always been there between them.

'You're impossible, Leo. Just, please try and be as invisible as you can and leave all the talking to me, or at least most of it. I'll signal when you can chip in. We don't want to... What we don't want is...'

'Don't worry. We'll find the right balance and maintain the charade until it quietly fizzles out. Now, what time are we going? The snow's not abating.'

'Mum's invited me over for lunch but we can get there earlier. Then we can leave as soon as we've eaten. She'll understand; you remember how much the weather here in winter dictates what people do.'

'In which case, if you could let me have your Wi-Fi password, I can get some work done. Time waits for no man.'

'It actually waits for quite a few of them who don't live life in the fast lane,' Cassie retorted, standing up to fetch the card with her Internet details that she kept on her fridge door. 'You can use my office—it's at the end of the hall—and then maybe we could leave by eleven?'

Leo stood up, reached out and circled her arm with his fingers, pulling her ever so slightly towards him,

'And are those the types you like?' he drawled in a low, husky voice.

Cassie blinked. Her brain was suddenly addled at the red-hot touch of his fingers on her, burning through her top and lighting her up from the inside out.

'The types I like...?'

'The ones who don't live life in the fast lane.'

'Maybe.'

'Liar.' Leo's voice was soft and amused, and his eyes burnt into her, dark, intense and penetrating through the mask she was wearing so that she felt suddenly exposed with nowhere to hide her feelings.

'What do you mean by that?'

'You're way too outspoken to settle for Mr Nice Guy. Learn from the last one you dispatched—you'd eat him alive. Even as a girl you knew how to keep me on my toes, and I have never been *nice*.'

'You enjoyed me keeping you on your toes, Leo,' she riposted without skipping a beat. 'If your advice is to steer clear from nice guys like my ex, does that mean you're volunteering for the role of the bad boy in my life, Leo?'

In a rush, Leo was catapulted back through time to when marrying this woman was all he'd been able to think about—having her to himself and doing all the stuff he'd never thought he'd have time for, such as having kids and settling down...becoming *house-trained*.

Those plans had crashed and burned, and lessons had been learnt. So why was he standing here now, *wondering*? He shifted, raked his fingers through his hair and reminded himself that this charade was a convenient ploy to get rid of his ex once and for all. He wasn't going to drift back into any situation that would make him vulnerable. He was well beyond any weakness like that, even though there were times when the past felt perilously hypnotic and the present woefully empty.

'I don't do the happy-ever-after, story-book romance,' he said, abruptly releasing her arm and turning away. 'Let's park that particular notion and I'll see you in a few hours when we're ready to leave.'

CHAPTER NINE

CASSIE HAD NEVER seen her mother so lively, at least not since her dad had died and even before then—weeks, months and years before then—Mary Farraday had gradually withdrawn into herself, constantly living on the edge with a disease that seemed to come and go at will.

Right now she was laughing at something Leo had said. Her head was flung back; there was colour in her cheeks and a sparkle in her green eyes. She was tall and willowy, as blonde as her daughter was dark, with sleepy green eyes that gave her a lazy, mesmerising appeal. Nevertheless, she was a muted copy of the woman she had once been, hollowed out and with lines of stress ageing her.

'Mum...' Cassie interrupted the flow of conversation. 'I think we should be going now. Leo has...er...a lot of work to get through—business deals; high-level, important stuff. He's already taken way too much time out recently, haven't you, Leo?'

They'd had lunch in the dining room and were now in the sitting room, one of the more frequented rooms in the house, and therefore still reasonably comfortable and well maintained. Most of the other rooms in the massive, rambling house had quietly been closed off as money problems had become more acute. A lot of the valuable paintings and artifacts had been auctioned, so there was an air of abandonment everywhere.

When they had arrived several hours earlier, Cassie had looked around her and seen it through Leo's eyes. It was a once-grand manor now reduced to shabbiness. She could only imagine how he must have inwardly gloated at the comparison between himself, the boy from the wrong side of the tracks, and her, the girl who had once had it all in a small community where her father had had his finger in a couple of very large pies.

Oh, well; in fairness, she had seen nothing in his expression to validate that train of thought. He had certainly taken everything in his stride the minute he'd walked through the front door and he hadn't really stopped. If this was his idea of not laying it on thick, then she couldn't begin to imagine what it would have been like if he had.

She stood up and began clearing away the coffee tray that Leo had carried in earlier after they'd finished eating.

'Leo, dear...remember all that work you mentioned that you had to do?'

She looked at Leo as he glanced across to where she was perched with raised eyebrows and a wry grin.

'It's been lovely catching up with you, Mary.' On cue, he stood up, even though Mary was already protesting, urging them both to stay a bit longer; reminding them that her visitors were few and far between, although now she felt so much stronger with all their money worries behind them.

There were tears in her eyes when she told them how happy she was that Cassie had found love, how regretful she'd felt over the years at the love affair she and Clive had ruined.

'We were selfish,' she admitted sadly. 'I was scared, so scared, so desperate not to lose Cassie when it felt like I was losing so much else at the time—all my security, my health, the very foundation of my life. We never knew just how serious you both were about one another. It was only after time, a long time, when Cassie never really seemed to recover, that I could see how hurt she'd been.'

She laughed then, lightening the atmosphere, while Cassie silently begged for the ground to swallow her up. 'But I'll see you before you disappear, won't I, Leo? Your engagement took me by surprise but, now that I've got my head round it, I want to sit you both down and discuss some of the nitty-gritty.'

'Oh, time enough for that, Mum!' Cassie waved aside that suggestion, that just wasn't going to happen. Come hell or high water, she was determined to avoid crossing that bridge for as long as possible so that the inevitable demise of their so-called relationship wouldn't need much by way of unravelling of arrangements. Or too much unravelling of hope on her mother's side, for that matter. She and Leo would have to agree on a timeline, just as they had done on Mustique for their devastating, short-lived affair.

'We'll head off now, but you stay put. Leo and I will take care of the kitchen, and we'll pop in before we leave. If we don't get going now, the snow…well…look at it out there. It's not stopping any time soon.'

'We once had help,' Mary said sadly. 'Those times are long gone.' She looked at Leo with shining sincerity. 'But these times now are wonderful.' She smiled. 'Looking forward to something…you have no idea what it means for me, because it feels as though I haven't had anything to look forward to for a very long time.'

'Okay!' Cassie said hurriedly.

She was lightly perspiring with prickly guilt and tension by the time she and Leo were in the kitchen, with her mum safely ensconced upstairs in the little sitting room that adjoined the master suite. Darkness was already falling outside, and a glance at the window told her that, if they didn't leave soon, they wouldn't be going anywhere, which would leave Leo in a predicament.

'Dear?' It was the first thing he said when the kitchen door shut and they were looking at a kitchen in need of tidying. 'Since when does a twenty-something use the term *dear* when referring to the love of her life, the man who's swept her off her feet, the old flame she'd never forgotten, whose ring she's now going to be wearing on her finger? Have we time-travelled back fifty years?'

'This is just awful,' Cassie said, sweeping stuff off the table without looking at him and ignoring what he'd just said. When she did finally stand still and caught his eye, it was to find him staring at her with an inscrutable expression. 'I had no idea Mum would throw herself into this whole engagement thing with such…such…*gusto.*'

'How did you think it would play out, Cass?'

'Not like this! Why did you have to be so *convincing*?' she said accusingly. 'We both agreed that you would keep the charm on the down-low, but it felt like the second you walked through the door your mission was to bowl her over!'

Leo flushed darkly and scowled.

'It doesn't come as second nature to be a bore.'

But Leo could see where she was going with this; she could see she was upset and was temporarily at a loss to explain how moved he had been to see a woman who, eight years on, was a shadow of her former self. He had judged Cassie years ago, and had been quick to rush to the assumption that the class differences between them had been the root of the problem. Why else would she have gone from excitement at the life ahead of them both to sudden retreat? A change of heart like that didn't spring from nowhere.

He had blamed them for manoeuvring Cassie because he came from the wrong side of the tracks, just as he had blamed Cassie for allowing herself to be so massively influenced by them. He had speculated, drawn conclusions and had felt powerless, and had subconsciously allied that powerlessness with the same helplessness he had felt knowing that his mother had walked out on the family unit—had chosen to abandon *him*. His heart had sealed over and he had cut Cassie loose, along with everything associated with that painful slice of his past.

He had had no idea of the circumstances at the time. Now he had met Mary Farraday, and the one-dimensional picture of her he had constructed in his head had shifted into something more nuanced, because he was finally in full possession of all the facts. He understood the fear she must have felt in the face of a creeping disease that could sink its teeth into her without warning, or else meander along for years, only revealing itself now and again. He saw how she might want to cling to her only daughter, because the alternative had been losing her at a time when life must have felt very uncertain and frightening.

He understood how Clive Farraday must have felt: like a rabbit suddenly caught in the headlights, distraught and out of his depth, so eaten up with unhappiness and confusion that he had allowed everything he had worked for to slip away. Hadn't his own father bolted from real life, unable to cope, bereft and helpless, when his wife had abandoned him? And desertion had surely been a lot more manageable than the prospect of slowly losing the person you loved to an illness that would only get worse over time?

And he understood how Cassie had been put in the position of having no choice in the matter, because sometimes difficult decisions had to be made, and she had made an incredibly difficult decision.

Still... He knew that he should have been more conscious of the role he had to play this evening, the role of a fiancé with just a hint of unreliability. He knew that they *both* had to play roles so that the ending of their fictitious relationship didn't come as a complete shock to Mary. There was no alternative because, whatever were his thoughts on the past and the way he now viewed it differently, he couldn't change it, and neither could he change the steel that had formed inside him when he and Cassie had walked away from one another.

'That's not the point, Leo,' Cassie snapped, driving him out of his introspection. 'We could have established the groundwork for us breaking up at a later date...which reminds me that we need to set a timeline for this charade of ours.'

'I suppose that makes sense. What do you have in mind?'

'I know you're not accustomed to doing anything domestic, but you're going to have to lend a hand here, because if you look outside the snow's not getting any lighter, and you might need to get to the airport directly from here. We can talk as we go, but we just need to clear this kitchen quickly. I don't want Mum over-exerting herself in the morning when she comes down.'

Leo sauntered over to the window and stared out at a panorama of white snow falling gently but steadily and settling on everything.

'Leaving for the airport from here is out of the question.' He turned to her. 'I can't leave without my laptop and, by the time we get back to your house, this snow is going to be even deeper and more impassable. We both know what it gets like here in the depths of winter.'

'You mean you're going to be around for another night?' Cassie cried.

'Why is that such a big deal?'

'Because...'

'It's also a little worse than you think, Cass. Come and stand here and have a look at what's happening outside.'

He waited until she was standing next to him. From here, there was an unimpeded view of white pouring down on open space, collecting on the trees and the tangled lawns at the back, with the looming dark mountains behind making it feel as though they were caught in a snow globe.

He could see her reflection in the window. She was tall and toned, her long, dark hair caught in a pony tail so that it was impossible to miss her fine bone-structure, the same as her mother's.

'We're going to have to spend the night here,' he said flatly, spinning round on his heels although, instead of tidying, he reached for the wine to pour himself another glass.

'What?'

'You don't live far away, but this snow's collecting, and I have no intention of getting stuck out in it because you're scared to share space with me.'

'I'm not scared to share space with you.'

'Sure about that? What do you think is going to happen if we're here together for a night? And, by the way, we're going to be sharing a room, because I don't suppose your mother is going to buy us sleeping separately because we've suddenly become shy. Not when she knows that we've been seeing one another for...what did you say?...a few months. And definitely not when we've just returned from a raunchy week away.'

'I never said to her that the week was raunchy!'

'I looked at your mother looking at us,' Leo said with silky-smooth conviction. 'And I can tell you that, whilst she might not be in robust health, she's not away with the fairies. She knows that we had fun together.'

'That's because you kept *looking at me*.'

'So you noticed, did you? I did wonder…'

Cassie glared at him, at the small, satisfied smile tugging the corners of his mouth.

A tense silence stretched between them for a few seconds. Cassie could feel the colour rush into her cheeks. Yes, she'd noticed those sidelong glances in her direction—lazy, assessing and *sexy*. Just as she'd noticed the way he'd brushed against her every so often, without actually blatantly resting his hand on hers, which would have been a lot better for her blood pressure.

'Did you enjoy that—me looking at you?'

'What are you playing at, Leo?'

'Am I playing? I thought I was just trying to establish why you're so skittish at the prospect of spending another night with me.'

He sipped his wine and stared at her over the rim of the glass, looking cool, collected and curious.

'I'm going to finish tidying the kitchen.' Cassie huffed before spinning round and whipping stuff off the table, conscious that she was as tense as a bow string. When she eventually looked at him, after several minutes of nerve-racking silence, his eyes were still on her and he was grinning.

'I can show you to your room, if you have no intention of helping out here,' she said with lofty indignation. 'I know you're allergic to all things domestic.'

His grin widened. '*Our* room,' he corrected. 'And don't

worry; I'm not so allergic to all things domestic that I can't pull my weight when need be...'

They tidied the kitchen in record time. When Cassie next peered into the darkness outside, it was impossible not to agree with Leo that trekking back to her apartment was out of the question, never mind him getting a taxi to the airport. They would have to share a room. He had been teasing her earlier, but underneath that ran a very real thread of curiosity about her behaviour around him. How on earth was she going to cope having him at such close quarters, when she was in love with him; when all she wanted to do was touch him?

'Okay.' She made a show of stifling a yawn. 'I'm going to head up; I need an early night. You might as well see where we'll be sleeping and then, if you're not tired, feel free to go back down and work.'

'Thanks for your permission to make myself scarce, but I'm afraid working is going to be impossible without my laptop.'

'Then watch telly,' Cassie said irritably, stalking off towards the door and out into the cavernous hallway that felt cold after the warmth in the kitchen. 'You might catch a good cooking programme so you can improve your skills.'

'I've never been much of a fan of television,' Leo informed her thoughtfully, exiting the kitchen behind her and catching up with her fast stride so that they were walking alongside one another. 'Usually feels like a waste of time when I could be doing something better.'

Cassie stopped dead in her tracks and looked up at him, arms folded. 'In that case, you could always while away your time painting your nails or doing your hair,' she snapped.

They stared at one another in the semi-darkness of the hall, the chill gathering around them, and just like that, without any warning—or she surely would have taken a few evasive tactics—he reached out and very softly trailed his finger along her cheek. All at once, Cassie heard the soft, trembling intake of her own breath and felt the heavy thud of the blood in her veins and the weight of her legs pinning her to the spot like lead columns.

She wanted to ask him what the hell he thought he was doing. Instead, her mouth parted, her eyelids fluttered and all she could think was how much she had missed this—the physical connection that had been left behind in his villa on Mustique.

Her breasts felt heavy and there was a tingling in her nipples that longed for the heat of his mouth clamped on them. Between her legs, the tell-tale warm pooling of liquid reminded her of a body that still craved his. Her nails dug into the soft flesh of her arms. She felt drugged with longing.

'I still want you, Cassie,' Leo murmured softly. He leant into her so that she could feel his breath tickle her ear when he spoke, and smell his aftershave.

'Please, don't,' she whispered back.

'Don't what—don't want you? Or don't tell you that I want you?' He cupped her cheek with his hand, gently urging her to look at him, which she did.

'I can't do either of those things, Cass, but don't worry; I won't come near you. I know you want me—I can feel it. A week wasn't long enough for either of us but, if you want to turn your back on what's going on between us, then I'll let you. You've laid down your ground rules and you have my word I won't break them. Unless you want me to…'

He pulled back, dropped his hand and Cassie blinked her way back to reality, which felt very cold, now that he was no longer touching her.

'It's cold out here.' He stepped back but his eyes were still pinned to her face.

'It costs a fortune to heat the house. We've become good at being careful. We—we should head up.' Her voice was jerky.

'Where's the bedroom?'

'On the floor above, left at the staircase. Leo…'

'Keep a light on and the door ajar. You go up and I'll follow in a couple of hours or so.'

Cassie remained frozen to the spot as he turned away to head back to the kitchen, then she sprinted up to the bedroom they would be sharing, her mind buzzing with a confusing tangle of thoughts and emotions.

She wondered how she had ever thought that someone who knew her so well, someone as intuitive as Leo, could ever miss the signals she'd been giving off. Not signals that she had feelings for him—deep, true feelings that went against everything her head was telling her—but signals that she was still attracted to him, still wanted him.

How could she have imagined that he would obediently fall in line with her request that sex remain off the table?

But he wouldn't lay a finger on her. Cassie knew that because she knew him as well as he knew her. He would wait to see if she would come to him, and that was an even more devastating thought, because it gave her the absolute choice to go one way or the other without him trying to persuade her. She'd made so many promises to herself. How could she jeopardise her heart with her eyes wide open?

She had clothes in the bedroom. She always kept clothes there because she spent so much time between the family house and her apartment, especially after her father had died and there had been so much stuff to do, so much to sort out. She had a lengthy shower, changed into warm pyjamas, because the bedroom was only slightly less cold than the hall and then, as she'd said, she kept the door very slightly ajar with the bedside light on to guide him to the room.

There was no chance of her falling asleep this early so she was still wide awake when Leo pushed open the door and stepped inside. His silhouette, looming in the doorframe, sent a shiver of sexual awareness rippling through her. She watched in absolute stillness as he quietly shut the door behind him and walked in, stripping off the jumper as he did so, and throwing it over the back of the chair by the old-fashioned dressing table.

He was a sight for sore eyes. Outside the steady fall of snow could just be glimpsed through the gap in the curtains, and inside the dull glow from the bedside lamp threw his remarkable body into alluring shadows. His broad shoulders tapered to a narrow waist. He was standing in full view of her avid gaze, having strategically paused by the dressing table to slowly undo the top button of his trousers.

She could hardly draw breath as his fingers lingered on the button, then down came the zip, and his trousers followed the jumper over the back of the chair, collected in one fluid movement that showed every ripple of sinew and muscle...

He had his mobile in one hand, and for a few seconds he looked at it, beautiful and semi-naked with just his boxers on. Then he switched it off and, as the blue light faded, he got rid of the boxers and Cassie almost choked at the sight of him completely naked. It was crazy, as she'd seen this man in the buff before and more than that—much, much more than that. It was crazy that she'd run her hand across the taut leanness of his chest, felt the compacted muscles of his thighs, taken him in her mouth and tasted the masculine essence of him. Right now, she was as turned on as though none of that had ever happened.

He strolled towards the bed, hand resting loosely on his impressive member, and then slid under the covers to join her. The mattress depressed. She was lying on her side, facing him, and now she couldn't find a way to adjust her position without calling attention to herself.

He was half-propped up on the pillow, one hand behind his head, staring off into the dark room.

'I'm guessing you're still awake.'

'No, I'm not.'

Leo grinned and then shifted so that they were facing one another.

'Did you enjoy the view?'

'I don't know what you're talking about,' Cassie lied breathlessly.

The silence hung between them. Staring straight into his eyes, Cassie blinked. Her hand trembled, reaching out to touch the naked body so close to her.

Why, why, why...?

Just as quickly, she pulled her hand away, but her body was on fire, burning up under the thick pyjamas that covered her from head to toe.

'You want to touch me,' Leo said softly, keeping his hands to himself.

'You should be wearing clothes.'

'Tell me you're not going to blame my lack of clothes for your wandering hands. I didn't come here with some pyjamas conveniently stashed in a bag. In fact, as you know very well, I don't even own a pair.'

'Leo, I don't want to fall back into bed with you. And don't forget, you said the same thing to me.'

'I did, and I certainly meant it at the time, because I

didn't want to add any more complications to an already complicated situation not of my choosing.'

'And now?' Cassie whispered.

'And now? Things don't seem quite so straightforward.'

Her heart leapt just a little. What did that mean? Things were always straightforward when emotions weren't involved. She could happily have had sex with him for a week when she'd told herself that she was in charge, that she was just doing what he was doing, getting him out of her system.

But then emotions had crept in and everything had changed. Questions had been asked, hopes nurtured and despair lay just round the corner because the heart was fragile and defenceless in the face of love. Was he beginning to have feelings for her? Was that why things weren't so straightforward for him any longer? She dared to hope but she wasn't going to probe any further because she knew that the shutters would slam down.

Maybe he needed to reach the same place as her but would take longer, because he was so proud and because he'd been hurt. Maybe, after all, he *had* agreed to this engagement because some subconscious stirrings of love had prompted him to. Maybe all he needed was a little nudge and he would get there; he would see that what they had was too good to let go. He would see what she saw.

'I still really fancy you,' she admitted huskily. 'I thought that a week would be enough, but maybe it's not.'

'And here we are. Me naked and you fully clothed in flannel.'

'It's cold in this house.'

'I'm pretty hot right now.'

Cassie reached out again and this time she leant into what her body yearned for. She wanted to silence that sprig of hope, but she couldn't, so she just abandoned herself to it.

She reached down to feel his arousal, hard and pulsing, and when he smiled as her eyes widened, hot colour scorched her cheeks. She couldn't wait to get rid of the thick pyjamas. He reached for the top and she brushed aside his hand to kneel and yank it off, then she slipped off the side of the bed and got rid of the rest of her clothes.

They made love. Slowly at first, touching as if finding one another for the first time, except there was a familiarity there that came from the time they had spent together at his villa. She knew what turned him on and vice versa. She knew how to stroke and where to touch and he knew how to make her body sing.

She came with his mouth pressed between her legs, his tongue exploring her and his hands touching her just the way she loved being touched. And then, when her orgasm had faded to lazy, warm contentment, he slowly stirred her up all over again and then took her with long, deep thrusts that had her bucking against him and stifling her cries with her hand.

Afterwards, she curled into him and wrapped her arms around his body so their bodies fused as one.

Lying like this, Leo could feel the beating of her heart and her soft breath on his neck.

He'd never liked the after-sex routine where, without fail, women wanted to cuddle. He'd never done cuddling. Post-coital activity, for him, had always involved a shower and then usually work. Anything to get out of bed and away from an intimacy that he had no time for. He'd long accepted that this was part and parcel of his iron-clad defences against encouraging the sort of relationship he would never entertain.

But, since Cassie had come back into his life, there had

been a lot of cuddles. There had been many hugs and the sort of post-sex, sleepy contentment he had never experienced before: talking with voices low; laughing; touching again; drifting into sleep; tenderness...

'Leo...'

'Mmm...?' His mind wandered and he lazily softened to the slow caress of her voice.

'This is good, isn't it?'

'I can definitely tell you that my body hasn't felt this good since...the last time we made love.'

'It's more than that, though, isn't it?' she asked huskily. 'Leo, I know we've put limits on this, but we don't have to, do we?'

'What do you mean?'

'I mean...we still connect. When I'm with you, the years fall away. Maybe that's why I mentioned the whole engagement thing to Mum. Maybe, deep down, something about us felt right. Maybe not *engagement* right, but we're here now, and this connection... We could explore it, Leo. We could see where it leads us. We're older now, and the past is the past, but this is a great present, isn't it—this thing we've got now?'

'What are you saying, Cass? You want to explore what we have?'

'Yes!' She propped herself up on one elbow and looked at him, stroking his hair and then gently kissing the side of his mouth. 'Maybe it was the same for you and you didn't realise it. Maybe that's why you agreed to this— because without even realising it you wanted to explore what we started eight years ago and is still waiting to be finished. To reach the place it should be—us together. I loved you then, Leo, and I love you now—and I'm not afraid to admit it.'

CHAPTER TEN

'I NEED TO get some air.'

Cassie froze at the tone of his voice. At the coolness, the icy detachment. The sound of shutters slamming, doors closing and a future that had shimmered tantalisingly close disappearing for ever.

'Get some air? But, Leo, it's late and it's snowing…'

But she was already retreating in the face of his rejection. She'd been carried away by her own love, by hope and by idiotic, misguided optimism and she'd been wrong in her assumption that he surely must be on the same page as her. How could the tenderness she'd felt not mean more to him than just sex?

But Leo was already shifting off the mattress, barely able to hold her gaze.

'I'll take my chances.'

'In my car? The one you said you'd be surprised if it made it here in one piece? The same car you swore was held together with masking tape and glue?'

'Cassie…'

'No, don't say it, Leo,' Cassie whispered.

He would rather get buried in falling snow than spend a minute more with her after what she'd confessed.

She remembered the way he had walked away from her eight years ago. Yes, she had broken things off with him, but now she wondered whether it had been easier for him to move on than she could ever have imagined. He'd told her about his mother—not a lot, but enough. Enough for her to have heard the pain in his voice and to understand the depths of his feelings of betrayal and abandonment by the one person whose love should have been unconditional.

If events hadn't worked out they way they had, would he really have stayed with her, married her and had a family with her? Or was he just too damaged inside by feelings of abandonment ever to trust that she could love him with all her heart, unconditionally, the way he should have been loved by his mother? Had the threat of being left again cast such a great shadow that he would just never be able fully to commit?

Cassie wondered now whether the possibility of real closeness and commitment, which required trust and vulnerability, would always just be something beyond his grasp.

Suddenly the torment of the past felt more straightforward because she knew so much more about him now. The space he had left behind on the bed was already icy cold and her body was rigid with misery and tension. As he began dressing quickly and efficiently, pride and defensiveness started slamming into place inside her, just as his own shutters had come down.

'This was never what it was supposed to be about,' he ground out.

'I know.'

'We did what we did and we both knew the rules of the game,' he continued grimly.

He'd moved to stand in front of her, towering and forbidding, arms folded, his face inscrutable.

'Sometimes it's a little hard sticking to the rules,'

Cassie said without defiance, quietly proud that she had been brave enough to be honest.

'Not for me.'

'No. I see that now.'

'What we had was good, Cassie.' He raked his fingers through his hair and stared down at her. She had pulled the covers up tightly but had sat up and was pressed back against the pillows.

'Where will you go to get your air? It's dangerous out there.'

'It's dangerous in here.'

'I said what I wanted to say. You don't have to be scared that I'm going to get clingy on you. I just thought that, like me, something in you wanted this phoney engagement…some unconscious pull you couldn't acknowledge.'

For a few seconds, seconds that felt like minutes, hours and decades, silence stretched as their eyes collided in the darkness, adding drama and danger to the atmosphere.

Leo reached for his phone. He felt as though he needed to support himself, lean against the wall, because he was suddenly overcome by a weird falling sensation.

He had no choice. Had he asked for any kind of emotional connection between them? He'd agreed to this crazy arrangement because he'd wanted to get rid of a troublesome ex. There was nothing to be read between the lines. He had made it clear from the start that what they had would just be a fitting conclusion to something that had started eight years ago but from which he had never achieved closure. And then, when this charade had started, he'd told her that it was just a charade.

Yes, uneasily, he had realised that there might be something more beneath the surface but he knew that, whatever that something might be, he was never going to let it escape and do all sorts of damage to his peace of mind.

He'd built his life on self-control and he wasn't going to let it slip through his fingers now like he had eight years ago. He would never be so weak again that he would allow his emotions to rule his life.

But, still, it felt as though he was staring down into an abyss as he handed his phone to her, having scrolled to just the right conversational thread between Aimee and him. She took the phone and he watched as she read the thread: his admission to his ex that he was engaged; the clarity with which he'd explained that she had to back away because he was unavailable. That, if she didn't believe him, just a couple of questions would sort that out because he was happily and openly engaged to be married to the girl he'd once known. Why would he lie?

Cassie handed the phone back to him and didn't say anything for such a long time that he could feel the incipient nausea inside begin to ripple through every bit of him.

He knew that he couldn't have severed things more completely between them if he'd tried. He fought against an untethered, falling sensation.

'So you see, Cass,' Leo eventually said grittily, 'There were no sentimental reasons for me agreeing to go along with your engagement charade.'

'No. I see that.'

'I was having problems with my ex-girlfriend.'

'Yes.'

'She wouldn't let go and I realised that getting on board with your plan, and making sure she knew about it, would probably be my best chance of getting Aimee to realise that I was never going to agree to giving what we had another chance.'

'I understand that now, yes.'

'Cassie...'

'Just go, Leo. The car keys are on the dressing table. You can take the car and leave it in town and spend the night... Actually, I don't care where you spend the night. You can park up at the side of the road and spend it in the back seat of my car if you want. But leave my car in the car park by the police station and I'll make sure I collect it when I next go into town. It'll be perfectly safe there.'

'Cass...'

'There's nothing left to talk about, Leo. I don't want to see you again, ever. Tomorrow morning, I'll tell Mum everything. I'll tell her just how extensive the financial problems were and what I did to solve them. I'll take my chances that she'll understand that, what I did, I did for myself more than because it was a way of getting Dad's debts sorted. I'll take my chances that she understands and...forgives me.'

'Cassie...'

'Just go.'

'We can talk about this more, if you want. Whatever you might think of me, it's worth bearing in mind that—'

'Go!'

Cassie looked at him with angry hostility as every shred of hope was washed away and her foolish love was exposed for what it was: a mistake; an idiotic, naïve, pathetic mistake.

'And take all your things,' she continued in the same low, hostile voice. 'If you have any reason to contact me, then please go through my lawyer.'

'Damn it, Cassie...'

She didn't answer. What was the point of a dialogue that wouldn't go anywhere? She stared at him with stony indifference, which couldn't have been further from what she felt, from the painful tumult of emotions tearing through her. Tears were so close that her eyes stung.

She watched in silence as Leo redressed in the very clothes he had removed only a short while before. His coat was in the hall. He went to the dressing table and hesitated before picking up her car keys and distractedly tossing them up and down, catching them while he looked at her as though tempted to carry on talking.

Eventually he shrugged and walked to the door. 'Where do you want me to leave the keys?'

'You can lock them in the car. I have spares.'

'This is a crazy way to end—'

'Not to me.'

'I never meant to hurt you, Cass.'

Cassie thought that those must be the most hurtful words in the English vocabulary, always spoken when the worst pain had been inflicted and solving nothing at all. Those were words spoken by someone who wanted to clear their conscience before walking away from a messy situation they no longer wanted to be involved in.

'Goodbye, Leo.'

She only sagged when the door had been quietly closed behind him. When she walked to the window and looked outside, it was to find that the snow had stopped falling, as though fate had taken it upon herself to make sure he made as safe a getaway as possible.

She wasn't going to collapse. She wasn't going to give him the satisfaction of falling apart, even though now that he was gone he wouldn't know whether she'd fallen apart or not.

For the moment, she was going to think about what she would say to her mother without breaking her heart.

***

The drive into town was slow and torturous, although thankfully the snow had stopped and the wipers didn't have to be set at full speed. The car might be a four-wheel drive, as most were in this part of the world, but he hadn't been kidding when he'd told Cassie that it was all just tin and metal stuck together with glue and running on a wing and a prayer.

He thought of her driving it in conditions like these and felt a little sick. He could buy her a new car. They might have parted company but that didn't mean that he liked the thought of her risking her life while she was getting from A to B.

He'd done the right thing. He'd broken off a relationship that had no place in his life. There was no point learning lessons if he then went and ignored every single one. That thought lasted about as long as it took him finally to make it to the car park by the police station which was in the centre of the small town, the nucleus from which everything else radiated.

He parked carefully. His computer was still at her house and he didn't care; that could be sorted.

He could barely spare a thought for work, anyway. His head was stuffed full with memories of Cassie, from the second he had seen her again to the second he had walked away from her for good. Memories of everything that lay in between, of her laughter and joy and the way she had made him feel.

Making his way to the hotel, which was buzzing, Leo felt the steady onset of emotions that he had stored on ice, always expecting that they could never, ever be thawed out. He hadn't banked on Cassie coming along and bewitching him all over again. He hadn't figured how easy it would be to remember every single thing about her he'd sworn he'd forgotten over time. How stupidly easy it would be to remember just the way she was. Remember the way he'd loved her and...now...the way he still did.

He'd turned his back on her and walked away and he couldn't see how he'd ever be able to rebuild all the bridges he'd burnt behind him with the reckless disregard of someone too blind and stupid to deserve a second chance.

He thought about his mother and all the unanswered questions that had settled in his subconscious, ruling the way he'd behaved towards Cassie and laying out a pattern of behaviour he could see hadn't freed him but had done the opposite: it had paralysed him.

He changed his mind about the hotel and instead headed straight to the airport. On the way there, from the back of the car that had collected him, he pulled out his mobile and hesitated, but only for a few seconds.

Right now, there was only one person he felt a driving need to talk to.

'*Papa, puedo hablar contigo...?*'

Cassie looked at her mother over the casserole which, so far, she had yet to touch. It was a little past one in the afternoon and right now she felt that she could do with a glass of wine instead of the glass of water next to her.

The conversation about Leo and the vanishing engagement had yet to be had. She had spent three days mulling over what to say. She'd covered his disappearance with, 'He's had to rush off to work... Remember I told you what a workaholic he is?' But she was just buying time and she didn't have much of that left at her disposal.

If only her head would give her some peace, but on and on it churned, replaying the ending of their relationship in grinding, remorseless detail. She was hollowed out by the fact that he had agreed to the engagement because it had suited him. He'd wanted to dispose of a nuisance ex and an engagement to her had been a handy excuse. She was mortified and crushed at the way she had foolishly thought that he had succumbed to feelings he hadn't yet consciously acknowledged.

He'd never had the sort of feelings for her that she'd had for him. Maybe eight years ago he'd been infatuated with her but had it been love? No. It hadn't been love then and it hadn't been love when they'd met again. He couldn't love anyone. Maybe back then he'd tried, but love and all the complications involved was something that was beyond him and the finality of that was like a knife driven into her again and again.

There was just no space inside her to come out with the truth to her Mum.

'Why are you looking so glum?'

Cassie blinked and half-opened her mouth.

'I suppose you're missing Leo. You'll have to get accustomed to those times when he's not around, Cass. As you've said, he's a busy man. Your dad did his best but I spent many an evening in because he had to cancel at the last minute when some work thing came up. Once you start a family, trust me, your life will be so busy you won't have time to sit and brood about him not being with you.'

'Mum, if and when I ever do have kids, I would never accept my husband *not* being present for them!'

'So does that mean that you're thinking of having children? I guess time waits for no one.'

'I never said that.' Cassie looked at her mother whose cheeks were pink and whose eyes were bright. She'd been moving better and walking faster, looking forward instead of back.

Cassie felt queasy.

'There's something, actually...something I feel I need to tell you, Mum.'

Her tummy lurched. She had contemplated holding off indefinitely on the explanation. She had debated whether to just let the whole engagement thing disappear in a slow series of excuses for Leo's continued non-appearance that would culminate in the sad demise of their relationship. But she just couldn't. She couldn't bring herself to have anything more to do with Leo, even when it came to having his name pass her lips. To talk about him would be to torture herself every single time, and she couldn't cope with that—not yet, anyway. Maybe a few hints at what was to come might work; a process of erosion...

She was about to speak when the ring of the doorbell came as a shocking intrusion and it took a couple of seconds for her to register that there was someone outside.

'Are you expecting anyone, Mum?'

'Who would be out calling in this weather, uninvited?'

'It's nearly Christmas.' Cassie began rising to her feet. 'You know what it's like here; someone always wants to drop something off.' She smiled weakly, backing out of the sitting room towards the front door, half-relieved that she'd been temporarily spared, half-annoyed because she was just delaying the inevitable and, now that she had settled on a way forward, she just wanted to get on with it.

It had stopped snowing. The skies were clear and blue and it was freezing. She pulled open the front door without checking to find out who it was, and then stood back and blinked in utter shock at the sight of Leo standing in the doorway.

Temporarily deprived of speech, Cassie could only stare at him with her mouth open, the silence stretching into incredulous infinity, then sanity returned and she rushed into furious speech.

'What are you doing here? What the hell do you think you're doing coming back here when I *told* you that I *never* wanted to see you again?'

She made to slam the door, only to find the flat of his hand on it, preventing her from moving it so much as an inch.

'I find there's more talking to do, Cass.'

'Too bad.'

'Let me in…please.'

'No; absolutely not.'

In a minute, her mother would come out and Cassie didn't even want to think about that.

'Leo, if you had any respect for me at all, you'd leave. I'm just about to explain everything to Mum. Please just go away. I don't know why you've come—whether you've forgotten something—and I don't care. I just want you to go.'

She glanced over her shoulder, a quick, surreptitious glance before returning strained, combative eyes to Leo.

'I'd like your mother to hear what I have to say as well, Cassie,' he told her quietly.

'I don't need you to share this with me. I can tell her everything on my own. It's all my fault anyway. I should never have got in touch with you.'

'Don't say that.'

'Why? Because you got the closure you wanted?'

'I don't want to spend the rest of the afternoon out here having a conversation with you when it's freezing cold.' He paused. 'You know if I just very, very gently push this door you wouldn't be able to stop me from coming in, but I don't want to do that. I don't want to force an entry here. I want you to invite me in because I've never wanted to talk to anyone more than I want to talk to you now.'

Cassie was overcome with a wave of weariness. Weary from her misery, from the stress of having to disillusion her mother; weary from Leo standing here for reasons she couldn't fathom but destroying her fragile composure just with his presence.

She stood back, defeated, as he brushed past her.

Leo paused and looked at her in silence. She'd stuck out her chin and postured but he could see that she was broken, and he had done that.

His stomach clenched and pain coursed through him. He'd turned away from her in the very moment when she had been most open, trusting and vulnerable. She'd confessed feelings that had thrown him into a tailspin and he had reacted predictably.

He would have come sooner but, after his conversation with his father, he had taken a few days to digest what he had been told. It was a conversation that should have been had a long time ago but this was the first time Leo had been driven to find out those details about his mother. He had seen how his past had put him in chains, and to break free of those chains he'd had to dive into dealing with what had happened between his parents.

His mother leaving, his father had explained to Leo, had actually been a release, in hindsight. It had been an unhappy marriage and she would have eventually become a toxic parent. The signs had already been there before she had even given birth to him. She had hated everything about the life she'd had and, yes, when she had finally walked out he had said goodbye to the married life he'd hoped he would have; but, even through his own unhappiness, he had known that her leaving was the best thing she could have done for both of them.

His father had described a woman who had been immature, selfish and narcissistic—the polar opposite of Cassie. Leo had turned his back on the woman who loved him because he had put her in the same category as his mother instead of seeing her as the wonderful individual she was.

He was the last person she wanted to see standing here now and he couldn't blame her. The little carrier bag in his hand felt incredibly weighty. This was the second time in his life he had felt helpless in the face of something overwhelming. The first time had been eight years ago when they'd broken up. He'd closed himself off then, determined never to feel that way again, but now he knew that feeling this way wasn't dangerous. Feeling this way, vulnerable and exposed, didn't make him weak.

He'd spent years shutting away his emotions and that had made him empty and dead inside. Cassie had come back to him and she had turned a key and opened him up but, instead of embracing the feeling of being alive, he had been so damn scared that he had turned his back on it. He had told himself that he couldn't allow anything to have the potential to hurt him the way he had been hurt as a child. He'd been a blind fool. He had ignored all the signposts telling him what he should have known a while back because he had known it for what it was: love. Love that had never gone away. Love that had lain dormant, just waiting for the only woman he had ever given his heart to to return and reclaim it.

'You're staring at me.'

'Where's your mum?'

'She's right behind you.'

Leo turned around and, sure enough, Mary Farraday had come out to see what was going on. She was smiling broadly, walking towards him with her arms outstretched in warm greeting.

Behind him, Leo could almost hear Cassie's soft, despairing intake of breath. He heard himself chatting, explaining away whatever important work situation Cassie had come up with that had supposedly demanded his immediate attention, telling her that he realised that there was no work situation as important as being here.

Mary bustled ahead of them and he turned when Cassie tugged him back and, coldly and furiously, demanded, 'What are you playing at?'

Their eyes clashed, hers bright and angry, his tentative, measured, determined and tender.

Cassie breathed in sharply and stumbled back.

'You...you're not meant to be here, screwing up my plans,' she began, suddenly thrown by something in his eyes she couldn't quite put her finger on, but refusing to trust instincts that had previously let her down. She could feel the heat emanating from him. Where had he spent the past few nights? What had he been doing—seeing who else was out there, what other fish there were in the sea?

'If you've come for your precious laptop,' she snapped, suddenly remembering that it was still in her apartment, 'Then you can have the keys to my place. Feel free to let yourself in, get it and then disappear. Mum has a spare.'

'I don't care about my laptop.'

'Then what...?'

'Please, Cass. Let's go through with your mother. She'll only come back out in a minute if we don't.'

'Only,' she returned tightly, 'If you can promise that you'll let me do this my way.'

'I will on the proviso that you look, *just look*, at what I've brought with me and hear me out.'

'You're not in a position to make any provisos, Leo.' She sucked in a painful breath.

'I know and I'm... Well, Cassie, you could say I'm begging you to just give me ten minutes of your time.'

Cassie felt it again—a stupid, stupid urge to trust what her gut was telling her. To soften and open up to the same guy who had rejected her and then headed out into the snow because it had been better than being with her after what she'd said to him.

She stormed off towards the sitting room but she could feel his presence right behind her. If he carried on with the charm offensive, then where was that going to leave her? She wondered whether his ex was demanding proof of his engagement. Was that it? Was that why he'd come back here—because it suited him to prolong the narrative?

Just the thought of it flung her right back into a righteous fury. But, still, she managed to pin a smile to her face as she led Leo through to where her mother waited and politely offered him coffee.

He declined. Instead, he sat forward with his arms resting loosely on his thighs and looked at them. Cassie cleared her throat while her mother watched in expectant silence...deafening silence...

Heart beating like a sledgehammer, she watched him reach into the carrier bag he had brought with him with hands just a little unsteady and pull out a little black box. He stretched out to where Cassie was sitting and handed it to her.

'What's this?' Cassie asked suspiciously, even though she still had that frozen smile pinned to her face for her mother's sake.

'Open it.'

Her mother glanced at the box with a beaming smile.

'You know what it is, Cassie, darling!'

She knew what it was. She just didn't know why he had given it to her. Was this some kind of joke? Fingers trembling, she opened the box and stared down at the perfect engagement ring. It was unfussy, unpretentious, just like her. The solitaire diamond glittered.

Cassie looked at him sitting there looking anxious, perspiring, and then she did give in to her gut instinct, which was telling her that this was the real deal, that what he felt was the real deal. It was there on his tense face, in the love she could see in his eyes, and she allowed herself a tremulous smile.

Leo moved forward and went down on one knee.

'I don't think I did this properly, did I, Cass, when it came to this engagement of ours?' He smiled crookedly and the look that passed between them was for her eyes only. 'So I'm going to try and set the record straight now and do it right, from the very bottom of my heart. Will you marry me? Because I'm in love with you and I can't think of life without you. The sooner you're my wife, the happier I'll be.'

The world disappeared as he waited for her to speak but he knew that she would be his because of the smile on her face, a smile that mirrored his. The touch of her hand on his cheek made him tremble and he clasped it and kissed her palm.

'I love you so much, Leo,' Cassie whispered, still smiling as he tenderly slipped the ring on her finger. 'And I can't wait to be your wife…at last.'

Lucia Mary Cruz was born nearly a year later. Leo had looked at his daughter, plump at a little over eight pounds with her mop of dark, curly hair, hands balled into fists and lashes that Cassie told him definitely came from him, and his heart had wanted to burst.

He had never thought about fatherhood but, then again, he had never thought about a lot of things being within his grasp until he'd met Cassie, first as a kid and then as a man who'd thought he had it all figured out: having a fling to finally kill feelings that hadn't been snuffed out, to forget the one woman who had meant everything to him once upon a time. He hadn't banked on lust camouflaging a love that had never died. He'd never seen himself as capable of handing his heart over to someone else, but he had, and now…

Lucia was three months old and as beautiful and as laid back as her mother. Cassie was curled up on the sofa watching television with their baby breastfeeding lustily, little chubby legs kicking. Her head was resting on his shoulder and he nuzzled into her hair and felt her smile.

'Have I ever told you how happy you make me?' he murmured. 'You and Lucia?'

'I think you may have done, just once or twice.'

'I can't say it often enough, my darling.' He felt the sting of tears behind his eyes as he gazed at his daughter's head bobbing as she fed. 'You've made my life worth living and I would be no one without the two of you.'

Cassie gently manoeuvred herself so that she could angle her eyes to meet his.

'Leo, my darling…it's the same for me. It feels as though we're here now because of a series of unexpected events but…'

'But…' he finished the sentence for her '…we were always meant to be, and we would always have found one another just the way we did, because we belong together. Now and for ever.'

* * * * *

THE GREEK'S
WIFE RETURNS

DANI COLLINS

MILLS & BOON

To my new editor, Jenny,
and the teams at Harlequin and Mills and Boon.

It takes a village to turn a story into a book.

Thank you for all the hard work you put into mine.

CHAPTER ONE

As the car stopped, Carmel Davenport closed her eyes against the craving that rose in the back of her throat. She didn't *really* want alcohol. She wanted the blankness. The numbness. Emotions were spiky and hot and heavy. They bombarded her as the door opened beside her.

She kept her eyes closed, concentrating on her breathing technique as she absorbed the slice of regret and the bruising ache of shame, the loss of time and the opportunities she had squandered. She drew a breath laden with nostalgia while technicolor images danced behind her eyelids. A man with black hair and tanned skin that gleamed with drops of water. A cocksure smile. A heated stare and a confident touch that made her feel thrilling, wonderful sensations. Caresses that told her she was worthy and special.

She exhaled melancholy because those moments were yet another thing she'd taken for granted and misused.

Darker voices tried to creep in and berate her for that, but she firmly reminded herself she was *not* worthless and stupid. She couldn't change the past, but she could move forward making better decisions.

She *had* to move forward. No more backsliding. No more wallowing in the purgatory of yearning and self-loathing and what-ifs.

"Sorry," Carmel murmured to her brother's driver as he continued to wait patiently in the hot Athens sun.

She snatched a few tissues from the holder in the console, blinking her eyes against the press of tears. She *hated* crying. It made her feel sloppy and out of control. Plus, tears would ruin the makeup she had taken such pains to apply.

Everything about her appearance from the low, twisted chignon to the power suit in navy blue had been debated to death by her inner critic.

What would Damian say about how she had aged? It had been five years. She was no longer twenty-four and stick-thin with bleached blond hair and a penchant for showing skin. What would he think of her natural brunette hair color? Her weight gain? Her sobriety?

Ugh. She didn't need his approval. She needed a *divorce*.

She didn't even need his approval for that. She could have filed the petition and waited to see if he would contest it, but she was hoping he would cosign so it could be rubber-stamped without delay.

So she could continue her trek forward, out of the past and into a more deliberate and fulfilling future.

She stepped her open-toed Ferragamo onto the sidewalk and accepted the hand the driver offered.

"I'll walk back after my meeting," she told him, not caring if the heat frizzed her hair out of its bun or turned her into a flushed and sweaty mess. No matter what happened, she would need to clear her head after she saw her husband.

"I'm happy to wait for you." The driver knew as well as she did that there were three licensed establishments between this office building and her brother's apartment.

"I'll be fine." She hoped. "Please let me tell Atlas in my own time where I asked you to drop me today."

"I'm sure you'll speak to him before I will. I would only tell him if he asked." But he *would* tell Atlas if Atlas asked, and Atlas *would* ask because he still didn't fully trust her. His wife, Stella, had been the one to say effusively, *Of course you can stay in our apartment while we're away.* Atlas had instructed the housekeeper to lock up all the alcohol.

"I'll text you once my meeting finishes, then." Gone were the days when she could bribe or charm her brother's employees into hiding her secrets.

Not that she wanted to be that person anymore.

Or that she had many secrets left. Only this husband she was planning to divest herself of.

She looked up at the building and her belly filled with a heavy, oily sensation.

Maybe she should have asked Atlas to handle this for her. She didn't think Damian would come after her fortune—which begged the question, "what fortune?"—but he could make a grab for the assets she had left, like the company she'd inherited from her mother or her flat in London.

No. She didn't want to tell Atlas about this rash, short-lived marriage of hers. They were finally in a good place. She didn't want to ruin it by asking him to clean up yet another of her old messes.

She was so *tired* of being humbled by her past. Of having to ask for help. She needed to do this herself, to properly make her amends with Damian.

Even though it scared her spitless.

She glanced in her shoulder bag for the millionth time, ensuring the envelope of paperwork was there.

A horn beeped to nudge her driver into moving from his spot in front of the building.

She let him go and hurried through the revolving door, then showed the envelope and her lawyer's card to the security guard.

Her assistant had finagled a five-minute appointment with Damian by claiming she was bringing paperwork from a London law firm that required his signature. Which was *true*, if not as forthcoming as Carmel was striving to be these days.

Heck, if she was as brutally honest as she should be with herself, she would admit the real reason she hadn't involved Atlas or allowed her lawyer to handle this was because she wanted to see Damian.

And she knew he wouldn't see her if he knew she was coming. He had said so the last time she'd seen him.

I never want to see you again in my life.

The antipathy in his expression had sat as a cold spike in her chest for five long years. Hot misery over earning his hatred had prompted her to get serious about sobriety, not that she'd succeeded right away. No, she'd stumbled in and out of treatment several times, trying to pull herself together only to fall apart again. She was taking accountability now, though. Facing her demons.

Or the one she'd married at least, she thought ironically.

She accepted the visitor badge and was escorted into an elevator. As it whisked her to the top floor, she tried to inject strength into her weak knees and willed her palms not to be so clammy.

Her apprehension only grew worse as she shot skyward. This was one of the tallest buildings in Athens and it hadn't escaped her notice that Damian's name was on it, including on the wall that faced her when the doors opened.

Growing up in a wealthy family, she wasn't intimidated by the marble floors and glass walls and hushed air of luxury as she followed the receptionist. She was impressed, though. Damian had been a scrappy start-up in green energy when she'd met him. Now he dominated that industry across Europe and had offices around the globe.

The receptionist stopped near the end of the hall and left her in the custody of an assistant who invited her to take a seat in a waiting area.

She almost didn't hear him, her pulse pounded so loudly in her ears. As subtly as she could, she regulated her breathing. Her hands longed to wring the envelope like a wet rag.

It would be fine, she reassured herself. Damian didn't want to be married to her. How could he? They had married on impulse after a few days of passion. He had had big ambitions, and she had wanted to fund them. She had believed that marriage would grant her access to her trust, and she had wanted to be free of her father's pressure to marry one of his toadies.

At no point had she imagined their marriage would last. Damian couldn't have thought so, either. He'd been indulgent and affectionate. Possessive enough to stare down any other man who looked at her, but he had already been realizing his mistake by the time they arrived in London.

Did you just put vodka in your mimosa?

She had. Because she had known that her father would be *appalled* that she had married a common working man she had met while vacationing in Greece.

Like father like daughter, she had said when Oliver

curled his lip at Damian. *At least I married my lover. At least there won't be a baby turning up fifteen years from now.*

Good, her father had said. *That means you can get rid of him.*

She sighed, no longer blaming Atlas for her father's philandering ways, but she had no one to blame but herself for the way Damian had looked at her as his father sneered at him.

Is that the reason you married me? To offend him?

The assistant's phone buzzed, startling her back to the otherwise silent office.

The young man answered in Greek, which Carmel understood better than she spoke. Atlas's mother had been Greek, and Carmel had learned enough to eavesdrop on him.

"*Málista, kyrie*, but your ten o'clock is here." The assistant flicked his gaze toward her. "She has documents from a law firm in London."

He made a noise of assent and an apologetic expression began to form on his face.

No. Carmel lurched to her feet.

"I only need two minutes," she said in English, rushing toward his desk. Her brain frantically tried to find the words in Greek. "*Dýo leptá.*" She held up two fingers. "*Parakaló.*"

"*Kýrie?*" the assistant said, frowning at his phone.

There was a loud bang as the wide doors that dominated the end of the hall were pulled inward so forcefully, they hit the walls.

Carmel jumped again, heart stalling in her chest because there he was, like an avenging god. Damian Kalymnios. Her husband.

She had stalked him online many times, rarely seeing his image in anything other than groundbreaking ceremonies or corporate headshots. None of those small photos had prepared her for seeing him in real life.

He was still tall and wide-shouldered, but he'd filled out with maturity. His muscles were even more powerful beneath his gray, bespoke suit. He was clean-shaven, not wearing a scruff the way he used to, revealing the cleft in his square jaw. His black hair was shorter, his mouth unsmiling. Grim. His gaze raked her, then slammed back to meet her own. His eyes brimmed with outrage. And contempt.

Ouch.

She had braced for his disgust, but it surprised her how much it hurt to see it so fiercely alive and well. It surprised her how sensitive she was to his regard and how badly she wished he had softened a little with time.

Not that she let him see any of that. If her history of being a shameless liar had been good for one thing, it was the shell of indifference she had developed to protect herself.

She lifted her chin and offered a cool, collected smile. "Hello, Damian."

"No," he said flatly in English. Then, to his assistant, he said in Greek, "I'll work remotely as time allows."

"Yes, sir. The pilot is preparing for takeoff. Is this a matter for security?" He darted a wary glance at Carmel.

"No." Damian switched back to English. "She's leaving."

He strode past her without another glance, heading down the hall toward the elevators.

"Damian." Carmel hurried after him, careful to keep

her heels from sliding out from under her on the polished marble. She waved the envelope at him. "I only came to give you this. Read it, sign it, then we never have to speak again."

"I already don't have to speak to you." He jabbed the call button, not even looking at her. "In fact, I distinctly remember telling you I never wanted to see you again."

"I know, but..." *I want to apologize.* "Please, will you take this?" She continued to hold out the paperwork. "It's time. You know it is."

He ignored it, exactly as he had the first set of divorce papers she'd offered.

The doors opened and he stepped inside.

She followed.

Now he looked at her. Straight down his nose. His cheek ticked as he seemed to debate whether to give her a hard shove out of the elevator. Out of his life. But that would require he touch her. He jabbed a button instead, expression dismissive, gaze aimed straight ahead.

Her stomach twisted, but she pressed on.

"Don't you want to close this chapter?" she asked.

"No. I would rather stay married and continue to bring shame upon your family name." He was quoting what her father had said of their marriage. "But wait." He pinched his chin in a mock ponder. "Have I got that the right way around?"

The severe sting of a hard blush hit her cheekbones and sent a withering path of culpability down her spine.

"I won't pretend I don't deserve that. But isn't that more reason to sever ties?"

"Did you just say you won't pretend you don't deserve that?" His tone balanced between spite and dark laughter. "That almost sounds like honesty, Carmel."

"It's a new thing I'm trying." She flashed a facetious smile.

"Good luck getting people to buy it."

The doors opened into a small waiting room with windows onto the roof where a helicopter waited. Damian strode straight out into the blistering sunshine.

Carmel didn't have time to think. She ran after him and shoved herself into the space of the open door to the chopper, blocking him from climbing inside.

"What the hell do you think you're doing?" He sounded as astonished as he was enraged.

"Getting what I came for. I want a divorce, Damian. *Sign this.*" She tapped the envelope against his chest.

"I know you're the ultimate spoiled rich girl who thinks the world bends to your will, but it does not. *I* do not."

They were too close. She could feel the animosity radiating off him, but there were pheromones within it that spoke to her body in ways that couldn't be explained. Her bones softened and her pulse tripped, and she was accosted by a sense of breathless anticipation.

"It will take five minutes," she said in a voice growing husked by reaction.

His pupils were pinpoints in orbs of bitter dark chocolate. In her periphery, she saw his hands flex. His whole body was coiled muscle that she expected to spring at her any second.

"I don't have five minutes. Move or I'll move you myself," he warned.

"And give me something to use against you?" It was beneath her to threaten him like that. She wouldn't, but she had a lot of practice fighting dirty and some habits were hard to break. "Right now, this is a no-fault, irreconcilable differences divorce. Let's keep it that way."

"You haven't changed, have you?" he said with tired spite.

It was the cruelest thing anyone could say to her. Coming from him, someone who'd seen her in ways she'd never revealed to anyone else, someone who'd made her *want* to change, it was even more hurtful.

"Is this how we're playing things? With intimidation and threats?" He crowded closer, voice turning low and menacing. "Are you absolutely certain you want to test me right now?"

She set her hand in the middle of his chest. The contact sent a jolt of white-hot electricity through her. If she hadn't been face-to-face with him, stares already locked in challenge, she might have missed the way his pupils exploded. The air crackled. A magnetic force tried to pull her forward. Her gaze dropped to lips she longed to feel against her own.

Maybe she hadn't changed, if she was longing for things that were likely to destroy her.

"Me synchoreíte," the pilot blurted as he came around the tail of the helicopter. He started to turn away.

Damian jerked his head up, flashing her an accusatory glance.

"Come back. I'm ready." He switched to English to say to Carmel, "I'm meeting someone important to me. I don't want to keep her waiting. *Move.*"

She tried not to flinch at the mention of "her."

"I'm sure *she* would want you to be free of me." She made a wild, split-second decision, turning to grasp the handle on the open door. She levered herself into the luxurious passenger cabin of the helicopter and took a seat.

"Do you have a death wish?" Damian asked in a growl of amazement.

"What are you going to do? Push me out while we're in the air?" Her fingers shook as she buckled in. "That's one way to get what I came for."

"Don't tempt me!"

"You seem to be in a hurry. I'm accommodating that." She tried to overcome the tremble in her voice. "You can read through the papers while we're in the air."

"Since when do you have an ounce of consideration for anyone else?" he asked as he levered in to sit beside her.

"It's another of those fashionable things I'm trying."

He jerked his head at the pilot who was hovering uncomfortably, silently telling the man to proceed with takeoff.

"I'm not flying you back here," Damian said. "You'll have a long walk to the ferry slip." He sent a pointed look at her shoes. "It departs at ten in the morning so you've already missed it."

"I'll manage." It wouldn't be the first time she'd found herself at loose ends in a strange place. She had credit cards. At least this time she'd be sober.

"I bet you will," he muttered, implying she would press herself onto the nearest man.

Which was not an unfounded accusation. She'd been taught manipulation by a master. She hid her shame over that behind a stiff mask of indifference.

The pilot locked the door, then closed himself into his own cabin. The rotors began to turn, causing the sunlight to strobe around them.

"Will you please read this now?" She offered the envelope.

"No." Damian brought his phone to his ear and told someone in Greek that he would miss their meeting. A string of business calls followed.

She took the opportunity to text Atlas's driver not to wait for her, then informed the housekeeper that she would be away for the night. She would have to offer some excuse to Atlas, too, but he was in New York. She had time before she had to reach out to him.

As they flew south across the water, she realized they were headed to Damian's island south of Mykonos. They had met while she'd been cruising the Cyclades with friends five years ago, but she'd stayed with him on Mykonos, never seeing his actual home.

The people she'd been with hadn't been real friends, either. They'd left while she'd still been in bed with Damian, not that she'd minded at the time, but their lack of regard for her was indicative of the company she'd kept back then.

Growing up with her father's fortune at her fingertips, Carmel had always had a lot of people around her. They'd all been up for adventure and partying, especially when she covered the bill, but none had ever stood by her with true loyalty or love. The ones who'd possessed any sense had quickly distanced themselves from her chaos while the rest were there for a good time, not a long time. She had pruned those hangers-on from her life once she began taking stock and saw how detrimental they were to her.

These days, she had one real friend: her sister-in-law, Stella. Their friendship was still new and, really, Stella was teaching Carmel *how* to be a friend. Stella was naturally warm and thoughtful and unconditionally supportive, which were unmastered skills in Carmel's repertoire.

Carmel aspired to be more like Stella, though. Her sister-in-law was *lovable*. Watching Atlas, a certified hard-ass, turn into a gooey-centered pushover around his wife was hilarious and stupefying and envy-inducing.

No one would ever look at her that way. Not if she didn't change.

Certainly not the man who ended his latest call and removed his jacket with impatience, tossing it to the seat across from him.

"Why now?" he asked flatly.

Oh, God. She had scripted this thousands of times. The words were there, but they were jumbled on her tongue and difficult to push past her lips.

"I...um..." She swallowed. "I've been making a lot of changes to my life. I'm..." She rolled her lips inward and carefully stacked her hands on the envelope in her lap, contrite. "I'm sober now. I'm running my mother's company and trying to..." She cringed inwardly, wishing this wasn't necessary, but it was. "I'm trying to make amends with those I've hurt."

He released a choked noise. "This is your idea of making amends? By lying your way into my office and forcing your way onto my helicopter?"

"Is this not how apologies work? *I'm joking*," she insisted when his mouth tightened.

Humor was one of her go-to defense mechanisms and one of her few good qualities, not that she always used it appropriately, but she couldn't be expected to change *everything* about herself, could she?

"Look. You're right," she conceded. "This wasn't the best way to approach you. I could have had the lawyer send this, but I wanted to speak to you. I wanted to face you and acknowledge that I behaved very badly. I knew that marrying you would upset my father. That wasn't kind to you. I genuinely did believe I could help you, financially, but I deserve your anger and dislike for pulling the rug on that. I should have been more honest about how he would react."

She was trying to hold his gaze so he would know she was being sincere, but he was wearing such a hard, implacable expression, it felt like she was throwing herself uselessly against a rough, brick wall. She was collecting nothing but bruises, but she swallowed the lump in her throat and pressed on.

"He's no longer in my life. My father." Cutting Oliver away had been like using a rusty scalpel for self-surgery, but she felt lighter these days, having excised him.

"I also wanted to tell you…" A hot pressure rose behind her eyes. The burn in her chest spread into her throat, thinning her voice. "I wanted you to know that I didn't actually, um, cheat on you."

He snorted disparagingly.

"What I mean is…" She nervously licked her lips. "I didn't have sex with that man. I kissed him. Obviously. You saw that. And I took my top off so it would look like we were having sex, but I didn't actually sleep with him."

She realized her hands were clenching the stiff white envelope into a cone. She smoothed it flat and dared a look at him.

"I'm very sorry."

"I'm no longer that gullible idiot you met on Mykonos."

"I never thought you were."

Another snort.

"No, I mean…" She held up a hand. "Okay, I thought

everyone was gullible enough to believe whatever I told them. I actually thought that it didn't matter what the truth was. Lying to you was never a personal attack. I wasn't trying to trick *you*. It was the way I lived." God, that was humiliating to admit. "This is what I'm trying to convey to you now, that I am genuinely trying to be a more truthful, sincere person. Letting you believe I cheated on you was a lie. I have deeply regretted it since the moment it happened. I'm truly sorry, Damian. I promise not to lie to you again."

"I cannot imagine why you think I'd care one way or another what you say, how you feel, or who you sleep with," he said with derision.

She dropped her gaze to hide how deeply that pierced her.

"Or that I could possibly bring myself to believe a word coming out of that deceitful mouth of yours. Here's what I know is true, Carmel. I've seen the headlines. Your father got sick of your spendthrift, devious, disgraceful behavior and kicked you off his payroll. God knows you couldn't possibly work for a living so you've come to the Bank of Divorce for a piece of the fortune that I built *without* your help."

"No—"

"I would also bet my hard-won fortune that you have another sucker on the line, one you can't marry because of this." He pointed at the envelope. "So, no, Carmel. I will not sign your papers. In fact, I will happily spend every last euro I possess on legal fees fighting that divorce. I will break both of us before I will give you anything you want. This is what you get when you poke the bear. Maybe you should have listened to me and stayed out of my sight."

CHAPTER TWO

"Okay, but if you could just sign this first?"

Theós, she was brazen, blinking with facetious innocence as she pushed her toe over the line.

"You really have no sense of self-preservation at all, do you?" Damian was trying not to look at her, refusing to fall under her spell again, but the small details of her appearance kept puncturing his wall of anger. Her hair was a rich, warm brown now. Her features were no longer softened by youth, seeming more pronounced, but maybe that was sobriety because she had collected a few kilos and they suited her. She had also traded in raw sex appeal and edgy fashion for refinement and elegance.

She looked like she was stepping into the potential that she'd been squandering when he met her.

Her voice hadn't changed, though. It still had that husky edge that swept across his skin like velvet. That voice was what had pulled him from his office as he informed his assistant that he needed to leave for the island early. He had heard Carmel's unmistakable feminine tone with its condescending accent insisting on two minutes, and his vision had gone white. His scalp had tightened and his abdomen had tensed and his shoulders had bunched with raised hackles.

Even as he told himself she wouldn't *dare* turn up like this, he had known damned well that she would. Carmel Davenport had no shame whatsoever.

Is this not how apologies work?

As if an apology would cut it when she had cratered his savings account, throwing away his hard-earned money on clothes and high-end booze and offered an empty promise to pay him back.

I get access to Mummy's money once I marry. I'm sure Daddy would invest in your expansion if I ask him to.

That had not happened. After her father had treated him like a street mongrel and threatened to ruin him, Carmel had come back to their hotel with papers very like the ones she was trying to foist on him now.

Daddy wants us to get a quiet divorce. Sign this and he'll give you ten thousand euros.

Damian had seen the advantages in marrying her. Or rather, the *apparent* advantages. It had all been a lie. All of it. He'd been so offended, so disgusted with himself for thinking he could profit off marriage, he had refused to profit off their divorce.

He had walked out of their hotel room only to come back two hours later to find her in bed with a Belgian tourist who was lucky to still be alive.

He should be over it by now. He knew that. After years of hardscrabble hustling, he had more than enough money to cut her a check and expel her from his life for good.

That wasn't enough to compensate for the humiliation of trusting her, though. She had used him. Betrayed him. Then she waited five long years to show her face and offer a weak apology in exchange for, once again, wheedling to get what she wanted.

He should put an end to this farce of a marriage. He knew that.

But vengeance sounded so much more appetizing.

How much did she want? he wondered. The suit she wore was couture, but it could have been purchased before her father's wallet had been closed against her.

Seeing the headlines about her falling-out with her father had been unavoidable. The Davenport family had always been a favorite with paparazzi. Her father had inherited a media conglomerate from his own father and an athletic clothing company from his late wife. Carmel and her brother had been models for the brand for years. Being a beautiful, notorious party girl, Carmel made enticing clickbait.

It really was a miracle they'd kept their marriage under the radar for five years, but they'd both been motivated to do so. Carmel had been trying to stay on her father's good side and Damian had kept silent out of embarrassment, hating himself for falling for her tricks.

He never would again.

She really wanted him to believe she was running her mother's company? It was common knowledge that it was under the umbrella of DVE, the global conglomerate her brother had recently taken over. At best, she was collecting a paycheck for the use of her likeness on the company org chart.

He glanced over to see her chewing her bottom lip. Crafting a plan, no doubt.

"Whatever this is, I don't want any part of it," he said flatly. Not now when he had other, greater concerns. His thoughts turned to his grandmother. "As soon as we land, I want you gone."

"If I send this through a lawyer, will you sign it?" she asked.

"I don't know how to state this more clearly, Carmel. *No.*"

The truth was always made out to be so noble and golden and pure.

It was not. It was messy and dark and covered in thorny barbs that shredded you when you tried to wrestle in it. The more you waded into honesty, the deeper you were in whatever reality was already drowning you.

Lies were easier. They were silk roses and false compliments and the oily bronzer that helped you slip out of a tight spot.

Until they piled up around you like the stinking garbage they were, of course.

So Carmel chose honesty over lies as often as she could, especially with herself. Even when that meant acknowledging she had come here hoping for forgiveness.

He would never forgive her. That was the bleak truth she confronted as the helicopter began its descent toward an island and a blinding white villa sprawled between olive and orange groves. The roof was covered in solar panels. The pool sat like a glittering blue sapphire next to a courtyard covered in pink bougainvillea. There were abundant terraces and paths to small gardens, and stairs cut into the hillside that led down to the beach.

This could have been mine, she thought.

So could the boxy mausoleum outside of London, if she hadn't chosen to side with her brother against her father last year. Now she had a flat in Barking that was trendy and secure, but modest by the standards she'd grown up in.

It was hers, though. It was enough.

She had no idea how she would get back to it. This villa seemed to be located well away from the nearest town. She'd need a taxi to a hotel where she could stay while she waited for the ferry, she supposed.

Should she leave the papers? Was there any point in doing so?

She glanced at Damian to see him scowling as the helicopter settled onto its pad. Looking for whoever he was meeting? She tried to ignore the searing jealousy scorching her heart. She had no claim on him! Who did? She looked for the beautiful supermodel she presumed was waiting for him.

As the rotors slowed, the pilot stepped out and nodded that it was safe to disembark.

Carmel followed Damian away from the helicopter into the shade of a nearby tree where a middle-aged man waited.

"Where's the car?" Damian demanded in Greek.

"Your grandmother refused to go to the hospital. The doctor is with her now." He motioned toward the smaller stone cottage that Carmel had assumed was staff housing.

Damian strode toward it without looking back.

"His grandmother," Carmel repeated in bemusement.

"Yes. Are you...?" The man was studying her clothes, trying to discern if she was a guest or staff.

She was about to faint with relief that Damian wasn't meeting a paramour, but she looked after him with concern.

His grandparents had raised him after his mother dropped him here and disappeared. He hadn't told her a lot about it, only that he'd been six and had always been confused by her abandoning him that way. He didn't know what he had done to cause her to reject him.

His grandfather had already been gone when she met Damian, but hadn't been the warmest man. She was a little surprised to hear his grandmother was still alive. And ill? That was distressing.

Damian had demanded she leave, but Stella would never walk away if someone was going through a difficult time. She would wait and offer emotional support—something Carmel had not given her husband in the past, despite the vows she'd taken to do just that.

She looked around, then pointed at the nearby bench. "I'll wait for Damian there."

Zoia Kalymnios had grown faint while walking in the garden. That was the call that had had Damian telling his assistant to clear his schedule and prepare the helicopter only to hear Carmel's crisp English demanding "Two minutes" of his time.

"But I didn't faint," Zoia insisted from the overstuffed, swivel rocker she occupied, sounding alert and impatient. "I *felt* faint and tried to get back to the bench to sit down. I caught my toe and stumbled."

The fall had been enough to scrape her hand and knee and alarm Renita, one of her caregivers, into calling Damian along with the doctor. Zoia had eighty-two years behind her and a number of conditions related to that age: arthritis, blood sugar issues and a heart that was liable to fail if she didn't have surgery.

The operation wasn't without risk so she was refusing it. She didn't want to spend her last days in a hospital in Athens, she kept saying. Or lose what quality of life she had by suffering through weeks of recovery. What if she never recovered at all?

Damian had to abide by her wishes, but it was frustrating. Worrisome.

"Renita shouldn't have troubled you," she continued. "*Or* the doctor." She glowered at the physician. "I'm perfectly fine."

The doctor wore a stoic expression as he folded his stethoscope into his bag.

"I'll walk you out." Damian followed the doctor through the kitchen to where the doctor had parked his car behind the cottage. "She's not fine, is she?"

"She needs that surgery," the doctor said.

"How soon could she get it, if I can talk her into it?"

"I'll speak to the specialist in Athens. He'll want some tests, which we can do here on the island. Two weeks, perhaps? You have my number. If she changes her mind, call me. I'll expedite it. Either way, you ought to stay nearby."

Damian winced. "I was planning to spend the summer with her, but I'll move that up."

The doctor left, and Damian reentered the bungalow that his grandfather had brought Zoia to when they'd married. They'd struggled for most of their lives to eke a living from their small pasture and olive grove. Zoia had supplemented their income with chickens and a vegetable garden, selling off what she didn't preserve for their own pantry.

Zoia and Eurus were Damian's mother's parents. When their only child had come home from her first year of university in Athens to announce she was pregnant, with no sign of the father, Eurus had been furious. How dare she throw away her future on an Australian tourist?

After a terrific argument, Hestia had left, swearing to make her way on her own. She had. Damian's memories of her were dim, but warm. They hadn't had much, but he had never gone hungry. He had believed she loved him.

Until she dropped him here one day when he was six years old and never came back.

"Something has happened," Zoia had said a thousand times in those early days. They had called hospitals and police to no avail.

Hestia had died. Damian knew that now, but for most of his life he had believed his mother had deliberately left him behind. She hadn't wanted him and neither had his grandfather. That's how he'd seen it, anyway. Life had been hard. His grandparents had already been aging. They hadn't needed the burden of a young child. Damian had learned to earn his keep from Day One, lest he be rejected again.

He had been ambitious, though. He had wanted more than a small farm and a lifetime of working it. He had quit school when he got on with a roofing company and, when a client asked about solar panels, he began to specialize in installing them.

Eventually, his fledgling company had grown enough that he was able to put a down payment on the run-down estate next to theirs. Over time, he'd renovated the villa, ensuring a comfortable apartment for Zoia.

Of course she refused to move into it with him. This was her home, she insisted.

As he returned to the living room, Zoia pointed to the window.

"Who is that?" The lines in her face deepened with

curiosity. "Why did you leave her sitting in the heat? Go get her."

Damian followed her gaze to see Carmel sitting in the shade of a tree, jacket off and draped over her bag on the bench beside her. Her white, sleeveless blouse exposed her pale arms. She sat with her legs crossed and was looking at her phone.

Typical. Of course she was still here despite his telling her to leave. Although, it was more her style to have changed into a bikini and jumped into the pool while ordering someone to bring her a daiquiri rather than sit on a bench as though waiting for a bus.

"That's Carmel," he admitted reluctantly.

"Your wife? You're reconciling? Oh, Damian." She set her hand over her fragile heart. "If there's one thing I've longed to see before I died, it was you settled down and starting your family."

"You're not dying," he reminded her. "You only *felt* faint."

The oppressive weight of the doctor's words hung over his head, though.

"She's here to ask for a divorce," he told her.

"You've agreed?"

"No."

"Good. You're right to give her a second chance." A misty-eyed smile lifted the corners of her thin lips. "I know how you felt about her."

An eely sensation squirmed in his chest, one that reminded him how trusting he'd been. Infatuated. That was the part that grated the most. Spending most of his life believing his mother had abandoned him, he'd been very careful about lowering his defenses.

Carmel had slithered around them, though. Before her, most of his hookups had been with tourists or older women who didn't want anything serious. Carmel had immediately become a sexual fixation. He'd thought they had a connection of sorts and had begun to believe he could trust in someone besides himself.

That's why it had been such a devastating kick when he'd found her with someone else. The nascent things he'd begun to feel for her proved to be unrequited and the height of foolishness.

And now?

"I don't feel anything for her." Except hatred. And a persistent sexual pull that wasn't something a man discussed with his grandmother. Especially when he intended to ignore it. "Our marriage is over."

"Then why aren't you divorcing her?"

To punish her. It was such a childish statement, he couldn't admit to it aloud.

"You would have found someone else by now if you didn't feel *something* for her." Zoia's body might be ailing her, but her eyes were still bright and penetrating.

He had painted himself into a corner, but he suddenly saw an opportunity. He wanted Zoia to agree to the surgery that would prolong her life. Zoia wanted to see him "settle down." Carmel wanted a divorce.

"If I make an effort to reconcile with her, will you agree to the surgery?" he asked. "At least have the tests and speak with the specialist?"

Her thin lips pursed with amused exasperation. "You're coercing an old woman who only wants to see her grandson happy? Shame," she chided. "I would feel comforted, though, if you at least *tried* to make this marriage work.

I don't expect to live long enough for you to divorce this wife and find a new one. Very well. If you make an honest effort with her, I will see the specialist. Now bring her in before she's fully cooked."

Carmel was browsing the hotel options when she looked up to see Damian striding toward her with the energy of a knight on a charger, jousting stick aimed at her heart.

"I know you told me to leave." She scrambled to her feet and collected her things. "I was worried about your grandmother. Is she okay?"

He halted, seeming taken aback by her question. His gaze struck where the lace of her bra was visible through the sheer fabric of her sleeveless blouse before rising to crash into hers again.

She'd been melting in the heat and removed her jacket. Now she hugged her things to her middle, defensive.

"She's not. She has heart trouble and nearly fainted. She needs surgery or she won't last the year, but she's been refusing it."

"I'm sorry to hear that." He looked very remote and contained, but she could tell he was deeply concerned. She thought about reaching out a hand to him, wanting to squeeze his arm in comfort, but hesitated, then lost the moment as he curled his lip in cynicism.

"How badly do you want a divorce?"

"What?" Her heart spun out and fell. All the oxygen seemed to evaporate from her lungs, making it impossible to speak. The sense of loss, of a light of hope winking out and leaving her in a sea of darkness, was profound.

"Zoia wants to see me happily married. If we attempt reconciliation, she'll agree to the surgery."

"I—" She swayed under the impact of that statement, trying to make sense of what felt like a one-eighty spin. Despite everything she knew about his hatred for her, a continent's worth of butterflies filled her chest. "That's not likely to happen, is it?"

"Absolutely not. But it's two weeks out of your life, Carmel. If you want a divorce, that's what it will cost you."

She was still in free fall, trying to gain her bearings.

"You want me to *pretend* to reconcile with you?" She shook her head. "I can't lie to her."

He released a disparaging noise. "Not if it benefits someone besides yourself?"

A vise pinched her heart, cutting into her air. "Lying was as much an addiction for me as alcohol—"

"Oh, you're sober from *lying*. I didn't know that was a thing," he scoffed.

"Don't." She held up a finger. "You can throw insults at me for the stupid, hurtful things I did to you, but do not mock my sobriety. Or my desire to be honest."

He narrowed his eyes, his gaze delving into hers so deeply her heart swerved in an effort to avoid being seen. It was hard to give up the shield of alcohol and subterfuge and stand in the truth of her past. It was even harder to admit she wanted something she had failed at more times than she could count.

She fought back the press of heat behind her eyes. Change was *hard*. It meant making difficult choices that the old Carmel would have refused out of selfishness. It meant evaluating every relationship in her life and deciding whether it was worth keeping. Worth fighting for.

"I didn't say I wouldn't help you." She felt her way forward as though inching onto thin ice. In the dark. While it creaked and cracked. "I said I wouldn't lie to her." That was no way to start a relationship with anyone. She knew that from experience.

She wanted to help him, though.

If she had a chance to make up to Damian for the way she'd treated him, if she could help him in a way that truly mattered to him, if she could give him more time with his grandmother, she wanted to do that.

Even if it would be hard for her.

"It sounds like your grandmother wants to see us resolve our differences. I would like to end our marriage on a better note, so I'm willing to make a genuine effort toward *that* kind of reconciliation."

His expression remained flinty enough to cause her confidence to falter, but she persevered.

"One that is civil and…" She cleared her throat. "Less angry. Spell out what you would need from me."

His expression hardened at the word "need." His jaw worked while he debated something, then, "She would expect you to stay in the villa with me. I mean that, Carmel. No flitting away for shopping and parties. If you step one foot off this property, keep going because the deal is off."

"Sounds like rehab," she said pleasantly.

"I thought your sobriety was not to be mocked?"

"Oh, I'm allowed to do it. It's the only way I can cope. But on that note, ask your staff to put all your alcohol in storage. Have a drink if you want one, but I'd rather not be confronted with temptation everywhere I look. This will be stressful enough. What about work? Can I set up a remote office here?"

"For the five minutes a day that you'll be calling in your career? Use mine." His mouth tilted downward with derision.

"See? I fully accept that insult." Because she would make him eat it. She cared deeply about Davenwear. He would soon see that. "What about…"

She lost her nerve.

His brows went up.

She cleared her throat. She toyed with a button on the jacket draped over her arm. Her chest began to burn. Heat rose to bloom in her cheeks. But she had to ask.

"What about sex?"

"I'm not going to touch you." His voice turned gritty, and his gaze lashed across her once before he looked away again.

"What a relief." Sarcasm wasn't a lie, was it?

"I'm doing what I have to, to persuade Zoia to get the treatment she needs. That's all this is. If you upset her, you're gone."

"I won't."

He snorted. "I'll be shocked if you're still here by morning."

Oh, she would be here. Every one of his little digs only hardened her resolve.

CHAPTER THREE

"Yaya," Damian spoke in Greek as he escorted Carmel through the door of the cottage. "This is Carmel. She has agreed to stay and work on our—"

Carmel caught the word *schési*, but knew it wasn't *marriage*.

"My grandmother, Zoia," he said, switching to English. "I told her we're going to work on our relationship."

"Ah." Apparently, he didn't like lying outright to his grandmother, either. "It's nice to meet you." Carmel made herself attempt the language, even though her accent was appalling. She hurried across before Zoia could rise. "Please sit."

"You speak Greek?" Zoia smiled with surprised pleasure. She wore glasses and a dark blue dress with a light cardigan and slippers. Her iron-gray hair was swept back into a knot. Her sharp gaze and reserved, assessing demeanor made Carmel aware of all her crimes against the woman's grandson.

"Very little." Carmel pressed the woman's soft, cool hand gently between her own. "How are you?"

"Much better now that Damian has brought you to meet me. Finally."

"Carmel will stay with me until you go to Athens for

your surgery," Damian said. "You'll have lots of time to get to know her, so you can rest until dinner."

"What happens after my surgery?" Zoia asked him.

"We'll see," Damian said mildly.

"Humph." Zoia's gaze moved between them, weighing whether she was being snowed, but her lunch was ready so she waved them out.

"Since when do you speak Greek?" Damian asked as they walked across to his villa.

"That's generous," she said dryly, considering she'd butchered every word. "My brother's mother was Greek. I was always afraid he was talking about me behind my back so I learned enough to eavesdrop. You'll be shocked to hear that I had an exaggerated sense of my importance. He never said one thing about me. Oh, this is lovely."

They walked through a stone archway into a shaded courtyard that accessed a side entrance into the house. Inside, the staff had opened the series of glass doors off the living room onto the walled terrace and pool.

The decor was white and bright, with accents of blue and yellow. The floors were an earthy stone, and contemporary paintings hung on the walls. The furniture was tasteful and comfortable. Inviting.

She caught him watching her take it in. "This is the property you were trying to buy when we met."

"Yes." His expression hardened. He cast a critical eye around the space. "I renovated so Zoia would have a suite here, but she's been in the cottage since she married and prefers it. Ah, here's Lethe."

A middle-aged woman in a simple beige dress came down the stairs and offered a polite smile.

"Lethe keeps the house running." He switched to

Greek so the other woman would understand. "Lethe's husband is my estate manager. You met Pirro when we arrived. This is Carmel. She'll be staying in the room next to mine. We'll have lunch by the pool when it's ready and dinner with Zoia in the gazebo. Before you do anything else, will you sweep the house for alcohol and put it in the wine cellar? Don't serve any with meals."

"Of course. Please tell me if there's anything else I can do to make your stay more comfortable," she said to Carmel before she moved into what Carmel presumed was the kitchen.

Damian led the way up the stairs to a huge bedroom with a king-size bed, love seat and full bathroom.

She dropped her things on the bed as she moved to open the double doors, and stepped onto the balcony. Outside, the fragrance of the geraniums in the box along the rail filled the air while she took in the stunning view over the pool and out to sea. The horizon was a blurred line between the rippled water and the dome of blue sky.

"This is really beautiful." Leaning out, she saw the wall of Zoia's cottage where a trellis was covered in flowers. Looking in the other direction, she asked, "Is the orange grove yours? Can I walk there?"

"Yes. The vineyard beyond it is also mine."

She glanced at him and saw his gaze come up from her backside. She didn't know whether to be flattered considering his harsh, *I'm not going to touch you*, but she definitely tingled under his notice.

He looked back into the bedroom. "I initially planned to make this room my office, but it gets all the midday sun. I'm mostly here in the summer so I prefer to work across the hall, on the cooler side of the villa."

"How do I get things delivered here?"

"That didn't take long," he said wearily. "What is it you think you can't live without, Carmel?"

"A change of clothes? My work laptop. Feminine protection." That one was nonnegotiable. She had some emergency supplies in her bag, but not enough for more than a couple of days. "Basically, everything I left in Atlas's apartment because I didn't know I was going to be confined here like Persephone."

"Are you calling me Hades? I haven't even started to make this hell for you."

"It sounds like you expect me to share your toothbrush so, yeah, I think you have."

His mouth twitched with reluctant amusement. "That won't be necessary. Give me your brother's address. My assistant will collect your things and have them delivered tomorrow."

"Thank you." She slipped past him to the bed where she dug into her purse for her phone. "Atlas's driver could probably drop my suitcase at your building. Let me make some calls, then I'll freshen up and meet you downstairs for lunch?" She kicked off her shoes and sat cross-legged on the bed.

"Make yourself at home," he said with irony.

She curled her toes, self-conscious, but if he noticed, he didn't say anything, only walked out and closed the door behind him.

She flopped onto her back and let out a breath she'd been holding since leaving London. For a few minutes, she simply concentrated on relaxing, allowing her adrenaline to subside and her limbs to go limp.

She had desperately needed this break from Damian's

dynamic presence to gather her composure, but how was she supposed to do that? She had agreed to spend the next two weeks with him! *Here*. In his home. Sleeping in a room beside *his*.

Through the wall, she heard faint, muted noises that suggested he was changing. Now she was picturing his naked chest and powerful thighs with a strip of black briefs—

Popping her eyes open, she gave herself a mental shake and forced herself to make the necessary calls, starting with Atlas's housekeeper, then a few key personnel in her office.

She contemplated how much to say to Atlas as she washed her face and brushed her hair, then repinned it. When she felt suitably back to full armor, she checked the time. It was still early morning in New York. She could get away with a voice mail, which would let him hear her sincerity better than a text would convey.

"I swear to you I'm fine," she began without any other greeting. "But I'll be working remotely for a few weeks, taking care of some old business. I won't be able to make Stella's birthday. I'm sorry about that. Genuinely. Don't be mad." She quickly rethought that. "Go ahead and be mad if you want to. I'm not the boss of your feelings. But I'll make it up to her. If anything comes up at work, you can call me, but I'd rather have some privacy while I deal with this so butt out." She almost ended it there, then quickly added, "Thank you for letting me stay in your apartment. Give my love to Stella."

Ugh. *Feelings*. She couldn't say she loved Atlas. Their relationship had been too contentious for too many years, but she appreciated him. Deeply. And she genuinely liked

Stella. She was the bridge they needed to get along, so Carmel regularly told Atlas how much she liked her. Men loved to be flattered on their decision-making, and telling her brother he had married well was never a bad move.

She listened to the voice mail, hit Send, then walked downstairs barefoot, not ready to face Damian, but she had to. How else would she make good on her promise and *try* to improve their relationship?

Damian had a well-developed core of cynicism, especially where Carmel was concerned, so he had to question whether she purposely left her balcony doors open so he could overhear the message she recorded from where he sat beside the pool.

As was his habit when he arrived at the villa, he had changed for a cooling dip—something he had needed more than ever today, despite the fact it was merely a warm spring day, not the height of summer. He was having second and third thoughts about asking her to stay, but reasoned that prolonging his grandmother's life was worth the strain of having Carmel in his home. He wasn't the naive idiot he'd been at twenty-six.

Still, it was strange to have someone in the villa with him. He was always aware of his grandmother nearby, always concerned about her well-being. He planned his days around spending as much time with her as possible without tiring her, but he typically had the house to himself. He liked it that way. His life in Athens was grueling. He traveled a lot and regularly put in twelve-to sixteen-hour days, breaking only to eat and sleep.

He'd been called a workaholic, but he didn't see it that way. From the time his mother had left him here, he'd seen his grandparents working long, hard hours. It was ingrained in him to do it, too. It had paid off. His grandmother was well cared for, and he lived a very good life. When he was here, he took some of the pressure off himself. Or rather, he shifted the focus of his work onto the estate.

Now he had this disruptive energy in his private space, though. Someone he couldn't trust.

He was especially suspicious of the way Carmel wanted to appear cooperative and selfless. As she played back her message, allowing the recording to drift as loudly through the window as the original message, he listened more closely. She claimed she was sorry she couldn't make a birthday party. He didn't doubt she hated to miss a party. Who was this lover she was so worried about offending anyway?

Then he heard again, "Thank you for letting me stay in your apartment," and realized the message was for her brother.

He should have picked up on that from the name "Stella." Atlas Voudouris had recently married a woman from Switzerland. Their affair had created a feeding frenzy online, as these things were wont to do. Damian had paid little attention beyond the end result that Atlas had taken over DVE and his interest there was only from a business standpoint.

It had nothing to do with keeping tabs on Carmel.

"Oh." She came onto the pool deck and halted when she saw him on the lounger. Her eyes were hidden by her black sunglasses, but he sensed her attention dropping to his blue, quick-dry swim shorts. "I didn't realize you were down here."

Her head angled as she self-consciously glanced to her balcony where the doors were still open, wondering perhaps if he'd overheard her.

"No?" He took in the fact she'd smoothed her hair and turned up the cuffs of her trousers to reveal her ankles and bare feet.

The first time he'd seen her, she'd been in a bikini with a sarong slung around her hips. Her blond hair had been falling in wisps from its topknot, framing her tanned face. She'd had the slender build of a model and a kittenish personality. He'd been drawn to her humor and confidence. Her unabashed sex appeal.

He'd been lust-struck, as had every other man in her vicinity. Damian had drawn his own share of interest from the opposite sex, being well-muscled from manual labor and full of confidence and ambition. He'd still been flattered that this beautiful woman with the posh accent singled him out for her attention.

He ignored the twinges of that old pull and rose, moving to the table in the shade where Lethe had set it with salad, pita and tzatziki. He held a chair for her.

"Thank you." Carmel sat and flicked her napkin onto her lap.

He took his own seat and reached to pour from the jug. "Would you prefer lemonade? Or a soft drink?"

"No, I like to keep the ice water in my veins at optimum levels."

"I had forgotten what a dark sense of humor you have." He sipped his own water, finding the taste noticeably plain.

He often added a splash of ouzo when he was relaxing by the pool, but he had decided to join her in teetotaling.

It wouldn't be a hardship. He wasn't a heavy drinker, but he drank when it suited him. This would be an interesting exercise.

Also, he wanted to keep his wits about him.

"How long have you been sober?" he asked as they tucked into the food.

Her expression grew circumspect. "Eight months. Before that, I had a full year."

"Oh? What happened eight months ago? Is that when your father cut you off?"

"No. That happened later and didn't really bother me. No, Atlas got married."

"Were you celebrating?"

"Ha. You don't remember much about my relationship with him, do you?" She set down her fork and sipped her water, studying him from behind her dark lenses. "I don't mind talking to you about my recovery, but is this a safe space? Why do you want to know?"

He wasn't sure. Maybe because he hadn't realized she had such a problem she'd sought help for it. In the short time they'd been together, she had definitely overimbibed, but that wasn't unusual for people in their midtwenties. Also, she'd been on vacation when they met, then they'd married. He hadn't liked seeing her drink to excess, but she hadn't been a mean or sloppy drunk. She'd been bubbly and flirty and given to undressing. That hadn't been a detriment until that last dark day.

"I need to know you won't use anything that I say against me later." Her mouth stretched into a flat smile. "You're angry enough to destroy me, Damian. I accept that, but the quickest way to do me in would be to spike my drink." She tilted her glass. "FYI."

"My taste for vengeance has its limits," he bit out, insulted.

"Don't take my suspicion personally." She shrugged. "I've been burned so many times in group sessions I refuse to take part in them anymore."

"Those twelve-step meetings? Aren't they supposed to be confidential?"

"They are, but stories on my dirty little exploits still earn good money. Some find it too tempting." She stabbed an olive and sealed her lips over it.

"If I wanted to capitalize on something like that, I would have revealed that we're married a long time ago," he pointed out.

"Why haven't you?"

"Shame."

"So this is not a safe space. Good to know." She continued eating.

The silence stretched for three long minutes.

"That was a cheap shot," he admitted. And not nearly as satisfying as he had hoped. "I won't do it again."

Lethe brought out freshly baked spanakopita and skewers of lamb souvlaki, then retreated again.

He thought Carmel was going to leave him in the dark, but she said, "You might remember that I lost my mother when I was twelve? That's the first time I got drunk."

"Her funeral?" That shocked him.

"No. But not long after."

"It was something to do with her heart, wasn't it?"

"She had a thyroid condition that caused arrhythmia." She nodded. "There was always a potential for an event. It happened while I was at school." She kept her eye on her plate while she pushed her food around, brow flinching. "I came home and she was just...not there."

He had felt a kinship over the abruptness of her loss. Like him, she had put up a lot of walls around herself as a result. At the time, he had thought that made them alike. Neither of them was capable of deep connection, but when he proposed, he had believed they could build a decent life on trust and respect and shared resources.

None of which they'd actually had.

"Daddy sent me back to boarding school as soon as the funeral was over, though." She sipped her water. "According to the legions of therapists I've seen over the years, I wasn't ready." Her tone turned pithy.

Boarding school. It should have been the first red flag that they came from very different worlds, but he hadn't thought it mattered until he'd stood in front of her father. Oliver Davenport had firmly slapped him in the face with the fact that where a person was educated mattered very much.

"I'd never been a very good student," Carmel continued in a smooth, unflinching way. It almost sounded rehearsed, but he had a suspicion it was simply something she'd told many times. "Mummy used to advocate for me. She would arrange for me to have more time on a test or would hire me extra tutoring. Daddy thought I needed to apply myself. One day I was crying over failing a quiz and an older girl offered me a drink. It tasted like a milkshake and made all my troubles seem insignificant. As an added bonus, I got found out so I was suspended and sent home." Her brows went up along with the corners of her mouth.

"A win-win," he drawled.

"Exactly. That started a cycle where I would drink and

get kicked out, then come back to even worse grades because I'd missed so much. I'd drink those away and…" She rolled her wrist. "The headmistress finally told Daddy to get me help or they wouldn't take me back. That's how I wound up in my first group session. I shared everything I just told you and two days later, there was a huge story in one of Daddy's rival papers. They eviscerated him as a horrible father who hadn't allowed his daughter to grieve. Daddy was livid."

"At being scooped?"

"Ha!" She leaned forward with a chuckle of delight, face so bright he had to tamp down on a sudden rush of attraction. "How have I never made that joke? I'm stealing it. It's like you've met him," she added with deep irony. "But no. It wasn't the betrayal of my precious privacy, either. He was angry I made him look bad."

That sounded exactly like the man he'd met.

My daughter is a Davenport. She can't be married to a carpetbagger like you.

"I try not to make excuses about why I failed at rehab so many times, but that was a genuine blow to my trust in the process. I tried to manage it on my own, which means I hid my drinking, fooling no one except myself. Those were the modeling years. I had dropped out of school, but Atlas finished his degree and wanted a real job in DVE. Daddy gave him one and said I could have one, too, if I got sober, so away I went to rehab again. That time I talked about how difficult it had been to learn at fifteen that my father had had an affair while my mother was pregnant with me. And that I found out about Atlas when Daddy brought him to live with us. I said I struggled with a sense of not being good enough because Daddy told me to my face that he had to make Atlas his heir because I wasn't smart enough to run DVE."

Parts of that story were common knowledge here in Greece. Atlas had been a competitive swimmer already winning junior games when his father stepped in to support his training. One of Atlas's first sponsorship deals had been for the Davenwear Athletic clothing line. Atlas had modeled it alongside Carmel.

She hadn't talked much about her brother while they'd been married, except in a disparaging way. Hell, they hadn't talked much at all, usually keeping their mouths busy in other ways, but, "That was a brutal thing to say to your child."

"Even more brutal to have that damning statement show up online before the words 'Atlas the Great' had left my mouth. Daddy was scooped *again*." Her lip curled with malicious amusement. "I went straight off the rails." She pointed into the distance. "That's when Atlas had the bright idea for the Davenport Foundation to fund an exclusive clinic outside of London. If they violate my privacy, they lose their funding. I checked in so often, they've given me my own set of keys."

"Really?"

"No." She snorted. "That was hyperbole."

"Not the keys. You've sought help several times?"

"Did you miss the part where I have learning difficulties?"

"Are you making jokes because you don't want to talk about this? Then say that."

"I'm not avoiding... Maybe I am." She sighed, then said flatly, "*I* didn't seek help until a few years ago. Before that, help was pushed onto me when I didn't want it so I didn't accept it."

"Why not?"

"Because I didn't want to change," she said simply. "I didn't have to. Daddy made it very easy for me to continue in my decadent ways. It worked for him. As long as I was unstable, he had a reason to keep me from accessing Mummy's money."

"The money you thought he'd release to you when we married."

"Yes. He also played me and Atlas against each other, telling Atlas he was afraid how I would react if he retired and put Atlas in charge. Then he would tell me that he was keeping Atlas from taking over for *my* sake, because Atlas would go on a power trip."

"But Atlas is in charge of DVE now, isn't he?" It had been all over the headlines a few months ago.

"Yes. The board had their issues with Daddy. He's a tremendous philanderer. That's why he never remarried after Mummy. It was one woman after another, my age or younger." She curled her lip.

So did he.

"The board was afraid Atlas would be the same, so they said he had to be married before they would support him. Daddy picked him out a wife, but of course it was a side deal that would have kept Daddy in place. Atlas married Stella instead. Daddy knew right away his goose was cooked and got in my ear that Atlas was staging a coup. I threw away a year of sobriety because…" She stared at her plate.

He couldn't read her eyes, but the way her mouth

turned down and the way her shoulders slumped spoke of very heavy emotions. Deep introspection and sadness.

"Because?" he prompted.

She drew a breath as though coming out of a trance and picked up her head.

"I thought it's what Daddy wanted. I had never wanted to see how he used my drinking against Atlas, but Atlas was always the one who took me to the clinic. He was furious that day, but he wasn't mad at *me*. And I was so mad at myself for throwing myself off the wagon I voted against Daddy with the board. They installed Atlas and Daddy cut us off as punishment."

"So you are broke."

"I have my salary as president of Davenwear. It's generous. And Atlas would help me if I needed it. I'd rather not ask because..." She wrinkled her nose. "Pride."

He studied her, filtering every word, trying to decide how much of what she had told him he would allow himself to believe. It all sounded plausible, but was delivered with her laissez-faire attitude that had him wondering if it was simply another story told to get what she wanted.

"I don't blame you for not trusting me," she said, reading his skepticism. "*I* don't trust me. I want to believe I can stay here and bring some comfort to your grandmother, but seeing you and facing all the things I did is hard. I was raised to believe that I was special and didn't have to do things that are hard." Her mouth twisted in self-deprecation. "But I've done some very good sharing today, so I'll end our session *here*." She set her fork and knife together on her plate. "And reward myself with dessert."

CHAPTER FOUR

SUSPECTING DAMIAN HAD overheard her calls through the open windows earlier, Carmel closed all her doors after lunch while she spoke to her therapist.

"You don't have to succumb to ultimatums," her therapist reminded her. "You don't have to do penance. You can leave this with lawyers unless reconciliation is something you really want?"

"I don't expect to stay married, no. But I would like a chance to mend fences." There were many people in the world whose opinion no longer mattered to her, but she would always regret that she had lost Damian's respect. She had killed it with her bare hands. If she could earn a shred of that back, if she could give him something he wanted, she was compelled to try.

They talked a little more about how she could work through some things with him, then Carmel ended the call and went to the kitchen to top up her ice water. She genuinely did drink a lot of it through the day, mildly addicted to the jolt of cold in her throat.

Lethe came in the back door while she was there.

"Oh." Lethe smiled with surprise to find her there. "This is for you." She shyly offered a cloth shopping bag. "The boutique at the bottom of the hill caters to tourists.

I picked up what I thought you would need until your things arrive. I had to guess at your size."

"That's so kind." Carmel peered in to see a number of toiletries atop a cotton sundress in shades of butter yellow and green. "How much was it?"

"*Kýrie* told me to put it on the household expenses."

"Oh. Um, thank you." Now she owed Damian? Ugh. "Do you know where he is?"

"Out with Pirro." She waved vaguely toward the hillside.

Carmel took the bag to her room and emptied it on the bed, finding fresh underwear, two swimsuit options, the sundress and some cheap flip-flops.

With quiet glee, she threw off her clothes and pulled on a swimsuit. Moments later, she was wading into the pool, sighing with relief.

After a few lazy laps, she moved to one of the loungers in the shade, thinking about how to smooth things over with Damian.

Their talk at lunch had been difficult. She was used to being the center of attention for one reason or other—she had a history of demanding it—but she had always felt his attention more intensely. It was sexual, but also something more difficult to articulate. She had ample experience with being pursued by men who had buckets of confidence, but Damian's self-assurance was justified. He knew his own worth because he had built it by hand.

The first time she'd met him, she'd been at a pool party on Mykonos. His solar panel company had already been the dominant supplier across the islands, and he had come by to check on an installation. His jeans and collared T-shirt had accentuated his powerful build, and his dismissive glance at the drunken antics of the guests had been the sort of challenge she couldn't resist.

"Join us," she had coaxed him.

"I have three more work sites to check." He'd paused, and the tingle in her breasts and stomach and thighs told her the gaze behind his sunglasses had taken a long look at the bikini she wore. "You're welcome to come with me. I'll bring you back when I'm done."

"I'll get my bag."

She'd been tipsy, of course, and given to following impulse in those days, but she was cautious about putting herself into dodgy situations with men. After a scary moment in her teens, she'd learned to either moderate her drinking or stick with a group.

She was bored with the people she was with, though. Bored with the lifestyle she had locked herself into. No one stopped her leaving, which told her exactly how much they cared about her.

Damian had intrigued her, and something in his casual strength and unapologetic boundaries had made her feel safe for the first time in a long time.

She pulled frayed cutoffs over her bathing suit and kicked into her sandals, then climbed into his boxy utility truck. He took them on a scenic route, windows open, music playing through the tinny radio.

When they stopped at a villa, he moved around the property with comfortable facility, explaining his work to her.

"What do you do?" he asked.

"I model for my father's company." She showed him some of her photos on her phone because they were sexy and flattering.

When she tried to climb a ladder with him, he stopped her. "You've been drinking."

"Not that much," she lied. She used their closeness to loop her arms around his neck.

He caught her around the waist and accepted the invitation of her uptilted mouth, taking her weight and her breath in the same moment.

She was suddenly suspended, captured by a kiss that stole her awareness of anything beyond the hardness of his body against hers and the commanding way he plundered her lips. He smelled sweaty and tasted salty and he was so *hot*. They both were.

When he finally let her slide down so her feet touch the earth, she was uttered dazzled.

"Stay here," he ordered.

"Or you'll do that again?" she teased.

"Or I won't," he warned.

Her heart skipped and her inner rebel thought about defying him, but she feared he might not actually kiss her again if she crossed him so she waited patiently until he came down from the roof.

When he did, he cupped her cheek and said something in Greek that might have been *Good girl* before he kissed her again, slow and lingering.

She glowed when he released her, certain he was pleased with her and that was more potent than any drug could ever be. Not that she did drugs. Alcohol was trouble enough for her to control. She knew deep down she'd be truly in danger if she went down those dark paths.

The rest of the afternoon progressed in the same amiable and sensual fashion. He set his hand on her leg as they drove. When he started to climb the ladder, she kissed him as though he was leaving for war.

At the last house, the owners had been away. They'd snuck into the pool and, since Damian hadn't had a bathing suit, he'd swum naked. She had stripped down, too. They'd heated up more than cooled down, kissing and caressing until she thought she would die.

"Do you have a condom?" she had gasped.

"In my shorts. Let's go into the cabana."

They had, but he hadn't been finished with foreplay. His kisses had trailed down her neck to her pebbled nipples. While the hot suction of his mouth drove her wild, he opened her legs and settled his wide torso there. He began peppering kisses down, sending heat deep into her aching pelvis—

Rain hit her skin.

She jolted awake, disoriented to find herself poolside, but at *his* villa. Her blood was pooled and thick, her loins throbbing with arousal.

Damian stood waist-deep in the pool, chest hair in fine whorls of black across his well-developed pecs. She could see his blue shorts beneath the surface of the water, but she was remembering a nest of dark hair and the thrust of his erection that magical day.

She yanked her attention to the view. Could he tell what she'd been dreaming about? Had she moaned? Had her hand moved in her sleep to anywhere telling?

As a culpable blush seared her cheeks, she threw her legs off the edge of the lounger, saying unnecessarily, "I fell asleep."

"Why?" he asked with suspicion.

"Because I didn't sleep well last night." She'd been nervous about seeing him.

Her stomach was fluttering with all those same nerves along with the jittery ones of sexual awareness. She surreptitiously glanced down at her breasts. They felt heavy and yes, her nipples were pressing against the cups of her top. Hopefully, he would attribute that to the splash of water.

As she entered the pool, he dropped backward and reached his long arms up in a powerful backstroke. She settled on a lower stair where the water came up to her chest, trying to cool her blood or at least hide her arousal.

He settled in the deep end, arms stretched outward against the lip of the pool.

"I spoke to my therapist," she said, trying to move as far from sexy thoughts as possible. "She suggested that I give you an opportunity to tell me how my actions affected you. She said I should just listen. Is that something you want to do?" She braced herself because she knew it would hurt either way.

He made a noise that was somewhere between a bark of laughter and a choke of dismay.

"Who the hell *are* you? I don't recognize this tentative version of you. It seems fake."

"Is that your biggest grievance? That I'm not offering reasons to hate me?"

He was very still as he stared her down from the far end of the pool. Then he snorted. "No."

"I ran up your credit card," she recalled. "I think it was around ten thousand euros. I had the bank cut a cashier's check for that amount with compounded interest at the average rate for the past five years. It's in the envelope with the divorce papers."

"I didn't take your father's bribe. I won't take yours."

"My father did insult you," she acknowledged. "And I let that happen. I set you up for it. I apologize. I can't make him say he's sorry, but I can promise it wouldn't happen again. Not unless you go looking for him yourself."

"The things you did don't matter to me, Carmel. What I can't *stand* is how stupid you made me feel. I couldn't fathom how I fell for so many lies. You broke my ability to trust anyone, especially women. All the fish in the sea became piranhas. *That's* my biggest grievance against you."

She swallowed, arms looped around her knees, lips sealed while she let him continue.

"All I want from you is for you to be polite to my grandmother for two weeks. This cute little trust exercise of yours is pointless. It won't change anything because I will never believe anything you say."

Her throat was too tight to speak. Her chest was in knots. She could only nod, accepting his harsh judgment and antipathy.

"For God's sake, fight back. Acting meek only makes me feel like a bully. Is that your intention?"

She lifted her gaze from the bottom of the pool, meeting his narrowed stare across the gulf between them. Did he really think she'd forgotten how to be mean? Or that the truth was the sharpest weapon of all?

"You married me for my money, Damian. I told you my father had promised to give me access to my trust once I was married, and you whisked me to Gibraltar the very next day. Daddy was the one who lied about giving me access to it, not me. And yes, when it came down to it, I chose him and the life of comfort he already offered me over gambling on your promise to do the same. He was the devil I knew. I'm sorry you came away thinking all women are as faithless as me, but that's between you and your ego because that's all I damaged. I asked you if you loved me and you said, 'How could I?'"

Another spike of anguish went straight into her throat as she recalled that.

"We'd known each other for eight days. You were holding divorce papers," he reminded her grittily. "You only said it after sex so don't try to tell me that *you* meant it."

Fair. In those days she had said it to anyone from the girlfriend emigrating to America to the pool boy who brought her a mimosa. The truth was, even though her mother had loved her ferociously, after she was gone, no one had loved her. The few good friends she'd had at school had dwindled away, and everyone else had loved her money. Her father hadn't loved her. She had made sure that Atlas never would.

What she'd felt for Damian had been the most painful crush she'd had on anyone ever. It had been new and sharp and frightening because it took up so much space inside her. Because she knew how much it hurt to love and lose.

She hadn't known how to handle it or express it so she'd used those words that had lost all meaning to her, afraid to find a more accurate vocabulary until she knew he felt the same.

He hadn't.

"The truth is, after losing my mother, I stopped believing anyone could love me," she said starkly. "It's the source of all my problems. Or so I've been told."

It took all her effort to make her stiff muscles stand. Water sluiced off her body, falling away like all the nascent hopes she had held close to her heart all her life.

She snapped out her towel and wrapped it around her middle, too flayed by this conversation to continue it.

"You're right. Trying to talk through things serves no purpose. It only makes things worse so let's not bother. What time is dinner? I don't want to keep your grandmother waiting."

The sun was setting when Damian walked across to collect Zoia.

Carmel was already in the gazebo as he passed it. Her back was to him and she was in shadow so he only saw her silhouette in a sundress, hair gathered in a ponytail at her nape.

I stopped believing anyone could love me. It's the source of all my problems.

She had delivered the statement with her signature, throwaway sarcasm. He'd resolved not to believe a word she said, or fall for ploys for sympathy, but that was as starkly truthful as it got. Which was an unsettling thought.

Because he could relate, having had doubts as a child about his own lovability. When his mother had left him here, his grandparents had kept him, but his grandfather had had a lot of mixed emotions, initially resisting Damian's presence. He had wanted to find Damian's father. Ignorance was no excuse for failing to take responsibility for the child he'd made. Clearly that shiftless man's attitude had rubbed off on their daughter if she had abandoned her son with them.

Over time, Damian had earned Eurus's respect by working hard without complaint. Zoia's warmth had made up for Eurus's ambivalence, but the nagging sense of rejection and being unwanted had stayed with Damian into adulthood, until he learned his mother hadn't deliberately abandoned him here.

Learning the truth didn't erase the fact that Damian had conditioned himself to eschew love. It wasn't an emotion he wanted or needed. He looked after Zoia because she was his family. She had given him a home when he had no one else. He had a duty to do the same for her.

Whatever he'd felt for Carmel had held shades of that sense of responsibility. He'd been enthralled by her and flattered by the enthusiasm she'd shown for his work. Her seeming willingness to invest in him had fueled his ambitions. She'd made it sound as though her father kept her on a leash by holding on to the purse strings so he'd thought he was solving a problem for her by offering marriage. And yes, she had promised to help him buy this estate. If she had, it would have been theirs together. In that respect, he had believed they were building a life together.

Their marriage had seemed logical and practical and maybe it had also been a shortcut to where he wanted to go, but he had accepted he was taking on a lifetime commitment.

He'd spent this afternoon thinking about all she'd told him over lunch, about her journey into recovery. When he'd returned to find her asleep by the pool, he'd been struck by how innocent and angelic she looked. And alluring with those new, lusher curves.

It had been hard to drag his eyes from her. When she didn't wake as he was washing off the field dust at the outdoor shower, he'd begun to wonder if something heavier than sleep was keeping her from rousing. A flick of water had had her sitting up, though. Her nipples had already been hard beneath her turquoise bikini top, and a guilty blush had risen to her cheeks.

Why?

His brief thought that she'd been having erotic dreams was titillating enough that he'd had to push himself into lapping the pool to cool his ardor. He had made himself stay in the deep end as he caught his breath, distancing himself as far from temptation as possible.

When she had invited him to air his grievances, he'd nearly howled. He was *furious* that she wasn't making it easy to hate her, but his greatest complaint was that he still found her so mesmerizing.

It was so misplaced! Either she was still a woman struggling to overcome personal demons by making amends, or she was here with a fresh batch of lies. Neither made her a woman he could or should pursue.

This was a ridiculous situation, one he never should have put himself in, but this wasn't about him, he reminded himself. This charade was for his grandmother.

"The doctor wants to see you in his office tomorrow," Damian told Zoia as they carefully navigated the graveled path to the gazebo. "We'll go tomorrow after lunch."

They liked to eat outdoors when the weather allowed. It wasn't too far for her to walk, there was a comfortable breeze, but also a sheltered corner where she wouldn't grow chilled. And it was a pleasant atmosphere, overlooking the water.

"You aren't wasting time, are you?" she chided. "What about spending time with your wife?"

"She's having dinner with us." He nodded toward the gazebo.

"*You* need to spend time with her. Woo her. Take her on a date."

"If she's still here tomorrow, I'll consider taking your advice," he said dryly.

Zoia didn't talk again until they had joined Carmel, then she said, "You'll still be here tomorrow, won't you?"

"I've never been someone who knows when to quit," Carmel said with an ironic twist of her mouth. She seated herself while he held his grandmother's chair.

Damian tried not to ogle the expanse of skin across the top of Carmel's chest and shoulders, bared by the simple dress. Of course, she was so naturally beautiful, she would look good in a burlap sack.

"Tell me about yourself," Zoia said once they were settled. "Tell me why you ended your marriage before it started."

"Oh." Carmel flashed him a look that was part disbelief, part question. *How honest do you want me to be?* "You may need to translate. My Greek may not be up to the task."

She wouldn't lie to his grandmother, she seemed to be telling him, but she would allow him do it, if he wanted to revise anything she said.

"My father disapproved," she said in English to Zoia, waiting for Damian to translate. "He wanted me to marry the son of his friend. He was angry that I didn't ask his permission before I married Damian."

"Why didn't you?" Zoia asked.

"Because I knew he wanted me to marry the son of his friend," Carmel said wryly.

"Ah." Zoia shot Damian an astute look, correctly understanding that he'd been cannon fodder. "Is that why you didn't ask for a divorce sooner?"

"I did. Damian refused." Carmel looked to him, perhaps wondering if he would prevaricate.

He didn't, even though he had never told Zoia that. He had called to tell her when the deed was done, explaining they were carrying on to London to tell Carmel's father. Damian had asked Zoia to keep the news under her hat until he brought his bride home. Whatever enthusiasm had been in his voice during that call was the source of her earlier "I know how you felt about her" remark.

Because he returned home alone. Furious. Spurned. Zoia had asked him a few times what had happened. He'd always said as little as possible. When she had occasionally asked if he wanted to marry again, he'd told her he was still married to Carmel, but he had never wanted to rock that boat.

"Daddy threatened to disinherit me if I didn't divorce Damian," Carmel continued. "I was afraid I would lose my mother's company. It was all I had of her, and I had already put a lot of my own effort into its success. So I told him it was done and, whenever he tried to push me to marry anyone, I made myself unpleasant enough my suitor would be turned off."

Meaning she would go on a bender and create a stir?

A sharp spear of concern went through him. He skipped relaying that part and explained that Davenwear was athletic clothing and wearable tech.

"Carmel's mother found a pocket of opportunity in

women's wear that was engineered for specific sports. The clothes were fashionable and well-made, so they became popular streetwear. Her father comes from a legacy of publishing. He provided the start-up investment for the clothing company, but soon the clothes were keeping his media operations afloat. When Carmel's mother passed, her father poured all his resources into taking the clothing brand global, which included asking his children to model for the line."

He saw why Carmel had wanted to fight for it. It was a profitable enterprise still capable of growth.

"I don't remember telling you all of that," Carmel said with bemusement.

"I can read," he said dryly.

"You're a model! No wonder you're so pretty," Zoia said.

"Thank you. You should see my brother, though. Oh! You may have. Atlas Voudouris?"

"The swimmer? He's your brother?" Zoia's voice rose with excitement, and she touched Damian's arm. "We watched him win gold, didn't we? I remember that very well. How did you never tell me we're related to someone so famous?" she chided Damian, then asked Carmel, "But how is your brother Greek and you are not?"

Carmel's mouth tilted into bitter amusement. "How do you think? My father had an affair with Atlas's mother. She reached out when Atlas was doing so well with his swimming, asking Daddy to fund his training. Daddy said Atlas had to come live with us and become his successor at DVE. He didn't want to remarry and start a new family with anyone else, not when he had a son who was perfectly capable."

"Are you not?" Zoia asked with surprise.

"No. Which used to be a bone of contention between us, but he's welcome to it. I prefer to focus on my mother's company."

Zoia asked about it and Carmel became more animated. She always had cheeky stories at the ready and soon told one about a prototype for a sports bra that came out laughably wrong, then a pizza party that was accidentally ordered from an establishment that used strippers for deliveries.

"HR was not happy with me," she assured Zoia, who was laughing with enjoyment. "Then there was the day I thought I'd put us into bankruptcy. Everyone knows my math skills are terrible. I usually have my staff check all my work, but we had this one deal that had to be closed by midnight. I double-checked everything and signed off on the quote. Two days later, I got a notice from accounting saying, 'This math is wrong.' I was *horrified*. The order was huge and our profit margin was *so* narrow. Backing out of the contract would have been a disaster."

"What did you do?" Damian asked when he caught up on the translation. He was as much on the edge of his seat as Zoia.

"I had missed a zero on the end of the profit estimation. It was actually ten times what I'd calculated. The whole thing was a huge success. But, based on my math skills, it could have gone the other way just as easily!"

Zoia clapped her hands, delighted.

Damian couldn't remember the last time he'd seen his grandmother so lively. Even if Carmel's story was pure fiction, he didn't care. He liked seeing that sparkle in Zoia's eye.

"It sounds like you enjoy your work a great deal," Zoia said.

"I do. It makes me feel like I'm keeping a piece of my mother alive."

"And do you ever think about becoming one yourself?"

"A mother?" She flashed another look at Damian.

"She doesn't want to answer that one," he said in Greek. "It's too personal."

"No, I don't mind." Carmel's hand rested on his wrist in the briefest of touches, like a butterfly that was gone before it had fully alighted, but he felt the contact like an ice burn. "When I was very young, I presumed I would have a family. I failed a lot while I was at school, though. That's another reason I gave up on our marriage so easily." She glanced at Damian, shoulder hitching in a pained acknowledgment. "Failing is the one thing I've always been good at. Since then, I've made many poor life decisions. I believe it's best if I don't become a parent."

"I hope you reconsider. Children are a great comfort when you're old." Zoia sent a misty-eyed smile to Damian. "Grandsons especially."

"I never think about growing old," Carmel confided wryly. "Should I?"

"It will happen whether you think about it or not," Zoia said philosophically. "And when it does, you tire easily and must excuse yourself from good company. Come see me tomorrow. I'll show you my garden."

CHAPTER FIVE

CARMEL TRIED TO help Lethe clear the table while Damian escorted Zoia home, but Lethe assured her she had it under control.

With little else to do, Carmel wandered to the top of the steps leading to the beach. They were long and steep, cut into the stone cliff, but were gated near the bottom. She climbed back up in time to see Damian crossing back to the villa.

"Are you keeping me in?" she asked, thumbing over her shoulder.

He veered toward her. "No, it's... I'll show you."

He went down to a small landing and showed her the small storage locker with rolled straw mats and a beach umbrella, then gave her the code to punch into the glowing keypad. He held the gate for her before following and drawing it closed behind them.

She meandered onto the pocket of sugary sand spread in a horseshoe of rough rocks. In the liminal light of dusk, with the purple sky turning the water inky blue, the atmosphere was spellbinding. Romantic.

"It's difficult to hike into, but there's a path from some ruins about two kilometers away," Damian said. "Not many bother, but it's listed on a few websites as a nude beach so the people who come here are looking for privacy."

"Oh? Is that something your grandparents started?"

He ignored that. "Visitors think our stairs are a shortcut to get back up so..." He pointed at the sign reading No Entry Private Property in a dozen languages. "There's usually a good patch of shade next to that rock. If you walk in that direction, watch for the tide coming in. People have been inadvertently stranded. The swimming is safe, though. It's shallow, and there aren't any dangerous currents."

"Did you swim here when you were growing up?"

"I wasn't allowed. There were nudists down here," he told her.

"Uh-huh. Were you one of them?"

"Sometimes," he allowed with a shrug of one shoulder.

"Ha."

His profile was difficult to read in the fading light, but she thought his expression softened. Either way, he was heart-stoppingly handsome, staring out at the water in his quietly intense way.

She remembered what Zoia had asked and hesitantly said, "I'm not trying to start anything, but have you never met anyone you wanted to move on with? Have a family and all that? For Zoia's sake?"

He sent her a flinty look. "There were many reasons I didn't bother asking for a divorce. I didn't want to make it easy for you. That's petty, but true. I didn't want the expense, especially if it became contentious. I didn't want to risk you taking a piece of what I'd managed to build."

She had to look to the water to hide the way his low opinion of her made her ache.

"As for children, I'm like you in that I'm not sure I'd make a decent parent, so why become one?"

"Am I wrong in thinking family is important to you?"

"Zoia is. My top priority has always been to ensure she was comfortable and secure. It's only lately, as I face that she's in her golden years, that I'm realizing I've built an empire that has no obvious heir."

"It's such a funny system, isn't it? Before Atlas came along, I was presumed to be my father's only successor. I felt a lot of pressure, especially because I didn't have the tools for it. That wasn't just on me and my learning struggles. That was on Daddy for not investing in me in a way that made me feel up to it. I think you'd make a good father, though. I haven't been around a lot of children. They kind of annoy me, to be honest. I prefer to be the cutest person in a room—"

He snorted.

"—but they're vulnerable and need to be loved. You're very protective of Zoia. Doting. I think you'd be the same with any children you had."

He considered that before saying, "She was never able to get pregnant after my mother. The original farm had been in my grandfather's family for generations. Pappous wanted my mother to marry a local boy and take over from them, but my mother didn't like the quiet island life. She went to university in Athens and came home to tell them she was pregnant by a boy who lived in Australia. Pappous wanted his name so he could call and tell the man he needed to marry her. They argued and she left, insisting she could raise me on her own. Yaya says my mother was her father's daughter, very stubborn."

"Oh? Did you inherit that trait, do you think?" He absolutely had.

"I'll never admit to it," he said blithely, making her smirk.

She wanted to ask him about his mother and whether he'd ever heard from her, but knew it was a difficult subject for him. He had barely mentioned it when they'd married and only because she'd already shared about losing her own mother.

"I remember you talking about your grandfather as being very strict." He had already been gone when they met, but he'd continued to cast a long shadow over Damian, fueling his determination to expand the estate. To *achieve*.

"He had old-fashioned standards. Children should be seen and not heard. Earn your keep. He instilled a strong work ethic in me."

She smiled at the faint praise. "Whereas Daddy kept me quiet by giving me anything I asked for."

"Who inherits your father's assets now that Atlas staged a coup and you sided with him?"

"I imagine we'll split whatever Daddy leaves, but the way he was talking, he was planning to spend every last pound on flying lessons for pigs, purely to spite us. Which is fine. I still have shares in DVE. With Atlas running it, I know he'll keep it solvent. I am supporting myself, you know. Ask Atlas if you want to. He'll confirm it. The paperwork confirms it. I left the envelope on your desk. Read it."

"It doesn't matter what it says." He spoke without heat, only stating a fact. "I won't sign anything until you've completed your side of the bargain."

"It matters to me if you believe me, though."

"I know what pressure tactics are, Carmel." He sent her a bored look. "I've used them myself. Sign now, before I change my mind. Otherwise, I'll up the price."

"I'm not threatening to change anything!"

"As long as I refuse to read it, you can't. Or you can and I won't know."

"Great. Let's stay in Schrodinger's marriage, then. One that's both alive and dead until you open the envelope."

"That's my plan."

"You really are stubborn."

"We should get back before it's too dark to see the stairs."

They moved up to the small landing where he opened the gate for her and waited while she passed through, then followed and firmly closed it again.

It was very dark here in the deep well of the stairs, but the heat of the day lingered, radiating from the stone walls. She found the rail and began the ascent, aware of his footsteps behind her.

She stumbled when she caught the toe of the slippery new flip-flops on the lip of a step.

Damian was right there, his strong hand looping around her stomach to steady her.

She caught her breath and straightened, whirling as his arm fell away.

Carmel was one step above him so they were eye to eye. Much too close in the narrow, hidden space. Her hand was on his shoulder. She didn't remember putting it there, but there it was, soaking up the solidness of him.

She told herself to turn and keep walking, but her feet wouldn't move. She couldn't read his expression in the shadows, could only see his silhouette against the twilit sky behind him. She could only feel the tension in him as they stood frozen, caught in a time slip where they were five years younger and touching each other was permissible and natural. Irresistible.

It was only when he drew a breath that she realized her hand had slid to his neck. She felt the tendons at the top of his shoulders contract. Wide palms found her hips, urging her to tip forward.

She did and he slid his arm around her. Her feet left the step, but he held her so tightly she had no fear, only the weightless sense of floating she'd experienced the first time they kissed.

And here was the heat and hunger of his lips. Damp and commanding as he consumed her, kissing her hard, but he wasn't trying to hurt her. No, she was the one who was pressing her mouth with bruising force to his, heart thudding with the shock of desire.

This was the crash of two elements that had been magnetized and held apart, but now they snapped together and melded at a particle level, orienting to each other. Trying to occupy the other's space. Attempting to become one.

He turned, and she felt the hard wall of bricks behind her. The angled rail was under her butt. She picked up her legs to grasp them around his waist and felt the column of his erection press to the notch of her thighs. The firm cup of his hand invaded the top of her dress, pushing the cotton aside to claim her braless breast.

He yanked his head up and gazed on the pale swell he had exposed. Her taut nipple was already at attention, eager for the pull of his mouth.

"No," he growled bitterly.

He pushed his hand against the wall, drawing back while keeping her from falling down the stairs.

She had to grasp at the iron-like rail of his arm as she struggled to get her feet under her, then shakily pulled her neckline over her naked breast.

He turned away and started up the stairs ahead of her, leaving her leaning on the wall, breathless. Stunned. Wanting to cry from deprivation. From embarrassment.

She made her way up on trembling knees.

He was already gone from her sight when she reached the top.

Carmel tossed and turned all night, reminding herself she was allowed to be attracted to the man she had married for that very same reason. Plus, she hadn't had sex with anyone since the last time they'd made love five years ago. Of course she was horny!

She was still mortified at how eager she'd been, though. How *easy*. Offering herself as though she was desperate.

And he had pushed her away with scathing anger, sounding repulsed.

Oh, that hurt. She had to breathe through the anguish and clench her eyes against tears because what would soaking her pillow do? Nothing.

Twice she rose, thinking to start walking to the ferry in the dark only to fall back into bed with a whimper. *You made a promise. Keep it.*

But how would she even face him?

At some point, she fell asleep, then slept in so late she was freshly embarrassed when she rose. Now he would think she hadn't changed a bit, lolling in bed half the day, recovering from a hangover.

This morning seemed cooler than yesterday, so she put on her pants and blouse and jacket rather than the sundress. She put on armor, really. And she used the little makeup in her purse to mask up with a game face.

When she felt presentable and in control, she went downstairs only to learn Damian was long gone, having left the villa before breakfast, out to view various worksites on the estate with Pirro.

She ate alone and walked across to visit Zoia where she spent a pleasant hour in the garden with her. They talked about innocuous topics since Carmel didn't have the vocabulary to bemoan kissing Damian last night and complaining that he'd rejected her—not that she wanted to confess that, but it sat on her chest like a heavy, jagged boulder.

The garden with its flowers and sundial and buzzing insects was very soothing, though. It grounded her, reminding her that life moved at its own pace. The things that she thought were monumental enough to destroy her rarely were. She was still alive, still sober, merely feeling the feels of being human.

"May I ask you something?" she asked Zoia as she was walking the woman back into the house. "Did you ever look for Damian's father after he came to live with you?"

"No," Zoia said with a small, pained frown. "Our daughter didn't tell us his name, only that he left for Australia before he knew she was carrying Damian. We learned it eventually, when she didn't return and we had to put him in school. We were able to get his birth certificate. By then..." Zoia shook her head, her gaze far away and filled with melancholy. "I didn't know where my daughter had gone. I didn't want some stranger taking my grandson. I didn't let Eurus look for him."

"Damian has never tried to find him?"

"I don't think so."

"That's sad to think there's a man out there who doesn't know he made such a good man."

Zoia smiled up at her and patted the arm she clutched. "He is good, isn't he? I'm glad you see that. I've been so worried about him. What if I have this surgery and I don't pull through? That would leave him with no one. Knowing he has you is a great comfort."

The way the older woman looked at her made Carmel's heart pinch with contrition.

"I promised him I would stay until your surgery and I promise *you* that I'll be in his life anytime he needs me, but I think you should know that we don't plan to stay married. I came here to tell Damian I'm sorry and ask for a divorce. We were never in love. We married too fast. It was never a real marriage. There's nothing to save."

"Then why be here at all?" she challenged lightly. "You wouldn't bother to give an old woman hope unless you felt some yourself."

Carmel smiled weakly, unwilling to argue and not quite able to deny it. She did have hopes where Damian was concerned. Foolish hopes she avoided acknowledging. She told herself she wanted him to forgive her when, really, she wanted him to like her. She wanted him to want her the way she wanted him.

Uncomfortable with those thoughts, she left Zoia in her chair and she went back to the villa to change. It was definitely not cooler today, but at least her things from Athens had arrived. She pulled on shorts and a tank top, then settled into Damian's office with her laptop.

Since she'd never been book smart, she tended to make

her decisions with her gut—something that drove people like Atlas mad. He was all about reports and statistics and whatever else could be charted on a spreadsheet.

His "show your work" mentality was the nightmare of school all over again, but Carmel had assembled a crack team of nerds to help her. It made for a tedious process of reverse engineering the decisions she had already made in her head and instinctively knew were sound, but it was always nice to prove she was right so she plugged in her earbuds and dug into the materials they had sent her.

With his blood ignited by their kiss on the stairs, Damian had barely slept. He'd been far too aware of Carmel in the room next to him, ears pricked for the sound of her leaving.

Or coming to him.

He had eased the worst of his libido's ferocity in a hot shower, but sexual hunger sat in his groin like a toothache. One that hadn't found proper relief in five drought-laden years. He'd dated. Kissed a few women. He *wanted* to have sex, but after Carmel, there'd always been something bland and mechanical in the process that wasn't any different than using his fist.

He'd always blamed Carmel for that, thinking she had put a stake through the heart of his sex drive. His mistrust of women had made it impossible for him to feel truly aroused by them anymore.

But no. His trust in Carmel was in the proverbial basement, but his response to her last night had been so strong, he'd nearly nailed her in the stairwell without a thought to the consequences.

Had she been trying to manipulate him by offering

herself that way? He hadn't stuck around to find out. He'd used the last shred of self-control he possessed and walked away.

Then he woke at dawn and threw himself into the kind of backbreaking labor he'd done alongside his grandfather while growing up: cleaning up fallen branches and digging post holes to repair a fence.

Pirro interrupted him midday. "Lethe asked if you'd like her to take your grandmother to her appointment? She has to run into the village anyway."

Damn, he'd nearly forgotten about that.

"No, I want to do it." He needed a shower, though. "Thanks."

He wiped his hands on the seat of his jeans and walked back to the villa.

As he climbed the stairs, Carmel's voice grew in volume, singing a pop tune about everyone in a bar getting tipsy.

He paused in the doorway to listen, unable to help himself.

She was engrossed in something on her laptop, brow pulled with concentration as she used the top of a pen to follow a line across the screen, voice clear as a bell as she sang about her history with a certain kind of whiskey.

Her gaze strayed upward and she jolted with fright when she saw him.

"Oh, my God!" She dropped the pen and pulled an earbud from her ear. "How long have you been there?"

"Since you ordered a double shot of whiskey," he said, referencing the lyrics. "I didn't mean to startle you."

"Was I singing?" She winced. "I don't realize I'm doing it. Sorry."

"Don't apologize." Her voice was beautiful. "I do have to question your choice of song, though."

"I know." She grinned cheekily. "But it's so catchy." She flicked her gaze to the damp patch in the middle of his shirt. Her expression sobered as though she suddenly remembered how they'd left things last night. Pink stole into her cheeks. "Do you need the office? I can move to my room." She started to close her laptop.

"No, I'm showering then taking Zoia to the doctor for some tests."

"Okay. Um, before you go…" She cast a wary look past him, but he'd already told Lethe to leave on her errands. Her gaze dropped to the laptop she had closed, and she ran her thumb along the seam. "About last night…"

This ought to be good. He crossed his arms and leaned his shoulder into the doorjamb.

She lifted her lashes to peek at him, chin still tucked. "Do we need to talk about it?"

"I thought I said all that needed to be said." "No" was a complete sentence, wasn't it?

"You did." The red in her cheeks deepened. "I only wanted to say that I agree with you."

Really. That was annoying. Some perverse part of him wanted her to whittle away at his control so they could have explosive sex and he could blame her for it. His gaze kept sliding down to the neckline of her green top while he remembered the feel of her nipple against his palm.

"I'll see you later, then." She opened her laptop and started to pick up her earbud. "Will we eat in the gazebo again? What time?"

He remembered what Zoia had said last night before dinner.

"Can your work wait? Zoia will be tied up for an hour or so, but you could wander through the shops if you come with us. Pick up anything you need."

"Thanks, but now that my stuff is here, I don't need anything." She glanced over the desktop as though taking inventory.

Damn it, he was going to have to spell it out.

"Zoia suggested we spend more time together. She told me I should woo you."

"*Woo* me?" Her cheeks went a bright red again. "That's sounds like a performance neither of us is prepared to give. Especially after you shut down yesterday's improv. I think the trick is to say, 'Yes, and.'"

She looked him dead in the eye, smirking at her own joke.

"I cannot believe the things that come out of your mouth," he said truthfully.

"So you've said." She opened the laptop again. "Explain to her that it's against our rules for me to leave the property."

"I'm willing to make an exception. Call it supervised parole."

"Is this you starting the wooing already? Be still my heart."

"Get in the car and let me buy you an ice cream," he said, abandoning patience.

She closed the laptop again. "Next time, lead with the ice cream. I'm ready when you are."

CHAPTER SIX

THERE WERE ONLY a thousand people living on the island. Damian knew all of them at least by name.

After walking his grandmother into the clinic, he came outside to chat briefly with one of the locals, but pointed across the square where Carmel was picking over an outdoor display of knickknacks, cheap jewelry and beach bags.

"I'm with someone, but come see Zoia when you have time. She would enjoy a visit." As he walked away, he was aware of the curious stare that followed him.

He hadn't thought this through. In trying to please one person—his grandmother—he was about to become gossip for the entire community.

Carmel had a wide-brimmed straw hat on her head when he came up beside her. She held it in place as she tilted her head to look up at him.

"To protect my delicate English complexion?"

"Good idea."

"I want to find something for Stella." She left the hat on and looked through the doorway into the shop. "Do you think they have T-shirts that say *My sister-in-law went to Greece for a divorce and all I got was this lousy T-shirt?*"

He shook his head at her irreverence, refusing to encourage it. "There's an art gallery down the way. Local artists. You might find something there."

She chose a sarong on her way to the payment counter and started to fish out her card, but he handed the proprietor some cash.

"You don't have to do that," Carmel said.

"It saves them some fees." He exchanged a few friendly words with the woman, then they meandered down the alley, which was paved in flat, pale gray stones between bright, whitewashed homes.

"This is so pretty," she commented.

It was. He couldn't recall the last time he'd strolled the streets of his youth. They hadn't changed much. Tiny gardens bloomed with flowers or held tidy rows of tomatoes and peppers. Some doors had a fresh coat of bright blue paint while others were faded. People sat on stoops or drank coffee at wooden tables. Some were eating a late lunch or enjoying an early ouzo. Music and the smell of cooking food drifted from different open windows.

They arrived at the art gallery and entered to find an eclectic mix of pottery, jewelry, paintings and stone sculptures.

"What are you thinking to get her?" Damian asked.

"A tasteful carving of a phallus? That's a joke. But I'd do it just see Atlas's face when she unwrapped it. *What has she told you?*" she asked with mock panic.

That playful sense of humor of hers had been as much a draw for him as the sex five years ago. He'd forgotten that she had made him laugh. Often. It annoyed him that she was so close to doing it again.

"You seem to like her," he commented.

"Stella?" She glanced up from tilting her head to better view an intricate knot of metal ribbons. "The first time I met her, I was genuinely horrible to her. I don't really remember it. It was five years ago. We took a ski holiday to Switzerland the winter after you and I..." She waved between them, then grimaced at how it had ended. "The second time I met her I was even worse. That was when Atlas brought her to home to meet Daddy."

She took the lid off a glazed bowl and peered inside.

"Daddy was a perfect gentleman to you compared to how he treated Stella. I wasn't any better. Atlas should have walked out on both of us, but he got me to the clinic and Stella was so nice to me while I was there. At first, I was highly suspicious. Like, what could she want, right? But she texted a lot and sent me little gifts. I've since learned that she's been knocked around plenty by life, but *she* never crawls into a bottle to escape it. She's too good for Atlas, in my opinion, and he's perfect, so that tells you how much I don't deserve to call her my friend. She insists, though. That's how nice she is."

"You talk down about yourself a lot," he noted.

She didn't say anything, only gently set down a blown glass sculpture and moved to study an abstract painting on the wall.

"Did I strike a nerve? I was only making an observation," he said.

"No, you're right. I'm overcompensating." She shifted to another painting, this one a colorful oil of a local beach. "Daddy is very superior. Nothing is ever his fault. I was the same way for a long time. Now I make a point of acknowledging my shortcomings to prove I'm not like him.

Also, I'm ashamed of my faults so I try to laugh at myself. That way I don't feel the embarrassment so deeply."

He actually hated to see her this humble. It was the boxer, bloody on the canvas. *Get up. Keep fighting.*

"You don't have to do that around me," he told her. "I'm already very familiar with your shortcomings."

She slowly turned her head, brows arched.

"Was that over the line?"

"No. Sarcasm is my love language. Which you know. Flirt. What do you think of this?" She nodded at the painting. "It takes you a minute to see that the mist is actually an image of Aphrodite rising from the water. I really like it." She tilted her head. "Also, I've called Stella a smoke show more than once so it works on that level, too. I'm going to ask if they can ship it to Athens."

As they emerged from the shop, Carmel saw Damian check his phone.

"Is Zoia ready?"

"Not yet. Do you want to walk to the church?"

She looked at the long, zigzagging path that went up the hill to the bright white building perched near the top. "Is that where they sell the ice cream?"

"You've developed quite a sweet tooth, haven't you?"

"It's called self-care, Damian." She did her best to sound condescending. "I'm staving off heat stroke."

"I didn't realize it was a medical emergency." He waved her into an adjacent alley.

When they had their cones, they made their way to a shaded bench overlooking the sea.

"Can I ask—" She cut herself off as she realized he was

watching her sweep her tongue along the ball of strawberry gelato atop her cone. Her heart lurched.

He moved his gaze to the horizon, his profile impassive.

After a moment, he said, "What did you want to ask me?"

"I wondered about your mom. I only bring it up because you mentioned her yesterday. I've always wondered if you ever heard from her," she said tentatively.

"She's dead," he said flatly.

"Oh, my God! I'm so sorry. When did you learn that?"

"Someone gave me a box of her things a few years ago." He bit into his orange gelato and crunchy cone, demolishing it without ceremony, then wiped his mouth and fingers with his paper napkin.

"Where was she? When— I'm sorry." She gave herself a small shake. "You don't have to tell me. It's just that I've thought about her a lot over the years, hoping there was a good explanation for the way she disappeared." At least when her mother disappeared from her life, it hadn't been deliberate.

Damian had confided his confusion over pillow talk. His mother had left him with his grandparents and he had never known his father. He'd channeled his sense of loss and rejection into making himself bigger. Proving his worth if only to himself where Carmel had gone the other way, letting the loss of her mother and her father's manipulations erode her self-esteem.

She'd seen this as common ground, though. They'd both struggled to believe they were loved. She'd thought it made them the same, or at least people who were twisted in a way that allowed them to mesh into something that felt more whole. Soul mates, almost.

Then she had broken those fragile threads of connection, sweeping them away like an unwanted cobweb.

"You don't have to tell me anything about it," she murmured. She knew it remained deeply personal. Still, she glanced up at him, concerned for how it must still affect him.

Their gazes tangled and she felt all those old, silvery threads tug inside her chest.

He frowned toward the water.

"It was strange that she left me here alone," he said somberly. "We usually stayed here together, but she told Zoia she had a job interview and would be back in a few days. They presumed she went back to Athens. That's where they called hospitals and lodged the police report when she didn't come back. She actually flew out of Paros to Malta."

"Paros? Why?"

"Probably because it was closer than going all the way back to Athens." He shrugged.

"But was there really a job interview?"

"We think so. She rented a room at an unlicensed boardinghouse and paid up front. When she never came back for her things, the landlord put them in storage and forgot about it. After he died, his granddaughter was cleaning out his house to sell. She found her bags and thought the photos in her purse might have sentimental value. There was a ticket stub for the ferry to and from our island so she started there. She got Zoia's details and Zoia called me. I flew to Malta and, once I knew where my mother had been, I was able to get a police report. There'd been a hit-and-run on a woman at that time, but she didn't have identification."

"Because it was in her room. And the landlord never reported her missing."

"Exactly. They filed her as an illegal immigrant. She was cremated and put in an unmarked grave."

"That's so tragic. I'm very sorry, Damian." She touched his arm.

His muscles flexed under her touch before he protectively pulled his arm into his body. "It's better than believing she didn't want me."

She searched his expression, hurting so badly for him, she might never recover from it.

Something tickled her knuckle and she realized her gelato was melting down her fingers. It was about to plop onto her thigh.

She hurried over to a nearby bin and threw it away, wiping her fingers with the napkin, but her hands remained tacky.

When she turned back, Damian was looking at his phone.

"Zoia is ready to go home." His expression was back to being remote.

"I'm sorry," she blurted. "I didn't mean to make you talk about something so painful."

"I don't mind. Really." His eyes were squinting in the light so she couldn't read his thoughts, but his mouth was tense, his body bunched. His voice was steady and cool, though. "You're one of the few people I've ever talked to about her. I thought you should have closure, too. Cliff hangers are cruel."

"They are," she murmured as she began walking alongside him.

She desperately wanted to take his hand, but her fingers were sticky and she had the sense that he was so far inside himself, he wouldn't feel the contact anyway.

Over dinner, Zoia urged them to go on a proper date. "Ice cream in the village doesn't count."

"I thought that was your first date with Pappous?"

"Because we were the children of farmers. You can afford to take Carmel to Italy for gelato. What about your award? When is that? Tell Carmel what it is."

"It's nothing," Damian replied. "My company is being recognized for innovation and engineering in the green energy sector. I had planned to attend the ceremony in Berlin before coming here for the summer. Things changed."

"When is it?" Carmel asked.

"This Saturday. But I don't want to be away from Zoia," he said firmly.

"It sounds prestigious." Carmel was impressed. "You should go. I can stay with Zoia."

Damian narrowed his eyes in a "what are you up to" look.

Nothing. It hurt to see his suspicion when she was trying to be a help to him in whatever small way she could.

She repeated in Greek to Zoia that she would stay with her so Damian could go.

"Nonsense," Zoia said. "All of this visiting is too much for me anyway. You must want to do something fun, don't you?" she asked Carmel.

"This is fun." Carmel pointed to the table. "I don't think many say 'no' to Damian and get away with it."

"I'm telling him to say 'yes,'" Zoia argued. "Will you really refuse to give me what I want when these could be my last days?" she demanded of him, then turned to Carmel. "Do you have a pretty dress?"

"I have this." She plucked at her cheap sundress. "I don't think it will work."

"You'll buy her something, won't you, Damian?" Zoia urged him. "I don't want you to miss out on something you deserve. You work so hard. Go have fun. Please."

He sighed. "You won't run any marathons while I'm gone?"

"I will keep my feet up and wait patiently for you to come back with your stories," Zoia promised.

"Damian." Carmel touched his arm to hit pause. "What sort of press are you expecting? You know what they can be like toward me."

"It's an industry award. There won't be any gossip rags lurking around, but it's an important networking event. I'd like to make an appearance. Will it be hard for you, though? To be around people who are drinking?"

"Not really." She was used to it.

"And what about a dress. I can cover it."

"Oh, please. I have a stylist on retainer in every major city around the globe." She flicked her fingers, blasé.

"It's settled then." He relayed the news to Zoia.

She was thrilled, especially when Carmel promised to bring her laptop across the next morning so Zoia could help her choose a gown.

Despite setting them up on the weekend, Zoia wasn't satisfied. When Carmel offered to eat lunch with her, she urged her to take lunch to Damian instead. Her grandson liked to be hands-on when he was home and often spent the day with the workmen, ensuring things were running well, but Zoia didn't like that Damian was neglecting his wife.

He was suspicious when Carmel turned up with a beach bag and a picnic blanket.

"Are you that bored?" he asked.

"Zoia is worried you're skipping meals. And I felt like a walk." She wafted the blanket across a shady patch of grass and knelt to smooth it.

"What happened here?" He crouched beside her and his hand touched her shoulder, frowning as he ran his touch over the tender bump on her shoulder blade.

"I had the bright idea to do yoga in Zoia's garden this morning. I didn't notice a wasp had landed on my mat. It's fine. I'm not allergic. It's just itchy." And his light caress sent tendrils of sensuality into her stomach. She hitched her shoulder to dislodge his disturbing touch.

"Check the bathroom off the kitchen when you get back to the villa. There's a first aid kit that will have some ointment to numb it."

"Okay. Thanks."

It was the most benign sign of caring, but she was deeply affected by it.

They sat to eat the food Lethe had prepared.

"Do you think Zoia used to bring your grandfather lunch?"

"I know she did."

"Really? That's cute. They were in love?"

"I guess. He was a difficult man to read."

"I wonder what it was like, being married to a man like that."

He slid her a side-eye.

She chomped into one of the stuffed pitas that Lethe had prepared for them.

"He thought the world of her. I know that," Damian said. "She was devastated when he was gone. I wanted her to come live with me in Athens. She could have gone anywhere. Done anything. Traveled. She wanted to be here. This is the home he gave her, she said. So this is where she belongs."

"Do you feel that way about this place?"

"I do." His restless gaze scanned the nearby trees. "Probably for the same reason. It's the home they gave me."

"That makes me jealous. Envious," she corrected. "I've never felt that way about any of the places I've lived. The house I grew up in holds as many bad memories as good. Everywhere else was transitory or belonged to someone else. My flat in London is the closest thing I have to my own home and I would be disappointed to lose it, but I wouldn't be crushed."

She caught him studying her.

"Don't worry," she said wryly. "I'm not vying for an invitation to stay. But I might have tried harder on our marriage if I'd seen this place."

She was being glib, but he was somber as he reminded her, "I hadn't bought it yet. I was going to use your money to do it, so it would have been yours."

"Ours," she corrected, accosted by thousands of what-ifs. What if she had placed her trust in him? What if they had been together all this time? "That was something that attracted me to you, though. The fact you knew who you were and where you belonged. I always felt so lost."

"I liked that you seemed to be on board with my ambitions. Coming from a little farm on a tiny island, raised by my grandparents… There was a generation gap. They were already baffled by my mother's desire for more. They didn't hold me back, but they didn't understand why I wasn't satisfied with working the land every day. You had an attitude that not only accepted that I wanted greater things, you seemed to want to help me get there. I thought we were going to be partners, creating that bigger world together."

"That's why you were so angry when I pulled the rug," she acknowledged with a pang. "I had no business marrying anyone, Damian. I hope you see that. Our marriage would have blown up eventually because of my drinking."

They heard some of the workmen returning from their own lunch so they finished eating, and she gathered everything up to carry it back to the villa.

It became a thing for her to walk his lunch out to him, though. It allowed her to see more of the estate and was a nice midday break.

"I'm avoiding Atlas," she said when he told her these picnics weren't necessary. "He saw I was online and tried to catch me. I said I had a lunch date, which isn't a lie if I actually have lunch with you." She shook out their blanket.

"What happens if you tell him where you are? Does the sky actually fall?"

"No. He probably wouldn't even be that surprised to learn I'd been married all this time. No one would. But I don't want to do that to you." She sat down and took the water bottle from her bag, handing it to him. "I'm a little worried about drawing attention in Berlin."

"I'm not. I'd rather keep our marriage private because

it's no one's business but ours, but if it came out, we'd make a statement and move on."

"You said you were ashamed to be married to me," she reminded him with a pang in her chest.

"I also admitted that was a cheap shot."

"There was truth in it, though." Otherwise, it wouldn't have been such a heavy hit that landed so squarely. She concentrated on setting the food between them.

He took several gulps of water, then lowered the bottle with a hiss.

"If I was ashamed to be seen with you, you wouldn't be here. I sure as hell would never introduce you to my grandmother. Are you that conditioned to think of yourself as a liability?"

"It's sort of been my vocation," she joked.

"Don't do that," he said sternly. "You think your father and brother are the only reason Davenwear became a global brand?"

"I was drunk or hungover at nearly every photo shoot. I can't take credit for its success. Not in those days. Atlas was the bona fide athlete, giving it legitimacy."

"Your looks and reputation didn't hurt, Carmel. I'm not saying sex appeal is the right way to sell a product, but Davenwear didn't succeed *in spite* of those things. Didn't you say your father liked to enable you? He had to see that any publicity was good publicity."

"Oh, God," she breathed as the extent of her father's manipulations struck her anew. She brought up her knees and hugged them, hiding her burning eyes against her kneecaps. She felt sick.

"You never saw that?" His hand rubbed across her bowed back.

"No," she said miserably, then fought back the tears and picked up her head. "He always acted as though everything I did had negative value. I married you knowing he wouldn't approve, but who cares? Nothing I did ever pleased him. At least I would gain some autonomy—money," she said on a guilty croak. "But he did that thing where he made it seem like he was *saving* me. You were an opportunist and I was the dummy and he was the reluctant hero. *Again*."

"Are you crying?" He found a napkin and offered it.

"No. I hate crying." She dabbed it to her damp lashes. "And he's not worth it. I'm just mad. I should be able to trust my own father, but I *can't*."

"True," he said quietly.

She glanced at him. "Have you ever looked for your father?"

"No," he said flatly, then he completely changed the subject. "I spoke to Zoia's specialist. The surgery is scheduled for the seventh. That's Monday, week after next."

"Oh. That's good, I guess?"

"I guess."

CHAPTER SEVEN

She was still thinking of his abrupt change of subject yesterday afternoon, when she was starting her workday the next morning.

Out of idle curiosity, she opened the envelope that she had left here on the desk, hoping he would be enticed to read it. She recalled that it contained their marriage certificate and that her lawyers had requested a copy of the long form, which—to her shock—had the names of both of their birth parents listed.

Damian's father was a man named Nicholas Gatz, birthplace "unknown, Australia."

She quickly shoved everything back in the envelope and looped the string around and around the little button that closed it, as if that would put all the troubles, woes and vices back in Pandora's box.

It was impossible to squelch now, though. The name floated from her eyeballs into her mind and down her fingertips into her laptop.

Dozens of profiles turned up from minor celebrities to social media to ancestry sites.

Maybe that's why Damian had never looked for him. It was a needle in a haystack.

Even so, Carmel couldn't resist digging deeper. This

was one of the reasons she had struggled in school. It wasn't that she struggled to read or learn. She just loathed doing what was expected of her. Why solve boring math equations when there was a far more interesting mystery to investigate—like a pop star's love life or how skirt length had changed through the ages.

It would literally be quicker and easier to jab Damian in his sleep for a blood sample and send it to one of those DNA sites than it was to figure out which of these men might be his father, but she couldn't help herself. Before she realized what she was doing, she had lost the afternoon to compiling a list of contenders based on age and photos that bore some resemblance to him.

Of course, she had her earbuds in the whole time. She didn't hear Damian until an alteration in the fall of light from the doorway made her look up and see him.

She quit singing and slapped the laptop closed, face hot as she pulled out her earbuds.

"Why so guilty?" he asked with amusement. He was covered in sweat and dust, and she liked the way his shirt clung across his chest as he braced his arm against the jamb. He didn't have a right to look so sexy. "Are you watching something kinky?"

"Christmas movies. Too early?" It was a joke, obviously, but it still felt like a lie because she was using it to cover up what she was really doing. She winced. Almost whimpered, but it was hitting her that what she'd been doing was a massive overstep. "I don't want to tell you. You'll yell at me."

He dropped his arm and his glimmer of humor disappeared. "No, I won't. Tell me."

"You will," she assured him dolefully. "I know when I've done something that will get me into trouble."

"Then why do it?"

"I don't know!" It was enormously frustrating. "Not enough boundaries as a child so I don't know where they are?" Her therapist would say she created chaos as a means of taking control. "I'm obstinate. I don't want to be, but I am. And sometimes, when the little voice in my head says, *You can't do that*, another voice says, *Oh, yeah? Watch me.*"

"Get to the point, Carmel."

"I just happened to look...at our marriage certificate." She swallowed. "And I noticed your father's name was on it."

His body gathered as tall as one of those black clouds grew to tower in the sky, promising biblical retribution.

"I didn't do anything!" she cried, holding up a hand. "I just wanted to see if I could find him. I can't. There's at least a hundred contenders." Of which, she had eliminated forty-three.

"Why the hell would you do that?"

"See, you're yelling."

"*Why*, Carmel? What were you going to do? Hold it over me in some way?"

"*No.* I just wondered if I could find him." Her voice faded because it was such a lame reason. "It's a puzzle. I'm chasing a dopamine fix that comes from solving a mystery. And I'm curious. I mean, I can guess what your mom was like because I've met Zoia. But how much of you is like her and your grandparents and what parts of you come from him?"

"Who cares? It's none of your business! If I wanted to meet him, I'd find him myself."

"I know. I'm sorry."

"You've cut your own father out of your life. Why would you presume I want anything to do with mine?"

"You're right. I didn't think it through." She bit her lip, trying to hide that her mouth was beginning to quiver.

"You have no right to my private life, Carmel. You are not my wife. You're nothing to me. Do you understand that?"

"I know." Hot, helpless tears seared the backs of her eyes. Her stomach churned with remorse.

He swore under his breath, looking away, then his gaze slammed back to hers.

"Get out." He stepped out of the doorway and pointed at her room. "Get your things and get walking. I don't need this."

Her heart swerved. Her stomach wrenched sickly because he was angry *and* disappointed. Because she had crossed a line. Because she was failing. She had done something wrong *again* and was rightly being punished for it.

She wanted to slink away in shame, but there was another part of her that sparked with fight. Sometimes she was thoughtless, but she wasn't mean. She might have done something wrong, but she wasn't *bad*.

"No," she said.

"What did you say?" he asked, astounded.

"I said, 'no.' I won't leave." She rose and lifted her chin in defiance. "I made a mistake, Damian. I said I was sorry."

"Oh, that makes it all better then, doesn't it?"

"People make mistakes. *I* make mistakes. You want to believe I had some master plan to ruin your life when I married you, but guess what? *I'm not that smart!* I made a dumb, stupid mistake. Same as you. And I *would* leave, but I promised Zoia—"

"Ha! As if you care about her," he shouted scathingly.

"You shut your damned mouth," she yelled. "I do care about her. Do you know how scared she is to have this surgery? Do you? She thinks it will kill her and leave you with no one. She needs to know you'll still have someone who cares about you if she doesn't make it. Well, you have had *five years* to find someone better than me. It can't be that hard! The bar is at the bottom of the ocean. But this is what you chose." She pointed at herself. "So quit acting like all of this is my fault. I'm here because you wanted me here. Live with it."

She barreled past him and darted into her room across the hall, slamming her door behind her.

Then she leaned on it, clenching her eyes and holding her breath as she fought the spiny sobs that crowded into her throat.

Damian was livid.

He stepped into a cold shower, purely to cool his temper.

Who interfered in someone's life that way?

Carmel did. Because she did whatever she wanted and didn't care who she hurt. She was selfish. Thoughtless.

Whereas he had been worried about her. She'd taken to bringing his lunch and, when she didn't turn up, he'd been concerned that she'd tripped or gotten lost.

He liked working with his employees when he was here. It grounded him to do the mindless work of physical labor and showed his employees he would never ask them to do anything he wasn't willing to do himself. It was a way to reinforce what he'd told Carmel, that this estate was his home. He was a part of it. This was where he belonged.

He had needed that sense of belonging as a child, when he had felt discarded. At least his grandmother had wanted him here. And, as he proved his worth and invested his own sweat into the dirt, his grandfather had wanted him here, too.

This was his home so he took care of it.

He had begun to enjoy the midday break with Carmel, though. Eating in the shade, talking about what they were working on that day and having lighthearted arguments over each other's taste in books and movies.

His mind kept circling back to her saying their marriage would have blown up anyway, because of her alcohol addiction. An egotistical part of him wanted to believe he could have helped her through that, but he hadn't even realized she needed help. He'd had blinders on because he'd been so focused on his own goals. In that respect, he'd had no business marrying anyone, either. Not when he hadn't been prepared to give her all of himself.

He'd wanted her, though. He could admit that there had been an element of not wanting to lose his chance. In the haze of anger that he'd kept kindled so fiercely through the years, he'd forgotten that he actually liked her.

When he had come in to hear her singing about dancing the night away, he'd been impressed by her voice again, and amused at how caught up she became in her work, not realizing she was belting out a song as though she stood on a Broadway stage.

That gave him pause.

He flicked off the water and stepped out, acknowledging she was naturally single-minded and driven to get what she wanted, not unlike him.

It didn't excuse her invading his privacy, though.

Telling her to leave had been a reflexive reaction. He hadn't thought it through, but Zoia wouldn't refuse the surgery at this stage. The date was set. They'd both spoken with the specialist. She understood the risks and that she would need time to recover, but ultimately, she could expect her life to be prolonged. Her quality of life would improve.

Carmel didn't need to be here any longer.

Except as emotional support for Zoia.

He'd been aware of his grandmother's reservations, but Carmel had called it fear. He only wanted Zoia to be well. And alive. He wasn't trying to bully her, but now he felt as though he hadn't been paying close enough attention to Zoia's concerns.

As he walked by Carmel's room, he glanced in the open door to see her laptop was on the end of the bed next to some strewn clothing.

He wanted to be angry at her defiance, but his reaction was more a sense of relief.

Downstairs, Lethe asked if he wanted lunch served by the pool.

"That's fine, thanks."

"And will Miss Davenport join you?" she asked in a wary voice that told him she had heard their shouting.

"She hasn't eaten yet? I'll text her."

He did and heard a faint ping from upstairs.

He went back to her room to see her phone was charging on her nightstand. Her bathroom door was open and the room empty. So was the balcony. Her yoga mat was rolled up in the corner so she wasn't doing that.

He could have texted his grandmother's caregiver to ask if Carmel was there, but he wanted to see Zoia anyway. He walked over.

"I haven't seen her since our morning constitutional in the garden," she said, from her rocker. "She's probably out looking for you. She brings your lunch, doesn't she?"

"She didn't show up so I came back to look for her. I saw her in the office a little while ago." He had yelled at her, exactly as he'd promised he wouldn't. "She said you're afraid to have the surgery." He sat down to face her. "Is that true?"

"Wouldn't you be?"

He sighed.

"I'm not afraid for me, Damian. Your mother and grandfather are waiting for me whenever I pass. No, it's you I'm worried about. As long as you have Carmel, though, I'm comforted."

He looked out the window toward the upper hills, wondering where she'd gone. "We argued."

"About my surgery?"

"No. I caught her looking for my father online." To be fair, she'd confessed to it, otherwise he never would have known. He was still angry, though.

"You're upset? Why? It would be nice to know something about him, wouldn't it? Especially once you decide to have children?"

"That is not going to happen," he said firmly. "Not with her."

"Not at the rate you're going, arguing with her when she's only trying to help."

"How does finding a complete stranger help anyone? Mamá didn't want you to know who he was. *You* never wanted him to know about me."

"I didn't want him to *take* you from us. That might have been your mother's reason, too. Australia is a long way away."

"There's nothing I need from him. There's no point in finding him," he muttered.

"Carmel said the other day that it was sad there's a man out there who doesn't know what a good son he made. I've been thinking about that a lot. I don't think she meant any harm in trying to find him."

It's still harm, he wanted to bite out. But what harm had she caused? She hadn't actually reached out to his father, only made Damian feel threatened and defensive at the prospect of it. Why?

Because he didn't want to be rejected again.

"You don't think she left, do you?" Zoia asked with concern. "How bad was your argument?"

Bad enough he had ordered her to leave. "Her things are still in her room."

"Good. Go find her and patch things up."

"Me?" Carmel was the one who had crossed a line.

"Be proud then," Zoia said with a sniff. "That's how your mother and grandfather dealt with things. They held their obstinate positions and I suffered, barely seeing my grandson for the first six years of his life. What was I supposed to do? Leave Eurus here alone and live in Athens without him, so I could see my daughter and grandson? What was the point in their being so stubborn? What did it accomplish?"

"I see your point." Damian used a mild tone, trying to calm Zoia's temper, not wanting her to grow agitated.

"*I* was the stubborn one when it came to finding your father." She pointed at herself. "Eurus didn't fight me on it, but you know he had strong feelings about how a man should behave. It didn't sit well with him that your father wasn't part of your upbringing. I know you think he didn't want you, Damian, but that's not how it was. We were blessed to have you. We knew that. But you were a puzzle to him. We always believed your mother's wanderlust would wear off and she would come home, but you wanted bigger things than we could ever give you. And the way your mind worked, so mechanical... We knew that must come from your father. It wasn't fair of me to hold you back from knowing him."

"You haven't," he said firmly. "I've been a grown man a long time. If I wanted to find him, I would look for him myself."

"You really don't want to? Not even for the memories of your mother he could give us?"

The pang in her voice was a sharp blade in his chest. He had lost his mother twice and still had very mixed feelings that prevented him from being sentimental about her. He would give Zoia anything within his power, though, especially at this stage of her life. Even if it was only the *hope* of a single fresh memory of her daughter.

"I'll see what I can find out," he promised in a voice that turned to a rasp.

"I'd like that." She reached out to pat his hand. "And don't be so hard on Carmel. Marriages have rough patches. Working through your issues makes your relationship stronger. You don't burn down the orange grove because you have a few aphids, do you?"

Their issues were a little bit bigger than aphids and yes, he was planning to burn his marriage to the ground in about ten days, but he appeased Zoia with a bland, "Of course not."

"Go make up with her, then." She nudged him.

He went back to the villa and texted Pirro to ask the workmen if they'd seen her, then called his lawyer to ask for a discreet inquiry.

By the time he got off the call, Pirro had reported back that no one had seen Carmel anywhere on the grounds.

Damian frowned. There were small hazards all over the estate. Outcroppings and gullies and low hanging branches. It didn't escape him that his need to know where she had gone bore an uncomfortable similarity to her drive to find a stranger online.

What a burr in his sock. And why had he thought he should give up drinking while she was here? He would love a shot of something to take the edge off right now.

Annoyed beyond measure, he walked out to the terrace to scan the grounds, trying to think where she might have gone.

His gaze snagged on the stairwell to the beach.

Carmel heard a clang, but she was reading so she stayed on her stomach on the straw mat where a tall rock blocked the sun from her bare back and legs.

In her periphery, Damian approached, but she stubbornly kept her eyes on her book, hiding beneath the brim of her hat.

"What are you doing here?" he demanded.

It seemed obvious, but she said, "Sulking," to dispel any doubt.

"Lethe wants to serve lunch."

"Shh. The hero is deflowering the heroine. Let them finish."

"Seriously?"

"I don't know how to answer that. Is he being serious about it? Yes, he is very earnestly attending to this virgin's pleasure."

"You are the most infuriating woman who has ever walked this earth."

"We're all good at something."

He swore and walked toward the water.

She looked over her shoulder, then closed the book and sat up to retie her bikini top and adjust her hat.

"What are *you* doing here?" she asked. "Felt like a skinny-dip?"

When he said nothing, she stood and wrapped her sarong around her hips, then crossed the warm sand to wade into the water alongside him, stopping where ripples lapped her knees.

"I really am sorry, Damian. I—"

"Stop apologizing for who you are," he said flatly. "Most people are sheep. You're a leopard." He looked down his nose at her. "You ambush out of nowhere and have claws that shred a man to pieces if you feel threatened, but you're powerful and graceful and necessary to the ecosystem."

"Do go on," she said with heavy irony, but he was liable to make her cry. *Stop apologizing for who you are.* She drew a breath that felt salty and fulfilling.

There was another long silence while he looked out to the water.

"When I was very young, when I thought she left me here, I couldn't understand why she didn't want me. I thought she might have gone to live with my father," he said quietly. "To my mind, *he* was the one who didn't want me. That's why she left me behind, so they could be together without me."

Oh, Damian. She didn't speak, didn't touch him, only waited while an ache squeezed her from head to toe.

"The older I got, the more I realized that wasn't likely, but what if I did find him? What if he made me go to Australia? I didn't need a father. I had Pappous. I was sixteen when he died. Yaya couldn't manage alone. Caring for her was my responsibility. It felt disloyal to even consider looking for my father. They had sacrificed a lot to give me as good a life as they could manage. I've never seen any way that finding my father would enhance or improve the life I've made for myself. And what about his life? You, of all people, should understand what a shock it could be for him and his family to learn of my existence."

"You're right," she murmured. "I should have asked you first."

"Tell me about a single time that you've asked first instead of begged for forgiveness later."

She stared balefully at him. "As soon as I can remember it, I will blurt it out."

"That's what I thought." He was still gruff, but he was begrudgingly letting go of his anger.

"Do you want my notes?" she offered. "Or should I drop it?"

"I've asked my lawyer to look into it. Zoia wants me to find him in case he has memories of my mother. I would like to give her that, if I can."

"Oh, Damian." She couldn't help curling her hands around his upper arm, which was solid as iron and filled with tension. She pressing her forehead there, knocking her hat askew as she absorbed how much he loved his grandmother. She had shouted at him about how scared Zoia was, but it hit her how afraid he was to lose the most important person in his life.

His arm moved. For a second, she thought he was going to scoop her close and hold on to her.

She would have hugged him. She wanted to.

He angled to pull his arm from her grip, expression still withdrawn, but his tone was dry as he asked, "Are we swimming with clothes on or off?"

"If that's a dare, you know I'm going to take it." She started to reach for the string on her top.

"God, you're a nuisance." He broke away from her and dove into the water, still in his shorts and T-shirt.

CHAPTER EIGHT

ON SATURDAY, Damian had his private jet collect them from the small airport on the island to fly them directly to Berlin. It bothered him to leave Zoia, but she was in high spirits. One of her good friends was planning to spend the day with her while they were gone, and the doctor assured him that he could be with her on a moment's notice if her health turned.

"Go be young," Zoia had ordered.

He didn't think he knew how. He'd had to grow up very quickly and still found it difficult to let go and enjoy himself. It struck him that one of the reasons Carmel had appealed to him in the first place was her willingness to throw herself into a moment. It was a frustrating quality at times, but an enviable state of mind.

In fact, that aspect of her personality was on full display from the moment they entered the suite, when she met her team there and began to wax poetic over the gown choices they'd brought.

"What can I say?" she said when she caught him watching her. "I'm a girly-girl. I live for— Ooh, yes!" She snatched up a shade of nail polish and held it against a silver gown. "Right?"

He left her to get ready while he ran out and did something he had sworn he wouldn't. He found a jewelry store and bought her a pair of earrings. He had never bought her an engagement ring, he reasoned, but there was something a little more self-serving in it. It wasn't a bribe. He wasn't trying to get her into bed.

Although...

He firmly shut *those* thoughts down, even as the vision of her in a bikini never left his mind's eye.

No, this was a point of pride. He had invited her to be his date, and he would cover her costs and buy her a thank-you gift. That's all this was.

She was still in the second bedroom when he returned. He checked in with his grandmother, then changed into his tuxedo.

He would typically nurse a scotch at this point, but his assistant had dutifully ensured there was no alcohol in the suite. He answered a few emails until he heard the door open, then looked up in time to see Carmel stroll toward him with an abundance of graceful confidence.

Her gown was liquid silver that ran from one shoulder across her lush breasts, clung to the indent of her waist and poured off her hips, splitting to reveal one thigh and the silver straps of her high heels.

He came back from that very pleasurable journey to see her pose with one hand on her hip, chin up, hair pulled back on one side and falling in a length of curls down the front of her opposite shoulder. Her scarlet mouth tilted in amusement and her thick lashes tangled into a line as she narrowed her smoky eyes at him.

"Like what you see, sailor?"

Too much. Everything about her was more than he could bear. In a very good way.

"You look beautiful." He had to clear his throat.

"I know."

"Except..."

Her brows went up, haughty.

He offered the earrings.

"Loaners?" She took the velvet box.

"They're for you. A thank you for being so kind to Zoia."

"I like her." Much of her saucy self-assurance fell away. "You didn't have to get me anything for that."

"I wanted to."

She opened the box and drew a soft breath at the cascade of pear-shaped stones from a cushion cut stud.

"These are really beautiful, Damian." Her voice was hushed and somber. "You have excellent taste."

"I know. I asked you to be my date, didn't I?" he said blithely.

She dipped her chin and smiled with shy pleasure. "Someone has been reading Wooing for Dummies."

He gave a rusty laugh.

She walked to the mirror and removed her artistically sculpted platinum earrings. They were admittedly eye-catching and interesting, but his were infinitely nicer. They sparkled the way she did.

After a long look at her reflection, she said, "I love them. Thank you."

She came toward him and every muscle in his body tightened. She was taller in her heels and only needed to lift her chin to touch the corner of his mouth with a peck of her lips.

He set his hand on her hip, tempted to keep her close. To turn his head and *take*.

"You're welcome." He drew back a little and lifted his

hand to the earring, desperate to touch *her*. The weight of the diamonds on his fingertip pleased him. The sight of *his* earrings on her appealed to the Neanderthal in him.

He had been lying about wanting to thank her for being kind to Zoia. As far as his ego went, he was marking her as his. That's what this was.

And it was a disturbing enough realization he had to take another step back from her.

"Shall we go?" He had to rummage for his voice in the depths of his chest.

The ceremony was being held in the ballroom of another hotel, but it only took the car a few minutes to get them there. The guests were executives from the tech sector, no pop stars or celebrities. Thus, there were only a handful of second-string freelance photographers taking photos against the prepared background that advertised the event.

They still recognized Carmel and began snapping and shouting questions at her.

"Carmel! What are you doing here?" one asked.

"I'm on a date," she said mildly.

"How do you know Mr. Kalymnios?"

"We've been acquainted a long time."

"Is it serious?"

"When have you known me to be serious?" she countered.

"Are you sober tonight?"

"That's enough," Damian muttered, appalled at the man's rudeness. He started to escort Carmel to the entrance, but the photographer persisted.

"You look like you've gained weight. Are you pregnant?"

"Do you want a broken nose?" Damian turned back to ask him.

"Don't." Carmel caught his arm. "It's not worth it." She urged him to come with her into the hotel.

"Who is he?" he demanded as they entered the lobby. "Do you know his name?"

"Don't even bother. They all heard what he asked me. They'll all pile on the same rumor. I did warn you."

She had, but, "It's always that intrusive?" he asked.

"That was nothing," she said dismissively. "I used to be a *Titanic* level disaster. Now I'm very boring so they try to get a rise out of me, hoping for an implosion they can capitalize on."

"I really do want to break his nose." They were already in the elevator and he'd never been a violent man, but it sounded really satisfying.

"That's sweet, but if you recall, I don't actually have any honor worth defending."

He started to admonish her for talking down about herself, but the doors opened on a greeter who took their names and gave them their table number, waving them to enter the festively decorated ballroom.

The evening passed pleasantly. Carmel was loosely acquainted with a few of the people in the room, either through women she knew from boarding school or other business connections she had made over the years. She made some useful introductions for him, and she was a vivacious date, capable of small talk and witty interjections that kept the evening from becoming dull.

Once the awards had been handed out and the speeches were made, the dancing started. Finally, he had an excuse to hold her.

He invited her onto the floor and she fit perfectly against him, exactly as she had five years ago.

He had been burning to feel her again since their kiss on the stairs that night. She smelled divine and moved perfectly with him, reminding him of exactly how well-matched they'd been in bed, not that he'd ever forgotten.

Their chemistry had predictable results on his body. She noticed when he had to pull her in to avoid a less adept couple. She flashed a questioning look up at him.

"Surprised? I already told you you're very beautiful."

"I'm surprised you let me know." She blushed, seeming discomfited, which was an unusual reaction from someone who seemed incapable of embarrassment. "You didn't want anything to do with me that night on the stairs." Her expression grew stiff. Hurt?

"I didn't want to want you."

"Didn't? Or don't?" Her lashes lifted.

He spent a long moment drowning in the deep pools of her eyes.

"I don't know if I have a choice." He drew her close, avoiding another couple again, and watched over her head as they continued moving. "I had forgotten you have such natural charisma. Everyone is drawn to you." He was making excuses for his own fascination. Even he could hear it.

"I'm a ham," she said, looking away. "A hack entertainer. I play the clown so people don't see the real me."

"I do," he said, because he did. She wore a sheen and sparkle as armor, but like her gown, it was actually a very thin, delicate layer. Beneath it was a vulnerable, naked, very human person.

She winced. He saw her gaze track a tray of champagne carried by a server.

"Should we go?" he asked.

"Are you worried about me?" she asked wryly. "I mistook that server for Stella's sister, Beate, but she's at school in Vienna."

"I'd still prefer to leave." He wanted her to himself.

He held her hand as they left the dance floor and wound their way back to the table to collect their things.

Back in their hotel suite, she opened the gilded box containing the light bulb–shaped crystal award and set it on the bar, then stood back to admire it.

"You should be proud of that."

"You know as well as I do that those things are subjective at best and mostly exist to self-congratulate and drum up friendly PR."

"It's still a signifier of how much you've achieved. You wouldn't have won it if you hadn't come this far. I should have believed in you. It's not that I didn't, you know." She turned to face him, hands clenching together. "I had every confidence that you would get where you wanted to be. It was me that I didn't believe in. Us."

"I know." He pulled at his bow tie. "Me either. Your father called me an opportunist, and I was. The minute I saw you, I knew you were out of my league. It came as no surprise that you would dump me as quickly as you married me. It was nice of you to give me a reason to hate you, though. Made it easier on my self-esteem."

"Please don't make jokes about what I did. I've hated myself a lot over it."

With a resigned sigh, he moved closer and touched her chin, tilting it up so he could see into her eyes. "Is it true? You didn't have sex with him? Just kissed him?"

"It was still a kind of adultery." Her brow flinched and

she delicately lifted her chin from his grip before turning her face away, showing him a profile that was stark and pained. "But yes. I could barely stand to be alone with him. You ruined me for sex with anyone else. Thanks for that," she said grouchily.

Don't believe her, his inner voice warned, but there was something so despondent in her expression, he had to ask, "What exactly are you saying? You haven't had *any* lovers since me?"

"Ego fully restored?" she asked, voice lofty, but there was a thread of tension in it.

"I—" He didn't know what to say. Didn't know if he could believe her. "Why not?" he blurted.

"A lot of reasons." She folded her arms defensively. "Lack of interest was the main one, but I also knew that if I did find someone I liked, I'd have to do this. Come see you." Her lashes lifted to reveal the clouds of anxiety in her eyes. Remorse. "I wasn't ready to face you. To atone. I needed to get sober first. I know you think I want a divorce so I can marry someone else, but there's no one waiting in the wings. Just me. My therapist says I need to learn to love Carmel. Date *myself*." She rolled her eyes at the concept.

It seemed too far-fetched to believe, but was it? *He* hadn't been with anyone else. And even though he'd seen her photographed with other men, it had usually been in the context of something like tonight—a fundraiser or a business function. He'd been on countless similar dates himself. They were polite but bland nonaffairs that met society's expectation for an evening, but did little else for him.

"I can't make you believe me," she said with a downturn of her mouth. "That's on me for failing to appreciate what we had. If you want the real, terrifying truth, I felt things for you that I thought I wasn't allowed to have. I'd done too many stupid things to deserve it. I didn't know how to handle it so I threw it away."

She looked too self-conscious for him to dismiss this as a ploy. What would she even gain by such a lie? The divorce she had already asked for?

No matter how many times he tried to disbelieve her, the things she said kept ringing true. He *wanted* her to be a liar because her truths were inconvenient. They forced him to change his view of her.

They forced him to feel some understanding and respect for her.

"I want this to be all your fault. I really do," he admitted. "But I was the one who proposed. I can say I was caught up in the romance of it. That I thought I was helping you get access to your own money, but I was hungry to get ahead. I saw marrying you as a cheat code. A way to jump the line. I'm not proud of that."

"This might come as a shock, but lots of people got close to me for my money. I knew that's what you wanted, but I wanted you so…" She shrugged.

"Don't let me off the hook. We're being honest here, aren't we?"

"Okay," she said gravely. "I was hurt that you were so angry about Daddy pulling the promise of giving me access to my money. I know he was insulting to you. You had every right to be angry, but I wanted you to stand up for me. To say it didn't matter. After the way I'd been treated all my life, I felt like the only value I had was the fact I had access to money. That's why I sided with Daddy when he told me it was him or you." She waved her hand in the air, then looked to the floor. "The only other value I seemed to have for you was sex, so I chose to hurt you that way."

"It worked. You did," he said without heat. "I wanted to kill that other man. He was touching what I believed was mine." He nodded at her.

"I was yours." Her voice grew thick and her eyes welled. She scrunched them closed with a pained expression. "But I knew I wasn't enough for you. Not for forever. Sooner or later, I would ruin it, so I got it over with."

Of all the things she'd ever said, that sounded like the truest. It sounded like something she would do, purely to drive the situation, rather than wait in a state of dread.

"Are you going to do it again?" he asked gruffly.

"Do what?" Her gaze came up to his, anxious.

"Take this little bit of trust we've found and throw it away."

"No. I hope not." Her shoulders twitched in a small shrug. "I don't want to. I want you to forgive me. That's all I've wanted since it happened."

"I do forgive you." It was less a decision than an arrival at a place he hadn't expected, but the doors opened and here he was. The air was lighter and his view of her softer. "I believe you're sorry, Carmel. So am I. Let's draw a line under it and leave it in the past."

Carmel heard a harsh gasp and realized it was her own gulp for air, even as her ears strained to hear what he'd said because she couldn't be sure.

Had he really said he forgave her?

She could hardly see him. She blinked fast, but the tears were gathering on her lashes, making it impossible to see him. Her mouth felt electrified. Her lips were numb and couldn't form words.

"Do you r-really—" She sniffed the tears gathering in her nasal passages. "Do you m-mean that?" she choked. "You f-forgive me?" *Me?*

"Yes. Are you crying?" He sounded shocked. Warm hands took hold of her arms.

"No. I hate crying." But he was gone behind a curtain of blurred vision. Something hot was spilling down her cheeks. The release—the relief—was so profound, her knees turned to melted butter. Her breaths shortened, becoming jagged.

She tried to look for a tissue, but she didn't know which way to turn. She clasped at his arms to keep herself upright.

"You're shaking. Carmel, it's okay." She found herself squashed into his chest.

He *hugged* her.

Which made something in her break open. She began to cry. Really cry. The wave inside her crested and she was overcome. Thrown to the bottom of the sea, limp and crumpling and unable to breathe even as he gathered her up.

He sat on the sofa with her in his lap and set a box of tissues in her lap. He plucked the first few out of it, trying to dab at her tears.

"Shh. Stop now," he chided.

But it meant so much to her, she shook. Cheating on him was the one thing she had never been able to forgive in herself. She'd used it against herself a thousand times, digging deep grooves inside herself that engraved the harsh truth into her soul: she didn't deserve him. She didn't deserve his forgiveness.

She didn't deserve to be happy.

That's what she had believed for years. Now he had dismantled that and what was she supposed to do? Not hate herself? It was too big to absorb.

"All right," he said in a gruff tone, holding her tighter. "Get it out, then."

He cradled her and rubbed her back and petted her hair while she fell apart completely.

She wasn't one of those women who cried pretty. She looked like a wounded hagfish, using tissue after mascara-stained tissue to mop her cheeks and blow her nose and still the sobs rose and burst, shattering her apart.

It was awful. Agonizing. But also cathartic as she keened out all her pain.

His patience was a layer of anguish in itself, hurting and healing at once, but eventually the storm was spent. Her sobs died to hiccups and a sensation of being utterly drained. By then, her shoulder was under his armpit, her arm bent against his rib cage. Her head was tucked under his chin and he was sifting his fingers through the length of her hair. It was really soothing.

All of this was so *nice*. She had never let herself believe he would show her this much kindness. As she soaked it in, she had to close her gritty eyes against a fresh scorch of heat.

She sighed, loathe to move because she was warm and comfortable and he made her feel very, very safe. She could have had this all this time, she thought distantly. If she'd been brave enough to accept it. To believe she deserved it.

She kept her eyes closed and memorized every sensation—the physical presence of his body surrounding hers, but also the feeling of calm within her. The sweetness of his forgiveness and the inherent acceptance in the way he petted her hair. Deeper yearnings stirred, and she let herself feel those too because this was what she wanted more than anything. A person who made her feel *good*.

She couldn't have Damian, though. She knew that. He could forgive her, but that didn't mean he could trust her or love her. That was okay. She understood that. But it was enough to bask in his caring and know she could revisit this moment each time her confidence flagged. Whenever the world grew too heavy and her commitment to sobriety flagged, she would remember this and realign.

This was what she would seek for the rest of her life.

She hadn't realized she'd fallen asleep until something snaked under her legs and the world tilted before the ground fell away. She was falling!

"It's okay," Damian said quietly even as she grasped at him. "I thought you were asleep. I was going to carry you to bed." He let her feet slide to the floor.

She wobbled on the heels she was still wearing and clung to his arms, disoriented.

"Do I look horrible?" She must.

"A facecloth wouldn't hurt."

For some reason, that offhand response, delivered without malice, made a huge laugh bubble up from her belly. It rose out of the pyre of her tears like a phoenix, releasing in a long, gusty roll that nearly made her cry again.

He steadied her, then trapped her hair against the side of her neck, thumb tilting her chin up so he could look into her eyes. His expression was concerned.

"Okay?"

"Uh-huh."

"That was a lot of tears."

"I know. My stomach hurts." She pressed the ache that lingered there. "But I'm going to tell my therapist that you deserve an honorary certificate. She's always telling me to cry more, but, as you just witnessed, I don't know how to stop."

"You're really okay?" His expression altered to something more tender, and his thumb caressed the edge of her jaw.

"I am," she assured him, patting his chest.

She yearned for the right to hug herself against him again, but they had arrived at a very fine balance. Grace. She didn't want to ruin it.

"I'm a lot," she acknowledged wryly. "I know I am. I have a lot of baggage, and I've spent most of my life expecting others to carry it for me. Literally and figuratively. I'm learning to carry it myself—no, I'm getting *strong enough* to do it. That's a better way to say it. But this…" She brushed at the damp stain on his lapel. "This was very heavy. I appreciate you taking some of it off me. Thank you. I mean that."

His gaze scanned her features, then snagged on her mouth. Her heart began to thud and the air between them became magnetized. Her lips began to tingle with anticipation, and she watched the tip of his tongue dampen his parted lips.

He drew back, pulling in a deep breath as he looked across the room. The hand on her neck dropped away.

"You should go to bed."

Disappointment crashed over her. It was his rejection on the stairs all over again.

She folded her arms and wobbled her way into her room.

CHAPTER NINE

IF HEARTS ACTUALLY BROKE, that was what Damian had witnessed in Carmel tonight. He could be as cynical as he wanted to be about her, but she had a conscience and it tortured her. The fact she'd felt that deeply about scorning him had impacted him profoundly.

He hadn't realized how much power he had over her. It was unnerving.

That's why he had balked at kissing her. He thought about sex with her constantly, certain it would be as good as he remembered it, but when they'd had a veil of bitterness between them, he'd been able to keep himself from going down that dangerous road.

After her storm of weeping, though, she'd drifted to sleep. All her deliciously soft curves had pressed into him, especially the curves of her ass in his lap. He'd already been drunk on the feminine fragrances of her shampoo and perfume. Arousal and fantasies had started to take root, so he'd thought he'd better put her to bed before he did anything stupid.

Then she'd awakened and stood before him with her eyes full of laughter instead of tears. She'd been bouncing back with a resilience that was awe-inspiring. The attraction he'd been fighting had nearly overwhelmed him.

He could hurt her, though. A week ago, he would have reveled in the knowledge he could do so. Now, he was shaken to realize how easily he could destroy her. And what a crime it would be to crush someone who was working so hard to come back from the battles of life.

He peeled off his jacket and threw his bow tie away, then toed off his shoes. Without thinking, he moved to the wet bar, only realizing he was looking for liquor when he didn't find anything except soft drinks.

Go downstairs to the bar? Some distance from the temptation of Carmel would be a good idea, but as much as he wanted the bite of alcohol on his tongue, he liked the sense of solidarity in staying sober with her. Maybe it had no effect on her at all, but he felt like he was supporting her by not drinking, so it was important to him to maintain that.

Her door opened and she came into the lounge.

"Oh." Her face was dewy and clean, her hair in a clip. She wore a silk robe in peacock blue with pink flowers splashed across it. "I thought you were going to bed, too." She moved directly to the shoulder bag she'd left on a side table and dug through it. "I think I left my book on the plane. That's annoying."

"The one about the guy deflowering a virgin?"

"You'll have to be more specific. That happens in all the books I read."

"Really?" He couldn't help the grin that tugged his mouth.

"Don't be a snob. Romance is uplifting and hopeful and gives me the happy ending I crave." She shot him a sly look. "Read into that however you like."

He barked out a laugh. "You have no shame, do you?"

"Why would I have shame about it? I've already told you, I don't have a sex life to speak of. Let me have this." She pushed the purse away in disgust. "Although, not tonight, evidently."

"You don't have anything on your phone?"

"I do, but I prefer physical books. Less chance of doomscrolling." Her shrug drew his eye to the way the silk cradled her unfettered breasts so lovingly.

He made himself look away and ignored the tug of raw, physical need that rang through him.

"Okay, I'm going to take this elephant by the *trunk*." She let the significance of her word choice hang in the air a moment. "I can't help being attracted to you—"

He had to look at her then and watched her falter slightly. She looked down as she played with the tail of her robe's belt.

"But we're in a really good place right now. I don't want to mess it up."

"Same." Damn it.

"I'm going back to London after Zoia's surgery. This reconciliation isn't *real*."

"Exactly. I don't want to mislead you."

"And I don't want to be impulsive and self-destructive. I want to be sensible. And disciplined. As if that's a color I've ever worn, but… I do."

"Good." He swallowed his disappointment and said with a dry throat, "I support you in that."

"But I still want to feel it again," she said in a helpless voice, shoulders sloping.

"What?"

"Pleasure." She shrugged. "And it's okay that you don't want me—"

"I never said that." His voice had dropped into the pit of his belly, where all his good sense was tangling in a net of growing desire.

"Would it be so bad? If we agreed it's just for now?" she asked in a voice so quiet and hesitant, he had to strain to hear it. So he had to move closer.

His feet just kept taking him toward her until he had her face in his hands and his mouth found hers and sensations crashed over him. Relief and hunger. Unleashed desire and a need to be careful. Incredible possessiveness even as he reminded himself it was temporary.

Just for now.

Carmel was startled at the way he had swooped onto her, but she slid her arms around his neck and opened her mouth beneath the ravenous scrape of his. Her heart was exploding with delirious joy and her back bowed over the arm that locked behind her. She went on tiptoe, trying to increase the pressure of their kiss, but he lifted his head.

"Don't stop. Please, Damian," she begged in a whisper.

He swung her up into his arms and walked toward his bedroom.

Dizziness accosted her. She hugged his neck and pressed her lips into his throat, kissing her way up to his earlobe and setting her teeth there.

His arms tightened and his chest swelled in response, then he set her on the bed and came down with her, supporting himself on an elbow as his free hand tugged at her slippery belt.

"All I do is steal looks at you," he admitted as he brushed aside the silk, exposing her torso and abdomen and thighs. "Do you know how hard it was to say no to you on the stairs? To say it *tonight*? There hasn't been anyone else for me either."

He cupped her breast and started to dip his head to brush his lips against the turgid pink nipple.

"Wait." She cupped his head and looked deep into eyes that shifted with shadows of self-consciousness. "Really? *Why not?*"

"Because I wanted you. This." He teased her with a damp kiss, a circle of his tongue. A gradual enveloping that had her combing her fingers into his springy hair, drawing him down while she arched herself into his mouth.

The light suction nearly lifted her off the bed. Maybe it was the knowledge that they had both been celibate for five long years. Surely that meant something?

Her mind couldn't land on a meaning when electric sensations forked into her loins, though. His hand flattened on her belly, then swept low to caress her inner thighs, stealing her last clear thoughts.

"Pale as whipping cream here," he murmured, lifting his head to watch his own hand caress her inner thighs. It was a tease, provoking heat and dampness and yearning to gather in her folds. "All I think about is the honey here."

She reached for the buttons on his shirt, but her hands were shaking and his knowing touch slid to her center, parting and spreading the abundant moisture, brushing the knot of nerves, sweeping her into a deeper level of desire.

Her fists curled into the fine fabric. With a sob, she yanked at it, tearing button holes, seeking the satin heat and mahogany smoothness of his chest with her palms.

"Do you want this?" His fingers strummed again.

"Everything. All of you. Everywhere," she gasped, growing urgent.

"Good." He nipped at the point of her chin. His finger delved, sliding easily into her channel while he buried his mouth in her neck and delicately sucked.

She couldn't stop the small climax that shuddered through her.

He lifted his head, but didn't laugh at her. Raw lust glazed his eyes. His nostrils flared and he eased a second finger into her, watching her closely, ensuring the way she bit her lip was pure, erotic delight.

The noise he made was animalistic. He began to kiss his way down, lingering at her breast, unmindful of the way she was pushing his shirt off his shoulders. He was on a mission and, unlike her, he was in no hurry. His mouth trailed down to join the caress of his hand, claiming her in the most blatant way. He tipped her thigh up, pinning it as he made love to her with his mouth and his fingers until another orgasm crashed through her, swift and powerful.

He didn't stop. His fingers slid away, but he continued to soothe and incite with his clever tongue until her abdomen was taut and whimpers of fresh need were resounding in her throat.

Rearing up on his knees, he took in her weak, flagrant pose with a long look of dark satisfaction, until her fist curled self-consciously into the linen coverlet beneath her.

Then he moved off the bed.

The slap of rejection was so profound, she cried, "Don't!" and scrambled to sit up.

"I need a condom." His voice was graveled and raw,

but the light brush of his touch on her jaw was tender. "Wait here."

He threw his shirt off as he walked into the bathroom.

She ducked her hot face against her upraised knees, shivering in arousal and panicked reaction. In need.

This was what he had done to her five years ago—made her forget simple realities like birth control. He destroyed her ability to think clearly in the most delicious way, but he wasn't as carried away as her. Not as quickly. Not as thoroughly.

And he stirred so much emotion in her. Not just those top-level feelings like attraction and arousal, interest and admiration. No, he had always made himself felt in the deepest currents of her being, where she kept her fears and secret longings. Where she wanted to feel someone close inside her. Where she wanted to be loved.

He walked back naked, bronzed and powerful as a living work of art.

The relief within her was only eclipsed by the burst of joy the sight of him provoked. *He's the one. The only one.* It was an elemental recognition that had been too big for her to accept five years ago. It had been too frightening to live with someone who could affect her this profoundly with a look or a touch.

Today, she surrendered to that force. To him.

He pulled the edge of the blanket down, and she moved onto the sheet he exposed. She watched him roll the condom down his erection and lay on her back as he loomed over her. Her arms lifted to welcome him. She parted her lips and enjoyed the sweet friction of her naked thigh as she stroked it along the outsides of his. She let her hands greedily feel all of him—the contours of his back and the hard hills of his buttocks, the tendons behind his neck and the shape of his skull. The taste of his kiss and the dark way their combined sensuality swallowed her whole.

When he lined up and pierced her, there was a small pinch because it had been so long. She caught her breath and he lifted his head, glazed eyes penetrating hers with concern.

He hadn't *really* believed her, but now he set a comforting kiss on her lips. And he cupped her face and set his brow against her temple and said in quiet Greek, "I missed you, too."

That's what their celibacy—their fidelity—meant.

Shaken, she curled her arms around his neck.

He tucked her beneath him with care and let her get used to the feel of him inside her again, murmuring, "Tell me when you're ready."

She was ready! Her body was singing with anguished joy at the weight of his hips and the nuzzle of his lips against her ear and the thud of his heart on her breast.

So much emotion rose within her, her eyes dampened anew.

This was love, she thought. It was this tremendous vulnerability and heightened elation and sense of safety all combined. It was this desire to please. To ease. To stroke him and pour herself into their kiss and be generous. To offer her entire being without condition.

That's why he had scared her so much. How could she be enough for him? How could she love him and not lose herself?

Five years ago, she had pushed him away as hard as she could. Now she embraced him. She lifted her hips in invitation and he groaned, taut body shuddering before he began to move.

They were still a perfect match, like dancers who had been partners for years. The bed was their floor and they moved around it with elegance and ease, kissing and rolling, parting briefly only to press close again, all to the beat of their hearts and the music of their pleasured moans.

He lifted her to the heights, pulling her to straddle his hips where she arched in climax, then tumbling her onto her back to drive her to the brink again.

And when she thought herself incapable of withstanding any more pleasure, he said, "You can. For me. Once more. Let me feel it."

She couldn't resist his urgent lips or intimate touch. His demand for her to give him everything. This time, when she quaked and broke apart, he was with her, shouting out his triumph, holding her in that stasis of pleasure for long moments so the whole world turned golden and promising.

Then they both collapsed like the fallen angels that they were.

They made love twice more in the night.

Damian should have been drained by then, but when he woke with a start to an empty bed, and found her in the shower, he prowled into the stall to join her, hornier than ever.

She welcomed him with soapy arms and a warm, wet kiss, but he saw the shadow of a bruise around her mouth. His fingerprints were all over her. When he slid his touch between her legs, her indrawn breath wasn't all pleasure.

"Sore?"

"A little," she admitted.

Remorse had him skimming his mouth to her cheekbone as he tried to rein in the arousal that was already thick and stiff between them.

"But I don't want *you* to be aching," she purred and slid to her knees.

Within about five seconds of her mouth enveloping him, he was lost.

Even so, when they dried off, he still wanted her. Acutely.

He pulled on his clothes and made himself exert some control, but rather than drink his coffee in the lounge, he brought one to her. She had moved into the other bedroom where her luggage was. He sat in the chair in the corner and watched her move around in a seafoam-colored bra and underwear that was lacy and pretty as hell.

"I wouldn't bother with makeup," she said, leaning her hips against the bathroom sink. "But they know I'm here. My team says there's chatter online, mostly wondering how we met. It puts extra attention on your award so that's something."

"That's not why I asked you to come with me." He wasn't interested in anything except the way the scalloped lace of her underwear sat against the pale globe of her ass.

When she bent to blow-dry her hair upside down, he nearly crawled out of his skin. A few minutes later, she flipped up, cheeks pink and gaze brightening with amusement as she caught him ogling her.

"What are you thinking about?" She sauntered toward him, making everything in him tighten.

In a deliberately provocative move, she stepped her

foot over his outstretched legs and dropped her hands onto the back of his chair, not touching him, but affording him a very nice view of her breasts swaying in the cups of her bra. The V of her underwear cut from her hips down to that paradisiacal place that so enthralled him.

He licked his lips and, with supreme effort, tilted his head against the chair back to say, "I want to get back to Zoia."

"Right." The light in her eyes dimmed, and she pushed the chairback to straighten up.

He almost caught her hand, but she was too quick.

"Did I hurt your feelings?" he asked, suspecting he had. He was learning that she bruised easily. In every way.

"Not really." She was back in the bathroom where she brushed her hair with quick strokes. "I just..." She came to the doorway and held the hairbrush in her two hands. "It's fine if we're not going to do this again. I just need you to say that so I know what to expect."

The beast within him came up against the length of chain he was trying to keep himself on and howled.

"What do you want?" he asked.

"To screw ourselves blind on every piece of furniture we encounter. *Obviously.*"

He chuckled at the ceiling. Same. He couldn't be more aligned with her on that.

"But last night we agreed it was just for now. I wasn't sure if that meant *now*, while we're here in Berlin, or until I leave the island." She moved to the bed and threw her hairbrush into the open suitcase, then shook out a pair of sage-colored wide-legged trousers and stepped into them. A matching crop top followed, leaving a glimpse of her midriff. "I don't want to give Zoia a wrong impression about our future, so it's fine if you want to leave things here."

As if Zoia wouldn't notice that his mood was a thousand times improved from what it had been for the last five, dry years.

Carmel threw a few more things in the bag and snapped it closed, then kicked into a pair of sandals and looked at him.

"I know that we don't really have a future. Forgiving me doesn't mean you forget. Wanting to have sex with me doesn't mean you want *me*. That's okay. I want the sex. Last night was fantastic. I really needed that. Thank you."

"Me too," he said with a rasp in his voice.

"I know," she said, holding his gaze long enough he began to regret telling her there hadn't been anyone else. It felt too revealing. Then her brows came together in pensive thought. "Zoia's situation is stressful for you. You need an outlet. I'm okay with being your distraction. I really am. It has its perks."

"That sounds like pity sex, Carmel."

"No." She sent him a sulky scowl. "Friends with benefits." Her frown altered to one that was more earnest. Apprehensive. "Do you think we could be friends?"

"I don't know," he said truthfully. "I'm worried that I'll hurt you. I don't want us to do that to each other again."

"Me either." She chewed the corner of her mouth.

"But unless you tell me very clearly that you don't want me to touch you…" He rose and moved to set his hands on her hips. "I don't think I can keep my hands off you." He sought the warm skin beneath the fall of her top, bracketing his hands on her smooth waist, thumbs reaching to caress her rib cage.

"I like it when you touch me." Her pupils dilated, and her hands slid up his arms to his shoulders while she leaned into him. "I don't want to stop until we have to."

They didn't stop.

Over the next few days, they spent every night and half their days making love.

While they weren't demonstrative in front of Zoia, she could tell. She teased Carmel one morning in the garden.

"I'm pleased you and Damian are getting along so well." Her smile was smug. "I knew Berlin would be good for you."

Carmel stuck her tongue in her cheek and changed the subject.

Lethe knew what was going on, too. How could she not? Carmel's bed was never slept in. Damian began coming back to the villa for lunch. They would swim and disappear upstairs to "change" before coming down an hour later, mellow and hungry.

One morning, while they were eating breakfast, Damian passed his tablet across to her, showing her a photo of himself. In it, he was ten years younger, sitting astride a motorcycle. His hair was overlong and his T-shirt held the name of a rock band she didn't recognize. He wore a cocky grin she hadn't seen since the first time they'd met, and there was something about his eyes and the filter on the photo—

"Is this your father?" she asked in shock.

"Potentially. He's an engineer. Owns a big firm in Australia."

"I mean... Do you really have any doubt? You look just like him." She compared the carefree smile in the image to his somber expression as she handed back the tablet.

"He's agreed to a DNA test, but he wants to tell his wife and family first. Don't say anything to Zoia."

"No. I wouldn't," she said faintly, then added, "He has children?"

"Two girls and a boy. They're all in their twenties." His expression was so stiff, she thought his face would crack.

"Are you okay?"

"Of course. But there are things I need to look at with Pirro today. I'll see you later." He rose and didn't kiss her the way he had been doing most mornings before he left.

She tried to work, but couldn't concentrate. When he didn't come back for lunch, she gathered a few things into her shoulder bag and asked Lethe to text Pirro so she would know where to find Damian.

He was off in a corner of the estate alone, rebuilding a rock wall. When she found him, he gave her a look of irritation.

"What are you doing here?"

"I brought lunch. Your knuckle is bleeding," she noted.

He wiped it on his trousers, then dusted his palms.

She ignored his mild hostility and unrolled the straw mat inside the wall, where the overhanging branches from a nearby olive tree cast dappled shade on the ground.

"I'm not hungry."

"Have some water, at least." She opened the water bottle and watched him drain half, then she held it so he could rinse his hands and splash his face.

"I don't need you to look after me," he stated as she

offered a cloth napkin from the bag so he could use it as a towel.

"My motives are a little more selfish than that." It was a half-truth, but still true. "I thought bringing food and water was the decent thing to do, if I plan to seduce you." She withdrew the condom from her bra cup and showed it to him. "If you're not into it, that's fine." She tossed it onto the mat. "I can leave you to your work."

He caught her wrist in his damp hand before she could turn away.

"Are you sure you want this? Because I'm not in a mood to be tender."

"I know." She cupped the side of his stubbled jaw, reading the conflicting thoughts and emotions swirling in him. "But why waste all of that energy on building a wall?"

He yanked her close and his mouth came down on hers, hot and rough.

Her pulse leaped in surprise, but if there was one state of mind she understood very well, it was the need to escape when emotional stakes felt too acute to bear. When it felt as though you were drowning in thoughts too stormy to articulate. When you felt like you needed to fight just to breathe.

She understood what it felt like to be alone in that and how badly he might need someone to swim all the way out to the middle of his personal lake and grab on to him and drag him to shore, whether he wanted to come in or not.

It was always a dangerous prospect to save a drowning soul. In their desperation for survival, they could pull you down with them.

Which was what Damian did in these first seconds. He

locked his arms around her and smothered her mouth so she could hardly breathe. His fingers dug into her hips and shoulder then buttocks as he pulled her in tighter and ground himself against her.

He was so hard! She didn't understand why she responded so carnally to that. It was a deeply primitive instinct, she supposed, but she groaned and moved against that hard shape, opening her legs for him to settle between them as he carried her down to the mat.

She wore her sundress and he yanked the strap off her shoulder, baring her breast so he could suck her nipple with enough aggression to make her gasp.

"Too hard?" He reared onto his knees and brushed her skirt up to her stomach, yanking her underwear down her legs and tossing them away. "I need you to catch up, *omorfiá mou*."

Kneeling between her splayed thighs, he tucked his hands beneath her butt and lifted her hips as he bent to claim her tenderest flesh with his mouth.

She flinched at the sudden intimacy, the spike of acute pleasure, the rawness of how deliberately he prepared her for what was to come. And when she was arched with only her shoulders touching the ground, heels digging into his back, so close to climax she was incapable of speech, he lowered her hips to the mat.

His expression was feral, his movements urgent as he yanked at his fly and released himself, then tore open the condom with his teeth.

"Roll over," he said gutturally. "I want you on your knees."

She did, equally frantic now. Animalistic in her desire for their joining.

He swept her skirt into the middle of her back and caressed her hips and buttocks with one hand while guiding the dome of his sex against her folds, seeking her entrance. Then he clasped her hip and entered in a smooth, forceful thrust.

"Touch yourself. Stay with me," he demanded.

She dropped her forehead onto her forearm and swept her other hand to where he was steadily thrusting and retreating, building a friction that made her feel tighter and tighter. Drawing her into a dark cavern where sparking lights danced on the walls.

She was dimly aware of his hand on her shoulder, the other on her hip, holding her in place for his unfettered lovemaking, but she was bracing herself into stillness, needing those hard thrusts. Caught in the moment and reveling in his loss of control because it meant the barrier between them was dissolving.

She was dissolving.

"Damian!" she cried as her world imploded at exactly the moment he held himself deep inside her, shuddering and shouting out his own release.

Damian sagged forward and squashed her flat before he made a superhuman effort and rolled off her. He was sweaty and filthy and so shaken, he felt stripped naked.

He was more than half naked. With a twist of his wrist, he removed the condom and left it in the grass next to the mat, then pulled his briefs over his softening erection, still trying to catch his breath. Mildly fearful his heart was going to crash through his rib cage before it settled.

"Why did you let me do that?" he asked when he was able to speak.

She was still on her stomach. Her dress was up around her waist, pale buttocks drawing his hand to pet her and provoke a latent shiver to rock through her.

She turned her head to face him, eyelids heavy with sensuality.

"Because you needed it."

He rolled onto his back again, wishing he could argue, but she wasn't wrong. He'd been throwing rocks around as if it was a vital exercise that would save his kingdom from the invading hordes, but really, he was just trying to ignore the fact that he was falling apart on the inside.

He wanted to know if that man was really his father. He wanted to know his father.

It was a very uncomfortable realization when he'd been telling himself something else entirely for thirty-odd years.

Carmel rolled onto her back and brushed her skirt down her thighs, then sighed.

"Did I hurt you?" He searched out her hand between their hips.

"No." She wove her fingers between his. "I'm just wondering how many of your workmen saw us."

They'd all gone for lunch and were working in the vineyard anyway, but he said, "I'm sure it was only one or two."

"Pity. That was a good performance on our part."

He snorted. She always had to take things a step farther than they needed to go, but he couldn't help adoring her for it.

He ran his thumb against her skin in appreciation. In gratitude. It wasn't just the orgasm or the fact she'd let him set such a hard pace. It was the fact she was here at all. That she'd come looking for him when he'd felt so unsettled.

They lay quietly for several minutes with only the soft rustle of a breeze in the trees and a few crickets breaking the silence.

"I think it's good that he wants to tell his family first," she said eventually. "Learning about Atlas was a horrible shock for me because of the way Daddy did it, never giving me any warning. Just, 'This is Atlas. His mother and I were acquainted.' That's the word he used. For real. Isn't that hilarious?" Her leftover outrage hovered in the rust of her laugh.

"Perhaps that's all that was between my parents," he said, putting voice to some of the thoughts that had been torturing him since he'd decided to look for Nicholas Gatz. "They were young. They might have been strangers passing in the night. Maybe he's doing the test because he hopes it will prove I'm *not* his son."

He was aware of her turning her head to look at him, but he kept his gaze on the mesh of the long narrow leaves against the bright blue sky above them.

Then he put voice to the thought that tortured him most.

"Maybe it wasn't consensual," he said very quietly. "Maybe that's the reason she never wanted me to know him."

Carmel rolled and pulled his arm out of the way so she could snuggle into his side and let her head rest on his shoulder. Her arm and leg went across him.

It was too hot for cuddling. He was sweaty and covered in dust, but he hugged her tight into his side anyway.

"That's the real reason you've never looked for him?" she asked quietly.

"Yes."

"I don't think she would have put his name on your birth certificate if that was true."

"That's what I've been telling myself, but I can't help thinking it. What if he's pure scum and I regret telling him I exist?"

"At least you'll know. You went into this wanting to find out, didn't you? Otherwise, you wouldn't have done it. This wasn't just for Zoia. Was it?" She tilted her head up.

"I've spent my whole life telling myself he doesn't matter. I don't *want* him to matter."

"And now you're worried he won't live up to your expectations, so you're trying to keep your expectations low. You don't have to invite him all the way into your life. It will start with a conversation. You'll know pretty quickly whether he's someone you want to talk to again."

"I don't even know what I'd say. I hate talking about myself."

"Oh, really?" She set her fist in the middle of his chest and propped her chin on it, sprawling even more fully across him.

"And yet you got all of that out of me." He could see now how she'd brought up the topic and asked an innocuous question to give him space to fill. *Isn't that hilarious?* "You're very sneaky."

"I prefer devious. It sounds more intelligent. Ground squirrels are sneaky. I have the potential to be a supervillain."

"You do. It's terrifying." He smoothed her hair behind her ear.

"Thank you." Her eyes were alight with humor and self-satisfaction.

A cascade of emotions stole through him—laughter and admiration along with a deep sense that she was becoming essential to him.

That thought caused a shift inside him, one that sent a chill of threat into his chest.

"We should go for a swim," he said.

Some of the sparkle left her expression. She sensed he was withdrawing, but she sat up and began to gather their untouched picnic back into her bag.

"You didn't even eat what I brought you," she scolded.

"I think I did," he countered as he tossed her underwear at her.

She smirked and pulled them on beneath her dress.

When there was no trace of their tryst except a patch of crushed grass, they walked back to the villa.

"Do you think having this much sex is healthy?" Carmel asked later that afternoon, when they were settled in their favorite shady corner of the pool.

Lethe usually went home for a few hours after lunch before coming back to make dinner so they were always comfortable canoodling in the privacy of the walled terrace. Carmel was balanced on Damian's knee, one arm looped around his neck for balance, lips pressed to the cleft in his damp chin.

"I think this much sex requires a robust constitution. We must both possess one." He tugged at the string on her top, releasing the bow behind her neck.

"Don't fancy it up. Call us the degenerates we are."

"That goes without saying."

"Maybe it's like that thing bears do." She lifted her arm so he could reach behind her for the catch against her spine. "When they're compelled to eat nonstop before they sleep for six months."

He froze. Their stares locked as she referenced that their time together was finite. They had only five more days. Four, since they were traveling to Athens on Sunday.

"You sure as hell aren't letting me sleep *now*, are you?" he said, abiding by their unspoken agreement to keep things light.

Below the water, her top floated loose, sinking between them while he slid his palm into the back of her bikini bottoms.

"Oh, poor baby," she mocked, arching and trailing her kisses into his throat. "And I hear *so many* complaints—"

"Carmel." His tone became abruptly serious. His hand left her bottoms and he stretched his arm across her back, holding her against him in a more sheltering way. "Did you call him?" he asked under his breath.

"Who?" She twisted to follow his gaze over her shoulder, but it wasn't easy. Damian was holding her so her naked torso stayed hidden against his own.

Her arteries jolted with guilty discovery as she saw Atlas and Stella coming through the arched opening that gave access to the path along the side of the villa.

"Oh, shoot." She fished for her bikini top and tried to get the cups in place while Damian gave her very little room to maneuver.

"You are here!" Stella smiled brightly from beneath

her black cat's-eye sunglasses and wide-brimmed hat. "When no one answered the door, we weren't sure, but wanted to check."

They were a spectacularly beautiful couple. Atlas was tall and fit and looked like he worked for MI5 in those mirrored aviators. He was dressed as casually as it was possible for him to get, which meant he wore tailored almond-brown shorts and a crisp, short-sleeved buttoned shirt with a stripe.

Stella was nearly as tall as her husband and possessed a figure that broke necks. Her golden-blond hair sat in a long, fishtail braid against the front of her shoulder, and her chic, floral dress clung to her curves as she moved.

Carmel glanced at Damian, certain he would be checking out Stella, but the angle of his sunglasses suggested he was studying Atlas. He released her with reluctance as she finished securing her top and rolled off his lap to kick herself to the ladder.

"Why on earth would you come all this way when you could call or text?" Carmel asked as she climbed out of the water.

"Because you're not replying to my calls and texts." Atlas looked to the view beyond the wall while she pulled her pale pink crocheted cover-up over her head.

Damian came out of the pool behind her and took the towel Carmel handed him.

"I did ask for privacy, if you recall," she said. "How did you know where to find me?"

"You leave more breadcrumbs than Hansel and Gretel. My driver dropped you at his building in Athens. The photos from Berlin. The painting you sent to Athens from a gallery here on the island. It wasn't hard."

So supercilious. But now she had to anxiously ask Stella, "Did you like it?"

"The painting? I love it so much. Thank you." Stella rushed forward to embrace her, always holding on for an extra second so Carmel knew she wasn't just being polite. Stella offered real friendship and affection. "He's worried," she whispered before she released her.

"Why would he be worried?" Carmel asked with loud annoyance. "I told you I'm fine. Totally sober. Ha." She mockingly left her mouth open as though inviting him smell her breath.

"Great," Atlas said impassively, then switched to Greek. "You must be Carmel's husband. I'm Atlas Voudouris." He reached past her to where Damian had wrapped the towel around his waist. "I apologize for turning up unannounced. I need to speak to my sister. This is my wife, Stella."

"Welcome," Damian said dryly as he shook Atlas's hand. "Damian Kalymnios. English is fine."

"It's so nice to meet you," Stella said warmly as she shook his hand. "I had no idea you were married," she scolded Carmel in an aside. "Not until Atlas told me when your photos from Berlin came out."

Carmel winced. "It's online?"

"The photos are. Not your marriage," Stella said.

"Then how do you know we're married?" She looked between them.

"I've always known," Atlas said in his pithy way, as though she ought to have known that he had known.

"Why do you always have to take that tone with me?" she asked with irritation.

"This is my voice. I can't help that you don't like it."

"It makes me want to push you in the pool."

"Have at it. I know how to swim."

If she hadn't tried and failed in the past, she might have given it a shot.

"Oliver told me," Atlas conceded. He never called their father anything but his first name. "He wanted me to help keep it quiet."

"Does he know I'm here now?" she asked with concern.

"No. But—"

"Why don't we let them change into dry clothes." Stella set her hand on Atlas's arm. "Rather than make them stand here soaking wet. Damian, would you mind if I help myself to that water?" She pointed at the jug on the table.

"Of course. Make yourself at home," he said with irony. "We'll only be a moment."

"I am so sorry," Carmel said as she walked with him into the villa.

"It's fine," Damian said, sounding impassive, but she could feel him withdrawing even further behind his shields.

She went into her room to slip on a sundress, then met Damian coming out of his room in shorts and a collared T-shirt.

Downstairs, Lethe had just returned and apologized profusely for not being here to greet their guests.

"We weren't expecting them, but if you could prepare some refreshments?" Damian asked.

"Of course. I'll be right out." Lethe hurried to tie on her apron.

"You have a beautiful home," Stella said to Damian when they returned to the terrace. "Is that a guest cottage over there? The garden looks beautiful."

"My grandmother lives there."

"Zoia," Carmel stated. "She rests in the afternoons, but I'll introduce you before you go. She's already a fan of yours." She flicked her hand at Atlas.

"Please sit," Damian said as Lethe came out with glasses and a jug of the citrus and honey flavored agora Carmel had begun splashing into her water. "Did you fly or come in by ferry?" he asked.

"We're on our yacht. We didn't want to be in Athens when the news broke." Atlas glanced at Stella then said to Carmel, "Oliver's likely to be charged with DWI."

"What! What happened? Is he hurt? Did *he* hurt anyone? Why was he even driving? Where was Costa?"

Atlas raised a hand and Carmel stopped blurting questions so he could explain.

"No one else was involved. Oliver bought himself a Jaguar. It arrived yesterday so he drove out to see Woodley in Oxfordshire. After imbibing through lunch, he stopped at every pub he could find on his way home."

"Why?" she asked with annoyed disbelief. "To show off?"

"Does it matter?" Atlas shrugged. "The point is, a lot of people saw him enjoying a pint. He rolled the car into a ditch around midnight, but managed to walk away with some bruises and a mild concussion. He called Costa to pick him up and get him home, but he was so drunk, Costa thought he might be having a stroke. He took him to the hospital. While he was there, the car was spotted. Oliver was still inebriated when the police came to question him. That's when he called his lawyer who called me."

"Where is he now? Home? Or still in hospital?"

"The clinic. To show he's addressing his problem," Atlas said with heavy sarcasm.

"You mean to hide from paparazzi." Daddy wouldn't seek actual help. His daughter might have a drinking problem, but that was because she was weak. He was perfect in every way. The world ought to arrange itself to recognize that.

"I wanted to tell you before we released the statement, but I want to stay ahead of it so…" He took out his phone and tapped briefly before pocketing it again.

"Have you talked to him? How was he?" she asked.

"The usual."

Carmel slumped in her chair, mind racing. There was no satisfaction in the irony of her father needing the very clinic their family had funded to take care of her, but she had a sense she ought to be with him, even though he'd never supported her when she'd been in there.

"I should have picked up your call." Atlas had texted this morning saying, *It's important*, but she'd ignored it. "Why didn't you say it was about him?"

"There's nothing you can do. It's better if you're off-grid and not linked to it."

"They'll drag me into it anyway," she said darkly.

"They'll try," he agreed. "That's why I wanted to warn you. And be sure you were protected from ambush." He looked at Damian. "I'm concerned that we were able to drive right in."

"Complacency on my part," Damian said. "Things are usually very quiet here. I'll have the staff start locking the gate."

"That doesn't always stop them," Atlas said with a dissatisfied curl of his lip. "You're welcome to join us on the yacht," he said to Carmel.

Which was when she saw this visit for what it really was.

"Oh, my *Gawd*, this is a rescue mission." She sent Stella a glare of exasperation. "Can't you control him?"

"You're funny," Stella said mildly.

"It's only a rescue mission if you need it to be," Atlas said. "Do you?"

"*No*. How many times do I have to say I'm fine?"

"You're staying here, then?" Atlas asked. "For how long?"

"If I answer that, can Damian grill Stella on *your* relationship?" she challenged.

"Damian can ask me anything he likes," Stella said with a warm smile across the table.

"I'm curious what the protocol is," Damian said to Stella. "Do we sit back and watch the show? How long does it usually go on?"

"Great question. I find it's best to wait it out, but a bit of misdirection can help. Oh. Before I forget." She touched Carmel's arm. "I brought a bag of books for you. They're in the car we rented."

"Really?" Carmel sat up with eagerness before she heard the men snort and realized she'd fallen straight into the trap. "I thought you were my friend, Stella."

Stella laughed and leaned over to hug her.

"*Kýrie?*" Lethe came out with a mezze platter of olives and grapes, cherry tomatoes and artichoke hearts, squares of feta, dolmades, wedges of pita and various dips. "Pirro said you wanted to speak with the winemaker the next time he was at the shed. Should I tell him you have guests?"

"I'd rather speak to him today. Care to walk up with me?" Damian invited Atlas.

"I'd like that. I'm curious about your operation." Atlas rose.

"Why do I get the feeling only one of you will come back?" Carmel looked between them. "We'll just sit here and talk about our moon cycles, then?"

"Do you want to come with us?" Damian asked.

"In this heat? Not twice in one day, thank you." It was a deliberate reminder of their tryst earlier.

He squeezed her shoulder in response. "We'll see you in thirty minutes."

To say he felt threatened by Atlas turning up here was inaccurate.

Damian was prickling with possessiveness and a sense of trespass, but there was something else underlying it. Guilt, perhaps. Sleeping with the woman who was his wife was not a crime, but sleeping with Carmel when they planned to divorce put him on a more defensive footing.

He wasn't surprised her brother was projecting a heavy attitude of "what are your intentions?" He was irritated by it, though. Mostly because he didn't have a clear answer.

He had promised to sign Carmel's papers once Zoia went into surgery. He considered himself a man of his word, but he wasn't allowing himself to think beyond getting Zoia to Athens. They were taking her across on Sunday, so she could settle in her private room and be prepped for the surgery on Monday. By Tuesday, he would have a better idea of her outcome. Then he would consider his own future and how much it might intersect with Carmel's.

"We're looking for something like this on Syros," Atlas mentioned as they hiked through the olive grove. "That's where I spent my childhood."

"Zoia's cottage is on a small plot that was in my grandfather's family for generations." Damian pointed out the surrounding tracts of land he'd purchased as they became available. "Carmel calls me a gentleman farmer for buying up all these groves and pastures, but I'm really just expanding my buffer zone."

"Because you like your privacy?" The corner of Atlas's mouth dug in with knowing humor. "You're entitled to it. So is Carmel. Her love life is between her and her diary, but she needed to hear about Oliver from me."

"Does she need to go to him?" Damian braced himself. Regardless of their deal or his profound dislike of the man, he wouldn't stand between her and her father.

"That's up to her." Atlas's expression tightened. "I hope she doesn't. I've never respected him enough to care what he thinks of me, but he knows how to play her. When I spoke to him, he tried telling me it was my fault he chose to drive drunk, that it wouldn't have happened if Carmel and I hadn't sided against him at DVE. Carmel has blocked him or he would have pulled her into this already. She desperately wants to believe he's redeemable."

"And your interference between them has nothing to do with the fortune you stand to inherit if you're on his good side and she isn't?" Damian asked.

"I don't need his money." Atlas didn't flinch or even glance at him, only continued walking up the hill at the same steady pace. "Neither does she. But I wondered if you might encourage her to mend fences with him, since her fortune was the reason *you* married her." Now he turned his head, but the sunlight only glinted off his sunglasses. "Or so Oliver told me at the time."

"I can't defend myself against that," Damian said grimly. "It's not untrue. But it wasn't as cold-blooded as that sounds, either. Carmel wanted to access funds from her mother. I saw a means to accelerate what I thought was our joint future."

"And when Oliver denied her that fortune, you split up, but you never divorced her. Why's that?"

Because she's mine. It was far too primal and sexist a thing to say aloud, but it sat in him as truth.

"That information is need to know," he said instead. "You don't."

"Did you separate because of her drinking?"

"No," Damian said with surprise. "I didn't actually know how much of a problem she had. We were young and met while she was on vacation. Too young to marry anyone, least of all someone we'd known for less than a week."

They were coming into earshot of the people hovering around the winemaking shed so he switched gears, pointing out the two different varietals, then introduced Atlas to the winemaker and the rest of the workers.

"Carmel suggested I look into making nonalcoholic wine," he told the winemaker. It was an emerging market and something Carmel thought could differentiate his small winery from the other boutique labels here in Greece.

The winemaker was eager to experiment, so Damian gave him the go-ahead to make some trial batches.

"Does that mean she's planning to be here long enough to try it?" Atlas asked once they were walking back to the villa.

"She doesn't trust herself to drink alcohol substitutes." It was a nonanswer. They both knew it.

"Everything I've read about you leads me to believe you're a decent person. I've made it my business to read extensively about you," Atlas added with dark humor. "Carmel no longer plays the blame game. If she has a stumble, she owns it. I'm not saying you caused her problems with alcohol. It started long before she met you, and the reasons for it are very complex. She's worked hard to get to where she doesn't fall back on drinking as a coping strategy, but that doesn't mean she can't be knocked off her stride, especially if she's hurt. Things were not good five years ago, Damian." His voice turned grave. "I don't relish seeing her like that again."

A chill moved into Damian's chest. "You think I'm toxic to her? Like your father?"

"I don't know. That's why I'm here, checking up."

They finished the walk in silence and arrived to find the women had moved to the loungers. They sat sideways on them, facing each other, both surrounded by paperback romance novels.

"All finished with your measuring contest?" Carmel didn't look up from the back of the book she was reading.

Stella moved a couple of books so Atlas could sit beside her. He braced his hand behind her and let her braid slither through the fingers of his other hand.

"I told Carmel that we brought our suits in case we found a beach and wanted to swim. She said we don't need them if we go down those stairs." Stella pointed.

"I'm game if you are, *agapi mou*. You're the shy one between us."

"She's misquoting me. I said we'd join you," Carmel said.

"With paparazzi about to hunt her like an escaped fugitive." Stella turned her head so she was nose to nose with Atlas. "Can you imagine the headlines if they caught the four of us down there like a bunch of pagans?"

"It's called taking control of the narrative, Stella." Carmel looked at Damian over her sunglasses and winked.

"Swim here." Damian waved at the pool. Carmel was obviously enjoying her sister-in-law's company, and maybe Atlas would be reassured that she was, in fact, better than fine. She was happy here with him. Wasn't she? "Stay for dinner. Zoia likes to eat early, but I'm sure she'd enjoy fresh company."

Zoia was tickled to have the exalted company of a gold medal champion, and she quickly warmed to Stella. Who didn't? Stella had a background in hospitality. She was a grand master when it came to engaging people in lighthearted conversation. Even Damian had been drawn into telling stories about his roofing days and how he got started in solar panels, then describing some of his ambitions for the future.

Atlas and Stella didn't stay long after dinner, though.

"We've imposed on you long enough," Atlas said to Damian, shaking his hand.

"Yes, you've been very gracious, letting us crash your corner of paradise. Thank you for dinner," Stella said. "I hope Zoia's surgery goes well."

Zoia had told them what she was in for.

"Thank you. Me too," Damian said.

"Text if you need anything," Atlas told Carmel. "We'll be back in Athens on the weekend. Come stay at the apartment if you want to." He issued that invitation to Carmel, but flicked his gaze to include Damian.

The men hadn't bonded like blood brothers, but they had found enough to talk about from business and sports to island politics that they had each other's respect.

"Thank you for inviting them to stay," Carmel said when they entered the villa after they were gone. "Was he rude to you when you walked up to the wine shed?"

"He gave me the courtesy of speaking plainly," Damian said blithely.

"Oof. That sounds awful. What did he say exactly?"

Damian seemed to debate a moment, then said, "He's worried you might go see your father and what could happen if you do." He watched her closely as he relayed that.

"So am I," she admitted, pacing across the stone tiles of the lounge. "That's why I was glad to have them here all afternoon, distracting me from wondering if I should reach out. Daddy never called me while I was in rehab. Or boarding school. He never really cared where I was or what I was doing. That doesn't make it right for me to ignore him in his time of need, though."

"Atlas said he was already trying to pin the blame on you and Atlas because you worked against him at DVE."

"That doesn't surprise me. But guess what? I thought the entire world was against me for *years* and never once drove drunk. He deserves to sit there and think about what he's done," she muttered, feeling guilty nonetheless. She was going to need a long session with her therapist to work through this one.

"What about sending him a message?" Damian suggested. "Do you know anyone on staff? Maybe they could relay something. That way you're not giving him an avenue to respond."

"Do I know anyone on staff," she scoffed. "We have a group chat where we share obscene and tasteless memes. But that's an excellent idea. Thank you." She moved across to hug him. "Do you mind if I do it now? To get everything I want to say out of my head?"

He gave a *be my guest* wave toward the stairs.

She let go and started to turn away, but turned back.

"Was that all he said? Because you seem... I don't know." She tilted her head, trying to read his expression. He was as unreadable as he'd been the whole time Atlas and Stella had been here. "Pensive?"

Damian played his finger in the tendril of hair that fell from her temple, then let his fist rest on her shoulder, looking as though he was going to say something.

"It can wait," he said, then pressed a kiss to her forehead. "Go write your letter. I want to walk down and make sure Pirro secured the gate."

She was a little disgruntled by that, but her mind really was spinning with everything she wanted to stay to her father. She nodded and ran up the stairs.

CHAPTER TEN

On Sunday morning, Carmel woke in the predawn hours, instantly melancholy as she realized this would be her last day with Damian.

She skimmed her hand across the sheet and found the warm satin of his back.

He stirred and she slithered closer, rubbing the inside of her thigh over the firm shape of his buttocks.

"What time is it?" he asked into his pillow.

"Early. Do you want to…?" She pressed a kiss to his shoulder.

"Always." He looped his arm around her and pulled her half beneath him as he buried his seeking lips in her throat.

They didn't have "always." They had today. One last time. It was enough to bring a sting of poignant heartache to her closed eyes, but she refused to let sadness infuse this moment. Her time here with him was a gift. It had allowed them to mend and learn to trust and, in her case, *love*.

She loved him. She knew it without a doubt and poured her love over him as they kissed and caressed and moved with languid friction against each other. She revered him, celebrating the feel of his hair between her fingers and the taste of his skin and the way they communicated without words. She welcomed him into her body and into her heart.

Time stopped as they made love. There was no urgency, simply closeness and incredible pleasure. Affinity.

And when climax approached, he was with her, knotting his fist in the sheet as he surged into her and cried out as helplessly as she did.

It was only as his shaking arms gave way and he let his weight settle on her, when his damp skin adhered to hers and his heart pounded against her breast that she realized what she had said in her moment of crisis.

Her heart felt as though it fell down a flight of stairs.

"Carmel," he whispered. It was more a protest. A prayer that he hadn't heard what he'd heard.

"It's okay," she said, because it was. "I don't want you to say it back. I just wanted you to know." She did. She loved him and she wanted him to know it.

He shifted off her, and she could feel how he was still trembling from exertion. Maybe that was her, shaking in reaction.

He pressed his mouth to her brow, holding her as though she was precious. She closed her eyes against his silence, though, trying not to feel tragic and forsaken.

He wanted her to be lying. That was the hellish part. Because her loving him put a daunting level of responsibility on him.

That doesn't mean she can't be knocked off her stride, especially if she's hurt.

Carmel relaxed in his arms and her breath evened out, telling him she'd fallen back asleep. He kept his arms around her, assimilating her words, weighing his own feelings.

He cared about her. Very much. Far more than he would have expected or admitted to when she had turned up in Athens two short weeks ago. He would have sworn then that he felt only hatred toward her.

But he couldn't have hated her that intensely without feeling something more in the first place. He couldn't call it "love." They had barely known each other then, and how well did they really know each other now? As much as he believed he could trust her these days, he was still cautious about fully letting his guard down with her.

He'd been toying with the idea of asking her to stay in their marriage, though, since it was working so well. Could he ask her to stay when she was more emotionally invested than he was? Or would that be taking advantage of her?

He had wanted to wait until he knew Zoia's future before considering his own with Carmel. Today was the day he was taking her to Athens and now he was thinking about it, he was fully awake.

He eased away from Carmel and pulled on a pair of shorts, then crossed the hall to pick up his phone off the charger. He checked his email out of habit, even though it was the weekend, and stopped midway down the stairs.

DNA Results, the subject line from his lawyer read.

Holding his breath, he opened it. His scanning eyes picked up the line in bold:

Probability of paternity: 99.99%.

He had found his father.

Carmel woke alone and felt robbed by Damian's absence, but also a little grateful. She wasn't ready to face him after she had told him she loved him.

She didn't regret it. Not really. She wasn't ashamed of her feelings, and telling him was only part of being as open and honest with him as she could be.

But she was very aware he hadn't said it back.

The hollow sensation that cold reality put in her chest was a preview of the loss she would soon experience unrelentingly.

She had already packed and Damian had gone over to Zoia's, so Carmel sat in the kitchen drinking coffee with Lethe until Pirro turned up looking for her luggage.

Two goodbye hugs later, Carmel boarded the helicopter where Damian was helping Zoia buckle in and get comfortable. Zoia's caregiver, Renita, was coming along to keep things familiar for Zoia and receive instructions about her recovery when she was cleared to come home.

It meant Carmel barely got a moment of eye contact with Damian, let alone room for a private conversation. She wasn't sure he wanted one. He seemed to have retreated into himself, and she tried not to feel responsible. Taking Zoia to Athens for this surgery had been weighing on him a long time.

The travel was uneventful. By lunchtime, Zoia was tucked into her room, urging them to leave so she could eat and rest.

Damian promised to come by in the evening and they dropped Renita at a nearby hotel on their way to his penthouse.

It was only a few blocks from Atlas's and was comparably luxurious with its tasteful, airy space, marble floors and a unified decor that created a sense of flow from one room into another. The furniture was modern in shades of blue and slate gray, and they had a beautiful view of the Acropolis off the terrace, but it wasn't "home" in the way the villa was.

She already missed being there.

As the silence between them thickened, she decided to bring up what they were both avoiding talking about.

"I didn't—"

"Will you do something for me?" he asked abruptly.

She blinked in surprise. "What's that?"

He took out his phone and tapped, then handed it to her. "Read that email and tell me what you think."

Her pulse skipped. "Your father?"

"Yes."

"This is why you've been so quiet today?" So it wasn't Zoia *or* her blurted words in the middle of the night that had him so preoccupied.

"The confirmation was waiting for me when I got up this morning. This came through while we were at the hospital."

She didn't ask him why he hadn't told her that Nicholas was his father. He hadn't had a chance.

"Have you read it?" she asked.

"More than once. I just…" He ran his hand down his face, seeming to work at keeping his emotions in check.

Warily, she sat down on the sofa and began to read aloud.

"'Hi Damian, I'm Nick. It's been a shock to learn I have another son, but a pleasant one.'" She liked him already.

"'I'll keep this short because I understand your granny is unwell. That's rough, mate. I'm sorry to hear that. Your lawyer said you were hoping I would have some memories of your mother that might bring her some comfort.

I don't have much, I'm afraid. I only knew Hestia for a weekend. I was at the end of my gap year when we met in Athens. The first night we slept together in the literal sense. No naughty business, if you catch my drift. The next morning, I sat in the café while she worked her shift, then we spent the rest of the day together. That night was less innocent and I'd like you to know I asked her to marry me. Twice.'" Carmel couldn't help smiling at that.

Damian stood with his hands in his pockets, profile tense.

"'She called me foolish for proposing. I suppose I was. Twenty-year-old men usually are.'" Carmel *really* liked him. "'I was smitten and very serious about wanting to see more of her, but I was meeting friends in Thailand and due to start back at school. I begged Hestia to visit me in Australia. She didn't want to carry on a romance with someone who lived so far away, though. She said her parents would never leave their island and her being in Athens was already hard for them.'"

That was sweet, Carmel thought. No matter her disagreements with Zoia's husband, Damian's mother had loved her parents and wanted to be near them.

"'I gave her my mother's number, hoping she would change her mind,'" Carmel continued reading. "'But not long after I arrived home, my mother moved to live with my sister, so that number was disconnected. I left a message at the café once, but Hestia never returned my call. By Easter that year, I had met my wife. We've been together ever since, but I've never forgotten my first love. It never occurred to me that Hestia could have been pregnant. We used protection. I understand she's been gone a long time, but this is fresh for me and it hurts a lot. I'm very sorry for your loss, Damian. Very.'"

She let that sit a moment before reading the rest.

"'Please tell your granny that we were a pair of silly young lovers who went dancing at a night club and ate street food at the flea market and that I hope I can meet her soon to thank her for raising my son.'"

Oh. She was going to cry. Carmel covered her mouth and scanned the rest. It was Nicholas's phone number and an invitation to call. *We're all very keen to meet you when you're ready.*

With her heart mangled in her chest, she rose and walked over to hug Damian's stiff body, setting her head against his heart.

Slowly, his arms came around her. They were angular and twitching. She had the sense he was staving off great emotion.

"He seems like a very nice man," she said through the thickness that had gathered in her throat.

"I wanted to hate him. To be right about not trying to find him." He swallowed.

"Now you want to meet him?"

"I do."

She smiled against his shirt. "Will you tell Zoia?"

"Tonight. When I go back to say good-night."

"Alone?" She looked up at him.

"Do you mind?" He smoothed his hand over her hair, then cupped her neck. There was turmoil in his eyes, but a calm sort of acceptance in his expression.

"No, I don't mind." Talking about his mother was very personal to them. She understood that. "I think she'll be happy to know…" Oh, God. Her throat was closing and her chest grew weighted with bags of cement. "To know that you have a whole family wanting to meet you," she choked out.

He would never be alone the way Zoia had feared. He had people waiting to welcome him into their fold. That's what struck Carmel like a hammer. He didn't need her to be his safety net. Perhaps he never had. She had only let herself believe it so she could have an excuse to be with him. Now she felt superfluous.

She began to pull away.

"What's wrong?" He caught at her.

"Nothing." It was a fib, one she couldn't allow herself to get away with, but she finished pulling out of his arms before admitting, "It's hitting me that we're at the end of our agreement."

"Does it have to be?"

She had spent the day steeped in dread of their parting, aware of the minutes ticking toward devastation. Instead, his words caused joy to explode through her entire being. Hopes she had barely allowed herself to acknowledge arrived in a vision that extended forward. A future with Damian. *Forever*.

"I thought..." She had to clear the huskiness of elation from her throat. "I thought you were mad about what I said this morning, but you..." She started to hug his waist again while tears glossed her eyes. "You love me, too?"

"I—" His hands closed on her shoulders, holding her off. "I care about you. Obviously. But... Carmel." His tone held a patronizing edge. "That word is very loaded. For both of us. We have to be careful how we use it."

"You don't believe me." She pulled away and might as well have fallen on her butt, she was so knocked breathless by what hurt more than the fact that he didn't return her feelings. "You still think it's something I say instead of 'thank you for that orgasm'?"

"I'm not trying to start a fight."

"This isn't a fight. This is us talking about how we feel. It's fine that you don't love me back, Damian. *That's fine.*" That was true. Painful, but, "I can't force you to feel anything, but don't you dare tell *me* how to feel. Don't *question* how I feel. I've been in too much therapy not to know myself inside and out."

"Fine. But you don't know me."

"How can you say that?" she cried. "Damian. You're terrified of loving and being abandoned again. That's why you don't want to love me. That's why you don't trust me, even when I say that I love you. *Especially* when I say those words. Because I betrayed you and left you once before. That's why I don't expect you to love me back. That's why it's *fine*."

She might have gone too far with that raw assessment of him. He glared at her, outrage flashing in his eyes. All of him looked carved from marble, but his cheek ticked.

"Why ask me to stay if you don't love me?" She hugged herself. "Because it's comfortable?"

"Hardly," he bit out.

She ignored the sting of that. "Because we're good at sex, then? I came here because I wanted you to forgive me. I didn't expect it, but I hoped for it. I wanted to tell you the truth and show you I had changed. That I'm not a spoiled brat anymore. That I am capable of caring about other people. But…" She took a breath that burned, shoulders hunched protectively. "You don't spend as many hours in therapy as I have without thinking about what you truly want from life. I'm trying to believe I deserve to be loved."

It hurt to meet his eyes as she said that. Admitting she wanted to be loved was deeply frightening. It felt arrogant while making her feel profoundly vulnerable. A fist closed around her heart and squeezed the air from her lungs as she continued to bare herself to him.

"I'm not saying that to put pressure on you. I'm saying that's what I want and need for myself. I need to be loved, Damian."

He still looked as if he were carved from marble, his expression so shuttered he was impossible to read, but his closed fist and clenched jaw told her how tightly wound he was.

"I think we were falling in love five years ago. I didn't believe I was lovable so I took whatever small kernel of feelings you had for me and stomped on them. I did that, I own it and I'm sorry. I'm sorry *now* because I can see what I might have had if I'd been braver. I understand why you don't want to risk your heart on me again." Tears were gathering in her eyes. In her throat. "But if you don't love me, if you can't love me, then I can't stay with you." There was barely any volume left in her voice. It hurt too much to say what needed to be said, but she managed to push it out. "I need you to let me go."

"Atlas said the last time we broke up—" His expression spasmed and he looked away.

She realized what he was implying and gasped, not having thought he could hurt her any more than he already had.

"Get over yourself, Damian," she snapped. "I don't need you to save me. Do you know how many times

I've gotten sober in the last five years? Enough that I'm good at it."

"Don't make jokes about that," he shot back.

"Then quit acting like you're the only thing that ever made me unhappy. And don't you dare keep me here as though I'm someone you're willing to tolerate so I won't hurt myself. I've been in that position and I won't stand for it again. I deserve better. I deserve *more*."

She moved to her bag, but there was a part of herself that stood at a distance, watching her burn her life to the ground again. Maybe she should shut up and stay with him. Maybe there was hope if she tried not to ruin it again.

No. She had played that game too many times to think this was the one time she could win at it. She hadn't changed until she'd had to. She couldn't expect someone else to change just because she wanted them to.

She found the envelope and slapped it onto the top of the kitchen bar.

"Sign these like you promised so I can find someone who actually loves me, flaws and all."

The air pulsed with the charged emotions between them. For a minute, she thought he would refuse.

Then he came across and removed the papers from the envelope. He plucked a pen from the nearby cup. The flourish of his signature was a rapier that shredded her insides.

"You're not going to read them?" The petition was very simple, declaring that both parties wished to dissolve the marriage with no settlements on either side, but she was begging for any stay of execution at this point.

"I read them the other day, after your brother left.

But—" He dropped the pen back into the cup. The sound might as well have been the blade of a guillotine crashing down. "You're right. We had an agreement."

He pushed the pages back into the envelope and handed it to her, then walked away.

She could hardly hold on to it. The pages felt too heavy. The entire package could have been on fire, the way it burned against in her numb fingertips. Her face ached with the effort to keep from crying.

Behind her, she heard Damian ask, "Are you home? Your sister is leaving my apartment. I'll have my driver—"

She snapped her head around to see he was on the phone.

"Yes. That's what I was concerned about. I'll walk her down to the lobby, then."

He ended the call. She stared in disbelief.

"I don't need a bloody chaperone to get from here to my brother's place. You think I'm going to head into the nearest bar? I will *never* give anyone that kind of power over me again."

"He said paparazzi are staked out at his building. He's sending his driver so you can go in through the underground."

"Oh." Aside from trolls making "like daughter like father" remarks online, she hadn't been bothered too much over her father's scandal, but that had been while she'd been at the villa on Damian's remote island. She supposed a reckoning on that front was coming along with everything else.

She threw the signed papers into her bag and shouldered it, then she marched down the hall to grab her suitcase. When he tried to take it from her, she slapped his hand away and rolled it into the elevator herself.

They rode down to the lobby in profound silence. When Atlas's car pulled up to the curb, the doorman hurried to open the door.

Carmel kept her chin high as she sailed out, not even saying goodbye.

Stella waited for her in the back seat. Her hair was in a messy clip atop her head. She wore one of Atlas's T-shirts over the damp outline of her bikini.

"You left the pool to come get me?" She could hardly believe it.

"Of course. Do you want to talk or—"

The door slammed behind her and Carmel fell into Stella's hug, letting her tears swamp her.

CHAPTER ELEVEN

DAMIAN WAS NUMB after Carmel left. He was tempted to stay that way by getting very drunk, but he had to see Zoia later.

He couldn't stay in his apartment, though. Carmel had only been there an hour, but she inhabited every corner.

He went to his office building, which was deserted on a Sunday afternoon, but he discovered she was there, too.

Two minutes, her tenacious voice insisted. *I only came to give you this. Read it, sign it, then we never have to speak again.*

He should have done exactly that. Then he wouldn't be feeling gnawed from the inside out.

After an hour of trying to read a report that refused to make sense, he stared out at the city until the shadows were long. Then he went to the hospital to see his grandmother.

He didn't tell her he'd ended things with Carmel.

"I wanted to come alone," he said. "To tell you I've heard from my father." He paraphrased the email Nick had sent.

Zoia shed a few tears at the small memory Nick had relayed of her daughter.

When Damian said good-night, Zoia cupped his face and said, "I'm not surprised he's a good man. So are you."

Then why does everyone leave me? He didn't ask it aloud. It was a childish question. His mother hadn't left him. It only felt that way. She hadn't meant to die, making him see her absence as abandonment. His father hadn't known about him at all. Age had caught up with his grandfather, the way it did with everyone. Exactly as it was doing with Zoia.

Carmel had left, though. Not just the first time, but today. He understood it. He even agreed with her. She did deserve better. She deserved to be loved.

It still hurt like hell.

You're terrified of loving and being abandoned again.

He was.

He breathed through the searing pain and went home, where he barely slept. His bed was empty and cold.

After a bracing shower, he went to the hospital; they had already taken Zoia into pre-op. That's when he picked up a text from Carmel.

Atlas has to leave for London this morning. I don't want to bring the paparazzi to the hospital unless you want me there?

You should go with him, he replied.

Three dots appeared, then disappeared.

It occurred to him that she might have ended their marriage, but she wasn't *leaving*. Not entirely. He was sending her away.

Finally, her message came through. Please let me know when you have news.

And that was it. She was gone.

***

One of the best things Carmel had done while staying with Damian was to teach Zoia how to send and listen to voice mail on her tablet.

Carmel had never known her own grandparents. Not in a way that felt like a real connection. Both of her grandfathers had been gone by the time she was born, and her mother's mother had had dementia. She hadn't recognized Carmel by the time Carmel was old enough to form memories of her. Her father's mother had been a very cold, critical woman who Carmel had learned to avoid at all costs.

Now she felt as though she had gained the grandmother she had always yearned for. At first, Zoia's messages were very short, saying only that she was feeling tired, but the doctors were pleased. Soon she was more chatty, leaving longer messages about how handsome her doctor was or that she was feeling good enough to work in her garden, but Damian said she was only allowed to sit in it.

Exchanging messages with her was a bright spot in otherwise dark days for Carmel.

She worked a lot, which helped the time pass, and she went to see her father twice, going with Atlas both times.

Oliver had negotiated a six-month stay at the rehabilitation clinic in exchange for avoiding jail time. He was furious about it.

It was odd for Carmel to go into the clinic sober and hear the same excuses she had once spouted coming out of Oliver's mouth. She sat in therapy with him and told him things he probably didn't really hear, but it felt good to get those old injuries off her chest.

It felt good to realize he had very little influence over her anymore.

When Atlas and Stella flew back to Greece, she was sad to see them go and jealous of their being that much closer to Damian, but she knew she would be okay.

She was lonely, though. Her heart wasn't broken, but it held an emptiness. She was pining for him.

The one rough day she had was when she received the Divorce Absolute. She stayed in bed watching comfort shows and eating junk food between crying jags.

The next morning, she woke with gritty eyes and an all-over body ache. It was a nonalcoholic hangover resulting from an overindulgence of self-pity, but it was over now. It was time to start afresh.

She knew how to do that. As she'd told Damian, she'd started over enough times to have a routine for it. The first step was always the same: she booked herself into a spa for a full day of scrubs, massages, nutrition and beauty treatments. Then she would buy herself a stunning outfit and a pair of obscenely expensive shoes. She might even spring for a new handbag.

Maybe Damian didn't love her, but she loved herself and, for now, that was enough.

Damian watched Zoia improve every day. Now that she was recovering, she was grateful to have the surgery behind her. Her color was good, she had more energy and her overall outlook was brighter.

He, on the other hand, was morose.

The villa, which had always been his sanctuary, was merely a dry place to spend his sleepless nights. He worked in the fields and in his office, finding little satisfaction in either. He looked for Carmel at lunch and listened for her singing as he walked up the stairs. He never lingered in the pool after his laps. He loathed his empty bed.

He missed her. Overpoweringly.

When Zoia questioned him on what had gone wrong between them, he told her what he believed to be the truth.

"She wanted a divorce." She wanted to *leave*. "I gave her what she wanted."

"I don't believe it," Zoia said. "I think she wanted you to fight for her."

"If she wants to see me, she knows how to find me."

"She already came to find you."

"To ask for a *divorce*."

His one consolation was that Carmel seemed to be handling their parting well. There were no reports of her turning to unhealthy coping strategies, which he was genuinely grateful to see, but it also told him that perhaps she hadn't loved him as deeply as she had proclaimed.

She wasn't suffering. Not the way he was.

"You should go get her," Zoia chided.

"You're still recovering," Damian argued. Until she was out of the woods, he wanted to stay close to her, and did.

He spoke to his father regularly, though. Their first conversations were stilted, but when he told Nick that his grandmother was seeming like her old self, Nick invited him to come meet the rest of his family.

Damian agreed, mostly because he couldn't bear staying here without Carmel any longer.

A week later, he landed in Melbourne. It was their winter, but the day was dry and sunny. He checked into his hotel, cleaned up, then made his way to his father's contemporary mansion in Toorak.

Nick met him at the door and shook his hand while catching him into a brief hug. The other man's eyes were wet as he introduced his wife and children. They all gathered around with great smiles and a buzz of questions while drawing Damian into their home.

It was overwhelming and heartening, and even though he felt welcome and wanted to be here, it was one of the most isolating moments of his life. He wished he had someone with him. He wished Carmel was with him. She had nudged him onto this journey, and he wished he could share this culmination with her. He should have asked her to come with him. She would have come, without question. He knew that as a certainty within him.

He kept thinking of Zoia telling him to go to her, but every time he did, he heard Carmel say, *If you don't love me, then I can't stay with you. I need you to let me go.*

He hadn't wanted to let her go. He had been honoring their agreement. Giving her what she wanted, so she could find someone who would love her the way she deserved to be loved. He kept telling himself that she couldn't love him because they barely knew each other, but she did know him. In some ways, she knew him better than he knew himself.

You're terrified of loving and being abandoned again... You don't trust me, even when I say that I love you.

She would have known that as much as he wanted to meet his family, it was hard for him. He kept himself so locked away from revealing anything personal, he struggled to tell his father how he began working in solar panels. He accepted a beer he didn't want and let it go warm in his hand because he didn't want to explain that his sobriety was a show of support for his ex-wife—who didn't even know that he was doing it.

Thankfully, there was a lot going on with Nick manning the barbecue and his brother and sister playing tennis.

"Can I ask you something?" his youngest sister, Faye, asked shyly. She was twenty-two and aspired to be a makeup artist on film productions. "Did you, um, ask Carmel Davenport to do that stitch with my video?"

His pulse took a swerve at the unexpected mention of her name, but he had to shrug.

"I don't know what you're talking about." He had a vague sense it was something to do with social media, but his PR team handled all of his online activity. It focused on business announcements anyway.

"Oh. Um…" She blinked, seeming bemused. "But you know her, right? I saw your photos with her in Berlin."

"I do, yes." *She's all I think about.*

"Well, somehow she found my makeup videos. She did one of my tutorials on her own channel, side by side with mine. I got, like, a bazillion followers from it. That was so nice of her I thought you might have asked her to do it."

"She has a channel?" Since when?

"It's the Davenwear Channel, but she's on there with a hashtag LTLY Challenge." She drew the letters in the air with her finger. "Learn to love yourself." Faye tapped into her phone. "It's affirmations and self-care. Like, it's really marketing for her clothes, but she makes it funny, too. This one came out the other day."

Faye hit Play and Carmel said into the camera, "I've been thinking about how good it feels when someone is nice to you. How it can turn your day around, especially when you're feeling low. Let's try something. Here comes my assistant. Hi, Maeve. I'm recording. Do you mind? I'll show you before I post it."

"Sure. What's today's topic?"

"Fishing for compliments. What do you think of these earrings?"

"Oh. Um. They're great."

"Say more," Carmel urged. "Embarrass me."

"Oh. Right. Sure. You always look fabulous, Carmel. You know that. I wish I had your taste. Also, you're a great boss. You give us French Exit Fridays and you're funny. You also sing really well. Everyone is loving your designs for next season. Marketing says you're killing it with this campaign. More?"

"No, that's perfect. Look, I'm blushing," she said as she pointed at her cheeks. They were bunched with her huge smile. "You're a superstar, Maeve. Thanks. Tell Marketing to buy you lunch for a month for being a good sport. See?" Carmel set her chin on her fist and spoke to the camera. "Ask people to tell you how great you are. Pay them if you have to. You'll still feel fantastic." Her eyes danced with laughter, exactly the way he loved to see most. "Keep watching for a peek at the winter collection Maeve mentioned."

"She's so shameless," Damian said on a choke of laughter, chest aching. "How many followers does she have?"

"Almost two million. She's only been doing this for a month. I can dream!" she said with a chuckle. "But I thought you might have told her we're, like, related or whatever. I just wanted to say thanks. I wasn't sure how well you knew her." She shrugged awkwardly.

I was married to her. He swallowed the words and tried to clear the lump from his throat.

"That was all Carmel. She's—" Nosy. Pushy. Generous and self-deprecating. "She's actually the reason I wound up looking for Nick." He glanced up to where his father was placing steaks on the plate his wife brought him. "She knew that I'd found him, so I imagine she got curious about all of you and came across your videos. She would have known that she could give you a boost, doing something like that, but she wouldn't have done it if she didn't genuinely like what you were doing. She doesn't lie."

Don't question how I feel.

"That's so nice to hear." Faye beamed. "I thanked her online, but will you tell her I really appreciate it?"

"Sure." He wanted to text her now, but texting her once, with an innocuous message, wasn't enough. He wanted more.

He wanted his wife.

There was a fine line between living a truthful life and owning up to being a maudlin wet blanket.

Carmel refused to be the latter. No matter how persistent her heartbreak was, she continued forcing herself to go through the motions of living a rich, fulfilling life—which was how she wound up at the opera house in Vienna.

Stella had purchased one of the premium boxes as a birthday present for Beate, her younger sister. When one of Beate's student friends dropped out at the last minute, Stella invited Carmel to take the empty seat.

Carmel liked music and lacked a good excuse. Besides,

she liked Beate, and Stella was treating all the women to salon visits. Carmel went along for the pampering as much as the company, then quietly booked the Emperor's Tea Room for a reception afterward as icing on the Sachertorte.

It was fun to be with the young women, too. Beate was turning nineteen, and she and her friends were quivering with excitement at wearing long gowns and updos. Their mood was contagious and kept Carmel from wallowing in despair.

The weather was edging into fall, so Carmel chose a gown in copper silk with gorgeous geometric beading. She added long black gloves that she cuffed with a coiled bracelet shaped like a snake, and she wore the earrings that Damian had given her.

If pressed, she would admit her entire reason for coming was for the excuse to dress up enough to wear these earrings and feel a little closer to him.

Atlas and Stella's younger brother, Elijah, joined them. Elijah was twenty-four, tall and blond like his sisters, very handsome in his tuxedo and far more interested in the other men in tuxedos than any of his sisters' friends.

As they all settled in the box, Carmel took a moment to admire the exquisite architecture of the auditorium. The sparkle in the air should have made it a magical night, but deep down, she was as blue as blue could be.

Damian had returned from Australia. Zoia had told her he had said it went well. Carmel was dying to ask him herself, but she didn't want to seem desperate. Maintaining their clean break was better.

Even though the silence between them was killing her. She longed for him so badly, she looked for him compulsively, not realizing she was doing it until a sighting turned out to be a hallucination, leaving her swimming in disappointment.

It happened again as the lights were turned down and the performance was about to start. She glanced into a box across the auditorium and saw Damian in a tuxedo, staring right at her.

Her heart skipped, but she quickly tamped down on the jubilation that tried to take hold. It wasn't him. It was never him. It was only a man who looked—

He rose and left his box with purpose.

"I think—" She abruptly stood. Was she deluded by wishful thinking?

"Where are you going?" Atlas asked her.

"I'll be right back." She shuffled past Elijah and out into the hall.

There were a few stragglers rushing to their seats, but as she strode toward the box where she'd seen Damian, she saw him striding toward her.

She stopped. It really was him. He wore a black tuxedo with satin lapels. His hair was freshly cut, his jaw clean and sharp, his mouth a stern line.

He stopped. For a long moment, they stared at each other while her mind crowded with questions.

"Is this a coincidence? Are you with someone?" she asked in horror.

"No. Zoia told me you were coming here with Atlas and Stella."

"For her sister's birthday, yes." She looked back. "Do you want to say hello?"

"No," he said flatly. Then, "Are *you* with someone? It looked like you were on a date."

Jealous? That shouldn't please her, but it did.

"Elijah is Stella's younger brother. But thank you for that. He's barely out of nappies and very not interested in women."

"Oh." He squeezed the back of his neck, gaze eating her up. "His loss. You look beautiful."

"Thank you." She brushed her gloved hands down the skirt of her gown. "How are you?"

"Fine. You?"

Her teeth found the edge of her lip to say "fine," but she let out a huff of defeat. "Terrible," she admitted. "I miss you."

"Then why the hell didn't you come back to me?" He took another urgent step forward.

"Sir!" an usher hissed and hurried toward them.

Damian looked around with annoyance, then jerked his head for her to follow him toward the ladies' lounge.

"I'm not going in the bathroom with you! Come." She waved the usher closer and told them she had booked the tea room. "Show us in, please."

Moments later, the usher walked them into an opulent room that was clearly the pride of the opera house.

"Have you been in here before?" the usher asked. "It was designed by Josef Storck—"

"Please come back when the rest of my party joins us. I don't want you to have to say it twice." Carmel practically shoved the poor man out the door and closed it behind him.

They both took a moment to absorb the sheer beauty of the room, though, with its columns and intricate detailing, the silk-covered walls and abundance of gold leaf, the paintings on the ceiling and the table set with tiered plates of pastries and other sweets.

She looked at him, thinking this was surreal, standing in this time capsule of a room.

"Zoia said your visit with your father went well."

"It did." He rubbed his jaw. "I actually had a really good talk with Nick. He said he doesn't regret marrying his wife. I can't fault him for it. She's very sweet. He loves the kids he had with her, but he feels terrible he didn't know about me. He said he wished he'd gone back to Greece at least once to see my mother. It made me think…"

"Oh, my God. I'm not pregnant, Damian!"

"I know. You would tell me if you were."

She smiled faintly. "It's nice that you know that. That you believe it."

He shrugged one shoulder, dismissing that, then continuing. "It was his talking about the time he could have had with my mother. Time when I could have known him if he had made other choices. I'm saying this badly." He pinched the bridge of his nose. "We've already lost five years that we could have spent together, Carmel. I don't want to miss another five years. I don't want to lose another five minutes. Ask me again if I love you."

Her knees went weak. Her pulse started to race, but she cautioned herself not to hope. The rise of anticipation, of excitement, was there all the same, elevating her to heights she might not survive if she didn't arrive where she thought he was going. She wasn't sure she could survive the plummet back to earth.

The risk made her too dizzy to say anything but, "How could you?"

"How could I *not*?" he responded with a crack in his voice that sent a fractured sensation through her chest. "You were right. We were falling in love. And I didn't trust it. I told myself we couldn't be in love because we didn't know each other well enough and that is such a lie. I *know* you, Carmel. Every bit as well as you know me. You're funny and arrogant and curious. You fight dirty because you're passionate. Because you hate to lose. You have a big heart, but you've learned to hide it because it's very tender and it's been crushed too many times. That heart is mine, though." He pointed at her chest. "You gave it to me. I want it and I refuse to give it back. I swear to you I will look after it."

She couldn't help but fold her hands over the spot where that organ was trying to grow wings and fly straight at him. Her eyes turned hot and filled with sparkling lights. Her throat thickened.

"Don't make me cry," she sniffed.

"Don't you make *me* cry," he countered sternly. "There hasn't been anyone else for either of us for five years. There never will be. So don't *leave* me, Carmel. Don't tell me to let you go. You said you wanted someone who loves you, flaws and all. You're perfect exactly as you are. I love your sarcasm and your truth bombs and your messy past because it's what makes you *you*. I love the way you're determined to claw yourself into a better future. I want to be part of that future. I want you." He reached into his pocket, then went down on one knee as he opened the ring box.

She gasped and staggered backward into one of the columns.

"Will you marry me, Carmel? Will you be my wife? Again? Forever this time?"

Tears flooded her eyes. Happy ones. She covered her trembling mouth, barely able to squeak out the one word that wound up muffled by her gloves.

"Yes."

He rose and swooped his arms around her. Her whole body shook.

It was pure joy to be here, back where she belonged. To wrap her arms around his neck and feel his lips seal hers in rough, sweet possession. He lifted her off her feet and she thought, *Yes. This is how it's supposed to feel.* Like she had lost her footing yet was perfectly safe. She opened her mouth, kissing him back with equally fervent passion.

There was a click and a "Sir!" and someone cleared their throat.

Damian slowly let her slide to the floor and looked over his shoulder.

Carmel peered around him and saw Atlas in the open door, one brow lifted in inquiry.

"What?" she asked him.

"What are you doing?" Atlas demanded.

"Trying to get arrested for public indecency. What does it look like?"

"I'm proposing," Damian said as he patted his pockets, then picked up the ring box from the floor.

Carmel hurried to pull her glove off and offered her hand.

"I want a proper wedding this time," Damian said as he threaded the ring onto her finger. "It doesn't have to be big, but I want our families there." He tilted his head toward Atlas.

"Me too." They kissed again, briefly, sharing big, joyous smiles.

Then Damian slipped his arm across her back and faced Atlas. "I think it would mean a lot to Carmel if we had your blessing."

"If this is what you want, Carmel, then of course you have my blessing." Atlas came across to hug her. *Hug her.* While she was recovering from that, he shook Damian's hand. "Congratulations. I'll let you tell Stella yourself. Are you coming back for the show?"

"No." She glanced at Damian, eager to be alone with him. "But this room is for Beate. Tell her 'Happy Birthday.' I'll see all of you in the morning."

Three months later, Carmel walked down the makeshift aisle on Atlas's arm.

She hadn't asked her father to give her away. He was still in rehab anyway, but Damian's new family was here. Zoia was hosting the ceremony in her garden. She beamed smugly as they took their position in front of the arbor.

Stella was Carmel's maid of honor and Nick was standing up for Damian, wiping his eyes with pride.

Damian's eyes were damp and hers were welling as she beamed up at him.

"Don't start," he whispered as he touched his thumb to the corner of her eye. "We'll be here all day."

That made her laugh, and they were able to complete their vows with only a few sniffs and chokes of deep emotion.

"I'm so proud of you," Damian said when he put his ring in her hand.

"I was always searching for where I belonged," she said as she threaded the band onto his hand. "It's not a place. It's here. With you."

Their mouths were trembling when they kissed and she thought her heart might burst from her chest, it was so filled with the glowing knowledge that this time it would work. That wasn't a hope or a wish or a prayer. It was belief. It was faith in them, an unwavering trust in her husband, and a deep, unconditional love shared equally between them.

EPILOGUE

Five years later...

CARMEL HADN'T PLANNED to get pregnant. She and Damian had talked a few times about having a family, but she had remained hesitant, even when she saw how happy Atlas and Stella were with their twins. Deep down, there was a part of her that wanted a family of her own, but her doubts in her ability to parent well lingered. Even though she was firmly committed to her sobriety, she knew things from her past could crop up to distress her.

Somehow, however, days after her brother's children were born, she woke feeling nauseous. For a full week, she'd attributed it to anything but pregnancy: food poisoning, the flu, a weird allergy. Finally, Damian insisted on taking her to the doctor.

One seemingly unnecessary test later, she was told they were going to be parents.

It was a shock, but a thrilling one. Aside from feeling hungover for nine months, her pregnancy was uneventful. Their son, Theodore, came out wailing and strong, and he brought out the best in both of them.

Today was his first birthday. His cousins were his guests, and it became an absolute zoo for a few hours before Atlas and Stella took their toddlers back to their yacht and Theo went down for his nap.

Zoia had enjoyed the chaos, but she needed a rest, too. Age was very much catching up with her, but she was strong enough that Carmel and Damian were planning a visit to see Nick and his family soon. Even so, they worked from the island as much as possible, preferring to be close to her.

Preferring to be home.

"I have something for you," Damian said as Carmel stuffed a wayward ribbon into a gift bag. She looked up to see he held a ring box.

"Damian!" She couldn't help her gasp as he revealed the stunning band of baguette diamonds set between rows of round diamonds. "I love it." It fit perfectly on the ring finger of her right hand and was a gorgeous counterpoint to the two on her left. "Why are you spoiling me? It's not *my* birthday."

"No, but it's a special day for us." He looped his arm around her and drew her close. "As of today, we have officially been married longer than we were the first time."

"You've been doing math behind my back?" She tsked in mock scandal. "How dare you."

"I'm surprised you didn't see the chalkboard and ask me about all the algebra."

She chuckled and slid her arms around his waist, loving him the most when he said silly things.

"Actually, I realized it was coming up a few weeks ago, when Zoia mentioned it had been five years since her surgery. She said she was glad she'd had these extra years with me, to get to know you and see us happy and hold Theo. I realized that I was happy to have these years with you, too."

"Oh." She curled into him, growing misty. "I am incredibly grateful for this life I have with you. I love you so much it makes me want to cry."

"Don't do that. I'd rather spend our son's nap doing something else." He kissed her, but it was a press of one smile upon another.

It altered, though. They were still a deliciously sensual mix. As they rubbed their lips together, the kiss deepened to a slow, tender, thorough precursor to what they both wanted.

When he lifted his head, she was breathless and dazzled and so in love with him, she could hardly speak.

"Shall we go upstairs?" he asked in the sexy rough voice that sent delight shivering down her spine.

"Yes, but I want to say first that even though I didn't know we were doing gifts today, I have one for you, too. You have to wait about nine months to hold it, though."

"Carmel." His brows quirked with deep emotion. His mouth kicked sideways in the cocksure grin her heart had tumbled over the first time she saw him. "I love it already."

He swung her into his arms and carried her to their bed.

* * * * *

MILLS & BOON®

Coming next month

THE HEIR AFFAIR
Heidi Rice

'Poppy,' he shouted.

The girl's head whipped around, responding to her name. Joy exploded in Xander's chest, as the need shocked him. Those eyes, that face. It was her. But as she turned toward him, depositing the tray back on the bar with a clash of glasses, his greedy gaze swept down her figure.

His steps faltered. And he blinked, exhilaration turning to shock, then confusion, then another blast of hunger. A compact bulge distended her apron where he had once been able to span her flat, narrow waist with a single hand.

He reached her at last, but it felt as if he were walking through waist-high water now as he tried to make sense of all the warring reactions going off inside his head.

But then his gaze snagged on her belly again—and the only question that mattered broke from his dry lips.

'Is it mine?' he demanded.

Flags of color slashed across her cheeks, but all he heard in her tone was the sting of regret when she whispered, 'Yes.'

Continue reading

THE HEIR AFFAIR
Heidi Rice

Available next month
millsandboon.co.uk

Copyright ©2025 Heidi Rice

COMING SOON!

We really hope you enjoyed reading this book. If you're looking for more romance be sure to head to the shops when new books are available on

Thursday 28th August

To see which titles are coming soon, please visit
millsandboon.co.uk/nextmonth

MILLS & BOON

FOUR BRAND NEW BOOKS FROM
MILLS & BOON MODERN

The same great stories you love, a stylish new look!

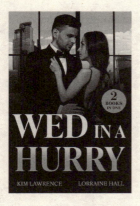
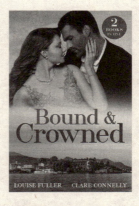

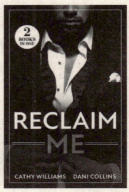

OUT NOW

Eight Modern stories published every month, find them all at:
millsandboon.co.uk

Afterglow Books is a trend-led, trope-filled list of books with diverse, authentic and relatable characters, a wide array of voices and representations, plus real world trials and tribulations. Featuring all the tropes you could possibly want (think small-town settings, fake relationships, grumpy vs sunshine, enemies to lovers) and all with a generous dose of spice in every story.

♪ @millsandboonuk
◉ @millsandboonuk
afterglowbooks.co.uk
#AfterglowBooks

For all the latest book news, exclusive content and giveaways scan the QR code below to sign up to the Afterglow newsletter:

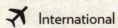 International

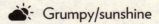 Grumpy/sunshine

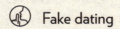 Fake dating

OUT NOW

To discover more visit:
Afterglowbooks.co.uk

LET'S TALK
Romance

For exclusive extracts, competitions and special offers, find us online:

- **f** MillsandBoon
- **X** @MillsandBoon
- **◉** @MillsandBoonUK
- **♪** @MillsandBoonUK

Get in touch on 01413 063 232

For all the latest titles coming soon, visit
millsandboon.co.uk/nextmonth

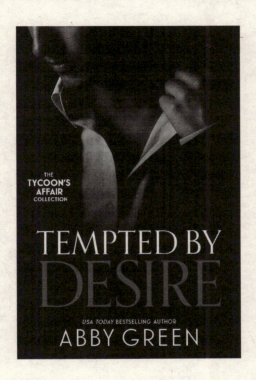

OUT NOW!

Available at
millsandboon.co.uk

MILLS & BOON